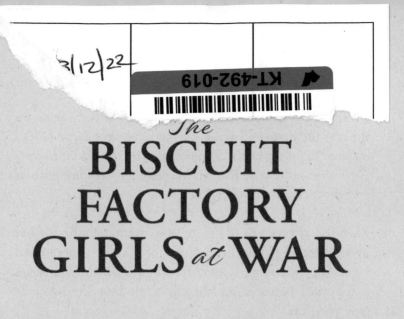

# The
# BISCUIT
# FACTORY
# GIRLS *at* WAR

Elsie Mason was born and grew up in South Shields on the real-life Sixteen Streets. Living beside the Tyne Docks inspired her story of the Farley family in *The Biscuit Factory Girls* series. She now lives in Manchester with her partner and their cat, and writes full time.

Elsie has always wanted to tell the dramatic story of her own extended family in the form of a multi-generational saga. After years as a writer, *The Biscuit Factory Girls* series is the most personal and heartfelt tale that she has ever embarked on.

# Elsie Mason

## *The* BISCUIT FACTORY GIRLS *at* WAR

ORION

An Orion paperback

First published in Great Britain in 2021 by Orion Fiction,
an imprint of The Orion Publishing Group Ltd.,
Carmelite House, 50 Victoria Embankment,
London EC4Y 0DZ

An Hachette UK company

3 5 7 9 10 8 6 4 2

A CIP catalogue record for this book is
available from the British Library.

ISBN (Paperback) 978 1 4091 9650 1

Typeset by Born Group
Printed and bound in Great Britain by Clays Ltd, Elcograf S.p.A.

For my mother, Joy, and my grandmother, Gladys.
With all my love.

# Chapter One

Ma Ada came in from the privy, washed her hands at the scullery sink and declared that she'd had a good idea.

'Listen, Beryl,' she said to her daughter-in-law. 'When our Sam gets in from work, I've got a little job for the two of you. You're to go up to the Merriweathers' at Number Nineteen and fetch back the cherrywood cradle. It's a family heirloom and they've no use for it now. I've told Mrs Merriweather to be ready with it and hand it back to you. We lent it to them decades ago and they've had good use out of it, and now it's time it was brought back here.'

So I'm going to have to start moving furniture now, am I? Beryl wondered. With one sister-in-law pregnant and the other one away down south, many of the heftier, more strenuous domestic tasks at Number Thirteen Frederick Street had fallen to her lately. Now she was expected to lug heavy old bits of furniture about. Ah, well. She didn't mind pitching in really. And it was all for a good reason. 'A cradle!' she smiled.

'Oh, it's a beautiful thing. A grand, hand-carved piece. My granda made it for me when I was expecting your Tony – all those years ago! It was about the only thing that anyone in my family ever did for me, actually, so it's quite a precious item, that cradle. It's one of the few nice things I have that wasn't

I

broken or pawned by that selfish drunken bastard who ruined my life when I came to live here in the Sixteen Streets.' The tiny old woman in the heavy shawls sighed and sat down in her usual chair by the dresser. Lucky the cat hopped nimbly onto her lap and arched his hairless back for a rub.

'A crib!' Megan smiled, rubbing her prominent belly. The blonde girl was the second of Ada's three daughters-in-law, recently returned from Hartlepool and her own family after a spell of conflict with the Farleys. Now she was reinstated at Number Thirteen Frederick Street and she was sitting at the dining table, looking rested and fresh, nibbling on a custard cream. 'How lovely!'

Ma Ada ignored her. 'It's to go in the top attic room, for Irene and her bairn. You'll have a right job getting it up there, you and Sam, Beryl. I remember the hassle we had getting it down to go up to the Merriweathers' in 1924. But it'll be worth it. It'll be a lovely welcome for Irene, coming home with her new bairn and seeing that cradle waiting for her. All polished and beautiful!'

The idea of getting an awkward and bulky piece of furniture down the street and up two flights of stairs made Beryl feel ill. But then she realised what the old woman had said. 'She's coming home, then? Irene has said when she's coming back, with the babby?'

Ma Ada couldn't repress her grin any more. 'Aye, lass! I got a letter this morning while you were at work. Here, you can read it. And yes – with Marlene, of course. We're gonna have a new bairn to look after!'

In the midst of their jubilation, Beryl clocked the tight, closed-up, nasty look on Megan's face as she pretended to smile and join in. Clearly the eldest daughter-in-law suddenly felt that she was about to lose her place in the limelight, and in the family pecking order.

So it was down to Beryl and her younger brother-in-law Sam to move the crib down Frederick Street, back to its rightful place. Everyone knew that the Merriweathers were a rough lot and Beryl didn't relish having to bang on their front door. It flew open to reveal the hostile face of Mrs Merriweather, as plain as a scoured front step. 'Yes?'

'I've come for the crib,' Beryl told her.

'It's not been used for years. Our Alan is my youngest and look at the size of him now,' said the woman. There was a hard-faced, skinny lad in a dirty vest standing behind her in the dark doorway. 'He's the only one I've got at home now. All my other boys are away at the war.'

'It's the same at ours,' nodded Beryl. 'It's the same everywhere.'

Mrs Merriweather glanced at Sam, who was clearly old enough to be called up, and strong-looking, too, but she didn't say anything. Sam looked uncomfortable, waiting on the pavement behind Beryl.

'We're to take it back to ours so that we'll be ready for Irene coming home with her new baby,' Beryl said.

'Oh, she's coming back, is she?' Mrs Merriweather frowned. 'I thought she'd run off for good, that one.'

Beryl shook her head. 'No, no, she just went back down south to Norfolk to visit her family. She was looking after her mum, because she was ill, and then she got stuck down there while her Tom was missing in action, and the next thing was, she was having her baby!'

'Eeeh, she's been busy, then.' Mrs Merriweather pursed her lips. 'Ma Ada must be pleased that her Tom and his wife have had the bairn. She's a grandma now. Their Tom's still missing, is he?'

'No, he turned up again. Out of the blue! And he went to see her and the baby and everyone was fine.' Why am I telling

3

this woman the whole story? Beryl wondered. She's just being nosey.

'What are they calling the bairn?' asked Mrs Merriweather. 'Little girl, wasn't it?'

'Aye,' Beryl nodded. 'She's called her Marlene, which she says we all have to pronounce the English way.'

'Eeeh, yes!' Mrs Merriweather gasped. 'You don't want to be saying it the German way, do you? Not while the Jerries are bombing Tyne dock every other night. Ha'way, then. You both better come inside and get this thing down. Mind, you'll have your work cut out for you. It's an awkward bloody thing!'

Moving the crib was a saga in itself.

Sam was used to manhandling all kinds of crates and boxes down at the docks. The slightness of his frame belied his actual strength. But the problem with getting the crib from one house three doors up the street and into its new home was that all the staircases and hallways of these houses were incredibly narrow. Ma Ada's granda had made a piece of furniture that really belonged in a much larger house.

Ma Ada was out on the street in the gloaming as Beryl and Sam wrestled and panted and cried out in annoyance. 'The bloody thing's wedged at the bottom of the stairs at Number Nineteen!' Sam declared, stomping down the pavement in his shirt sleeves and sweating profusely.

'Don't you dare swear in the street!' his mother hissed, scandalised. 'Everyone's listening!' It was true that there were faces at all the windows, and many of the denizens of Frederick Street had drifted out of their front doors to watch the palaver of the antique cherrywood crib.

'It's wedged solid,' Beryl told her mother-in-law. 'I don't think we're gonna get it through the front door.'

Ma Ada was resolute. 'It went in there easy enough and it'll come out again, too.'

Mrs Merriweather was out on the pavement by now: burly and mithered with the great ham hocks of her forearms folded. 'You'd better get it out of my front hall. We can't get upstairs to our bedrooms now.'

'What?' Ma Ada's eyes bulged at the woman's belligerent tone. 'What are you saying, Alice Merriweather?'

Mrs Merriweather was wary of rubbing Ada up the wrong way, but she couldn't stop herself sounding peeved. 'All this upheaval over an old bloody cradle. We've all had the best use out of it. It's good for nowt but firewood by now. I'll get our Alan to fetch the axe and make short work of it.'

Ma Ada gasped like it was her own flesh and blood that was under threat. 'You'll do no such thing! How dare you! After the kindness I've shown you, letting you have this priceless heirloom in that horrible old midden of yours. Letting you lay down your dirty little brats in my lovely antique crib. And this is all the thanks I get, is it? You're gonna chop the bugger up for firewood?' Ma Ada was rolling up her own sleeves now. 'Over my dead bloody body. Sam! Beryl!' She rallied her troops. 'We're gonna get this crib out of her stinking cesspit of a house in one piece, even if it's the last thing I do.'

There were cheers from some of the spectating neighbours as Ma Ada thundered up Frederick Street. 'Don't you step one foot inside my door!' threatened Alice Merriweather.

'I'm just getting back what's rightfully mine,' Ada growled. 'Get out of my way!'

Alice Merriweather pushed her scrawny son out into the street, in order to defend her. One look from Ma Ada made him step swiftly aside. Beryl hurried after her mother-in-law, trying to placate her. 'Look, maybe we should just let them keep the crib, eh? Maybe it's more bother than it's worth?'

'Never!' roared the old woman, and there was just a hint of Churchillian resolve in her voice.

They were deadlocked. The antique crib was wedged in the hallway and suddenly the Merriweathers and the Farleys were at war.

It was just at that moment that Sam saw a familiar figure rounding the corner of Frederick Street.

She was in her long coat and was laden down with a heavy suitcase and a carrycot. She looked exhausted, dead on her feet. But when she saw all the neighbours out on the street, the young woman grinned broadly.

Sam cried out jubilantly. 'It's Irene! She's back with Marlene! They've come home!'

# Chapter Two

'Eeeh, pet! It's like the family's not been the same, without you here. We've missed you, hinny. We really have.'

This was the highest praise from Ma Ada. Beryl and Megan stared in astonishment at the old lady. They'd never heard her welcome anyone so effusively into her home, not even her own sons. And she was smiling, too. She actually had a great big broad grin on her face, the Friday evening that Irene returned to Frederick Street.

Of course, the biggest factor in all of this was the presence of the baby. Right now she was asleep, swaddled in beautiful blankets knitted by Irene's ma, and perched in the old woman's lap. Irene had deposited her precious bundle in Ma Ada's arms as soon as she had arrived. She placed Marlene in her grasp like she was giving tribute to some goddess of a native people she was visiting.

Ma Ada sat there beaming and blushing and hugging the bairn to her. 'This is the first babby round here since our Sam was born,' gasped Ma Ada. 'And how long ago was that?' She glared across the parlour at Sam, as if she'd forgotten how old he was, and couldn't quite forgive him for insisting on growing up. 'Too long! Too long!' she cried happily. Tears were running freely down her coarse cheeks. 'There's been no child's cries or bairn's laughter round this house for far too many years. It's been a house of adults, with all their grown-up carrying on. I've longed for the blessed innocence of an infant. It's like a benediction on this house.'

The old woman sounded like she was going a bit peculiar and religious, but Irene decided it was best to let her get on with it. As she dumped her bags in the hall and took off her coat and hat at last, she felt like she was removing burdens that she'd been carrying for weeks. She straightened up and heard her back and shoulders clicking into their proper positions.

For too many hours Irene had been hunched into tiny compartments and squashed into seats with all her belongings and her baby. The journey up from Norfolk had taken over twenty-four hours and each stage had been more cramped and arduous than the last. More people than ever were moving up and down and across the country, looking worried, harassed and scared.

This time it had been harder than ever for Irene, not just because she was alone, but because she had had the care of her new baby. She was still getting used to the feeling of being responsible for this little helpless life, as well as all the para- phernalia the bairn required. At any moment she expected to be tapped on the shoulder by someone in authority who would tell her, 'I'm sorry, miss. You're not sufficiently adult to have the care of this precious item. We're taking her back off you. What do you think you're doing, running away with her?'

But as it turned out, no one paid her a blind bit of notice. Everyone had their own concerns and were bound up in their own troubles.

Oh, but it had been hard leaving behind her family in the tiny village of Hunworth. Last time she had left, following her marriage to Tom, she had been only too glad to get away from their cloying, over-familiar world. She was keen for the adventure of travelling north and settling into a whole new exciting world. How long ago had that been? Not even a year yet, and it felt like a lifetime. Back then she had thought she'd had enough of all her sisters and her noisy mother and her old da, living under that low roof in their ancient house.

These few weeks back there had been very strange, though. They reminded her of everything she had missed about the family she had grown up with. Irene had started to count her blessings. Her ma's brief health scare had rattled her, and she'd been glad to nurse her back to full strength. She'd been incredibly glad that her ma had been there when it had been time for Irene to give birth.

In some ways she had timed everything exactly right. She had been home, in the heart of her family, and that had made everything about having her baby seem much less frightening. The birth – though it was still terrifyingly painful and fraught – felt like it was part of a larger continuity going back decades and generations. Many, many women from her family had had their children delivered there, in that room, in that little house.

Everything had worked out fine. Marlene was perfect. Irene counted her toes and fingers a million times and stared into those bright blue, shining eyes and she had been astounded by the cleverness of the look that came back. She knew it was just the baby trying to focus, really. She knew it wasn't really an expression of blazing intelligence that seemed to look into her very soul . . . but still, it touched Irene deeply when she stared into her baby's eyes and the baby looked back. It was like peering up into the stars in the sky at night and wondering how far all that space and glittering wonderfulness went on for. It gave her the same shivery feeling.

And the way the baby gripped hold of her! Those hot little fists, grabbing hold of her fingers, her wrists, pulling at her hair. She was a strong little bugger, and no mistake! Also, she'd been born with some tiny, sharp toothy-pegs already pushing through her gums, so breastfeeding was a painful business, right from the start. But even this didn't matter too much to Irene. She was swollen, bleeding, scratched and exhausted, but she was in love.

She felt like she had come through a time of great trial. She had produced life in the midst of wartime at a point when she thought her husband was missing in action and, setting down her beautiful burden in Ma Ada's lap, she did feel very proud indeed.

Up in the attic later that evening the fancy cherrywood crib was installed at last. Irene was amazed at how much palaver it had been, getting it back to Number Thirteen.

'You should never have gone to so much trouble!' she laughed, once Marlene was installed inside the soft blankets, deep within the polished cage. 'She's been sleeping alongside me in the bed, back in Hunworth.'

Beryl shrugged. 'For Ma Ada it was a point of principle. That Merriweather lot up the street have had the use of this for years, and it was the best piece of furniture in their whole scruffy house, apparently. The rule round here is that everyone pitches in and helps out when there's a bairn born. There's a whole bag of clothes and bits and pieces waiting downstairs that various folk have brought round for you.'

'Oh, lovely!' Irene said, sitting down on the bed and taking a long look at her sister-in-law. Beryl had been one of the closest friends and allies she had made, since moving to South Shields last autumn. The older woman looked a bit more care-worn and tired than she had just a few months ago, Irene thought. Perhaps it was to do with her new job at the docks? Perhaps it was all taking it out of her, more than she had been expecting?

'Anyway, if you'd seen me and Sam earlier today, wrestling with this thing for ages,' Beryl went on. 'And then when it got stuck in the bloody hallway! Eeeh, it was awful.'

'Then I turn up, right in the middle of the whole carry-on . . .' Irene chuckled.

'That's the best thing that's happened in ages round here,' Beryl grinned, and peered through the glossy wooden bars at the sleeping bairn. 'Just look at that angel! She's perfect, Irene.'

Irene felt a deep sense of satisfaction at Beryl's words. There was something so honest and heartfelt about everything she said. From the first time she had met her last year, Irene had known that she would always be able to trust Beryl.

Now Beryl was laughing again about the crib and how, as soon as they had finished welcoming Irene and her new daughter home, Sam had been struck by a miraculous thought. He had suddenly burst out: 'Hey, maybe it comes apart? Maybe that's how they got it up the stairs in the first place?'

They had all stared at him. Then Beryl had laughed, and so had Irene, holding her hand over her mouth in her usual way. Then they had to send out to borrow a screwdriver from the Robin Hood pub at the end of Frederick Street. Sam's elder brother, Bob, who was the pot man at the pub, suddenly appeared with all his tools, and he made short work of it. 'I've never seen our Bob so bloody pleased with himself!' Beryl was laughing now.

'Ahh,' Irene said. 'I'm glad it was Bob who came to the rescue.' She was very fond of the slowest of the Farley boys. Before her trip to Norfolk she had been worried that he'd got himself into serious bother with the military police, and was glad to hear that all that business was sorted out. The army understood what he was like and had been lenient on him. There wasn't a spot of badness on Bob's soul and Irene was relieved that his superiors had realised that. 'How long is he home for?'

Beryl didn't know. 'He spends most of his time over at the Robin Hood with the landlady, Cathy Sturrock. Helping her out, even though he's meant to be on leave.'

Irene nodded. She knew that it was with Cathy Sturrock that Bob had placed all his hopes for future happiness. There was no love lost between him and his wife Megan any more, even though she was so heavy with her own bairn. 'Poor Bob,' said Irene. 'For such a simple soul, he's got a bloody complicated life.'

Beryl chuckled. 'I'd forgotten how much I love the way you put things, Irene. You've got a habit of seeing through stuff and putting the right words to them.'

'Have I?' Irene was shoving aside her bags and all her unpacking. It could wait till tomorrow. She was in no hurry to start folding things nicely and putting them away. She'd enjoy neatening everything properly over the weekend.

'It's true,' Beryl said. 'I've missed you and hearing your opinion about everything that's been going on, these past few weeks.'

'Well, I'm back,' Irene laughed. 'Surely I've not missed too much, have I?'

Beryl thought about it for a moment. 'That daft Mavis who works next to you at the biscuit factory . . . she's been running after our Sam. She's mad daft on him and won't let him alone.'

'She's not daft!' Irene laughed. 'She's quite an innocent lass, really. She's never had much attention or affection in her life, I don't think.' Irene felt quite protective of her biscuit factory friend. She was very pale and small, with lank, stringy hair and a raspy voice. 'It was because of her that I made everything worse between me and our Megan,' said Irene regretfully. 'Megan kept picking on poor Mavis, and that was why, eventually, I shot round to Megan's side of the work room and slapped her in the face. It wasn't like me at all to hit someone, but I hate seeing anyone being a bully.'

'Megan's never forgiven you for that!' Beryl chuckled. 'She hates anyone getting the better of her. She'll never let you forget what you did to her. And now here you both are again! Living under the same roof!'

Irene pursed her lips. 'Aye, well, me slapping her in the face isn't the only reason she hates and resents me so much.' She lowered her voice and peered again over the polished wooden rails to see that Marlene was settled. Ah, bless her. She was deeply, contentedly asleep. 'Hey, I think this family heirloom is working its magic.'

Beryl stared at the babe and beamed. 'Ah, sweet dreams, hinny. She'll be sharing the dreams of generations of the Farley family, lying there in that crib.'

'Aye, maybe . . .' whispered Irene.

'I bet your Tom was crackers for her, when he saw her?'

'It was love at first sight, of course,' Irene grinned. She was quiet for a moment, thinking of her Tom, and the few short days they'd shared down in Norfolk. It had been a blissful but all-too-short reunion. She thought about his reaction to first seeing the baby. It was a priceless moment. A moment that had stirred her heart and made her breath catch now, even as she thought about it. He should be here right now with the two of them, where he belonged, she thought. But he wasn't, and he couldn't be, and Irene had to fend off her sorrow and fight down her tears and simply smile at Beryl. 'Aye, he went on daft with her. He adores her. The silly fool is helpless. He's gonna have a life of misery, giving in to his daughter's every whim!'

'That's how it is, with fathers and daughters,' Beryl smiled, and felt a pang of sadness for her own dad, and how much she'd always loved him. He'd always been too preoccupied to return the love she had for him. 'Ha'way, we can leave her to sleep in peace. You can get a break downstairs and a cuppa with the grown-ups.'

Irene wasn't used to sitting with grown-ups, lately. She tiptoed away from the cradle in the attic almost reluctantly . . .

*

'Megan's got a headache,' Ma Ada sighed. 'She's gone to bed early, and she says, can we keep our shrieking and laughing to a minimum while she tries to get her rest.'

There was an ironic twist to the old woman's mouth as she passed this message on. Beryl rolled her eyes. Megan's whingeing self-centredness of recent months had been getting on everyone's nerves.

Irene was relieved Megan was out of the way. It allowed her to sit in the warmth of the parlour with Ada and Beryl, to sip strong tea and ask questions. She wanted to know all about Tony's recent leave, and Bob's tribulations. She even loved getting an update on the health of Lucky, the bald cat.

Ma Ada's voice took on a doleful, ghoulish tone as she enumerated which streets and families had been hit by bombs in recent weeks, and which had narrowly escaped. After an hour of this Irene felt updated with almost everything she had missed.

'And how's Bella getting on at Franchino's?' she asked. 'Have you been down there to see her?' Irene had received only brightly chatty letters from her friend in the ice cream parlour, as well as the most beautiful handmade congratulations card when Marlene had arrived. Still Irene was dreadfully worried about Bella. It was only a few months since her entire family and her home had been wiped out overnight. Her reaction to the devastation had been profound and frightening. She had been like a zombie, camping out in the derelict home of Mavis and her brother, Arthur.

The combined efforts of Irene and all her friends had seen to it that Franchino's was given a lick of paint and a fresh new look, to entice Bella back to work, and back into life . . . and it had seemed, miraculously, to work. But since then Irene had started to wonder whether the orphaned Bella was being a bit too bright and determined. She was working too hard, perhaps, to convince everyone that she could carry on as before.

Ma Ada had been into Franchino's most recently. 'I had a funny thing to eat. Something she'd been experimenting with. Horrible, really. Semolina with something strange on top. Anyway, I told her it was nice, but it wasn't really.'

'How did she seem in herself?' Irene asked.

'Seemed all right to me. She wears a lot of eye make-up, but that's Italians for you.'

Ma Ada wasn't very observant when it came to other people's emotions. 'I'll go and pay a visit with Marlene tomorrow,' Irene decided. 'She'll love that, seeing the bairn.'

'Good idea,' Beryl nodded. 'And what about going back to work there, Irene? Or the biscuit factory? What do you think you'll do about work?'

'Well, I'm not staying home with the baby all day,' Irene said, biting her lip. 'With both your help, I'd like to try to work as much as I can, in my two old jobs. But I'll have to depend on the two of you to help me . . .'

Ma Ada looked delighted. 'Nothing would make me happier, hinny!'

Beryl smiled, but she suddenly felt chilled all through her body. It was the thought of being left in charge of someone else's bairn, and having all that responsibility. She felt dead sick.

# Chapter Three

Irene had never seen summer in South Shields yet. When she walked into town on Saturday the sudden brightness and warm breeze came as a surprise to her. She had weathered a damp autumn and a long, frozen winter, and she had missed the spring. Summer made the town surprisingly green. She found herself longing to go and visit the park. When she reached the top of the hill she marvelled at the blueness of the wide sky above her.

Then it was down the steep lanes of red bricked houses, into the bustling streets and Ocean Road. She was wearing a too-thick woollen coat, and she was gamely getting the hang of the pram.

Ah, the pram! Bless her brother-in-law, Sam! From somewhere – he wouldn't quite admit where – he had magicked up a push-along pram for her daughter. It had freshly painted wickerwork and an oval shape with a rounded hood to protect the baby from the elements. The wheels were large and the metal had been scrubbed with iron wool until it almost shone. 'That lad's been out in the backyard, every spare minute for two weeks,' Ma Ada told Irene. 'He wanted to get that pram perfect for when you returned with the bairn.'

Irene had been shocked and delighted when Sam rather humbly, and shyly, presented the gift to her. It was, it had to be admitted, a rather old-fashioned kind of thing. It was like a contraption from twenty years ago, Irene thought to herself, as she examined the pram. In fact, she remembered seeing ones like this in the town of Holt, going up and down the pavements when she was a kid. But the point was that Sam had really put himself out to refurbish this pram. He had thought ahead about what Irene would need and he had worked a miracle on what would otherwise have been a piece of old junk.

'Thank you so much, Sam.' She made him blush when she hugged him.

'It's not much,' he said, with a shrug. 'But I wanted to give you something practical. I knew you'd want to walk her miles around the town. I know you love walking . . . and so I knew you'd need this.'

Sam touched her heart, and reminded her of why, when she first moved here, he had become one of her earliest allies and friends among the Farley clan. As her first year in this house had gone on, things had turned rather complicated between them, and Irene had worried that their friendship could never be the same again. She knew too much about a certain scandal that Sam had foolishly let himself become involved in, and the knowledge sat awkwardly, embarrassingly, between them. Still, this wonderful pram, with its non-squeaking wheels and its fresh coat of sea-green paint, went some distance to endearing him to his sister-in-law, all over again.

She went down Fowler Street feeling proud as Punch of her new baby in her new pram. Heads turned and people she only half knew stopped her and demanded a look at her new bairn. They peered into the pram and exclaimed over the bundle of blankets and the tiny bit of cross-looking face belonging to the baby they had woken up. There were many compliments and congratulations and Irene felt herself glowing red with embarrassment. She was delighted, really, though she would always say she hated to draw attention to herself.

I should have asked Sam to join me, she thought. That's what he was waiting for. He's just kicking his heels at home today. He presented me with the pram, and I bet he expected to be asked to join me on its maiden voyage, and I neglected to ask him . . . Irene bit her lip and shook her head. I should have thought of that. Beryl, too. I could have asked her to come along. I don't think she has any plans she mentioned for Saturday afternoon.

Irene hadn't thought to ask either of them, though. She knew that deep down she wanted this afternoon for herself and her child. She wanted to push her baby around the town, exploring her adopted home alone, and introducing Marlene to its sights and sounds. Of course, the baby was far too young to take anything in, and the hood on the pram obscured any view she might have had. But Irene hoped that the sea air and the atmosphere would seep through the wickerwork of the wheeled contraption and fill her daughter's senses with the feeling of belonging to this place. She wanted her child to have roots here: to properly belong.

Belonging somewhere was the most important feeling in the world, Irene thought.

The radio was playing in Franchino's, blaring some kind of big band sound, as Irene wheeled her pram through the glass doors. In the past, when old Tonio was in charge, he'd never liked music playing in his ice cream parlour. He loved the sound of spoons tinkling in coffee cups and cut-glass dessert dishes. He loved the whooshing, gurgling noises of the cappuccino machine and the chatter of his customers. That was the only kind of music he loved to hear.

But he had gone, and times had changed and now his daughter Bella was in charge. She had mourned her family and missed them dreadfully, but now it was her turn to make her own rules and traditions for Franchino's. She was building on everything she had loved about the past, but she was ringing the changes, too – and lively, loud modern dance music was a part of that. Bella thought it was a lovely innovation. Her heart lifted up with excitement at the sound of Al Bowlly and his orchestra.

Then there came a scream from the dark-haired girl behind the glass and chrome counter. 'Irene!' Bella dropped what she was doing instantly and came hurtling round to grasp her friend and employee. 'You're here! They said you were due back with the baby and . . . and is this her?' Her voice went quiet, almost reverential, as she crouched over the pram.

Irene laughed. 'Of course it is! Who else is it going to be?'

There was another figure hurrying round from the counter, one just as familiar as Bella. 'I can't wait to see her!' came the raspy little voice belonging to Mavis. She had been Irene's work colleague at both the biscuit factory and Franchino's, though they hadn't overlapped very much at the ice cream parlour yet. The strange, pale girl was proud of telling everyone that she was Irene's best friend in all of South Shields. Irene was embarrassed because she wouldn't quite put it that way: she had felt sorry for the girl at first sight, and had somehow become her protector. Looking at her now though, she did feel fond of Mavis. She was glad to be back within the coffee-coloured walls of Franchino's with both her friends.

The few customers waiting to put in their orders stood patiently and indulgently as the girls made their exclamations over the beauty and the health of Irene's new baby. She was picked up and yanked out of the pram and whirled through the air first by Bella and then by Mavis. The baby wore an expression of mute outrage at being handled by strangers. She didn't cry out or start bubbling, though. 'Isn't she a wonder?' Mavis squawked. 'I could eat her all up, I could!'

With relief, Irene took delivery of her baby and popped her back into the pram. Bella was laughing, 'I don't think baby-eating is something that we should encourage on these premises, Mavis.'

Mavis sometimes missed out on other people's ironic jokes. 'Ooh, you know what I mean, Bella! She's good enough to gobble up, isn't she?'

Bella ushered Irene and the pram over to their favourite corner of the parlour, and the banquette where they would always choose to sit for their coffee breaks and pow-wows after work was over. Irene sank gratefully into the leatherette seat, realising that she'd quite worn herself out with her bracing walk this morning. She was out of practice for walking miles across town during the course of her days. She was looking forward to getting back to full fitness.

'You look really well,' Bella told her, as she brought them both a frothy coffee, leaving a reluctant Mavis in charge of serving customers. 'You've got a lovely colour about you, and you seem to have your figure back, too!'

Irene pulled a face and pressed her hand to her mouth. 'I'm not sure about that! I've put on pounds, living in the country. They don't have the same shortages as we do here. So I've been eating like it's going out of fashion.'

Bella asked about Irene's mother's recovery from her illness, and about her father and all her sisters. She had quite vivid pictures in her head, of how Irene's family must be. She had only seen a few smudgy photographs, but the stories Irene had shared about her life in the Norfolk countryside were all very vivid. These days Bella was drawn to hearing about other people's families. After her own terrible losses at the start of the year, she wanted to tell them: make the best of your folk. Treasure them all every day, every single one of them. Even the annoying and horrible ones . . .

'How's Arthur?' Irene asked, referring to Mavis's eccentric brother and Bella's best friend. It was to Mavis and Arthur's scruffy, almost derelict, house that Bella had decamped, when her own family home had been destroyed in the air raid.

'Arthur is just the same as ever,' Bella chuckled. 'I'm sure he'd have come down here this afternoon if you'd given us warning of your arrival!'

Irene hadn't wanted to make too-firm plans for her first few days back in South Shields. She wanted to make up her days as she went along, seeing how she felt, and putting no pressure on herself to acclimatise immediately. Soon enough she'd have to fit into a new, strict work routine, blended with her responsibilities in looking after Marlene. But for now she was happy, just drifting for a day or two and enjoying the seaside town. She wanted to explain this feeling to Bella, but couldn't quite find the words. 'Ah, you know,' she said, instead. 'I'll see him when I see him.'

Then, with a hint of mystery, Bella dashed off and quickly returned, presenting her visitor with a special dish. She set it before Irene with a dramatic flourish. 'This is on the house – don't worry!' She smiled, knowing how Irene would want to pay her way. 'And besides, it's my first batch, and a bit of an experiment. I wanted to try it out on you – and baby Marlene, too.'

Marlene was out of her pram and lying on the bench beside her mother, swaddled up and supported by her bundled-up blankets. Her expression was mildly cross as she glared at Bella and her mother, as if demanding to know why she had been brought out of her comfy pram.

Irene stared at the silver dish with its two elegant spoons. Inside the dish were two delicate scoops of the most perfect, almost translucent, ice cream. The very sight of it made Irene's mouth water.

Bella pushed it closer to her friend, explaining: 'This was made using the sacred Franchino family recipe. It's the special recipe, Irene! I actually managed to make it, just like Papa used to!'

Irene gasped. 'So the recipe was in the safe upstairs, after all?'

'Oh, yes. Thank goodness! If he'd taken it home, it would have gone for ever. But I found it, Irene. Scrawled and smudged on a piece of brown paper that looked like an old treasure map. It must be fifty years old, that piece of paper, and God knows how old the actual recipe is.' She beamed at Irene. 'Go on, try it, hinny. And give the bairn a little taste.'

It was like a magic ritual. Irene squinched up her eyes as she took her first taste of genuine Franchino recipe ice cream.

'Oh, that's . . . wonderful!'

'Isn't it?' Bella said. 'It's a hundred times nicer than the usual stuff we used to sell here. Not that we've even had the ordinary stuff since rationing started.'

Irene took another small taste and felt a shiver of pure delight go through her. With no exaggeration at all she could tell Bella that it was the nicest thing she had ever tasted in her whole life. She took another tiny scoop and presented it to her daughter, who seemed to have noticed that something was being shared around and was eager for her own try. Marlene's eyes went wide and bluer than blue at that heavenly taste on her tongue.

'I can't believe it,' Irene said. 'But . . . why didn't your papa always serve this here? Why didn't he always make it like this?'

Bella shrugged. 'This is proper gelato. What the Italians call fior di latte – flower of milk. There's no eggs in this at all. Just cream, milk and sugar. Maybe he thought the Brits wouldn't like it? They wanted ice cream like they were used to? I know he was always keen on fitting in, my papa, and giving people just what they thought they wanted.'

'But that . . . that ice cream is just like heaven,' Irene said again. 'And no eggs! You've been thinking all along that you can't make ice cream because of the shortage of eggs, Bella. And you don't even need the bally things!'

'Just sugar,' Bella said. 'That's the major sticking point. We just need lots of sugar. But if we can sort that out, and I can keep churning up this beautiful stuff, I think we can do really well, don't you?'

Irene nodded, and helped herself to another taste of that perfect gelato. 'Oh, yes. I agree!' She couldn't wait to be back in her black and white pinny, serving up this glorious stuff to her customers. 'But what can you do about the sugar?'

Bella sighed, 'Aye, that's going to be a problem.'

However, when Bella was away at the counter serving a customer, Mavis suddenly lowered her husky voice. 'The sugar! That's where your clever brother-in-law Sam comes in,' she said shiftily. 'It turns out he's made a few helpful connections, working down at the docks.'

'Connections?' Irene said. She wasn't sure she liked the sound of that at all.

# Chapter Four

Ma Ada didn't much enjoy leaving her place by the hearth. Her legs and feet were painful, and marching up and down the steep hills of South Shields was a chore. She bitterly resented the regular trips she and her family had to make to the air raid shelters. That seeping damp cold as they sat in those gouged-out tunnels wasn't doing anything to ease the aches and pains in her joints.

However it was warm outside and, with the advent of her first grand-bairn and that smart new pram her Sam had provided, suddenly Ma Ada felt much keener to be out and about, walking everywhere. All of a sudden she was like the Queen of Sheba, parading around in the afternoon, pushing the pram in front of her, proudly displaying the most wonderful new member of her clan.

She grimaced as she walked, with her stout shoes gripping her bunions, but she had her best hat and costume on, and even a dab of make-up, courtesy of Megan, the most glamorous of her daughters-in-law. Walking about on those summer afternoons, Ma Ada felt like she had recovered her youthfulness, and there was even a spring in her agonised step.

Everyone stopped and turned as she came by, to exclaim over the infant, examine her and fill the air with fulsome praise. Ma Ada just took it as her rightful due, nodding calmly and watching as people paid tribute by pushing coins into the baby's hand. When Irene had first come across this custom she had demurred, thinking of how dirty coins could be, but Ada had told her: you can't refuse them. That's bad luck. And so now, after day after day of wanderings around the town, the bairn had enough coins to fill up a tin tea caddy.

'It's like I've sent the old woman out with the baby to go begging . . .' said the still-uncomfortable Irene.

Beryl nudged her arm. 'It's like nothing of the sort! Don't worry, pet. It's what everyone does. It's traditional, honest.'

Irene pulled a face, and tried to enjoy the film matinee she had come out to see. 'I've never heard of such a thing. Taking money off people in the street!'

Beryl smiled. 'Eeeh, I remember when our Fred was a baby, I was only a bairn myself. I used to love taking him round the park in his pram. The whole thing would be jingling by the time I got home! And my mam was like you, she was scandalised by the whole thing. I would tell her, though – you take him out yourself and see if you can stop people peering at him and pressing coins in his hands. It's just what they do hereabouts, when they see a bonny bairn! It's for good luck.' Beryl's voice suddenly stopped with a little hiccup and Irene glanced at her.

'Who's your Fred?' Irene asked, surprised that Beryl had never mentioned the name before.

'Oh . . .' said Beryl, in a lower voice. 'He was . . . my brother.'

'You never talk about him. Where is he these days? Is he grown up?'

'No,' Beryl said, focusing on the screen ahead and shaking her head quickly. 'He . . . erm . . . no, he isn't. It's a sad story, Irene. Let's not go into it now, hinny.'

Irene hurriedly agreed and mentally kicked herself for asking questions. 'Of course, love,' she whispered, and returned her attention to the movie.

The two of them ate a small packet of chewy mints and Irene half-heartedly attempted to follow the plot of the convoluted film, but she couldn't help wondering what had become of this child Beryl had mentioned. What had happened to her little brother?

As she chewed and watched and wondered, all the while Irene was feeling peculiar about not having her own baby with her. This was one of the few afternoons since the birth she had been separated from Marlene. It was the third one in a row that Ma Ada had taken the child out walking. Irene felt like she was missing a part of herself on these afternoons that Ma Ada went perambulating around the town, but she knew she had to get used to the feeling. Soon enough (next week, already!) she would be back at work at the biscuit factory, and she couldn't let herself get all teary and upset at being parted from Marlene. It just wouldn't do. She couldn't let herself go soft and silly.

The film rattled on: it was all people in long coats and big hats, kissing each other and then shooting guns. She wasn't really following it at all, but at least Beryl seemed to be enjoying herself a little more now. During the intermission she was keen to get a tub of ice cream to share, and Irene found herself thinking about that glorious dishful of homemade gelato she'd been given by Bella. This would bound to be horrible, synthetic stuff in comparison. However, the best thing about queueing to buy a tub and two little spoons was realising that the person selling ice creams was a good friend of hers.

'Arthur! They've got you doing everything here, now! Weren't you the usherette before?'

He shrugged and sighed theatrically, straightening his smart purple, braided uniform jacket. 'Ice cream seller, box office, bottle washer, everything!' He ignored the rest of his queue and hugged Irene awkwardly over his tray of intermission goodies.

'How are you doing, lovey? I'd heard you were back, from our Mavis. I was wondering when you were going to come over and see us?'

Instantly Irene felt a small pang of guilt. Why hadn't she gone round to their place, to show the bairn off to Arthur? Almost as quickly the answer popped into her head – and it was to do with the fact that Arthur and Mavis lived in a part of town that Ma Ada always described as 'a bit rough'. Their house inside was messy with all the old junk they collected, and none of it was too clean. Both brother and sister were a bit slapdash in their house pride and, Irene realised, she had been reluctant to take her baby round to some mucky place. She'd be breathing in all kinds of dust and nastiness. Thinking of this now, Irene blushed with shame in the light from Arthur's usherette torch.

'Ah, well, never mind!' he grinned. 'I bet you've been dragged round all over the place by that family of yours, catching up with everyone. And anyway, I'm seeing you now, aren't I? Hey, you haven't brought the baby with you here, have you? Not to the pictures?'

Irene shook her head and explained about Ma Ada's afternoon meanderings about the town with the pram that Sam had cleaned up.

'I bet that's a sight to see! That auld wife going about with a new-born!' Arthur chuckled. The people queueing behind Irene were getting impatient by now, anxious for their ice cream. 'Hold your flaming horses!' Arthur snapped at them. 'Look, lovey. When are we all getting together, then? When am I going to see this miniature Marlene of yours, eh? I feel like her uncle, really. That's what I am, aren't I? Or maybe I could be a godfather, eh? Who have you got down for godparents?'

Suddenly the film was coming back on and the amber lights were going down again. Irene had to hurry back to Beryl with the tub of rather inferior ice cream. Beryl was chuckling. 'I could hear that Arthur's piercing voice from back here! God, he's an embarrassment, isn't he? What's he like!'

Irene smiled as she settled down, holding the ice cream between them and giving Beryl her little spoon. She didn't like it when people took the mick out of Arthur. Yes, he was brash and annoying sometimes, but he was her pal, and it hurt her when people were even casually horrible about the ways in which he stood out from the crowd.

Sam had been Irene's usual movie-going partner during her first months in South Shields. If she was honest, she preferred seeing films with him, because he talked less through the important bits than Beryl did. Beryl let her mind wander and she tended to remember important things from real life that she suddenly had to tell Irene, no matter how exciting or complicated the plot unfolding on the screen was.

This afternoon Beryl startled Irene by bursting into tears towards the end of the movie. Her distracting chatter stopped about fifteen minutes from the end of the last reel, and when Irene turned to look at her, she realised that Beryl's face was wet with tears. She wondered if it was about Fred, the mysterious child she had mentioned earlier.

Irene squeezed her hand briefly as they left their seats and went down the steps, blinking, back into the afternoon brightness of the foyer. 'Are you all right, pet?' Irene asked.

Beryl was smearing her make-up with a fresh handkerchief. 'Oh, I'll look a right state. Sorry for making a show of myself. I don't know what came over me. I think maybe because it was a happy, romantic ending to the film, I was thinking about Tony. His last leave . . . it was just a fortnight ago. It wasn't a huge success, really. It was like he wasn't really here with me at all. I mean, he was physically here, but his heart and mind were somewhere else.'

Irene tried hard to think of the right thing to say. She knew how difficult it could be, with men coming back from leave and only being home for a short period of time. It was tricky, clicking back into the usual way of carrying on. Things could go wrong. You could feel like you were wasting precious time, or hitting the wrong note somehow. Perhaps that's what had happened with Tony? She was about to ask Beryl more when she noticed Arthur gliding up to them in his belted raincoat. His shift had finished and he had decided to catch up with them.

'I always get weepy like that when it's a Joan Crawford picture,' he commented, interposing himself between the two girls. 'I'm walking your way, do you mind if I join you?'

'Erm . . . no,' Irene said, watching Beryl dabbing her face clean, leaving it puffy and vulnerable-looking as they emerged with the crowd onto the street. Irene blinked in the bright sunlight as she got her bearings.

'You don't mind me tagging along, do you, Beryl?' Arthur asked, in his loud voice.

Neither of them had much choice, as they set off from the Savoy at the Nook, past the row of shops, and down the hill towards the docks and the area they lived in, which was known by everyone locally as the Sixteen Streets. Arthur breezed along, chatting away at twenty to the dozen, updating Irene about all his goings-on in the time she had been away.

It was all rambling nonsense, as far as Beryl was concerned, but Irene seemed to listen with great interest. Beryl wasn't sure why Irene even bothered being friendly with such an extraordinary person. She understood that he was the brother of Mavis from work and Irene was fond and protective of her, but there was something about him that was so peculiar that it sometimes set Beryl's teeth on edge.

Next thing they knew, they were back on their street and Arthur was with them, clearly intending to be invited indoors to have a look at the baby. 'Ah, go on, then,' he smiled, when Irene took the hint and invited him into Number Thirteen.

'Though I don't know that Ada will be back from walking her around the town yet.'

'She'll need to feed her before long,' Beryl pointed out. 'It's almost five.'

'Are you breastfeeding?' asked Arthur with interest, and Beryl tutted at his nosiness. Fancy saying 'breast' out in the street where anyone could hear!

They found Number Thirteen quiet and empty, apart from Lucky mewling for his tea from the top of the dresser. That cat was forever hungry, especially as he got older. Beryl hurried into the scullery to sort out his dish (urgh – fish scraps!) and Irene stood looking perplexed as she diddled with the kettle. 'She's out a long time with the baby,' she frowned.

'She's just carried away with her marching all over town,' smiled Beryl. 'You know how proud she is. There's probably some old croney of hers up at Seahouses who she hasn't showed off to yet. She's probably lost track of the time.'

'You're right,' said Irene, and started to make tea.

Arthur was looking around with great interest at the back parlour, where the Farley clan spent most of their time together. He inspected the faded pictures on the walls and the knick-knacks that lined Ma Ada's sideboard 'How the devil does your entire family manage to live in a place this size?' he asked, shaking his head. Indeed, his own presence seemed to fill up the whole of the back parlour as he loomed over the table. The last of the afternoon sun was peering through the lace curtains and there was something rather faded and dull about that little room.

'With some difficulty!' Irene admitted. 'Though we try to keep the dramas and fights down to a minimum.'

As if on cue the third sister-in-law, Megan, appeared then, from her tiny bedroom under the staircase. Her baby-blonde hair was awry and her face was twisted with a sleepy scowl. 'All your noise woke me up from my nap. Is that tea on the go?'

'Good thing you're up and about,' Beryl told her. 'It's no good dozing all day.'

Megan sneered at her and lit a cigarette. 'Ah, shurrup, man. I've got a stonking headache, and this thing in my belly's been kicking like mad.'

Arthur was staring at Megan with great interest. 'Goodness, you look like you're going to pop!'

Megan glared at him. 'Who let you in?' she snapped.

'I've come round to see the baby and to give it my blessing.'

The blonde-haired girl scoffed at this. 'It's like the wicked bloody fairy coming round to curse the bairn. You shouldn't have let him come indoors, Irene. Ma Ada won't be pleased about him being round.'

Irene was mystified, setting the heavy tea pot down on its trivet in the middle of the parlour table. What was Megan on about? Why would she care about Arthur visiting?

Arthur didn't seem to mind Megan's bad-natured ribbing. 'You're one to talk about being the bad fairy! From what I hear, you're not above putting curses and spells on folk yourself, Megan Farley!'

She glared at him. 'You're not natural, you.' Her eyes twinkled spitefully. 'Our Sam's told me about you.'

For a tiny moment Arthur looked discomfited, and his mask of blithe assurance slipped. Irene watched him suddenly rear up haughtily against her sister-in-law. 'What would Sam know about anything? He's still just a lad. He doesn't know what he's on about.'

Megan smirked and blew out so much smoke it seemed to fill the whole parlour. 'He knows enough. And he's told me plenty. So just you think on, Arthur Kendricks.'

Beryl and Irene exchanged a glance, both having no idea what these two elders of theirs were even on about. A current of obscure communication seemed to flow between Arthur and Megan: there was a hint of darkness, of unspoken things that went between them. Something about it made Irene feel very uncomfortable, and she wished that Megan would bugger off elsewhere and stop having a go at everyone.

Beryl said, 'Ah, Megan man. You've just got the hump because you're feeling poorly. Let's all have some tea and get along nicely. We saw a smashing picture at the Savoy.'

Sometimes Beryl had the knack for smoothing things over. With her rushing gabble of friendly chatter she made it easy for the four of them to gather round and share tea and biscuits, and gradually the tension that had been in the room petered out.

Soon enough, the ancient carriage clock bonged out for six o'clock. The sun had vanished over the backs of the steep rooftops opposite the back window.

Suddenly Irene was alarmed. 'So where is she? Where's Ma Ada . . . and where's my baby?'

# Chapter Five

Megan stood stirring pans in the scullery and refused to get involved in their ridiculous panic.

'Look, she'll come home when she comes home. What's the point in getting your knickers in a twist?'

Irene and Beryl couldn't believe how uncaring she was being. 'But look how late it's getting! She should have her home by now,' cried Irene. She had a sick feeling in the pit of her stomach, and Beryl had gone very pale.

Megan pulled a face and carried on making the supper. She wasn't a very good cook, and tended to leave a rotten mess all over the kitchen when she did. 'She's hardly gonna get lost, is she? She knows this town like the back of her wrinkly old hand. And nothing bad's gonna happen to her, is it?'

'You don't know that,' snapped Irene. 'Anything could have happened.' She whirled away from the scullery and started dragging her coat back on. 'Oh, why did I let her take the baby out? It's been every afternoon for days on end. Something was bound to go wrong . . . She's probably had a funny turn or a fall or something.'

Beryl said, 'Here, let me come with you.'

Arthur added, 'I'll come along too, and help you look.'

Megan couldn't believe her ears. 'What are you three dafties gonna do? Search every street in town for them? How are you gonna manage that?'

'I don't know,' said Irene, tight-lipped. 'But it's better than sitting here waiting for them. It's half past six already. I've got to get out looking.'

'Fools,' Megan tutted. 'Ma will think you're being daft when you come running up, lathered in sweat, all in a panic.'

But Irene didn't care what Ma Ada would think. She should have been home two hours ago. She had reneged on her promise.

Arthur caught her arm as she went hurrying into the hall. 'I'm sure everything's all right, hinny.'

'But how can you know that?' Irene shouted at him. 'You don't know. I don't know. And you don't know what it's like – any of you! None of you know what it's like to have a bairn . . . So don't go telling me how I should be feeling, or how upset I should be!' With that, she hurried down the hall, and threw open the front door with a bang.

Beryl and Arthur looked at each other worriedly.

'Silly cow,' Megan muttered, and returned to the scullery. Beryl opened her mouth to remonstrate with her, but there wasn't time. 'Come on, Arthur,' she said, and they hurried after Irene.


'What if the sirens go off while she's still missing?' Irene was saying as she led the way down Frederick Street. The last of the summer afternoon sun was being leeched out of the narrow canyons and the colour was fading from the red brick walls.

'They won't go off tonight, hopefully,' was all Beryl could say in reassurance, but there was no guarantee of that. As they all knew, the sirens could go off any time of day or night.

'She would just go to the nearest shelter to where she was, that's all,' said Arthur, sounding as measured and reasonable as he could manage.

34

'But the bairn's little gas mask!' Irene burst out. 'That horrible thing . . . it's in the pram all right, but I don't know that Ma Ada knows exactly how to put it on. She even needs help getting her own on right.' Irene stopped in the street and clutched her sides. She had a stitch and horrible waves of dread going through her. It almost felt like phantom labour pains wracking her body, reminding her of what she might have lost. 'Oh God, Beryl – what if something happens?'

'Nothing's going to happen,' Beryl said, but her voice sounded weak and worried, and she knew it.

It was teatime and most families were indoors with the radio. Smells of other folk's suppers were drifting out of opened windows and only one or two people were to be seen on the street. Beryl, Irene and Arthur called out to them: 'Have you seen Ma Ada this afternoon? Have you seen our Ma?'

Mrs Blenkinsop and Nana Ritchie shook their heads and clucked worriedly. 'Eeeh, why, hinny? What's going on? Is there something the matter, pet?'

'Ah, it's something and nothing, man,' Beryl told them, but they could see she was fibbing.

On the corner of the street they bumped into Sam, who was coming home for his tea. He looked worn out from his day's labouring, his clothes all scuffed and dusty and his hair thick with some kind of ash. He was alarmed at the sight of them hurrying down the hill towards him.

'It's your mam!' Beryl told him.

'Is she all right?' he panicked, thinking she'd been taken bad.

'She's not come home with the bairn,' said Beryl. 'She's been out all afternoon and she's not come back yet!'

Sam took in this news and stared at the three of them. He nodded a frosty hello at Arthur, though the girls hardly noticed it. Arthur pursed his lips and folded his arms. 'It's true, Sam.

Everyone's in a right flap over it. She should have been back hours ago.'

'It's not like her,' said Irene. 'We think something awful must have happened.'

'Well, you shouldn't jump to conclusions,' Sam said, rubbing his neck and trying to think straight. His senses were dulled by hours of routine donkey work, lugging boxes around at the docks. 'Now, where did she say she was going this afternoon?'

But no one knew. Ma Ada hadn't told anyone. She had been out most afternoons this week, taking the pram all over the place, and no one had been appraised of her itinerary. 'I just go where my old feet take me,' Irene remembered her once saying.

'I don't see why you're all getting so worked up,' Sam said. 'It's not like the bairn's gonna come to any harm, is it? It's not like Ma can't be trusted or relied upon.'

'It's not about that,' Beryl said. 'It's not a case of being reliable or trustworthy. Things just happen. Things go wrong. There can be accidents or things that no one ever saw coming.' She shook her head and tried to stay calm. 'Will you help us look for her?'

'Of course,' agreed Sam. 'But I dunno where you'd even start, pet. There's the whole town to choose from. Ma can walk for miles when she sets her mind to it, even with her bunions.'

'Oh, come on!' Irene urged. 'We're wasting time here. We've not even reached the end of the street!'

Clouds were massing over the docks – a good thing, Beryl thought. A cloudy, overcast evening means it's less likely there'll be an air raid. It's the last thing we need tonight, with everyone aerated and the bairn not home . . .

The four young people set off towards the town centre, figuring as they went that the best thing might be to split up and take separate parts of the town to search individually. While

Sam was starting to allot separate areas for each of them to go to, Irene was thinking to herself: I'll kill her when I see her. I'll wring that old witch's neck. It was the most horrible and violent thought she'd had for ages, and it shocked her with its suddenness. She couldn't concentrate on what the others were saying.

'Irene?' Sam asked gently. 'Are you going to be okay searching by yourself?'

No! she wanted to tell them. Don't leave me running about by myself through the streets.

'I'll stay with her,' Beryl said. 'I think someone should be with her.'

The fellas agreed, and Sam altered his plans for the search. Arthur muttered something admiring about his keeping a cool head in a crisis, but Sam ignored him.

And then, as they were hurrying, chattering, by the dark edifice of the town hall, a voice called out to them.

'Oh, yoo hoo! Hello, you lot! Helloooo!'

The search party stopped at once in their tracks.

'What the devil?' frowned Arthur.

They all blinked and stared, and Irene gave a strangulated yelp.

The voice called again. 'Eeeh, look at you lot! What are you's all doing, eh? Come out to give us a welcome?'

Irene, Beryl, Arthur and Sam stood in front of the town hall and simply stared in mute surprise at the figure inching her way towards them. She was moving at her own speed and pushing the green pram ahead of her a few inches at a time.

'Hellooo, there!' Ma Ada cried. 'What on earth are you all doing out? Who's getting the tea on, eh? We're gonna be starving, aren't we, Marlene, pet?'

They dashed up to her at the foot of the Queen Victoria statue. The old queen was indomitable, standing proudly with her sceptre and crown. Ma Ada looked not unlike her, pushing the bairn along with great care like she had all the time in the world and the whole world belonged to her.

'Where the hell have you been?!' Irene's voice crackled through the air and shocked them all. None of them present had ever heard her yell so loudly before.

'What?' Ma Ada looked genuinely mystified as she reached her welcoming party. Her daughter-in-law elbowed her out of the way and rummaged through the covers to heft her baby out of the pram. Marlene, shocked by the sudden noise and attention, started wailing at once.

'Mam, man! Where have you been?' Sam asked Ma Ada.

'We've all been worried sick!' Beryl added.

Arthur didn't say anything, conscious that he wasn't really a member of this clan at all. He was just a friend, helping out. They didn't need him shouting out and asking questions as well.

'But – we were just out walking the town,' Ma Ada said, in a confused voice. She looked at each of the young people in turn, amazed at how upset they seemed. 'I wore myself out a bit and my feet are a bit gyppy, so we might have taken a bit longer than I wanted to.'

'Look how late it is!' Irene cried, shielding her baby's face in the crook of her neck. Marlene was really howling by now. 'Didn't you keep a check on the time? Didn't you realise how worried I was gonna be?'

The small family gathering at the feet of Queen Victoria was causing an awful lot of noise. The few passers-by took note of them and assumed it was some kind of family squabble going on: not unusual for the denizens of the Sixteen Streets. The people there were known for their endless dramas. An ARP warden, hurrying by, going about his duties, considered breaking them up and seeing what was transpiring – and then thought better of it. Best not to get embroiled in family tiffs.

All of a sudden the old matriarch of the Farley clan looked very shrunken and helpless as she stood there in the road, with everyone's attention on her. The white cardigan that Beryl had knitted for her last Christmas was hanging on her baggily and her tiny feet looked sore and misshapen. Her face was twisted in sudden anguish as she realised how cross everyone seemed to be with her. 'There's no harm done,' Ma Ada said. 'We've had a lovely afternoon out. She's seen the sea today. I took her right along the coastal road and she looked at the North Sea. She loved her day with me, the little mite.'

Irene shook her head. 'You should have got her home on time!' she shouted. 'You stupid, stupid old woman. You should have been back when you said you'd be.'

Sam put his hand on her arm, and Irene shrugged him roughly away. 'Hey, now, pet . . .' he murmured.

'Get lost, Sam,' Irene snapped. 'What would you know about anything?' She watched him flinch at her words and just then Irene gave in to one of her worst instincts. She couldn't resist having one more jab, just to cause an extra stab of hurt. 'What would know about caring for babies? You've got one of your own coming, haven't you? And you couldn't give a toss about that!'

There was an audible gasp from Ma Ada at this, but Irene didn't care if she was blabbing about secrets or not. She turned on her flat heel and, clutching her whimpering baby in her arms, hurried in the direction of home.

'Now, what did she mean by that?' Arthur asked, looking perplexed.

'Nowt,' Sam grunted, and took hold of the pram he'd lovingly restored, and that Irene had left standing there on the pavement. 'Ha'way, Ma. Take me arm. I'll walk you back home.'

The old woman suddenly seemed twice her age and half her usual size. Irene's words had robbed her of her usual confident presence. 'A-all right . . .' she muttered. 'You know, I really didn't mean any harm, Sam. It . . . it just took longer to walk along the coastal road than I was expecting . . . with me feet . . . They're really hurting now. Maybe I was wrong to go so far . . . But I didn't mean to cause any bother.'

'I know, Ma. I understand that,' Sam said.

Beryl and Arthur were left looking at each other. He frowned. 'What did Irene mean about Sam having his own bairn coming? Is that true?'

Beryl shook her head quickly, defensively. 'She's mixed up. She's been in a right panic and she's saying stuff that she doesn't really mean.'

But Arthur's mind worked quickly. He was used to watching convoluted melodramas and mysteries at the Savoy, time after time, as he stood in the dark with his torch. He was used to figuring out secrets and surprises. His eyes widened suddenly. 'Megan's baby!' he gasped. 'Megan's unborn baby has Sam for a dad, doesn't it? That's what Irene meant, wasn't it?'

'Nay, of course not,' Beryl protested.

'It's true! I'm right!' Arthur crowed. 'Whey, that mucky little bugger. I'd never have thought such a wicked thing of Sam. I'd never have thought it in a million years!'

Beryl hissed angrily at him, 'Don't you say a bloody word to anyone, Arthur. We don't need this gossip getting out. We've got enough bother round our house as it is. And we don't need any more of your help tonight, thanks. Just you hie away home!'

'Aye,' he said. 'I will! I reckon I've heard enough from you Farleys and all your funny goings-on for one night. What a bloody bunch. What a family you are.' Then, with a whirling flourish of his long raincoat he hurried away from her, seemingly delighted by a scrap of scandal, and eager to be home.

Beryl sighed as she watched him go. What a family indeed, she thought.

# Chapter Six

It wasn't that she regretted her new job, but sometimes Beryl found herself wishing she'd simply stayed at the biscuit factory.

She still did some hours at Wight's each week. They wouldn't let her leave completely. Her expertise in the bake house was valued, and she stayed there to teach others what she knew. Mrs Clarke the supervisor had suggested that the newly returned Irene might be trained up to work in the bake house and take over Beryl's role, but as time went by, Beryl was stretched too thin, and soon she would have to decide to give up her original job and work full time at the shipyard.

But did she really want to work full time at the shipyard?

She had been so keen to work there. It was all she had wanted to do. She had talked about it enough: telling all and sundry that she wanted to be a welder. And now? Now that she had actually been granted her wish?

Oh, come on, she told herself: admit it. You regret it, don't you? You're wishing you'd stayed on the biscuits. It's nothing to be ashamed of.

But maybe it was? She'd gone in all gung-ho and full of bravado. I can do this! I can do as well as any man at this job. I'm not scared of heights, of cold, of heat. I'm not frightened of machinery or electricity or cables or wires. I'm not too terrified to clamber down into the deep hulls of ships or up into their towers, and to trust my life to rickety stepladders and planks braced between scaffolding. None of that stuff can faze me.

But the truth was, she found all of it quite daunting. Right from the first day, when Mr Hardy demonstrated popping out his glass eye and warned all the new recruits in a plangent tone of voice: 'Now, you don't want an eye like mine, do you?' He glared at them furiously once he'd popped it back, and she could have sworn she saw his glass eye swivel in its socket. 'Then wear your flamin' goggles at all times!' he roared. 'Get your goggles on!'

She was almost the only woman there. Somehow she thought there'd be more recruits like her, wearing their boiler suits with the legs and sleeves rolled up and their hair up in headscarves, braving themselves against all the boisterous banter and jeering of the men. But, in the weeks and months that she had been there, Beryl was still only one of two women in the place. She was holding out hope that more would come to join her.

The only other woman was called Lily Johnson, and Beryl didn't like the look of her. She was short and wiry, with jet black hair done up in a turban and a tight, belligerent expression. Also, she belonged to the Johnsons. Theirs was a famous clan in the town. Criminals and ne'er-do-wells, that was the rumour. On her first day at the shipyard Beryl had clocked sight of Lily Johnson parading about in her overalls and her heart had sunk. So that's the type I'm mixing with now, she had thought. And I've brought it all on myself.

Beryl had barely said a word to the other girl. She was too scared to. And every time she passed by, Lily Johnson seemed to glare at her with utter scorn.

The men weren't very friendly either, nor were they very supportive. One or two had been downright nasty: hissing at her and complaining that she was taking some poor fella's job away. Beryl didn't have the strength or the technical know-how. No daft lass could do the job in the way that a fella could do it.

None of that stuff hurt her. It was all sticks and stones. Let them say what they wanted. She was the girl who'd grown up being picked on all her time at school; who was aware of other kids muttering behind their hands each day. She was the girl who was quite used to being hectored and badmouthed in public. None of that stuff bothered her.

Though, kept up day after day, that barrage of abuse, seeking to undermine her confidence – it all mounted up. Especially when she was perched on ladders in some gloomy, freezing expanse, trying to keep her concentration as she hacked away at wires with her crafting knife. It was hard to keep her mind solely on the task in hand, and cutting through the plastic sheathing of the cables, when all she could hear were the men down below, hooting and laughing at her. That particular gang of them: she'd known some of them at school. They hated her being there. They were going to make her life a misery.

'We don't want you here, simple as that,' said their ringleader, a fat-faced fella called Chapman, who she vaguely recognised from big school, ten years before. 'You're a conniving minx. Coming down here, trying to do a proper man's work.'

'Oh, you're a proper man, are you?' she smiled sweetly, but her heart was pounding inside her chest.

As time went on, Beryl found herself less able to brush this kind of thing off. When it came day after day, from all the men she saw, it was tough to stand up to and laugh off.

Once, there was an air raid during daylight hours, while she was down in the damp, freezing bowels of a ship. There was no time to evacuate, and all the shipyard workers had instructions to hasten to special tunnels in the docks. There she had sat for three hours, by herself, quite apart from the men, as they waited out the duration of the raid.

The noise of the planes and the bombs far above had been terrifying, but almost as bad were the things that the men were saying amongst themselves.

Their voices carried down the echoing passageway, to where Beryl sat by herself. They were laughing and joshing each other like the daft lads at school used to, about getting hold of her and kissing her and doing all kinds of horrible things to her, just to pass the time and amuse themselves. All about how she wouldn't be able to resist them all. About how she wouldn't be able to put up a fight.

A cold rush of fear went through her as their giggles and hooting went on and on. It was all just bravado: silly boys saying meaningless stuff to make them feel that they had some power.

But it was terrifying, all the same.

They didn't come and find her and make her submit to them. That raid went by and no one was hurt, and the shipyards weren't damaged. They all emerged into twilight at the end of the day, and Beryl never mentioned to anyone the horrid things she had heard them saying, down in the tunnels. But she remembered those things each day, when she worked amongst the men.

Oh, what am I even doing there? Beryl wondered. She had a constantly streaming nose because of the chemicals and the horrible metallic tang seemed to cling to her hair and her skin no matter how much she washed. When she undressed at night she was horrified by the sight of the little burn marks all over her shoulders and arms and at the top of her chest. They were from the sparks that flew up, and then slipped past her mask and her overalls; they stung her like little fireflies, turning nasty on her skin and scorching tiny reminders on her flesh. Maybe they'd leave permanent marks on her body?

She couldn't just give up now, though. Not after making such a big fuss about getting in, and being nearly the only girl there. She couldn't cave in and let those men have the satisfaction of watching her go slinking back, full-time, to the biscuit factory . . .

It was all because of Tony that she was there, really. That's what she was having to admit to herself. She had been so determined to become a welder because that's what he was. He had been called away to war, and she'd had some daft, crack-brained scheme in mind. She thought she could take his place, and do the work he'd been doing. Like she wanted to prove something to him, somehow.

And then, the last time he'd been home, he hadn't been at all bothered, listening to her tell him all about it. He didn't congratulate her. He didn't look proud. He didn't hardly listen to her at all, she felt.

Tony's home leave had turned out to be a big let-down. Beryl blamed herself, really. She was so intent on everything being perfect for him that she felt harassed the whole of his long weekend at home, and neither of them could relax and enjoy it.

'He just looked exhausted the whole time,' Beryl complained later. 'All he wanted to do was lie in bed, in his old room. Even when the summer weather was glorious outside and all the flowers were out in the park and everything. He didn't want to go anywhere or see anyone. He couldn't have given a tuppence ha'penny whether I was there with him or not.' She blushed then, feeling awful for finding fault with him. The truth was, she'd been shocked at how skinny and tired he looked. It was like he hadn't eaten or slept for weeks.

'I heard what he was saying about the noise on the ship,' Megan said, nursing her bump under a crocheted blanket in the warm parlour. 'All that noise. It stands to reason, those hundreds of men cooped up inside all that metal. All that shouting and banging about. And sleeping under the waterline. What he told us gave me the absolute horrors. You know, Beryl, it must be hideously noisy all day and night. It would drive anyone out of their minds.'

Tony had been very sparing with the details he had divulged about his everyday life at sea. He certainly hadn't told them where he'd been, or where he was shipping out to next. Beryl knew that it was unreasonable of her, and unfair, but she resented him for not telling her the whole story. All she got was this tired man, who could barely rouse himself to do anything at all besides eat and sleep the whole weekend he was home.

'And now he's gone back to war . . .' Megan shrugged. 'Were you two even on good speaking terms by the end?'

'Of course we were!' Beryl narrowed her eyes at her sister-in-law. Megan was mixing it, as usual. 'There was no fight. Just a funny, strained feeling the whole time, like neither of us were saying what we really meant to, and neither of us were having much fun.'

Megan nodded, and winced. She was getting a lot of pain at this stage in her pregnancy. Their doctor had prescribed even more rest than she'd already been taking, and it wasn't helping much. 'It can't all be fun, though, Beryl,' she said patronisingly. 'That's not what marriage is like. Even in peacetime, it can't always be fun.'

'What?' Beryl gasped. 'You're actually lecturing me on marriage? You, hinny?' The words leapt out of her mouth unbidden, and she surprised herself.

'What's that supposed to mean, like?' Megan frowned. She wasn't used to Beryl answering her back. Irene, yes. Irene had made a bit of an enemy of Megan. But Beryl had always proved dependable, and never gave Megan any backtalk. Now she was glaring down at her blonde sister-in-law. 'Why is it so odd that I should have something to say about marriage?'

Beryl's laughter was bitter. 'Because your own marriage is a travesty, pet, that's why!' Suddenly she was on her feet. All the frustration she felt from Tony's brief leave, and all the anger that had been welling up in her was suddenly finding an outlet. Megan's mute, outraged face stared at her through the late afternoon gloom and Beryl was glad to yell at her. 'That's right! A bloody travesty! The way you've treated our poor, daft Bob. He knows no better, because he's got a heart of gold and he's not all there. But believe me, hinny, the rest of us know how you've mucked him about. We know what you're really like, Megan, and I wouldn't give you a tuppence for your marriage advice. You're no better than an alley cat, you!'

Beryl had shocked even herself. The two of them were suspended for a moment, both short of breath. Megan was longing for all her strength and vitality back, so she could launch herself at Beryl and rip her hair out. Who the hell did she think she was, talking to her like this?

'If I wasn't in this state, I'd batter you,' she warned her.

Beryl tossed her head. 'Aye, well, you are in that state. So you can't budge an inch, and you're depending on all of us lot to look after you, so just you shut your rotten gob.'

Megan narrowed her beautiful green eyes. 'You've changed, Beryl Farley. Time was, you were a sweet-natured girl. When I first moved in here you were so lovely, loyal and helpful. We were like two sisters, us two. And lately it's all spoilt. It's all ruined, because someone has driven a bloomin' great wedge between us. And do you know who that person is?'

Beryl shook her head. 'Don't you go blaming Irene. You've always had it in for poor Irene, though God knows what she's ever done to you.'

'She's a nasty girl,' Megan spat. 'She slapped me – twice! – round the face, in front of everyone, at work.'

'I daresay you asked for it.'

'She started a fight with me, and I still got the blame!'

'And so you should!' Beryl snapped.

'And ever since she's been back from Norfolk these last couple of weeks, you've been sucking up to her, Beryl, and carrying on like you're best mates with her. But it was always you and me who were mates. We were close. We were good sisters-in-law to each other before that little bitch came here!'

Beryl flinched at the language and stared at Megan. She also started to feel a little guilty. Maybe Megan had a point. Maybe she did really prefer Irene's company to Megan's, and she had allowed herself to show it. Megan was simply feeling left out in the cold.

Suddenly there was a kerfuffle in the scullery as Ma Ada came beetling back indoors from the lavvy. She was gasping with the cold. 'Eeeh, it's breezy out there!' She'd been in the khazi for so long that the two younger women had forgotten she was out there. 'It was that pastry on the pie you made, Beryl. It set like cement in my insides, it did. What did you put in it, pet?' As she shuffled through the curtain that insulated the warmth of the parlour against the draughty kitchen she saw at once that the two women were at loggerheads. Megan sat defenceless, clutching her blanket, and Beryl was standing over her with both fists clenched. 'What on earth is going on in here?' Ma Ada demanded. 'Are you two having a barney?'

There was a long pause as Beryl and Megan glared at each other. Then Megan said in a very sweet, small voice, 'I was just explaining to Beryl that it was no wonder that her Tony wasn't the life and soul of the party while he was home on leave. It isn't really a holiday for him, is it? She shouldn't be surprised that she's feeling so disappointed and dejected now that he's back at sea. He wasn't here just for her benefit, after all.'

Ma Ada frowned, listening to this. She glared at Beryl, who looked furious at Megan's words. 'Is this right, Beryl? What Megan's saying?'

Megan was stirring things up as usual, but Beryl couldn't deny the essence of it. Not really. She was disappointed, upset and frustrated. The man who'd come back to sleep under her eiderdown hadn't seemed much like her beloved Tony. It felt like she'd had a visit from a stranger. Beryl knew it was hopeless, explaining this to Megan and Ma Ada. 'I just feel confused,' she said. 'And really sad. I feel like we never made the most of the time that he was here.'

Ma Ada came over and patted Beryl awkwardly on the back. 'Don't upset yourself, hinny,' she said. 'We don't have time to go getting ourselves all upset. It doesn't help anyone.'

Over the tiny old woman's shoulder, Beryl could see Megan's smug grin. She was looking ever so pleased with herself, and Beryl again felt the temptation to wipe that smile off her face. Irene had been right about her the whole time, Beryl thought. Megan was like an incubus in their house. She had latched onto them and was leeching all of the goodness out of them all, turning everyone as horrible as she was.

Then Ma Ada was saying, 'Anyhow. No more pastry. Not for me. I've had an hour at least sat in the netty, and it wasn't much fun.'

They returned to their kitchen tasks.

Eeeh, I wish my spirit would return, Beryl thought. I used to feel so strong and capable. I could fettle anything! That's why I wrote to the shipyard in the first place. What's got into me? Why am I feeling so wobbly at the moment? Why do I feel just that bit more vulnerable and unsure?

# Chapter Seven

For a few days it had been rather awkward between Ma Ada and Irene.

Ma Ada went into and stayed in one of her moods. 'It seems that I'm not to be trusted!' she told Megan, making sure that everyone else could hear. She had sat in her chair by the dresser and refused to budge. She ate sparingly and glared at everyone.

'Please don't be upset,' Irene tried to reason with her, three days after the business of her coming home late with the baby. 'Maybe I over-reacted the other day.'

'Maybe!' Ada cried, and rolled her eyes. 'Bring me some tea. I'm parched.'

In the scullery, Beryl told Irene: 'She'll snap out of it. I've seen her like this before. It's whenever anyone criticises her. She's ruled the roost for so long round here, she's not used to someone knowing better than her.'

Irene nodded. She hated anyone causing tension for no good reason. She'd grown up with her own ma causing fights with the neighbours seemingly just to amuse herself, and to pass the time. She had seen quite enough of people wallowing in bother. The worst thing about this huff of Ma Ada's was that suddenly her favourite person to talk to was Megan, who was, in Ma Ada's eyes, blameless.

'Here, you just put your feet up, Megan pet. You must be exhausted. Eeeh, but you're glowing, mind. Look at your lovely complexion. You look like an angel.'

Megan adored all this solicitous attention. 'But I feel so fat and horrible.'

'Nay, lass, you've never looked more bonny. And I bet your bairn will be bonny, too.'

'She plays daft games sometimes, my mam,' sighed Sam. 'She did this when we were all kids. Playing us off, one against the other. Pretending to have favourites.'

'Well, I don't like it,' Irene said firmly. She was pushing Marlene about in her pram herself, today. They were visiting the park, which was looking the best it had for some time, with all the flowers in bloom. The bandstand was gone, the lake was boarded over, and all the railings were gone for armaments, but the park was looking as nice as it could in the straitened circumstances. Sam was walking out with her today, and she was glad to spend some time with the youngest brother alone.

'Ma will come out of her sulk soon,' Sam promised. 'She always does.'

'She'll have to,' Irene worried. 'I'm back at work in a day or so. I'll be relying on her to babysit for me.'

'Ah, she'll be delighted to. You'll just have to butter her up a little bit. Tell her you're sorry or something.'

The thing was, Irene wasn't very sorry for losing her temper. She had meant every word of it: Ma Ada had indeed caused unnecessary worry and fuss, the day she had come home so late. What was worse, Ada still couldn't really see what she had done wrong.

'She was confused, pet,' Sam said. 'She'd hurt her feet. You saw how she was hobbling. She had to admit that she walked too far that day. She's not as fit as she once was. That's a big

51

admission for a proud woman like her to make, you know. She's smarting inside.'

Irene pursed her lips. Yes, she could understand that. She knew Sam had a point.

'And you were pretty harsh with her, you know. You were shouting at her in the street. You made her feel foolish.'

Irene blushed at the memory. 'I did, didn't I? Oh, God . . .' She shook her head. 'But I was just scared, that's all, Sam. It made me so scared, not knowing where my bairn was.'

'Aye, I know,' said Sam. 'But you have to watch out. Ma's not as tough as she makes out. And you have to trust others, Irene. You have to learn to trust the rest of us.'

Irene glanced at him, but didn't say anything. Sam was lovely but she didn't really think of him as dependable and trustworthy. This wasn't a topic she was going to open up right now, though.

No one could really understand that stabbing pain she had felt when she thought her baby was missing. No one seemed to appreciate the panic she had felt. Except, maybe, for Beryl.

Beryl had understood. In a way, Beryl had seemed almost as badly affected as Irene was. She had turned very pale and shaky, the whole time it had seemed that Marlene was missing. It had taken her all evening to get her colour back, as if she had had a shock.

Irene had a sudden inspiration.

'Maybe we could go back via Franchino's, and I could take home a tub of Bella's special recipe ice cream? That might salve the old woman's feelings.'

Sam threw back his head and laughed. 'I reckon it would!' For an instant he looked handsome and carefree, just as he had when Irene had first met him. He hadn't been at all like that for weeks. Months, really. Ever since he had let Megan get her hooks into him, and Irene had spied something she shouldn't nave, and realised what was going on between them . . . Ever since that time, Sam had seemed haunted and unhappy.

Right now Irene was desperate to quiz him about how he was feeling, living under the same roof as the sister-in-law who had seduced him, and how he felt about the baby inside her, and having to pretend he was an expectant uncle, rather than a father . . .

But as they strolled around the busy park Irene couldn't quite find the exact words. Maybe it was best to let the boy forget all his woes for an afternoon, and to simply enjoy the sun?

He was dressed up in his best shirt and tie, and it was novel to see him neat and tidy, and out of his labouring clothes. Irene was wearing a new two-piece that her mother had skilfully run up for her on her ancient machine. The lines and the cut of it weren't perhaps the most fashionable, but it was very nicely done, as all her mother's homemade garments were. It was in a deep lawn-green cotton that suited Irene very well. The baby was all in brightly laundered immaculate hand-me-downs that had come via Mrs Clarke at the Women's Voluntary Service, and Irene felt that the three of them made a remarkably handsome grouping for their walk out around the park.

'I just wish the beaches weren't covered in barbed wire,' Sam sighed. 'You never saw this place before the war, did you? You've never actually been down on the beaches?'

Irene smiled and shook her head. She'd heard so much about the beautiful golden beaches here from Tom, Beryl and Bella, that she'd even started to have dreams about being on them. They made everything sound so idyllic: the sand soft as unrefined sugar, and the cold water frothing like lace as it ran in and out with the tide. It was true: several times Irene had woken up with the clear impression that she'd been walking along at the water's edge, hand in hand with her beloved Tom, or she'd been lying in the soft, warm sand, watching Marlene playing in the seaweed and clarts.

'One day!' she laughed. 'One day, when this is all over, and everything goes back to normal. Then I'll see this town as it's meant to be.'

Sam nodded. 'So long as it's all still standing by then . . .' he added worriedly.

They drifted away from the park and up Ocean Road, where they found a steady queue waiting at Franchino's counter. There were squeals of welcome and a delay to anyone getting served as both Bella and Mavis had to dash around the counter to exclaim over the baby.

'Hasn't she grown! Doesn't she look wonderful!' cried Bella.

'She's looking at me funny!' croaked Mavis. 'The baby's giving me a look like she knows something I don't!'

They all laughed at the daft things that Mavis always said – though Irene thought it was true, Marlene had in fact given Mavis a strange, sidelong look. She was probably surprised by the sound of her raspy voice, she thought. Then the queue of people started looking anxious and impatient about getting served, and Bella waved her visitors over to sit at their favourite banquette.

Mavis came shooting over, bringing their coffee. 'Franchino's finest blend,' she gabbled hoarsely. 'Plus, a fancy little wafer, on the house.' She was talking to all three of them, but only had eyes for Sam. 'Hello, Sam,' she said shyly.

He smiled at her and made the pale-haired girl feel queasy. She had been nurturing a passion for the youngest Farley boy for months. Tactfully Irene had tried to suggest to her that Sam had enough complications in his life as it was, but Mavis wouldn't be deterred.

'My brother Arthur says you were proper cool, calm and collected the other day, when the old woman ran off with the baby, Sam,' she said, trying to flatter him.

'She didn't run off with the baby.' He frowned. Mavis wasn't going to endear herself to him criticising his mother.

'Well, you know what I mean. Arthur says that all the girls were going hysterical, like, but you kept your head.'

Sam shrugged. 'I don't know about that.'

'I'd have gone bananas!' Mavis gasped. 'If it had been me. And it had been my baby gone missing. If I had a baby, that is. I'd have been worried sick. No wonder you were going crackers and shouting at people, Irene!'

Irene usually loved Mavis's daft chatter, but today she thought they'd maybe heard enough. 'Can we get our coffee in peace, pet?'

'Eeeh, yes, of course. It'll be going cold. I'll leave you's to it. And look – I brought an extra wafer for the babby to chew on. Can she have that, or will it choke her?'

'It'll be lovely. Thanks, pet.' Irene waved her away.

'Eeeh, Irene!' Mavis wouldn't go. 'I meant to ask. Are you back next week, working with us? At the biscuit factory?'

Irene nodded and smiled. 'That I am, Mavis.'

'And here, will you be back at Franchino's in the evenings with us?'

'Uh-huh,' Irene agreed. 'And we'll have lots of time to chatter and catch up when we're working together again, pet.'

'Oh, aye,' Mavis grinned, and took the hint at last. She scurried away, and Irene and Sam studied her back view. Somehow she made the smart black and white uniform of Franchino's look rather slipshod when she was wearing it. Her ankle-length socks were shabby-looking and her shoes were scuffed.

'Poor lass,' Sam said. 'Something about her always makes me feel a bit sorry for her.'

'I don't think she's had much of a life,' Irene agreed, sotto voce. 'From what I can work out, she and Arthur were left alone to fend for themselves from a really young age. Both their parents went off and abandoned them as soon as they could. The father was barely ever there, and I don't know what happened to their mam. Apparently she came from something like a gypsy kind of family.' Irene shrugged. 'I don't know what would happen to Mavis if Arthur ever chose to go his own way.'

Sam frowned. 'Is that likely, do you think?' he asked. 'I mean, has he said anything about that?'

'A little,' Irene said. 'Well, you grew up with him. You know what he's like more than I do.'

'What do you mean?' Sam frowned.

'His talent, for one thing. You've heard him sing. He sang here, on the night that we reopened Franchino's. And you heard him that day in the snow, when those boys were threatening to beat him to a pulp. His voice is amazing, isn't it?'

'I suppose so . . .'

'I think the day will come when Arthur will leave us all behind,' said Irene. 'He'll have to go off and seek his fortune down south, or somewhere.'

Sam sipped his coffee thoughtfully. He looked as if his thoughts were miles away. Irene couldn't read his expression at all. More secrets, she supposed. More secrets and stories from a time that predated her own time in this town, amongst these folk.

Perhaps she'd get to hear them in the end. For some reason, secrets and stories belonging to the Farleys and those around them, always seemed to find their way to Irene in the end.

She didn't say anything else for a while, just concentrated on feeding the wafer biscuit to the baby. Time to get back home to feed her properly soon. No way was she doing it here, where everyone would be able to see, even if she was mostly hidden away in a booth.

Before they left Irene asked for a tub of the homemade gelato, the *fior di latte* that came from Tonio Franchino's ancient recipe. Bella filled a paper tub and tightened its lid with waxed string and warned her that it would start melting almost immediately.

'We're going home right now,' Irene promised. 'And I'll give it straight to Ma Ada.'

'A peace offering?' Bella asked.

'A sweetener,' Irene smiled.

Bella nodded. 'I'm sure it'll work magic on her.'

Then they hurried out, Irene pushing the bairn in her pram, across the town centre and back to the Sixteen Streets. The last of the day's glorious sun was beating down on their backs, but they hurried for the sake of the ice cream.

'What's this?' asked Ma Ada suspiciously as they came hurrying in and immediately fetched her a dessert dish from her sideboard. The gelato was still mostly intact, a pale, delicate island of cream.

'Eat,' Irene told her, and passed her a spoon from the silver drawer.

The old lady sat down at her table heavily, looking like she might prefer to refuse and carry on sulking. She was weighing up which she would enjoy the most: a longer huff, or this unexpected treat.

She ate the ice cream.

'Eeeh, that's delicious, pet,' she said, smacking her lips and making the gelato last as long as she could. 'That's like nothing I've ever tasted before . . .'

'Good,' Irene told her. 'So, then. Are we friends again, Ada?'

Ma Ada pulled a rueful face. 'Aye, lass. Of course we are. You'll forgive an old lady for being daft, won't you?'

# Chapter Eight

It was back to routines and regular days. Sunday night was spent queueing in the downstairs hall for a bath in front of the range. Irene was used to the rigmarole by now, of everyone at Number Thirteen getting themselves ready for the week ahead. There was only one of the boys at home at the moment, as Bob had gone back to the army again. These were quieter days in the Farley household, but Sunday evening still filled Irene with gloom, trepidation and a vague excitement for the week ahead.

At the crack of dawn, with their hair bound up in curlers and headscarves and their lunch wrapped in greaseproof paper, Irene and Beryl set off for Wight's biscuit factory, joining hundreds of other girls hurrying down towards the docks. It wasn't as much of a wrench, leaving baby Marlene behind, as Irene had been expecting. Old Ma Ada had been up and about in her candlewick dressing gown, ready to take the baby in her arms, and looking very set on taking her babysitting duties seriously. The bottles of milk were ready in the scullery, and clean nappies laid out on the table. It had the makings of an efficient-looking operation, and Irene felt confident that her baby was going to be looked after properly.

'Just look how many bairns she's brought up,' Beryl said, as they bustled along.

'I know, I know . . .'

'There's nowt she doesn't know about looking after babies.'

Irene nodded, but she'd never forget that fear she felt on the day when Ada and Marlene were late coming back home.

It was a bright, beautiful morning, with yellow sunlight slanting over the dirty rooftops and the dingy walls of the docks. It was promising to be a gorgeous summer's day, and Irene thought about how they'd be spending the whole time indoors, busy at their noisy workstations.

'Did I tell you?' Beryl laughed, as they went in through the tall factory gates. 'In Tony's letter – the one I got on Friday. He never said much about the ship he was on. Or where he is, or what they're up to . . .' Beryl shook her head. 'And there were bits blacked out by the censor, so there was hardly anything to read in his letter. But one bit stood out, where he said, "Hey, pet, guess what? We've got Wight's ginger snap biscuits! That's what they passed round the other night. And I thought: my missus made these, probably. These biscuits come from our Beryl's factory, right at the end of our street!"'

Irene laughed. 'Well, that's what old Mr Wight always says – we're doing it for their morale! Sending out our patriotic biscuits!'

For the rest of the morning, as Irene settled back into her accustomed role in the packing room, she kept thinking of the picture of Tony that Beryl had painted. The eldest, most earnest of the Farley boys. The cleverest and most handsome, too, if you listened to Tom describe his brother, who he'd always worshipped. Crunching on ginger biscuits with his mates, and telling them about his wife and the other girls at the biscuit factory. It was almost absurd, but Irene did feel a small measure of pride that they could touch their lives in this way, and be thought of by men in the middle of the sea, and in the midst of danger . . .

'Irene!' croaked Mavis, delighted to be reunited with her work room buddy once more. She had her hair in a lopsided net and she looked paler than ever. 'I can't believe you're back, hinny!' She hugged her warmly, and some of the other girls smirked at her enthusiasm.

'I told you I was gonna be!' Irene laughed.

'Oh, I know . . . I just couldn't believe it was true, until I saw you in person. It's wonderful that you're back here. I've been missing the company. No one ever talks to me like you do.'

Irene was pulling off her coat and readying herself for work. She'd forgotten quite how much Mavis liked to gossip through the working day. They didn't have Beryl as a buffer, either, because Beryl's expertise was required in the bake house. My, that would be a stuffy, steaming hot place to work today. It was apparently quite a good place to be in the winter, but this time of year it must be punishing. Beryl was made of strong stuff, Irene thought approvingly. She did her mornings in the bake house, and then her afternoons welding at the shipyard. She had mastered the art of welding, she claimed, and found the whole thing was a doddle. Irene was very admiring of her expertise, and felt rather less accomplished, sealing Penny Packets of biscuits together with her brush and her pot of glue.

'Eeeh, your brother-in-law Sam was looking handsome the other day.' Mavis broke into her thoughts as work began. 'What a looker he is!'

Irene smiled as she thought back to that visit they'd made to Franchino's, with Mavis hovering around them, keen for approval, and to get a look at Sam. She tutted and shook her head. Sam had never really looked twice at Mavis, and didn't seem likely to. Maybe it would be kinder to tell Mavis that she was holding out false hope that he would ask her out. But what right had Irene to shoot her down? 'Aye,' she agreed. 'He's grown up into a very handsome young man. And he's a kind-hearted soul, too.'

Also, she thought, he's got a complicated life. The way he's tangled up with Megan. Irene herself couldn't understand what went on inside Sam's mind and heart, so she doubted that Mavis would ever be able to figure him out.

'One of these days, I'll ask him out,' said Mavis. 'Dancing. At the Alhambra or Albert Hall. I'll ask him right out. Come out dancing with me. And he won't be able to say no, will he? Not if I ask him right out?'

Irene wasn't so sure, but she smiled encouragingly.

'I'm a smashing dancer these days,' Mavis chattered on. 'Our Arthur – well, you know how wonderful he is at dancing – he's been giving me lessons in our front room. We push all the furniture back and he's been teaching me . . . slowly. It's the counting that I find hardest, and keeping it all in me head.'

The first morning back at the biscuit factory seemed to last for days. It wasn't Mavis's fault, but her endless talking made it harder for Irene to settle to her tasks. Luckily, she was so used to the routine of packing and parcelling biscuits that it took hardly any concentration, but the girl's voice was starting to grate at her nerves. Irene felt sorry for her and the way all the other girls gave her a wide berth.

At lunchtime they sat outside in the sun with their door-stop sandwiches and there was blessed quiet for a little while. 'I've got jam in mine today,' said Mavis, and opened up her sandwich so Beryl could see, and then she was off chuntering again.

'Erm, Mrs Farley?' called the supervisor, as they headed back to the conveyor belt, thirty minutes later.

'Mrs Clarke,' Irene smiled, hurrying over to the big-busted, formidable-looking lady. 'Thank you for all the baby clothes. They are perfect. Hand-stitched, some of them! Better quality than I'd ever be able to afford.'

Mrs Clarke nodded. 'I got the pick of all the donations to the WVS that week. Don't tell everyone! All that stuff came from Newcastle way. A better class of donation than you get round here.'

'Well, I'm very grateful, Mrs Clarke. And so is Marlene.'

The supervisor's eyes shone. 'Oh, how is the little mite doing?'

Irene happily updated her, and was glad to talk to the woman on a human level, and to see her smiling. She was used to seeing Mrs Clarke looming over everyone, tutting at their work, passing out instructions, and bellowing at them all in terrifying, stentorian tones.

'I feel robbed by never having had children of my own,' sighed Mrs Clarke. 'I had so much to give, but it was never to be. My Arnold . . . well, he never came back from France in the last war. That was my chance gone. But it does my heart good, to see lasses like you, Irene Farley. Getting on in the world, having your bairn and still working hard and doing your bit for the country.'

Irene smiled. There was something about Mrs Clarke's bossy tones that made her feel like she was still at school, being hectored by the teacher. 'Now,' Mrs Clarke went on, 'since your Megan has seemingly given up all her work for the foreseeable, can I put your name down to replace her in the WVS? Can I put you down for tea duty in the Sixteen Streets air raid shelter?'

Hoodwinked! Irene thought. She's lulled me into a false sense of security, with all that flannel about the bairn, and now she's trapped me into a corner. There was no way that Irene could refuse her suggestion now. 'Yes, of course,' she said. 'That's fine.' Beryl had told her it was bloody hard work, doing the teas and Bovrils in the tunnels all night. But at least it was better than sitting still on those wooden benches in the parky draught with all that noise echoing round the bends. It was better than trying to sleep down there in the bowels of the earth.

Mrs Clarke nodded with satisfaction. 'There's a good lass. Now, how are you doing, settling back at work today?'

Irene shrugged. Everything was fine. 'It's like clockwork. I know what I'm doing with my eyes closed.'

'You might well get moved over to the bake house,' Mrs Clarke confided, as if she was promising some kind of deserved promotion. 'Our more dexterous workers end up there eventually. You've no objection?'

Irene shook her head, though her heart sank. She'd heard enough about the heat and the noise of the bake house to put her off ever wanting to set foot in the place.

'I'll let you get back to your workstation,' said Mrs Clarke. 'But Mr Wight asked me to tell you to bring your Marlene in to see him one day soon. He loves bairns, and he took a special interest in you, back when you started.'

'Oh!' said Irene. 'That's kind of him.'

Mrs Clarke softened her sergeant major tone slightly. 'He's a lonely old soul, if you ask me. All his family are gone, nearly, apart from his nephew and that lot. I think Mr Wight would like to think of all you girls as his extended family, somehow.'

Irene thought about the strange-looking old man she'd encountered a couple of times. Once she had been invited up for a meeting in his wooden-walled inner sanctum. She had felt just like Dorothy entering the Emerald Palace to meet the Wizard of Oz, and finding the all-powerful ruler to be a doddery, kind, old man. 'Of course I'll bring the bairn in to visit him,' said Irene.

'I think he's particularly sad at the moment,' Mrs Clarke sighed. 'With it being summer, and the time of year that we'd usually be closing the factory and going on our annual summer jamboree. Of course, there's no chance for frivolity like that, with the war and everything.'

'A jamboree?' asked Irene.

'Oh, you're too new to even know about the jamborees!' Mrs Clarke smiled sadly. 'Why, it's been tradition here at the biscuit factory for over a hundred years! All the workers get the day off, and we all get on the train together for a day in the countryside. We take dozens of picnic hampers and everything we need, and everyone mucks in together. Bosses and workers, and we have a day in the sun, miles from anywhere. Oh, they were wonderful days. Perfect days.'

The two of them were now back in the work room, where everyone was intent upon their tasks once more. Mavis was watching Irene and the supervisor's hushed conference. She worried that Irene was somehow in bother and getting told off, and was surprised to see the large-busted lady suddenly wiping tears from her eyes with a corner of her apron.

'Oh, look at me! Getting all misty-eyed!' Mrs Clarke laughed hollowly.

'Oh, never mind,' said Irene consolingly.

'It's just that, sometimes . . .' Mrs Clarke breathed deeply. 'Sometimes it seems like we'll never get things back to normal. All those wonderful things about our lives that we've lost. All the things that we ought to be able to take for granted – like days away, or holidays, or having our loved ones at home. Can it ever get back to normal, do you think, Irene?'

She was looking with beseeching eyes at Irene, who in turn felt completely out of her depth. Her first day back and her scary supervisor was crying on her shoulder. 'There, there,' she said awkwardly, and rubbed Mrs Clarke's shoulder. The woman seemed to take some comfort from the gesture.

'Right!' she barked suddenly. 'It's back to work! Back to work for all of us!'

Somehow, with all the busyness and noise and the various conversations that came her way, Irene didn't find time, all that first day back, to feel sad and teary on her own account.

It wasn't that she didn't miss being with her tiny baby, it just didn't feel as bad as she might have expected.

She got through her first day and was delighted when the hooter sounded for home time. Then she flew up the cobbled incline of Frederick Street to see her bairn.

# Chapter Nine

It wasn't too many nights before the air raid sirens were going off again, and the inhabitants of the Sixteen Streets were trooping off to their shelter once more. The nights were warm, but everyone still took plenty of blankets and jumpers with them, knowing just how chilly and damp those tunnels were. For those at Number Thirteen there were extra considerations to make, and extra stuff to take with them, because of baby Marlene.

Irene was berating herself for agreeing to work the tea urn. She'd have much rather stayed close to her baby through the night underground.

'She'll be absolutely fine with me,' said Ma Ada, hefting the bairn in her capable arms. The old woman was a lot less complaining than previously about spending a night in the shelter. Previous times, her family had just about had to drag her there. Now she was marching up Frederick Street at the head of her family, looking like she'd gained a new lease of life.

This time it was Megan causing a fuss about having to vacate the house. 'Just leave me to die,' she scowled.

Beryl frowned at her, and then saw that she was in real discomfort. 'Can you manage, pet?'

'Does it look like I can manage?' snapped Megan. 'I'll bloody well have to, won't I?' She grimaced painfully, and it looked like every step was agony to her.

'Sam, help Megan,' Ma Ada commanded him. She ignored how awkward he looked, putting his arm around his sister-in-law and easing her along the street. She relaxed into his grip only slightly, and wouldn't even look at him in the face. Bad blood between them two, Irene thought to herself.

All around them, folk were streaming out of their houses, and calling out greetings to each other in hushed voices. They were used to the routine, but that didn't make it any less terrifying. The sirens were still whining, and there was only a short amount of time before they'd start hearing the drone of airborne engines and the ack-ack-ack of anti-aircraft guns on the coast. They had precious few minutes to get down below ground to safety.

Relative safety, thought Irene. It's no guarantee for anyone, being underground. She remembered Bella's family, and what had become of them. They had felt safe in the cellar under their house, but it had been no protection at all.

She dispelled these awful thoughts and took Marlene in her own arms. Oh Tom, she thought. Why can't you be here?

There was barely time to see the baby settled with her grandma in a busy corner of the shelter before Irene was taken off by Beryl to report to Mrs Clarke and the other ladies of the WVS. There was a tiny kitchen alcove, with a sink and a vast urn and a few cupboards stuffed with the most basic supplies. Here, instructions were issued swiftly and efficiently. Mrs Clarke was glaring at the few volunteers over her clipboard, defying them to miss a single word of her commands.

Irene's job was pretty straightforward. Teas and beef teas for those who queued nicely at her urn. Whenever the demand went down she was to scrub as many of the tin cups as she could, ready to start again.

'We expect everyone to bring their own tea bags and beef stock cubes, as you know,' said Mrs Clarke. 'But there are always one or two who forget to bring supplies, or who reckon they're too impoverished. For these poor souls we keep a small, secret supply of these things. Though you mustn't let that knowledge become widespread, otherwise everyone will be wanting something for nothing!' Her voice sounded thunderous in the rough-walled tunnel.

Beryl and Irene smiled weakly at each other. The pomposity of their supervisor seemed even less amusing than usual down here.

The shelter was almost full to capacity now. People were so well-accustomed to filtering down into the tunnels that the process took them only a few minutes. Already the twisting, turning tunnels were echoing with hundreds of voices and the cries of babies and the excited shouting of bairns. There were queues already at the primitive latrines and somewhere, deep in one of the tunnels, it sounded like some people were already starting up a sing-song.

'Probably it's them who's been dragged out of the pubs,' Beryl pointed out. It was chucking-out time, and that always brought a bunch of beery drunks underground with the rest. 'At least they cheer the place up,' Beryl shrugged. 'So long as they don't start fighting with each other or being sick.'

Irene smiled tightly, and turned her attention to wrestling with the controls of the urn. She was really regretting being here, and not in the next tunnel with her baby and the rest of the family. All she wanted was Marlene in her arms, and then everything would be better. Not perfect, not fine. They'd still be in danger. But better than this. To be parted from her was agony, and she bit her lip hard, trying not to show it in her face. She mustn't complain. She mustn't kick up a fuss about taking her turn to help out.

The giant vat of water was rumbling and bubbling deep within. It sounded like a volcano preparing to erupt. It was resting on a flimsy metal shelf. How easily could it be upset, spilling scalding water everywhere, Irene thought. It was a lethal object down here, and here she was, standing right by it, ready with her trays of tin cups.

'Listen, that's them starting up,' Beryl said with a nod, and when Irene listened, above the echoing hullaballoo, she could hear the explosions going off, across town. There was no telling where they were coming down, and no use in trying to guess.

'Kettle's almost boiled,' she said, with false cheeriness.

In the end Irene found that it was actually better, having something to work at, and concentrate on, throughout the raid raging above ground. To focus on ordinary things like tea bags and milk supplies and scrubbing cups clean – that was a kind of blessing, taking their minds off what might be going on upstairs.

Then there were the small scuffles that broke out over who had brought Oxo cubes and who hadn't, though people were remarkably patient and good-natured on the whole.

Now and then the tunnels would rumble and vibrate. Showers of horrible sandy dust would fall down onto their heads. There was gritty sand in every cup of tea they poured and passed around. 'I'm swilling that dust around in my mouth,' Beryl shuddered, as she drank her own tea.

Irene hated to think of what they were breathing in down here. She thought about Marlene, sweetly sleeping in Ma Ada's lap. Her tiny little lungs, filling up with the foul, dark air of underground. It gave her the horrors. But at least there wasn't oily, scorching smoke and fumes down here. That was one thing, at least.

'You want to go and check on her, don't you?' Beryl smiled, noticing the look of abstraction on Irene's face.

'Would you mind?'

'There's a lull – you go on,' Beryl urged her. 'And take Ma Ada a beef tea. She'll need it to keep her strength up.'

Irene hurried away down the tunnels, hoping against hope she wouldn't lose count of the twists and turns, and end up in the wrong passageway completely. Every single corridor had benches lining both walls, and every inch of wooden bench was occupied. As Irene made her way through the semi-darkness carrying her tin cup of Bovril she was aware of faces looking at her go by. Pale, watchful faces, like birds sleeping on branches. They propped each other up and some were snoring, somehow managing to blot out the reality around them and sink into blessed dreams. Others sat there alert, worried-looking, clutching scarves and blankets around their necks and holding each other's hands.

There wasn't a single face that Irene actually recognised, but she nodded and whispered hello to many as she went by. Just that nod and smile could make the difference, she knew. Someone saying hello and being human and ordinary. That tiny something could counteract the awfulness of the present moment. It was all too easy to sit down here with your own dark thoughts welling up around you: picturing what it might be like above ground, with the whole town razed to the ground, and no home to return to. It was easy to fixate on the horrible absurdity of clinging together underground like animals in burrows.

Luckily Irene's family were in the stretch of corridor where she remembered leaving them. Her sense of direction was pretty good, and she was glad to find Ma Ada sitting there with the bairn on her lap, with Megan beside her, looking incredibly uncomfortable.

'Where's Sam?' asked Irene.

'Helping out,' Ma Ada told her. 'There's lots needs doing down here. He's got strong muscles, my lad.'

Irene nodded, conscious of Ada's slight prickliness about Sam, and why he wasn't away in the services. There had been remarks recently from some of the neighbours. None would dare say anything outright to Ma Ada, but she knew that folk were wondering why Sam was still at home. All the Farleys knew that there was something wrong with his heart, and that's why the forces wouldn't take him. Ma Ada didn't see why strangers or anyone would need this explaining to them, and she had found herself growing defensive on Sam's behalf.

'It's good he's busy,' Irene said. 'If people see him busy and doing good volunteer work, then they won't say he's . . .'

'Say he's what?' Ada snapped, slurping her beef tea. 'A coward?'

'No one's said that!' Irene gasped.

'I'm not ashamed of my lad!' the old mother said, waking the baby with her sudden movement. 'I'd never be ashamed of any of my bairns! It's a bad heart he's got.'

'I know, I know . . .' said Irene soothingly, conscious that others were stirring and listening in. 'Drink your Bovril.'

'He's got a bad heart in more ways than one,' Ma Ada said darkly. 'His heart has led him into some bad places.'

Next to her Megan stiffened at these words. 'What's that meant to mean?' she started to say, and then her face twisted suddenly. Irene thought she was just grimacing in anger, and it took a few moments before she realised that Megan was in pain. 'Oh God,' her sister-in-law suddenly gasped. 'Oh God. Not now. Not down here.'

Ma Ada scowled. 'What's up? What's wrong with you?' She glared at Megan. The goodwill that had existed between them for the past few weeks was frittering away fast in the darkness and discomfort of the tunnel. Both women had been getting on each other's nerves all night, and Ma Ada had no patience with any more fuss from her most troublesome daughter-in-law.

'Megan?' Irene asked, worriedly. There was something about the way the girl was sitting forward and clutching herself, and the way she'd suddenly gone quiet that was terrifying to Irene. 'Megan, are you all right?'

The girl had her jaws clammed together and her teeth clenched shut, as if she could seal all the pain deep inside her. But the noise and the pain was getting too much for her and she had to let it out in a horrible, guttural roar that filled up the tunnel and silenced everyone at once.

'Oh bugger,' said Ma Ada, as she realised what was going on. The baby in her arms started to wriggle and gripe.

'Megan?' Irene asked again.

'Stop saying my name over and over!' Megan shrieked. When she lifted up her face it was lathered and gleaming with sweat. She was panting like a carthorse as she pushed out her words: 'Go and get help! Get me some help, Irene! I think . . . it's coming! My baby's coming . . . right now!'

Irene stepped away from her in shock. There was a moment of horrible tension as everyone stared at the suffering young woman, and then she screamed again, rocking forward on the bench.

'Go on, Irene!' Ma Ada shouted. 'You heard the girl! Go and get help!'

# Chapter Ten

There were two nurses in the tiny infirmary that night, Nurse Finch and Nurse Thompson. They were ready, as ever, for just about anything that a night in the shelter could throw at them, from broken limbs to asphyxiation. Their infirmary was a portion of tunnel almost the same size as the kitchen Irene had been serving hot drinks in, and she was appalled at the sight of it.

'Is this it?' she gasped, as they delivered Megan into the nurses' hands. Luckily it hadn't been too far to drag her.

'We've got everything we need here,' said Nurse Finch, in a clipped and businesslike tone. Behind her, Nurse Thompson was looking a lot less sure of herself. Megan was quiet for the moment, in a blessed lull between bouts of screaming. Her cries had unsettled them all, and nearly everyone in the Sixteen Streets shelter had heard her by now. 'Let's get her settled and comfortable.'

Easier said than done, on a tiny, canvas-covered gurney that was the closest thing the infirmary had to a bed. Irene stepped forward with her heart in her mouth as the two nurses helped Megan to lie down. She looked as if she was going to be doubled up for ever with the worst case of cramp. As she tried to lean back on the gurney she started wailing again. Her eyes looked wild as an animal's in pain. 'Irene! D-don't you leave me!'

Irene stepped closer. 'Of course not,' she said, and was surprised at herself. But her sister-in-law needed her tonight. It was as simple as that. Irene would be there to do whatever she could to help. There were no two ways about it. No matter how much of a bitch Megan had always been to her, Irene wasn't about to let her down in her hour of need. 'I know what it feels like, Megan. I know what you're going through.' She tried to brush the damp hair out of Megan's face. She was sweating profusely, drops standing out on her forehead.

'You hate me though,' Megan said, wrenching her face away from Irene's touch. 'Why would you help me out? You've always hated me, from the very first time you saw me.'

'That's not true!' Irene recoiled. It was on the tip of her tongue to shoot back, 'It's the other way around!'

Beryl was hovering anxiously at her side. 'It doesn't matter now, who hates who!'

'Y-yes, it does!' Megan wailed piteously. Her beautiful face was twisted and pale. 'She hates me! I'm going to die and she's still hating me. She's like the Angel of Death hanging over me!'

'Megan!' Beryl gasped, horrified. 'We're only trying to help.'

'I don't hate you, Megan,' Irene said, stoutly. 'I mean, it's true, that you've been a real cow to me, over the months, I must admit.'

'Irene!' hissed Beryl.

'No, no, it needs saying!' Irene said.

Nurse Thompson was looking alarmed, trying to push past to get to her patient.

'I knew it!' gasped Megan, breathing hard. 'I knew she thought I was a cow.'

'But you are!' Irene crowed. 'You've done some awful things to me. You've been a proper bully.'

'Look here,' said Nurse Finch insistently. 'We have to find out how far on she is. Contractions and so on.' The nurses were both rather posh-sounding, Irene realised. Nice lady volunteers with immaculate uniforms, working in a hell hole like this. Irene moved aside reluctantly.

'Don't you go away, Irene Farley!' Megan shouted at her. 'We can have this out at last. All this bad blood. You can tell me exactly why you hate me so much.'

Irene rolled her eyes, feeling harassed as the nurses fussed around Megan. 'I don't hate you. I told you that!'

'You wish I was dead. You're hoping that I die horribly in childbirth. And then you'll all be free of me!' Megan roared this in the most awful voice.

'That's just not true!'

'It is. I know it. You'd rather I was dead!'

Then suddenly, Ma Ada was in the room, stepping quickly around the curtain that divided the infirmary from the dirt tunnel. She was clutching baby Marlene and Irene had never been so glad to see the old woman in all her life. 'What's all this bloomin' noise about?' she cried, passing the baby straight away to Beryl, who took her awkwardly and retreated to stand by the curtain as if she wanted to make a quick getaway.

Suddenly the room was over-warm, as well as too noisy and there was a flurry of activity as Nurse Finch solemnly announced: 'That's her waters broke. The baby's on its way.'

Ma Ada was rolling up the sleeves of her heavy mustard-coloured cardigan and advancing on the gurney. 'You're insisting on giving birth tonight, are you, pet? That's just typical of you. But I know from experience that babies will be born just where and when they want to be.' She was muscling in on the nurses' territory as if she was expecting to play midwife herself. 'Come on, lasses. Let the dog see the rabbit.'

Nurse Finch reared up and told the woman, 'I am quite capable, with Nurse Thompson's help, of delivering the infant myself.' She said this in such a dignified voice that Ma Ada stared up at her in admiration.

'Well!' said Ma Ada. 'Is that so?'

Nurse Thompson didn't look quite as confident, Irene noted.

'And besides, who the devil are you, traipsing in here?' Nurse Finch asked haughtily.

'I'm the girl's mother-in-law!' roared Ma Ada, drawing herself up to her full height, which was only as tall as the watch pinned to the nurse's chest. 'I'm standing in for her mother, and I'm very experienced in matters of this kind.'

'Well, so are we!' glared Nurse Finch. Miss Thompson hurried away, looking anxious, to fetch more towels.

Another new arrival was suddenly pushing herself into the infirmary, edging nosily around the curtain and looking avid for details. 'I'm Mrs Clarke,' she said, confident that everyone would recognise her senior status. 'I understand this girl is going into labour.'

Megan cried out once more: a jagged, piercing cry that had a different quality to it than before. Her breath came in savage little bursts after that, and Nurse Finch shoved Irene out of the way so she could instruct her on how she should control her breathing.

'You – don't – have – to – tell – me – how – to . . . breathe!' gasped Megan.

'Yes, I do!' commanded the nurse. 'And don't start pushing yet. Just wait and do precisely what I tell you.'

Mrs Clarke was standing right beside Ma Ada now, and both were filled with great curiosity. 'You haven't even got her things off yet!' gasped Mrs Clarke. 'She's not going to give birth to anything with her knickers still on!' Her voice was incredulous. She looked like she was about to insist on taking command of the situation at once.

Nurse Finch rounded on her furiously. Her young face was suffused with red. 'Look here! Everything is in control here. I know exactly what I'm doing, and so does Nurse Thompson. Isn't that true, Nurse Thompson?'

Nurse Thompson nodded, looking white, as Megan let forth another volley of screams and panted desperately once more.

'But we are here to help you,' protested Ma Ada.

'Indeed!' shouted Mrs Clarke. 'We are very experienced in this kind of thing.'

Nurse Finch raised her voice once more: 'I don't need a whole bunch of fish wives fussing around me. Now, if you don't mind! Kindly – get out of my infirmary!'

Ma Ada and Mrs Clarke looked appalled. They fell silent at once and simply stared at the young nurse. Never had their help been refused in such circumstances. They were used to everyone looking hugely relieved at their reassuring presences as they arrived to boss everyone around.

'We have everything perfectly in hand,' the senior nurse added, in a slightly softer tone.

Hugging Marlene to her, Beryl stepped forward nervously to suggest: 'Let's go and wait out in the passageway, shall we? They haven't really got enough room in here, with everyone standing about.'

The older women were still in a state of mild shock at their apparent redundancy. They let themselves be led out into the dimly lit tunnel, and Beryl found them a spot on a bench they could occupy together as they waited for news. 'They'll tell us everything that's happening,' Beryl told them, jogging Marlene on her lap. 'I'm sure everything is going to be fine.' Secretly, she was relieved that they'd been turfed out of the infirmary. She hadn't wanted a ringside view of all the gory details.

Poor Irene, though. At the very last moment, as the others had been ushered out, Megan had reached out with one steely claw and grasped hold of her hand. 'No, not you! Please, stay with me, Irene. C-can she stay, nurse? I can have one f-family member, can't I? I can have one sister to stay with me and hold my hand?'

Nurse Finch had looked over and relented, giving a quick, supportive smile. 'Of course, dear. Only one, mind.'

'I want Irene to be here with me,' Megan said, with a queer, inscrutable smile. She gripped Irene's fingers tightly in her own, before submitting to another wave of agony. Irene's fingers cracked painfully in her fist.

Irene smiled wanly back and wondered what on earth she was doing here, making calming, loving noises into the ear of the girl who hated her guts.

Beryl felt awkward holding baby Marlene at first. The child wriggled and wouldn't settle. It was as if she was alert to Beryl's discomfort at being made responsible for her.

But Beryl managed to calm herself down and regulate her own staccato breathing as she sat in the dusty darkness with the baby. Her calm spread out to encompass the child. Soon Marlene was nodding off miraculously and Beryl found that her clinging warmth was making her think about the baby she had once been responsible for, so many years ago. Her baby brother, Fred.

Suddenly the memory of him was with her once more as she sat there drowsily, eyes tickling tearily with dust from the tunnel.

Beryl used to carry her little baby brother around like he was her teddy bear. She was seven years older than Fred and had fallen in love with him at first sight. He was noisy and bright red and he brought light, laughter and hullaballoo into their little house that overlooked the sea. When he got a bit older he grew fair, reddish hair in a curly calf lick that would never quite lie down.

Her mum wasn't well after the birth and stayed in bed a lot. She was weakened from then on and didn't go out of the house much. Same with dad, though his sickness was all down to shell shock from the trenches. He hadn't been right for years.

Their little house stood on the prow of the hill above South Marine Park. The best spot in the whole of town, Beryl always thought. They were at the very top of South Shields where the air was freshest and the seagulls were noisiest. She knew her family was lucky to live there, within spitting distance of the North Sea. Every morning she could watch the sun rise over the horizon, filling her room with its golden glare.

She was a happy kid, counting her blessings every day and wishing her dad was better. Then wishing her mam was better. It would have been a gloomy house of invalids if Fred hadn't been born. He lit up his sister's life and made her happy.

'Dragging him round like a rag doll,' her mother had muttered and rolled her eyes. Beryl carried tea trays and soup plates into her mam's room and watched her eating. Little dolly bites and sips. She usually left most of what Beryl cooked for her.

Sometimes Mum would be fond and loving, other times cross and almost envious at the way Beryl had taken charge of her brother, the home and various household tasks.

Her dad simply let her get on with it. He didn't know or care how things got done round their house. The little boy he merely blinked at with bewilderment, as if wondering how such a strange new person had suddenly appeared out of nowhere.

Fred was a kind of magical person. A little sprite who had floated into their lives. He was too good for this world, Beryl had sometimes thought. The perfect kid. No bother at all.

'Beryl, pet, you have to make friends your own age, you know,' her mother tried to tell her. 'You can't just carry around your little brother all your life. You've got to get to know other girls of your own kind. I don't want you acting like a little mother all the time. You've got to be a little girl as well. You're still just a bairn yourself, you know.'

Beryl didn't really get what her mum was going on about. And besides, she wasn't really bothered about making friends with other girls her age. They seemed young and babyish to her. Then, as they got older, they were a bit snippy with her, like they wouldn't want her around them, even if she'd had the time. She didn't fit in, but she couldn't have cared less.

She didn't have enough hours in the day anyway. Besides her own schooling there were meals to fix and rooms to sweep. There was laundry to scrub and the mangle to turn and all the pegging out in the yard to get done. Really, it was far too much work for a girl her age. But she never complained. She had Fred with her all the time, and that made everything easier.

Mum would grow gloomy and wish that it was her pushing the pram around town, and accepting everyone's compliments on her bonny bairn. Then there was the walking and the running and all the new words Fred was learning. He was learning it all from Beryl and not his own mum. Gradually Mum let all that go. She couldn't be envious, and she couldn't let herself get too twisted up about all of that. She was grateful to Beryl. Thank God they had a sensible lass to take over all the everyday business of running their house. Whatever would they have done without her?

Beryl's mum and dad lay in their beds in separate rooms, with a wall between them. Sprigged flowers on his wallpaper, Regency stripe on hers. They'd knock on the wall to message each other, but never really had much to say. They were bonded in the shared sickly enterprise of simply getting through their days. Both of them were gladder of Beryl than they could say.

Birthdays, Christmases, and some special Saturdays the family would assemble in one room of the house and sit together. The little lad looked surprised when his parents emerged, fully dressed, from their rooms. They looked shaky and shy. He was nervous of them. He secretly preferred it when it was just him and Beryl.

Especially when the two of them were out together. And especially when they were on the beach at South Shields. Their happiest moments were spent down by the sea and Fred, from the earliest, felt very at home with his bare feet in the gritty, warm sand and dipping his toes into the bone cold water.

It was down on the beach at South Shields that they had spent every day of their summers together. So long ago, it seemed to her now. So many years ago, when she was just a little girl.

The lapping of the waves and the bronze sheen of the sky filled up Beryl's horizon as she slept in the air raid tunnel. She hugged Irene's baby to her as if the child was Fred himself, even as the tunnel rocked with distant explosions and silt fell through the dusky air. Marlene slept through the cries of fright and surprise from the townsfolk, and even the piercing shrieks that were still emerging from the infirmary.

Then the screams from Megan grew more urgent and fearful, and Irene was back in the tunnel, looking scared. The child woke up and started crying for her mother, and this jolted Beryl awake.

'I-is everything all right?' she asked blearily.

Irene was gaunt with fear. 'Megan's lost a lot of blood,' she said hoarsely. 'There's been complications. It's like the bairn doesn't want to be born.'

'Who can blame it, in this hell hole?' Beryl let Irene take her own baby, and saw the splashes of dark, wet blood on her sister-in-law's clothes. 'Oh my God! Is she going to be okay?'

Irene nodded as she held Marlene close. She was just about squeezing the life out of her baby, seeking reassurance from that tiny body. 'They're trying to slow her down. She'll rip herself apart unless she does. It's like she can't get the kid out fast enough.'

'Typical Megan,' Beryl found herself saying. 'Causing a fuss.'

'Where's Ada and Mrs Clarke?' Irene asked.

As far as Beryl knew, Mrs Clarke had returned to her endless task of bossing everyone about, and Ma Ada had said something about going to find Sam, and telling him the news about Megan. They had left Beryl all on her own with Marlene. That sudden realisation – that she had been left with sole responsibility for the baby – sent a thrill of cold fear through Beryl's stomach. She quelled it and counted herself lucky that she hadn't been in Irene's position. She hadn't had to be in that infirmary, watching Megan bleeding and howling.

'It's a horrible scene in there,' Irene said, as if reading her mind.

'Sh-she's not going to die, is she?' Beryl asked.

'She's too bloomin' selfish to go and die!' Irene laughed bleakly. 'Can you imagine her doing that? No, she'll be fine.'

Another scream rent the air then. A new bout of agony and effortful work was beginning behind the curtain. Irene took it as her cue. 'I'd better go back in. She wants me there. Even in her delirium. Sweating and screaming and not even knowing what's happening to her. She wanted me there, so I'd best get back. Will you be okay with Marlene?'

'Of course . . .' Beryl nodded, and took hold of the child again. Her heart was thumping hard, though. What she really wanted to do was flee from this scene, as far and as hard as she could. But she forced herself to sit there, stolidly, holding the bairn, watching Irene disappear back inside the noisy infirmary.

Oh God, Beryl found herself praying. Please make everything all right. Please stop Megan bleeding and pushing too hard. Make her listen to what those nurses are saying, and make her do what they tell her to. Make her stop fighting her own child. Make the birth go easier for them both. Make everything come out right. Please, Lord . . . Beryl was startled at herself for addressing the almighty, even in the privacy of her own mind. She hadn't prayed like this . . . She hadn't prayed so fervently since . . . Well, since a long time ago, anyway . . .

Then Ma Ada was bustling back up the duckboards of the dimly lit tunnel towards her again. 'Any news?' she gasped, and sat heavily beside her.

'Irene's been out to see us, just a moment ago,' Beryl said. She weighed up whether to be fully honest or not. Would it do any good to alarm the old woman?

'What did she say? And don't try to soft-soap me, Beryl. What's going on?'

'Irene says Megan's lost a lot of blood. She says it might be a hard birth.'

The old woman was back on her feet. 'I'll go and help them!'

Beryl dragged on her tiny, claw-like hand. 'No, you stay here with me. They've got everything they need. They don't need you as well.'

A new volley of screams rang out, and Ma Ada stiffened. Then she sagged and sat down on the bench again. 'Eeeh, I hate being helpless. I hate seeing anyone suffer. But when it's someone in my family, and I can't do anything . . .' She shook her head tearfully. 'You know, I'd do anything for you lot, don't you? Any of you. I'd cut off my limbs if I thought it could relieve any of you of a moment of suffering. That's true, you know, Beryl. Even Megan.'

Beryl nodded, and put her arm around the old lady, and let her hold Marlene for a while.

The screams from the infirmary seemed to run on and on, all through the night . . .

'Ma?'

It was her son, Sam, looking tired and rumpled after a night of lugging sandbags and God knows what else about in the deepest recesses of the tunnels. He was shaking his poor, exhausted mother awake, and the old woman took a few seconds to remember where she was. 'Sam! What time is it? Is there an attack on?' She looked terribly old and afraid.

'It's nearly morning. No, there's been no bombs nearby. Not tonight. We've got through another night. But, Mam . . . I saw Mrs Clarke and some of the other volunteers. They were telling me that . . . Megan's having her bairn in there! Is she?'

'Aye, that's true.' Ma Ada sat up and pulled her shawl around her shoulders. 'I went looking for you, hinny. When the birthing started, and they chucked us out of that infirmary because we were no help nor use to them. So I went hunting through all the tunnels for you, to tell you what was going on.' Ma Ada was shivering with the damp cold of the sandstone wall at her back. Horrible place to fall asleep. She marvelled that she had even been able to. Beside her Beryl was sleeping sitting up, with Marlene curled at her breast.

'I–is Megan all right in there?' Sam asked. 'I've heard screams, but . . .' He looked very young.

'There's no more news yet,' she said. 'They'd have come out and told us, if there had been. But listen, son. Before there is any more news this morning, I've got to tell you what I was going to say to you in the night, but I couldn't find you in all the maze down here.' Ma Ada gestured for him to come and kneel by her, so he could hear what she had to whisper to him. 'Listen, lad. We've got to hope the birth goes well and both Megan and her child are healthy and safe. That's the most important thing.'

'Aye, of course!' he said.

'But there's more to this business as well, though,' she added, looking shrewdly at her youngest boy. 'Now, son. You know that I know, full well, that the bairn being born through there doesn't belong to your brother Bob, Megan's lawful husband. You and I both know that you are the father of that babby.'

Sam gulped, hard. Of course he knew his secret was out in the family. But everyone had agreed to keep it within the walls of Number Thirteen, for the good of everyone involved. It made him flinch to hear his mother speak the truth out loud to him like this. He nodded, with his eyes cast down at the earth floor.

'Now, we've got to trust in God that the bairn's born healthy with no problems,' Ma Ada went on. 'That's the first thing. But after that, you have to remember that the baby isn't yours. It's Megan's and Bob's. You have to stand back and renounce all claim on the bairn.'

'I know that,' he whispered. 'I realise that.' His voice was hollow, like this was something he had thought about long and hard. It was a thought that was torture to him, his mother saw.

'Aye, lad. But you've not seen that babby yet. You've not seen your own flesh yet, and you don't know how it will make you feel. Just listen to your old mother as she tells you, son. You'll find it so hard to step back. To keep away. To pretend that it's hardly owt to do with you, beyond you being its uncle. I know, you see. I know you, Sam Farley, and I know how it will feel. I know how it will feel in that tender heart of yours.'

She watched tears running down his face. He was a soft-hearted lad, she knew. And she also knew that this business was going to end up breaking him in two.

'Sam?' she said, taking his face in her hard, crabbed hand. 'Now, I've forgiven you. I don't know what you thought you were playing at with that damned Megan, but we all have to put that behind us. Now there's another bairn about to be born, and you're its uncle, and that's all. All right, son?'

He nodded, and realised that the screaming that had been coming from behind that heavy curtain had suddenly petered out. Beside them Marlene stirred on Beryl's lap, and both Sam and his mother realised that Beryl had been awake these past few moments.

She had heard every word that had just been said.

'Are you all right there, Beryl?' asked Ma Ada calmly.

'Yes, Ma,' said Beryl. 'I'm fine. Are you?'

'We're grand, aren't we, Sam?'

Sam nodded and wiped his eyes on his sleeve.

'We're both waiting here for news,' Ma Ada said. 'And we just know it's going to be wonderful news.'

They were interrupted by the thin, reedy cry of a baby, coming from beyond the curtain, inside the infirmary. Ma Ada gave an excited shout in response and jumped up onto her feet. 'Is it born?' she gabbled, and at that moment an exhausted Irene tottered out into the corridor to see them all. 'Irene! Is it all right? What is it?'

They clustered around her, and Irene's own baby girl started crying then, disturbed by the tension and the excitement in the air. 'It's . . . fine,' Irene told them. 'It's very small, and there was some worry at first, but it's fine. It's a little boy.'

Ma Ada shrieked with jubilation, kicking up her feet on the wooden duckboards in a dance of glee. 'Can we go in? Can we all go in and see him yet? He has to see all his aunts and his uncle and his cousin and his nanna!'

'In a moment – they're just cleaning Megan up.'

'Is she all right?' Ma Ada asked sharply.

'She lost an awful lot of blood early on,' Irene said. 'It was quite a drama for an hour or so. I've never seen anything like it. But it's all right now. Nurse Finch is stitching her right now. We have to give them some time before we all go dashing in.'

Ma Ada nodded with understanding. She settled back down on the bench and beamed at them all. There was a strange kind of glow about her face. All the tiredness had simply melted away from her. 'A little boy! Another little boy in our house at last!'

# Chapter Eleven

Megan and her baby got a lot of attention. As was traditional the women of Frederick Street and all the surrounding streets came round as soon as possible to coo over the tiny bairn and to hear the story of his birth.

They crowded into Ma Ada's parlour and chattered about how South Shields had fared compared with Sunderland under bombardment the night the baby was born. Beryl and Irene were busy making pots of tea for the gossiping women, and Megan sat there beatifically, holding her tiny red baby in her arms, and submitting to all their attention.

'Johnny indeed,' Beryl muttered, as she stirred the tea leaves in a fresh pot. 'That's not a name for a bairn. Though thinking about it, perhaps it's what they should have used, the pair of them.'

Irene didn't get it at first, and when she did she squealed: 'Eeeh! A Rubber Johnny!' And her voice carried out of the scullery, into the parlour, where Ma Ada heard them and scowled.

Aunty Winnie was visiting, holding a little glass of sherry and making pronouncements over the bairn. 'He will have a wonderful life. Doors will open up for him. He'll have health, wealth and happiness, will little Johnny.' Then she sat down heavily and clinked her glass to Ada's, prompting a top up. 'Mind, he's a poor little scrap of a thing to look at, isn't he?'

Still pale and peaky-looking, Megan scowled at her. 'He was early and it was a tricky birth. He put up quite a fight. He didn't want to come out.'

Mrs Merriweather from up the street shuddered. 'That's the same as I was, every time, with my lot. None of them wanted to come out! I'm like a war zone, down there.' She mouthed the words 'down there' and glanced downwards as if that explained things.

The other women pitched in then, bringing out their child-birth stories: the gorier the better. They relished dispensing the horrible details as they slurped their tea. It was one of those conversations they could really glory in while there were no men around.

Irene said, 'The thing is, if childbirth is so bloomin' horrible and painful and dangerous, why don't you older women warn us younger ones? Why don't you ever tell us how bad it really is?' Her voice sounded so earnest, rising above the jeering, laughing voices of the women.

'If we told you all the truth, there'd be no more bairns at all!' chuckled Ma Blenkinsop. 'That's one good reason, right there!'

General merriment broke out at this, and Beryl opened the biscuit tin and handed round broken ginger snaps.

'I'd have thought twice, if I'd known how bloody awful it was going to be,' said Megan, staring down into the sleeping face of her infant.

'Ah, nay, pet,' said Ma Ada. 'How can you say that, looking into your own bairn's bonny face? You'd do anything for him now, wouldn't you? He means the world to you, doesn't he? You'll soon see – the scars and the memories will fade, given time.'

'Maybe,' frowned Megan.

'I mean, you had a particularly awful time,' Ma Ada went on. 'With it being in the air raid shelter and all. Admittedly, that made it a bit more tricky. But them lasses there, them nurses – they were more than capable. They rose to the challenge marvellously, I thought.'

Irene bit her lip. 'They certainly did. I was there the whole time and they were incredible. You were lucky to have them, Megan.'

Megan shrugged and pulled a face as her baby woke up and started to mewl. 'They were doing what they're trained to do, I suppose.'

Ma Blenkinsop, the old dame from across the way, piped up in her wheedling voice, 'And I heard that Irene was a star, as well, that night? She was on hand to help you through it all, like a proper sister, eh?'

'That's right,' nodded Ma Ada. 'She held Megan's hand throughout the whole thing and shouted at her when to push, and when to breathe, and all of that. The nurses said she was – what was it? A stalwart help.'

Irene blushed and gathered in the used cups and saucers. 'Anyone would, under the circumstances.' Her hands were still all bruised.

'It's a relief to me,' sighed Ma Ada. 'To see you lasses getting along like this, and helping each other in your hours of need. What with all the lads away at war – and your own fellas away, fighting abroad – you lasses need to look after each other, and be on the same side.' Ma Ada shook her head and pointed at Megan and then Irene and Beryl, making sure that all their visitors were paying attention. 'Because, you know, they didn't all get on at first, these girls. Not at all. And it wasn't easy at the start, when they all came moving into my house, one at a time. Why, Megan and Irene didn't like each other one little bit, and there were terrible scuffles and argy-bargy at the off-set!'

The female visitors chuckled and muttered and nodded their understanding. 'It's often the way with lasses,' said Aunty Winnie. 'Oftentimes they just don't get on. It's the same with cats, I've noticed. And it's like me and my sisters. We could never see eye to eye. That's because my sisters were a pack of flamin' bitches, of course.'

There was laughter at this, and others pitched in to talk about their own complicated relations. Irene stood in the scullery doorway with her trayful of dirty crockery and realised that Megan was giving her a simpering, sickly smile. It was a defiant look, she thought. Megan hadn't made her peace with anyone, least of all Irene. It was plain on her face, if anyone had cared to look. All the old women here are too busy mulling over their boring pasts, Irene thought grimly, and she turned into the scullery to have a few moments alone.

'Buck up,' Beryl nudged her. She'd been out in the yard, sneaking a Woodbine. 'Megan won't be queen of the house for very long. Let her enjoy her moment in the limelight.'

'It's not that,' Irene said. 'I don't care about being centre of attention. You know I don't. I couldn't stand it when that lot came round to get a look at Marlene, and went pawing at the two of us. No, I'm just dreading having to share a bedroom with the cow, that's all.'

'Ah,' said Beryl.

To Ma Ada it seemed the obvious solution. The attic bedroom was wide and spacious, and the double bed up there was being used by only one while Tom was away. And Megan could hardly be expected to carry on sleeping in that tiny staircase room with a newborn baby.

'You want Irene and me to *share*?' Megan had burst out laughing at the proposal.

'It makes sense in terms of feeding the babies and sharing stuff, and having enough room,' Ma Ada told her beadily. 'All it takes is a bit of willingness to get along.'

The younger women felt the force of the old woman's blazing willpower. This was her house and it was up to her to order everyone about. In recent weeks they had felt her grip of power almost slackening, as if she was getting too old to enforce her will. But now, only a day or two after Johnny's dramatic delivery, she was laying down the law. Megan was to move with her baby up to Irene's room in the attic, and they were to share nicely.

'And whose baby is to have the antique carved crib?' asked Megan.

'Well,' the old woman frowned, 'Johnny is little and brand new. Irene, your Marlene is growing at a rate of knots and she's the picture of health. She can go in the bed between you lasses. I think the newborn should be in the crib.'

That was Ma Ada's final word on the matter, and Megan had turned to flash Irene a look of triumph.

'That's settled then,' Ma Ada had sighed contentedly. 'We'll have a wonderful nursery, up in the attic.'

'I won't be able to stand it,' Irene told Beryl. 'She'll drive me crackers. She hates me!'

'No, she doesn't,' Beryl smiled. 'She's difficult and selfish, but she doesn't hate you. I bet you'll end up getting up in the night to feed both bairns while she sleeps right through, the lazy devil. But that'll be the worst of it.'

Irene wasn't so sure. She didn't want to keep going on about it, and making everyone think she was complaining all the time, but it felt like a nightmare. It felt like she was attached at the hip to Megan now. All she'd done in holding her hand through the birth had been what any decent person would do. Megan had been like a screaming, suffering animal, and Irene's heart couldn't help but go out to her. She'd clutched her hand and yelled at her to push and push, and keep on pushing. She'd urged her on with every scrap of her own strength, and the whole thing had gone on for hours.

When Irene compared it with her own delivery, in the sunny bedroom in Hunworth, with her mother at her side and far fewer hours spent screaming in agony, she felt sorry for her sister-in-law. Even if the girl had been her sworn enemy for several months on end.

It was no use harping on about the past, though, and nursing old hurts. Especially in wartime. Especially when their fellas were abroad and suffering God knew what. It was the least the women could do, to bury the hatchet at home.

That night, when the two were alone in the attic room, preparing their bairns for bed, Irene said as much, in a bright, cheery voice. Megan lay on the bed, wincing with pain from her stitches and her swellings and she frowned up at Irene. 'What are you saying?'

Johnny was in the crib, quiet with surprise at being left alone for a moment in his blankets, with no old ladies prodding and probing at him.

Irene smiled patiently at her new room-mate and said, 'I think it's time we started getting along, me and you, Megan. We've had our differences in the past, but we were just silly girls, really. We were like schoolgirls, being envious of each other and carrying on daft.'

'Speak for yourself . . .' Megan muttered, and closed her eyes.

'Well, now we've got proper responsibilities,' Irene went on, 'and we can be a great help to each other.'

Megan sighed deeply, with her eyes closed, and Irene wondered if she'd simply fallen asleep.

'And maybe it's not perfect, that we have to share this room, and everything,' said Irene, 'but we can make it work, can't we? We can get along all right?'

There was a pause, and in the lamplight Megan's eyes seemed to be moving under her closed lids, as if she was thinking over what Irene had said.

'Megan? I want us to be friends. Like me and Beryl are. Like you and Beryl are. We're all sisters together.'

Irene bit her tongue to stop herself from gushing on any further. She was trying really hard and Megan wasn't responding at all. She felt like picking up her glass of water from her nightstand and dashing it in the girl's face. See her respond then!

Megan's eyes fluttered open and fixed upon her sister-in-law. 'Aye, pet. Whatever you want. I never wanted any antagonism in the first place. I really didn't.' Her tone was sweet and calm. It was a voice quite unlike Irene had ever heard her use before. 'So, I'm sorry for the things I've said and done, and all the things that have upset you. I could have been kinder to you at work at the biscuit factory. I could have made things easier for you when you were new here in the house.'

Irene drew in her breath sharply. She was amazed at her success in getting Megan to say this stuff. It sounded so heart-felt! It was like she really did regret that she'd been so much of a cow in the past. Maybe this was actual repentance from Megan? 'Th-that's all right . . .' Irene said. 'Let's just call a truce between us, and get along from now on, shall we? For the sake of both our bairns?'

'Aye, let's,' said Megan. 'Now, get into bed and turn the light off. We'll need to get all the sleep we can before we've got to do the feeding.'

Both babies were being angels tonight. Johnny was oddly self-sufficient and calm, lost inside the giant wooden crib. Marlene was hugged into Irene's side, dozing deeply as Irene turned out the lamp and settled down.

There was a moment of utter darkness until the room's shadows resolved themselves and the cloudy moonlight filtered under the ill-fitting blackout curtains. Then Megan said softly: 'I suppose I've been a bit crazy, this past year. I don't know what it is. Realising that my own husband doesn't love me, I suppose. Learning that he had a thing for that old floozy from the pub. My feelings have been all over the place.'

'I-I suppose that's natural . . .' Irene said. She realised she'd never really thought about things from Megan's point of view before.

'I suppose I've just been feeling a bit lost . . . and lonely,' came the older girl's voice, with a catch in it. She was sobbing, Irene thought. She's actually upset!

Irene touched her arm and tried to say the right thing. 'We never have to be lonely ever again, Megan. Don't you see? We're both mams now. That means we've always got someone to love, and someone who will always love us back.'

# Chapter Twelve

Beryl was jealous. There was no other word for it, and she couldn't help herself. She lay in her little room – the one she should be sharing with her husband Tony – and wept bitterly.

Fancy envying those lasses having sleepless nights! The babies took turns waking up and screaming down the whole house. They made each other worse, bawling and shrieking, and filling the place with their hungry, anguished cries. Some nights Beryl felt like joining in with their noisy wails.

How had her life wound up like this?

Not too many years ago she had met a young man in a pub, and he had talked nicely to her. He had inclined his head towards her so he could be heard over the convivial racket of the Robin Hood. He was warm, funny and cocksure. She had liked him at once.

'I'm one of the Farleys,' he had told her, laughing and shaking her hand. He said it like it was natural that everyone should know who the Farleys were, like they were a famous family or something.

The pub was along one of the ramshackle streets of red brick back-to-back houses, just up from the docks. Beryl wasn't used to those streets back then. They ran up the hill as far as you could see and everyone called them the Sixteen Streets.

Their chimneys smoked lazily, filling the skies with orange and purple smoke as the sun went down after the factories and the shipyards shut. Usually Beryl would hurry home from the biscuit factory across town to the hill overlooking the sea and make dinner for her two parents, who both tended to pick at her meals until they pushed them aside.

But one Friday night, for some reason, the girls in her work room asked her to come along with them to the pub. It was a dingy little backstreet pub called the Robin Hood. Nothing special. But Beryl felt as if she'd been asked to go to Buckingham Palace. For once she felt like she'd had a proper invite, and that people wanted her to come somewhere with them specially. For once she was going to be included. She agreed without a moment's hesitation, surprising herself. She had been missing company. She had missed being treated like one of the gang. She'd had years of feeling like she'd been denied the chance to be just like everyone else.

That night one of the girls had had a windfall, and she was buying all the lasses a half of mild each. Twelve of them were milling about in the dark little bar and huddling by the fire in the grate and, looking round, Beryl decided that the Robin Hood on Frederick Street was actually rather a cosy and welcoming place. She even loved the smell of the cigarettes and the hopsy beer. The grown-up scents of the place seemed welcoming to her, as did the people gathered around.

Just as she was starting to relax at last: that was the very moment that she met her Tony.

'What does that mean? "One of the Farleys"?' she asked, sipping her half and feeling cheeky.

'We live on this street, at Number Thirteen,' he said, jutting out his chin almost proudly, and puffing on his tab. 'We're renowned round here, us lot. There's so many of us, and we've all been here so long, our clan.'

'Oh, yes?' she smiled, giving him a slow, appraising look up and down. Beryl had to admit that he was a fine specimen. Six foot tall, in his early thirties, a little thinning on top, perhaps. But steely blue, deep-set eyes that seemed to be looking straight into her. That stare of his made her look away and take another deep swig of her drink.

Urgh . . . it tasted a bit like cold black tea, but she liked the way it made her head spin slightly. She liked the way her thoughts were being reordered and she almost felt giddy, for the first time in a very long while indeed.

But I was a young fool, Beryl thought. Let's face it, he was the first grown man who ever took any notice of me. He was the first to talk to me like I was a grown-up woman and worthy of notice, let alone desire. That was the first public bar I'd ever been into, and my first night out, with the girls from the biscuit factory. I knew nothing. I'd been nowhere. I was a fool! Anyone could have paid attention to me, snapped their fingers, and I'd have followed them slavishly.

The truth was, she had just wanted to be away from her mam and dad and the life she'd already had. Tony was her chance to do that, and she'd grabbed hold of him.

Yes, she loved him. Of course she longed for him to come home from his ship – wherever it was – every single day. She missed that closeness to him.

Warmth. That's what she had felt from the very start when she was with Tony, and just a little later, when he first took her to his home to meet the rest of his family.

Beryl wasn't used to feeling warmed through. Often, when she dashed into the house after work, she found that the pilot light on the boiler had puffed out at some point during the day. All the pipes and the rooms would be chilly and, of course, neither of her parents would have done anything about it. Almost every day Beryl crouched in front of the boiler clicking the noisy buttons and waiting for the blue flame to catch light. She would listen for the cold pipes gurgling into life.

All of South Shields had felt chilly to her in those days. Dashing in her warmest coat from home to the factory, walking as fast as she could in the early hours to be at her shift on time. Her breath fanning out in white plumes. Standing at her workbench in the chilly shed, working the machines and shuffling on the spot to keep her feet from freezing. Sometimes she even longed to work in the bake house where the biscuits were cooked and everyone complained about the extreme heat and the smoke and the fumes. Beryl would have volunteered, just in order to keep warm.

But it was a very strange thing. From her first moments with Tony Farley, standing in the corner of the snug of the pub, somehow a feeling of warmth entered into her. Some deep shiver that she'd been holding inside for years started to relax and thaw.

He liked the look of her at once, she could see that. He admired her dark, glossy hair, which she'd kept long, even though it was a faff to look after when you had to wear hairnets and things at work. He liked her slimness, and what he could see of her figure in her work pinny and overalls that first day in the pub. She had a gentle expression, and a kindly look about her. Her face wasn't pretty exactly, but there was something about it that appealed to him hugely. Beryl's was a face Tony could imagine looking at every single day of his life. Her eyes were huge and understanding, and she had a way of biting her lip when she listened to you. It was like she was reserving judgment until she heard your whole story, and she was wary of the surprises that the world may chuck her way.

From that very first teatime in the Robin Hood, that spring day in 1938, Tony wanted to put his arms around her and tell her that everything was going to be all right. To him she looked like that was exactly what she needed to hear.

He took her to his mother's house, just a few doors down from the pub on Frederick Street. At Number Thirteen it was always warm because of the great big iron range in the back room, and the comings and goings of all the people who lived there, or who passed through during the course of the day.

It was noisy and confusing, but Beryl was thrilled by all the friendly hullabaloo of friends and relatives noisily drinking tea, eating meals, laughing and telling tales about each other. Tony had three brothers and, together with their old mother, Ada, and her hairless cat, Lucky, they packed out that little house to the rafters. There always seemed to be double the number of people inside than there was supposed to be.

As the guest and possible sweetheart of the eldest brother, Beryl came in for quite a lot of attention. She was invited for tea in the back parlour, and the four brothers and the old woman watched keenly as she sipped her tea from a porcelain cup and saucer fetched out from the top shelf. She was fed biscuits and dainties from the very best china and her demure, undaunted reaction to them all went down well with the Farley clan.

She was used to hiding her reactions, but Beryl did find the old mother rather frightening at first. She was a tiny woman, heaped in shawls and layers of shapeless garments. She wore cameo brooches that dated back to Victorian times. Her hair was kept neat under a hairnet with curlers most of the time, but for Beryl's first visits she had it set into an elaborate do with perfect little waves that softened the deeply etched lines of her face. She studied the young woman with a speculative air, and her dark eyes were merciless.

'Tony's the first of my lads to bring home a girl,' Mother Ada told her, chewing a square of dark, moist Parkin and smacking her lips. 'It's all very novel, this.'

How old were the other lads? Tony was thirty-one, Robert was a year younger. Then there was Tommy, who was slightly younger again, and who seemed nervous and shy. And the youngest was Sam, who was still really a bairn, or rather a rangy, awkward youth, who was all arms and legs. He crammed all the cakes and sandwiches into his mouth that he could, and nodded hello to Beryl, and couldn't wait to go racing out to meet his friends in the streets again.

'I'm very proud of my four lads,' the old woman said. How old was she, really? The youngest boy couldn't be more than seventeen. Mother Ada couldn't be truly ancient, in that case. But there was something in the way she sat there and held herself, that made her seem monumentally old, like she'd always been here in this house observing centuries unfolding. 'It's been just me and them for ever. Since their daft bloody addle-pated dad ran out on us all and died a beggar's death in a ditch. It's just been us, looking after each other. And they're all devoted to their mam, these lads. It would have to be a very special woman who came along and turned the head of any of my boys.'

'Mam . . .' Tony gently reproached her. 'Beryl's only a friend, come to tea. It's early days, yet.'

Ma Ada snorted. 'Early days, he says! It's always early days, it seems like. And then time whizzes on faster than you'd ever believe, my lad. There's barely time to catch your breath before it's moved onto the next thing, and you get swept up in it all. All the choices you make and all the roads you choose. So think on, and choose wisely. The pair of you.' Then she looked down at her plate and picked up all the cake crumbs with the end of one stubby finger and sucked it thoughtfully. 'That's your Aunt Winnie's parkin, that. Not as moist as it might be.' Then she narrowed her eyes at Beryl. 'Have you got brothers and sisters, then? Did you grow up in a big family?'

Beryl gulped. She felt like she was about to cough and choke on Aunty Winnie's crumbly cake. For a moment she didn't know how to answer. Something about those ancient eyes boring into her compelled her to tell the truth, which she hadn't even explained to Tony yet. 'I . . . once had a little brother. Fred. And I loved him so much. I did everything for him because my parents are both quite ill.'

'Oh, yes?' Ma Ada perked up as Beryl seemed to warm to her theme. Ada liked a good tale-telling and appreciated folk with something to say for themselves. 'What happened to him, hinny?'

But on that occasion Beryl didn't say anything else, about her brother or her parents. She dipped her face to stare at the immaculate tablecloth and felt the ache that she always felt. She had an ache in her palm every day and she knew it was because her brother's little hand used to fit there, when she walked along the street with him, when he was in her care. That ache was never going to go away.

Now she could feel Tony's eyes upon her. She didn't dare look at him.

Mother Ada broke the silence, 'Eeeh, hinny. You're welcome here, with my lot.'

Her tiny brown wrinkled hand reached out across the table, and Beryl stared at the mother of the four Farley boys. There was something very steadying and calm about her. For once Beryl didn't feel like she was whirling around, her heart pattering away on the verge of panic. She took a deep breath and said, 'Thank you, Mrs Farley.'

'Call me Ma,' smiled the old woman. 'Everyone does.'

And that was the beginning of Beryl settling in and finding a place here at Number Thirteen. Almost five years ago and, in that time of great upheavals, she felt like she had changed and become someone else. She was no longer that cowed and biddable little thing she had once been. She was no longer simply grateful that people treated her like a grown-up and someone worthy of respect.

She had become a wife. She had been loved. She had felt her spirit lighten and she had even started to enjoy her life. Even after the war had begun, Beryl felt like she was experiencing real life at last, and loving it.

Then Tony had gone away to war, of course, and that was hard. Beryl had to spend some time alone and struggled along, finding her own feet. Though she always had the Farley family around her, there was a special loneliness to having a husband away at sea. All these experiences of recent times couldn't help changing her.

Even her work had changed her. She was a welder now! She'd been determined to be one – to take on the work that Tony had been doing, as if she could stand in his place and prove something to herself, stepping into his hob-nailed boots.

And she had. She could do it. It had been tricky at first, and almost frightening, wielding those tools and becoming expert with the fiddly controls, but she could do it all brilliantly now. She was used to training the thin blade of her welding torch into just the right spot and increasing the intensity until the iron went dull red and orange and yellow and finally white hot, and then started to run like melting cheese. It was like being powerful and God-like, almost. She was controlling elements and changing one substance into another.

Surely, surely, it was better than boxing up bloody biscuits, anyhow. Though she still did some hours at Wight's, so as not to lose her foot in the door there. She had kept working at the bake house, where they valued her expertise. Irene was in with her too, now, and she was teaching her the ins and outs of sending those perfect little pale discs of dough into the fiery furnace, and bringing them out perfectly baked and shaped and smelling like heaven. Of course, Beryl was sick to death of the smell of biscuits by now. When that sickly sweet smell came rolling up the hill from the docks it even turned her stomach. The aroma that made everyone else start salivating and grinning made her feel ill. However, that scorched metallic tang of the shipyards! That was a smell she was having to learn to love.

What will Tony even think of me when he gets back at last? To have a wife with muscles in her forearms and biceps like I've got?

Well, he'll just have to lump it, she thought. I'm strong and I've learnt so much, and I'm no longer the daft little haunted girl he met and married a few years ago. I've changed a lot and really, thank goodness.

It was no use moping in bed, half-heartedly trying to sleep. She was going backwards and forwards through her life, trying to figure out how it was she'd ended up here. Now it was dawn and she'd not sleep any more than she already had, and so she got up, even though her shift started later today. The screaming of the bairns in the attic had kept her awake most of the night and she was bright as anything right now. She went downstairs to make a big pot of tea. She'd take all the others their tea in bed, and try to sweeten their start to the day. These mornings, all the women were beginning their days so grumpily, all because of broken nights courtesy of Johnny and Marlene . . .

Downstairs she fed the noisy cat and set about making tea. The scullery was a litter of dirty baby's bottles and dishes. What a state! Time was, you'd come downstairs in the morning and the place would be immaculate. Ma Ada was a stickler for leaving downstairs tidy before you went up to bed. Since the coming of the babies, however, things had slipped.

Beryl pulled a face at the whiff from the bucket of steeping nappies by the back door. She ducked under the clammy linens hanging from the lines above the range. It was like a little forest of baby clothes she had to negotiate as she carried the tea tray back to the stairs.

The babies had taken over the Farleys' world completely. Perhaps it was inevitable, and perhaps she should be less complaining about it. She never said anything aloud, of course. In her worst moments she imagined that she was turning into the old childless maiden aunt in a big, busy family. Like in a story from the olden days, maybe. She was the dry-as-dust aunty that everyone feared turning into, but who everyone depended upon . . .

This was no good! Moping about and thinking things like this. She was no maiden aunty. She was an aunty, yes, and maybe she'd never have bairns of her own. She'd always been afraid of having the responsibility of bairns of her own . . . after Freddy, and everything . . .

At last she reached the top of the attic stairs, holding the tea tray awkwardly as she knocked on the door, and tried to sound cheery. 'I've brought tea for you!' she shouted at the lasses, and opened their door.

Everyone in the attic was flat out asleep, exhausted after another turbulent night of crying and feeding and begging for peace. In the early morning light from the attic window they looked so peaceful and perfect in the tumbled sheets: two babies and two mothers, resting so sweetly.

In their waking hours, the lot of them were anything but sweet . . .

'Tea!' Beryl tried again, but no one was waking yet. She left the cups on their nightstands, and went off to take Ma Ada's cup to her. And then maybe she'd get on with rubbing through the whites that were steeping. She liked to keep busy. It stopped her from thinking too much.

*

Megan was, in fact, awake, but she'd pretended to be fast asleep when Beryl knocked. She couldn't face talking to anyone yet. Her head was thick and claggy with the little bit of sleep she'd managed to eke out of the darkest hours before dawn.

That little brat in the crib. She could smother him. That's how she'd felt in the middle of last night. Only for a second. Only for the briefest moment as she'd put him back down for the hundredth time and his eyes had flicked open, brilliantly awake and furious again. He was a raging ball of endless neediness, this kid. His tiny arms lashed out and his legs kicked and he roared out his demands constantly through the night. Not the daytime. Oh, hardly ever the daytime. He was a perfect angel in the daytime. But at night . . . when he knew that he had his poor mother at his mercy. When she was yoked to him body and soul and he knew that he could really make her suffer . . . that was when he chose to let rip. The little monster.

She had tried breastfeeding for a while. But his hard little gums bit and chomped so hard he'd left her sore, cracked and bleeding. Blood had leaked into her milk, but that little vampire couldn't have cared less. Megan felt like he was leeching all the life and vitality out of her, and the very thought gave her the horrors. She pictured him as a winged bat creature lying in the night beside her, growing pointed, tiny fangs, and dreaming of sucking all the life out of his poor mother.

After that, it was bottles all the way. And all the palaver of sterilising them and fiddling around in the scullery. Well, luckily there was Irene in the same boat, and willing helpers in the form of Beryl and Ma Ada. Why, those two were such fans of the babbies that they'd do anything. They'd even scrub up dirty nappies and be glad of the job. It made them feel like they had a share in the new babies.

All of these things were reason enough for Megan to be content to live back here in this midden with the Farleys.

She knew she was on to a good thing here. They were glad of her baby in the house. They would do anything to get to look after him.

Megan knew that if she went back to her parents' small-holding in Hartlepool the welcome wouldn't be as warm as all that. Her parents were under no illusions about Megan. They didn't want her back, she knew, and they weren't about to feed another pair of mouths.

This was the place Megan had to be. She had no choice. She had to make the most of it, and rely on the excitement of the women of Number Thirteen over another new baby. She could exploit that happiness they shared, and worm her way back into the heart of the family. Even after all the damage and hurt she had caused. Megan was amazed that they were so foolish, coming to trust her again.

If you had a baby, it seemed you could get away with anything.

For Ma Ada, she knew, it was all about nostalgia. It made her feel young again to have bairns in the house. And for Beryl – well, she was barren, wasn't she? She'd seemingly never get bairns of her own, and this was her chance to enjoy getting close to someone else's. Megan supposed that Beryl was enjoying this whole business much more than she was herself. It must be nice, just to take part vicariously in the business of bringing up a baby. Without the pain and the anguish and the howling, sleepless nights. Beryl must be happy as anything, having all the fun of babies without any of the pain and anguish that real mothers felt.

Megan sat up and reached for her tea. It was strong and dark, just how she liked it. Beryl was a pretty good housemaid, as it happened. She remembered what everyone liked, and how they liked it. Megan supposed it was all down to her years running after her mum and dad.

Megan had met them once or twice – a meek-looking, sickly pair. They lived in a house by the park, didn't they? What a waste of space, Megan tutted. Two old incapacitated fogeys like that, having a whole house to themselves! They must have a load of money, to languish about like they did. They'd never worked apparently, and yet they lived in a great big house. With a view of the sea! Clearly Beryl had some kind of a fortune behind her, that she would presumably inherit some day. That was another reason, clearly, for staying in with Beryl and keeping friendly with her. There would be profit in it eventually.

As Johnny started to wake up in his crib, and his first cries woke up the other one, Megan's mind started mulling things over. She could fancy living in a house by the park, overlooking the sea. It'd be much better than living down here by the dirty dockside . . .

Suddenly they were all awake. Irene was up and slurping her tea, all in a dither as she tended to her bairn. Marlene seemed to be growing every single day at an alarming rate. Now she had thick, curly dark hair, just like her dad's. She was chirping away merrily, clucking and burbling, as if she thought she was using actual words. 'Get her to shut up, will you, Irene?' Megan frowned, taking her last few glugs of tea. 'That voice of hers grates on me.'

Marlene was sitting up on the pillows beside Megan's head. There was an ominous smell wafting over from her nappy, just to compound the irritation Megan already felt at her inane babbling.

'Oh, leave her be!' Irene laughed. 'She's just happy, waking up with us all. She's a merry little soul.' Irene was hurriedly dressing herself, flinging on her jersey and skirt over her slip. She was hiding behind the wardrobe door, as usual, and as usual Megan was amused by her ridiculous modesty. What had Irene got to be so modest and shy about? Megan couldn't give a hoot who saw her in the nuddy.

Why, Irene had seen her in all her glory with all her bits hanging out down in the air raid shelter infirmary, hadn't she? There was precious little for any of them to be modest about, but still Irene went behind the wardrobe door to hurriedly dress and undress herself.

The open wardrobe door had a full-length mirror on the reverse, and this was what confronted Megan now. A bright reflection of her own scowling face as she sat up in the rumpled sheets. Oh my God, she thought. Look at the state of me. I look like absolute hell. Look what these bairns have done to me already. Her blonde hair was hanging in tatters and her eyes were black like a panda's. My life is utterly ruined, she thought.

Then, as she did most mornings, Irene started singing to the bairns, clapping along to her song: 'Stop hiding behind your pillow! Whenever the dawn looks grey!'

The dawn didn't look grey this morning. It looked brilliant and blue, but today Megan's mood was so bad, that brightness only added to her irritation.

She swore loudly at Irene as the younger girl laughed and sang: 'Get up! Get out! And meet the sun halfway!'

# Chapter Thirteen

The rest of that summer saw the residents of Number Thirteen getting used to their routines and settling down to a new rhythm of work and chores. The radio was on every night, filling the parlour with the yellow light from its dials and its cultured voices intoning gloomy news.

The battle of El Alamein, which was somewhere in Egypt, seemingly. And casualties in Dieppe in France. The news was bewildering and mind-boggling. Ma Ada fetched out a huge, musty old atlas from the bookcase in her front room. It had been a school prize won by Tony once upon a time and was being used more these days than it ever had before, as the old woman laid it out on the dining table and slowly turned the pages, looking for faraway places mentioned on the radio.

It was so strange, not knowing where their men might be. Somewhere fighting on the face of this huge world. One on land, one at sea, one in the air. Beryl knew her Tony was somewhere near Africa. That much information had crept through the wires. But more than that, it was impossible to establish.

The summer's warm breath started turning just a bit chilly, and the very tips of the leaves of the trees were beginning to turn yellow. Ma Ada started going to church with Sam, who silently went to take his place in the pews on Sundays.

Repenting for his sins, everyone in the family surmised, but no one ever mentioned it. His mother felt a resurgence of her faith that autumn. She prayed like billy-o, supposing that every little drop would help. The priest nodded approvingly at her return to his house of worship, and she gave him an affable scowl.

'It mightn't hurt you girls to get down to church, too,' their mother-in-law told them, putting on her shapeless church hat, pushing long bobby pins into her hair. To Irene it looked like she was doing voodoo on herself.

The girls demurred over the church business, and hoped she wouldn't insist. None of them could see the point in sitting in that draughty place. Prayers didn't seem to accomplish anything. The Luftwaffe still kept coming back in wave after deadly wave. You still heard awful, harrowing stories from members of the congregation. No one's family, it seemed, was left untouched by death and tragedy. Church, to Irene, seemed like an excuse to wallow in all the misery, singing turgid songs and beseeching an absent Father, and that was absolutely no use.

Beryl and Irene kept busy. They filled their hours at home with chores, which mostly involved cooking and cleaning; scrubbing and mangling and trying to get the washing dry; riddling out the grate and manhandling the range and getting all the ashes out into the bucket; lugging coal back and forth in the scuttle. All of this was tiring enough, even before they set foot outside to do their actual jobs of work.

Megan, of course, was on lighter duties, following the rigours of the birth. She had a tin of Brasso and a pile of old duster rags made from dresses that she said she'd never fit back into, now that the child had for ever ruined her figure. She sat sighingly polishing up the old tarnished silverware and all Ma Ada's pots, kettles and ornaments. It was just busywork, Irene thought uncharitably. Hardly work at all, but it made it look like she was doing something. Megan was listless and mopey in the weeks following Johnny's arrival.

'I've seen this before,' Ma Ada told the other two. 'Some women can go a bit off their heads, after they've had a bairn. It's just natural, but it can be very nasty. Sometimes they look like they're going to do something silly to themselves, they get that bad, and they don't bond with their bairn. We shall have to keep an eye on her . . .'

So Ma Ada kept a very careful watch on Megan, as she sat rubbing the old tableware until it shone, and ignored the cries of her baby when he woke from his daytime naps. It was Ma Ada who had to go thundering up and down to see to him, cracking her arthritic knees so much it sounded like gunfire going off on the stairs.

'Ah, I bet she's putting it all on, that Megan,' Beryl snapped, smoking fiercely on the way down the hill to work one morning. 'She's not really miserable. She just likes to see everyone else doing all the work.'

Irene wasn't so sure. 'I see her more than you do, what with sharing that room, and I don't think it's a pretence. She's really miserable from the moment she wakes up in the morning. She sighs and moans even in her sleep. And she'll barely look at that lovely bairn of hers. She acts like she even resents him.'

'That's a shame,' Beryl gasped. 'What a bloomin' pity! That bairn will grow up knowing how his mother feels. That kind of thing communicates itself to them. Babies know.'

'Well, he gets lots of love and attention from the rest of us, anyhow,' said Irene.

'Especially his uncle Sam,' Beryl added.

'Aye,' Irene agreed. 'Sam's devoted to him. I've never seen a fella like that with a baby.'

'He's got reason to,' Beryl lowered her voice as they joined the crowd of lasses entering the factory gates. 'He's his real dad, isn't he?'

Irene nudged her in the side. 'Don't! Someone'll hear!'

'But it's true, isn't it? We're so used to not mentioning it, but that's the reason Sam's crazy about that tiny little lad, isn't it?'

Irene had to agree. 'Of course it is.'

At first it had seemed that Sam was going to do everything he could to keep out of the way of the Farley clan's newest member. Those first few days after their most dramatic night in the air raid shelter, Sam had only peered once or twice into the cot where his secret son was sleeping. He feigned uninterest and tried to get along as if nothing unusual had occurred.

But his heart ached for the baby, he couldn't help it. His insides felt hollowed out and red raw with anxiety at the thought of his illegitimate child.

He knew the family's strategy of collectively ignoring the truth of the matter was the correct one . . . but still that couldn't change his feelings. When he picked up that baby for the first time – cajoled by his mother, some days after the arrival – his heart had exploded inside his chest. He felt a massive blooming of hot, bright joy going right through his body. He tried to hold it in, and not even smile or give himself away, but it was impossible.

That tiny fragile body was someone who belonged inextricably to him, even if he could never say so, even at home. This helpless, somewhat premature child was linked to him profoundly and he felt it like an electrical shock when he held him close.

Pretending to be merely an uncle was proving very difficult for Sam. He went to church and prayed. He went to the pub and drank everything he could lay his hands on. Bitter was rationed out amongst the locals at each pub in the Sixteen Streets, making it harder to get bladdered. But he did his very best. He went through the secret cache of old liquor bottles in his mother's dresser when she wasn't looking, topping up each one with cold tea.

He spent his working hours down at the docks, building up sinewy muscle and bulk, lugging sacks and boxes off and on ships, in and out of warehouses. He learnt to steal and to do dodgy deals. He took sugar to the people who needed it – like Mavis, who wanted to take it to Franchino's. He took nylons to sell in the pubs he frequented. He was sinking daily into a shadier way of life than he'd ever been used to, and he even found he was enjoying it.

Sam started doing business with the Mad Johnsons. That was how far he had sunk. He could still hardly believe that's who he was working with. There was even a little secret thrill to it. Me and the Mad Johnsons, he thought. I'm mixing with a proper criminal fraternity. They were like gangsters in a movie. Tall and broad as coffins and ugly as mortal sin. They were a true fraternity of wicked brothers: the Johnsons were famous in their town. And I'm carrying goods for them, Sam thought, with a queer twinge of pride. I'm hiding stuff. I'm turning a profit. I'm squirelling boxes and bottles and parcels away. It's all for the good of my family. They'll thank me one day. He was hiding money away for the future. Surely that was worth the risks he was taking? He tried to convince himself he was doing nothing wrong. These were desperate times. The Mad Johnsons needed a lad like him, who worked at the docks. It was easy cash. No one was hurt. He could handle this all right . . .

Irene sensed that he was changing, and she fretted about him.

One rare day off in the middle of September, she suggested they take a walk to his favourite spot, like the two of them used to do, when she had first arrived in South Shields. What he called the top of the town. By the old, forbidding Victorian school behind the park.

He liked to sit where the Roman remains were, looking out over the mouth of the Tyne. He felt it connected him with something much older and enduring, and helped him forget all the turmoil in the present. He never quite put it in those terms, but Irene knew instinctively what he meant. Just standing on those old stones and looking at the faraway sea allowed him to forget his own troubles for a little while, and so that's why she suggested a walk up there one morning.

'It's so hard, Irene,' he said.

Oh, the cool breeze from the sea was lovely here. She closed her eyes and let the air caress her face. She'd had days on end in the bake house, and her skin felt like it had been cooked.

'The sight of Megan – being so casual and dismissive of little Johnny. She's got no patience with him, she's got no feeling for him.'

Irene opened her eyes and looked at his anguished face. He was right, of course. Megan was rejecting her own son. And here was Sam, longing to be even able to acknowledge him. It was all too cruel.

'You just have to hold on and be patient, Sam. Don't go getting upset and making a scene.'

He laughed bitterly. 'When do I ever go making scenes? In our family, it's everyone else who makes the scenes!'

'Things will settle down,' Irene said. 'At least, this way, you still see Johnny every day. You're still a part of his life. That's more than most fathers can be, in this day and age.'

He groaned at this. 'Oh, don't make me feel even more guilty, Irene, man!'

She hadn't meant to, but it did hurt her, to think of how very little her own man had been able to spend time with their daughter. Yes, she thought that Sam had every right to be upset – though he'd brought all his troubles on himself. But at the same time, at least he was at home, and saw his secret son every day. There was a certain point where Irene's sympathy with Sam ran out, and the young man sensed it.

'I'll not go on about it any more,' he said. 'I'm sorry. I shouldn't have bent your ear.'

'I asked you to,' she smiled. 'I brought you up here so you could get things off your chest.'

He smiled at her. 'Thanks, pet. At least I know that you're always on my side.'

She nodded. 'I always will be, Sam.'

They walked back down into town together, stopping at the butcher's on Fowler Street, to pick up the week's meagre rations, as they'd promised Ma Ada.

The old man in the butcher's was quiet as ever, but it was his son, Alan, who served Irene. He was a proper charmer, though he was nearly bald and his red ears were huge. He popped an extra bit of scrag end in with her cuts of meat. 'For a broth for the babbies,' he grinned at her. 'Because you've got a proper house full of them now, haven't you, bonny lass?'

Irene blushed, quietly delighted to be called bonny.

Then a cry went up as a new customer came hurrying into the shop, her heels clattering on the sawdusty tiles underfoot. 'Irene Farley! It's ages since I've seen you, lass!'

It was the tall, vivacious figure of Cathy Sturrock, landlady of the Robin Hood at the end of their street. Irene greeted her and stammered a reply about not having much time to go drinking in pubs these days. Even as she said it, she thought she was sounding unfriendly. She really didn't mean to: Cathy had been good to her, even if it had been she who'd blabbed out the secret of Johnny's paternity in the middle of Ma Ada's parlour, causing all that bother.

She greeted Sam with a nod. 'Hello, Sam.' And then she was drawing Irene aside and gabbling excitedly at a more discreet volume: 'I've got to tell you my news! He's coming home at the end of the week, Irene.'

'Wh-who is?' Irene frowned, though straight away she guessed. To her shame, her heart sank in an instant.

'Bob! Your brother-in-law! My fella!' Cathy jutted out her chin defiantly in case anyone in the butcher's shop queue happened to be listening in and was about to question her claim on Bob Farley. Cathy Sturrock was a formidable figure, famous in these parts, and of course no one said a word.

'Oh!' Irene gasped. 'That's great news.'

Cathy nodded. 'He's going crazy with impatience. He's got a three day pass . . . and he can't wait to see me. But he also can't wait to see that new little babby of his! Will you tell his ma and everyone, Irene? Or will I pop round myself and give them the news? Or shall I let him turn up unannounced and surprise everyone?'

'No, no. I-I'll tell them,' Irene stammered, getting out her ration book and her purse so she could pay Alan behind the till, who was waiting to hand her the small paper-wrapped bundle of meat. 'I'll let them know he's coming,' Irene said, and she couldn't help imagining the look on Megan's face when she did. 'Bob's staying with you, isn't he, Cathy?'

'Of course! He lives with me now. Under the brush, as they say. Living in sin, as I'm sure all the old biddies will say. But I couldn't give a flying fart about that. And you can tell who you like I said that, as well. We're in love, us two, and that's all that matters. The two of us deserve a little bit of real love, I reckon, after all the things that we've endured.'

Then she produced her own ration book and bustled up to the glass counter. She would want to order extra meat for this weekend: what with her fella coming home at last.

# Chapter Fourteen

They had an understanding. That was the best way of putting it.

Bob Farley was the pot man at the Robin Hood, and he'd worked there for several years before the war began. He had been there when Cathy Sturrock's husband, the awful Leonard, was still with her. He had been working for her back in the times when Cathy was feeling like she'd had a bellyful of Leonard's cruelty and his philandering ways. He was there when she first started fantasising about throwing her weedy little fella out into the night. Leonard was such a little scrap of a man, and he'd be no match for her.

Of course, there were many who were keen to court her. A fine, vivacious redhead like that. She'd been beautiful all her life, and now, in early middle age, she made a very striking, handsome figure. She behaved just like the queen of the Sixteen Streets, presiding over her bar with a regal air. Both her supporters and her enemies said that about her, and there were plenty of both around those streets. Some said that she gave herself airs and thought she was something special, but many thought that she embodied the spirit and the gumption associated with the people of the place.

'Mind, not that she's even really from here originally,' Ma Ada was heard to gossip, once or twice. 'I've got a long enough memory to recall when she turned up here on the arm of that Leonard Sturrock and she was the new lass in town. She came from up Northumberland, somewhere. Somewhere fancy and grand. That's what the tale was, back then. She'd taken a big step down in the world to marry that piddling little fella Sturrock, and she reckoned to be in love with him, and so she was happy . . .' Ma Ada drained her stout philosophically. 'That's how many women reckon to be at the start, but the scales fall off their eyes pretty soon.'

The word went round that Cathy Sturrock came from a family that was well-nigh nobility, and she'd given up a life of luxury and ease to come and dwell in an old boozer in the middle of the Sixteen Streets. Half the folk felt flattered by that, that she'd abandon riches to come and live in their midst, while the other half thought she must be a fool.

Leonard Sturrock wasn't very popular as the landlord of his pub. There was talk of watered-down beer and all kinds of illegal rackets. Cathy had been charmed by him, somehow, though no one could ever see why such a glamorous woman would ever fall for a runty little thing like him. But that was all down to the mysterious workings of love, surely. And then she put up with him for years, even with all his boozing, gambling, swindling and running around after the mucky women who frequented the inns right down by the docks.

Cathy must have realised she'd thrown her life away on a bad'un pretty early on, reasoned the women from the Streets, but she stuck by him, and they gave her credit for that. She weathered the storms that he brought to her door, and she became a strong, resilient figure that others came to depend upon.

Cathy's husband grew older, more sickly and decrepit: his wicked life telling on him physically, and she was forced to take on the bulk of the work in managing their pub. Len became an embittered shadow of a man who sat reading the racing pages of the paper all day long, drinking Scotch at the bar, and occasionally nipping out to fritter away all the money they made.

They needed a pot man, and it was Ma Ada herself who suggested her lad, Bob. He wasn't the youngest of the Farley boys, but there was something naive and soft as clarts about him. It wasn't that he was simple-minded, though that's what some cruel souls said. There was an innocence and a sweetness that was rare in a lad. And by, he was strong and he liked to work! He was perfect for lifting those cripplingly heavy barrels from the back of the brewery's wagon on a Monday morning and lugging them down into the cellar. All Cathy had to do was snap her fingers and he'd be at her beck and call, fetching a new barrel or a jingling crate of light ales. He seemed to adore working and pleasing the boss.

Bob had been extremely well-trained by his bossy old mother, Cathy thought admiringly. Such a huge, strapping lad! Twenty years her junior, of course, or thereabouts, but that didn't stop her looking at him. He was young and beaming with healthy vitality and rippling with muscles.

And he beamed at all the attention he was getting from the landlady.

'He's a daft lad,' said her awful husband from his place at the bar to anyone who would listen. He cackled nastily. 'Story is, he got dropped on his head when he was a bairn and he was never the same again. Simple-minded, like.'

Cathy was horrified that Leonard was saying such things when Bob might hear him. Any minute the lad might reappear from the cellar and realise that he was being discussed in such unflattering terms. 'You just hush your mouth,' she warned Len. 'You don't know anything.'

'Oh, don't I?' he snarled, turning the page of his racing paper.

'You don't know what happened to Bob when he was a bairn,' she told him. 'I do. I was there when his daft father knocked seven shades of shite out of him. I was one of them who went running when all the screams were coming out of their house and Bob had his head banged against the fireplace. I was there, man. I know more than you do.'

Len glared at her. He didn't care about all her old stories. He just cared about what was going on today. And as far as he was concerned, his wife was making a show of him by mooning after the pot man. She was batting her eyelashes at some daft bloke. Probably flashing her knickers and what-all else, too. Leonard growled at her: 'I know enough, lady.'

The redhead's eyes flashed dangerously. 'What's that meant to mean?'

'I know enough when I see my woman getting all steamed up over some dafty with muscles and nothing going on between his lugholes. I know enough when I see some trollop slavering like mad at the sight of him in his shirtsleeves!'

Cathy Sturrock was known for her quick temper, and though she was careful not to let it get the better of her, her husband knew all the quickest and easiest ways of winding her up. 'Just you shut your cake hole, you nasty little bastard,' she snapped.

'You're man mad, you,' Leonard threw at her, not caring that several of their early doors patrons heard him slagging her off.

'Chance would be a fine thing!' she flung at him.

Just then Bob returned from the cellar, bounding up the stone stairs, and he needed to be given fresh instructions. Cathy hurried to help him. He wasn't very good at working on his own initiative, and needed to be told very clearly what to do next, all through his work shifts, but Cathy never minded.

'See?' her husband jeered. 'Daft. Crackers. Addle-pated.'

She silenced him with a deadly look, and turned back to her loyal pot man.

And the years went by. 1936, 1937, 1938 . . . It was like she could feel time itself passing through her, like how the coloured sand in an egg timer must feel against the glass.

Now she was in her forties, and she could imagine living in this loveless, empty, hopeless marriage until she was dead. No, that was no good, she decided. She really had to do something about the bitter disappointment of Leonard. She had given him long enough to buck himself up. More than enough, in the opinion of most. She was worth twenty of him, most of the locals believed, and great was their relief when he let her down one last time, and she finally threw him out on the cobbled streets.

It was over the holiday money. He'd flung it away on a horse. A useless nag that was already shot and chopped up for cat meat after falling at the first hurdle in the race that Len had piddled away their savings on.

It wasn't even that much money, but it was money she had saved from her tips and popped away in a toby jug on the top shelf in a corner of the bar. She thought he hadn't noticed it.

And it wasn't even a holiday she was after. Just a day away at the seaside. The lasses from the biscuit factory had asked her along on their annual day trip and she had been so glad. She had nothing to do with Wight's factory, apart from serving their workers with beer all these years, and she had made quite a few friends from the work force. It was quite a badge of honour, and gave her such a sense of belonging, to be included on their day trip to the coast.

It was to be quite the jamboree. They were to dress up in their Sunday best and pack lunch baskets, and then they were to catch trains to Newcastle and on up the coast to her beloved Northumberland. The trip was to take them to the wild and beautiful beaches she had known as a lass, and that she had never seen since her youth.

The few pounds she'd saved in her pint pot would be well spent. Just a day with her friends, revisiting the scenes of her girlhood. It would be a well-earned tonic.

But Len had discovered her secret hoard of coins, and gleefully pissed her money away, and she couldn't afford to go.

It was this that made her temper snap. When he snickered and told her the news – that the money was gone, and so she could whistle for her day's outing – she had roared like a lioness. Legend had it later that people dropped their drinks in shock at the noise. Then she picked up her little scrap of a husband in both arms and carried him out into the dark street and threw him as far as she could.

Friends and neighbours and other drinkers came tumbling out of the pub to watch the fracas. Leonard tried to stand and berate her like a man, protesting his being bundled about like a bag of old rubbish. But she had had quite enough. She booted him in the knackers – as she delicately put it later – and then up the arse, for good luck.

'And don't you ever, ever darken my door again, you little shite!' she'd roared. She – who rarely swore or even said boo to a goose. Brawling and swearing in the street like a fish wife!

Oh, but it felt good. She had basked in the applause from her regulars when it came; when they all watched horrid Leonard Sturrock realising he was beaten for good. They laughed as they saw him go scurrying off in the direction of the docks and the nearest fleabag hotel.

She felt liberated that night. A great weight lifted off her and she bought everyone in her pub a drink on the house to celebrate. Someone struck up a tune on the piano and there was a great celebration: the landlady was a free woman at last!

And so Cathy Sturrock found herself alone. Blissfully,

joyously alone. With her loyal pot man to help her, she was queen of all she surveyed at the top of the Sixteen Streets.

Life rolled on, and the years swept by. Pints were sunk, barrels emptied, ships were built and repaired in the boatyards and then they went sweeping majestically in and out of the docks. Leonard was barely heard from again – bar a few snide begging letters, some tricky legalistic wrangles as the bar passed into her name and she became the sole landlady of the Robin Hood. But on the whole her life was smoother than it had been for years.

The world was going to hell, of course. There was war coming again, and she, along with everyone else, couldn't believe that all that horror could be started up once more . . .

And then, out of the blue, came a blonde bombshell from Hartlepool. Megan was new in town, and she turned everyone's heads when she fetched up. She was from a farming family somewhere down Durham way, and she behaved like she'd come to the bright lights for some excitement. She was living with her aunty on Armstrong Terrace, and was trouble with a big T, said some. Cathy saw her coming into the saloon bar of the Robin Hood, once she'd started at the biscuit factory, and on the whole she had to agree: she was trouble. Cathy knew that sort.

Unfortunately, her pot man Bob wasn't wise enough to know the sort. He took one look at Megan and fell for her, hook, line and sinker.

To Cathy's astonishment as well as her dismay, the feeling seemed to be reciprocated.

Even to this day, not many people could explain why it was that Megan had married Bob. He had few prospects, that was plain. He lived in a tiny room under his mother's staircase, for God's sake. Was Megan so intent – even desperate – to worm her way into that infamous clan?

Maybe she just liked having a fella she could boss about. A fella who would be devoted to her because she appeared to be sweet on him.

Either way, not three months after moving to the Sixteen Streets and first meeting the sweet-natured Bob, Megan and he were wed, and she was welcomed into the family. It was right before war was declared on Germany, and Cathy Sturrock had shed bitter tears for both developments.

But three years had gone by, and things had changed.

And now Bob was no longer Megan's. There had been shenanigans round Number Thirteen Frederick Street, and Megan had left him. It was no fault of Bob's, but he felt ashamed and confused by the whole thing. Then he'd gone away to war, and Megan had come back. Like the bad penny she'd turned up at Number Thirteen, begging to be taken back in.

She'd been pregnant with a bairn that wasn't even Bob's and it was decided that Bob was never to know. That's what all the women in his life had decided for him. The paternity of his bairn was never to be questioned: Bob wouldn't understand and it would hurt him too much. The problematic situation would be kept secret from Bob at all costs.

Even Megan herself was prepared to go along with the deception. Her mother-in-law had warned her: 'You play along, and there'll be a home for you under my roof still, Megan Farley. Just you play along.'

Now Bob was due to come home for the first time since the birth.

And he's coming to me, thought Cathy Sturrock excitedly. At last – he's coming home to me!


Bob arrived a little late on the Friday afternoon, with his kitbag, looking neat and tired, and stinking of the sooty railways. Cathy flew to him and he folded her into his arms. 'Can I go straight over and see him?' he grinned. 'Can I go now, straight away, and see my son?'

'Of course you can, Bob,' she smiled. 'So long as you remember you must come back here after. This is your home now, not over there.'

'Aye, aye,' he said vaguely, dumping his bag in her hall, and then lumbering happily out of the door, and down the street towards Number Thirteen.

# Chapter Fifteen

Mrs Clarke was visiting; emptying a shopping bag of second-hand baby outfits onto the dining table. Megan was a lot less grateful than Irene had been, to receive a bunch of strangers' cast-offs. Her wrinkled nose and sour expression wasn't going down well with the local head of the WVS.

'There's nothing wrong with these that a good boil wash won't sort out, Megan Farley!'

Megan poked around in the pile of musty old woollens and tried to summon a smile. This wasn't how she'd pictured motherhood, at all. She had a lump in her throat the size of a roast potato and when she tried to look suitably contrite and humble, the words just stuck in her throat. We're poor people, she thought, and we're living in a slum. We're crowded in a little two-up two-down and now I'm stuck here with this bairn. I was a fool for wanting to live here with this lot. Was I really ever that desperate?

Ma Ada had hold of the baby, over in her usual spot by the dresser. Johnny was swaddled up in blankets, which made him look more like the size of a normal baby, but he was still too small. He was a puny little thing, and he was dopey, too. It seemed as if he wouldn't even look at you properly, like he couldn't focus right.

'Are you listening to Mrs Clarke, Megan?' Ma Ada prompted. 'She has trooped all the way up the hill to bring these to you.'

Aye, this bag of old rags, Megan thought, and gave the bossy woman a sickly smile. 'Thank you very much, Mrs Clarke. It will all come in very useful, I'm sure.' Oh, how she longed to put them all on the fire, those wrinkled garments with their nasty, faded stains. She hated the way Mrs Clarke came round here, patronising them all, acting like she was someone special and she'd come visiting the worthy poor.

There came a knock at the front door then, a hesitant one, followed by someone fumbling at the lock. Ma Ada jerked upright, 'What the divil?' Her nerves were on edge all the time nowadays. It was as if she was expecting the Jerries to come marching up her front hall with their bayonets out every time someone came knocking.

Beryl hurried to answer with Lucky in her arms and, within seconds, was crying out: 'It's *Bob*!' She sounded delighted, and there was a squeal as she hugged her brother-in-law, squashing the cat between them.

'Eeeh, Bob, why are you knocking on your own front door, lad?' his mother gasped, clambering to her feet. 'This will always be your home, you know.' She was having some trouble rising to her feet, still holding onto the baby. 'Megan, take Johnny!'

Bob stood blinking in the doorway of the dusky parlour, looking befuddled as ever. 'Hello.'

'Hello there, young man,' Mrs Clarke nodded at him self-importantly over the pile of discoloured jumble with which she'd toiled up the hill. At least she was rewarded with being able to see a hero's welcome home.

'Bob,' Megan said in a flat tone, and presented the swaddled-up baby to him. 'This . . . is our Johnny.'

The women paused and watched very intently as the large, uniformed man stared at the baby. He boggled comically, as if he couldn't quite comprehend what he was seeing. The baby, meanwhile, was so wrapped around in covers that he could barely see who was looking down at him.

'This is my baby?' Bob asked uncertainly, stepping further into the room. His voice had gone very husky, streaked with emotion.

Ma Ada took a deep, shuddering breath and sat down heavily in her worn chair. 'Aye, lad, he's yours.'

'This is Johnny,' Megan repeated. Then she tried to lighten the moment by adding, 'And you'd better like him, because I went through absolute bloody agony, down there in that shelter, squeezing him out.'

Mrs Clarke tutted involuntarily at her coarseness.

Bob's hands were reaching out. Two scarred, work-hardened paws were inching cautiously towards Megan's bairn. For just a split second she wanted to whisk him out of reach, but she quashed that feeling. Let him take the bairn! Let him keep it! She'd feel happier if she could get someone to take the wretched mite full time, and that was the truth of it. Her feelings were all over the place, but one thing she was sure about: this kid was a menace. She was sick of the whining noise of his cries. They ripped right through her whenever he kicked off. Her belly seethed with pain when she heard his whingeing.

'Be very careful, mind, Bob,' his mother warned, as Bob took hold of the tightly wrapped bundle. 'He's very precious and delicate.'

'Of course,' Bob whispered, and brought the baby's face close to his own, the little bit of it that could be seen through the blankets. It looked to everyone there as if he was trying to read that tiny face, and he wore the same befuddled expression as when he was trying to read the print in the *Shields Gazette*. 'My baby.' He looked again at Megan, who was having that problem swallowing again. 'Our baby.'

'Aye,' she said, gulping.

At that moment Bob would have done anything. He would have come back home to Megan. Somehow. He would have begged her to try again to love him and take him back. If he was honest, he didn't quite understand what had happened to their marriage to end it all. He just knew that Megan had decided that she didn't want him any more, and didn't want them to be married any more. Well, perhaps for that he couldn't really blame her. He'd always known she was too good for him. That's what it was, at the root of it all. He'd always known that one day she would come to her senses and wake up and realise that she was in the wrong place and with the wrong man. It was obvious. It was bound to happen. He wasn't right, was he? He was defective, somehow. He knew that.

But look at this, now. He had a child with her. This baby was theirs. Why did it have to be now they were separated?

Why had this split had to happen right in the middle of their baby coming here?

At least Megan was still around. At least she had come home to Frederick Street. She might hate and despise him as her husband, but she had come back and she was still a part of the family. She hadn't taken the baby away, and for that, Bob would be eternally grateful. When he looked at her he had tears shining in his eyes and he burbled a few words, trying to express all these thoughts simultaneously, and failing hopelessly. 'Thank you, thank you, Megan,' he mumbled.

Megan shrugged her shoulders. She wasn't sure what that was supposed to express. She was aware of the eyes of the other women boring into her. She knew they weren't impressed with her. So what? I'm not the naturally maternal type. Who cares?

'I'll get some more tea on, and feed Marlene,' Beryl suddenly said, and she broke the silent spell of the moment. She bustled through to the scullery, and this was Mrs Clarke's cue to heave herself out of her place at the table.

'No more tea for me, Beryl, or I'll be wanting to go while I'm sitting on the tram. It's a long ride to Cleadon Park.' She smoothed down the jacket of her worsted suit, while Ma Ada repeated her solemn thanks for the donations. Mrs Clarke nodded graciously. 'We are only too pleased to help out. It can't be easy, what with two babies under one roof, in these extremely trying times.' As she eased past Bob she smiled at the baby while admonishing the father, 'Now, you do your very best, young man, and help out as much as you can while you're here. You might be on leave, but you can still do night-time feedings and so on.'

Bob shook his head. 'It might be hard, miss. You see, I live down the street, at the pub.'

Mrs Clarke blinked. 'I beg your pardon?'

'I don't live here no more. Megan won't have me now. We're not together any more. I live upstairs at the pub now, with Cathy Sturrock.'

His mother broke in, 'Ah, now, Bob. Mrs Clarke doesn't need to be hearing all our news.'

Bob clamped his mouth shut. He'd said something wrong. He did it almost every time he ever opened his mouth. No wonder Megan didn't want him.

Mrs Clarke was frowning at him. 'You live upstairs at the pub, you say?' She was obviously imagining that he was so far gone in some kind of raging alcoholism, even worse than his infamous father's. So much so, that he had taken up residence in the public bar full time.

'Don't listen to him!' Ma Ada said chirpily. 'He's a bit daft, as you know. Now, thanks again, Mrs Clarke. Don't go missing the bus!'

When she wanted to be, Ma Ada could sound even bossier than the head of the WVS. Reluctantly the big-busted lady allowed herself to be scooted out of the house.

'You don't have to blab all our business to the whole town,' Megan scolded her husband. 'Especially not to that old cow.'

'Megan!' Ma Ada cried. 'Don't be so ungrateful. That old cow brought you all those nice things.'

'Nice things!' laughed Megan. 'Look at them. Mucky old rags! Would you have dressed your bairns in stuff like this?'

'Beggars can't be choosers.'

'Oh, and I'm a beggar, am I?' Megan sneered.

Ma Ada's eyes narrowed. Her patience was thinning rapidly. 'You're a trouble-making Jezebel, and you ought to be glad to get anything at all, as far as I'm concerned.'

The baby started crying then, wriggling energetically in Bob's hands. He held him awkwardly, like he was trying to pacify a boa constrictor. Beryl swooped back into the room to help. 'Here, let me.'

'Beryl's an angel,' said Ma Ada. 'She's got the natural touch.'

This brought Beryl up short. She stared at Ma Ada as the baby settled down contentedly in her arms. The natural touch? She thought. *Me?*

Megan jeered. 'Then it's a bloody shame Beryl's not got any bairns of her own.'

Beryl felt this like a slap. Sometimes Megan could be so spiky. So nasty.

'Come and sit by the range, Bob,' his mother called out to him. He was looking rather lost. 'Come and tell us how you're getting on, lad.'

'Aye, all right,' he mumbled.

Then the front door was going with a clatter, and Irene was home from work. She looked dead on her feet, and she only had an hour before it was time to head out to Franchino's for an early evening stint. Nevertheless, she was delighted by the sight of Bob. She hugged him hard, and he beamed at this.

'Well, what do you think of the new baby?' she asked him.

'I've only seen him for a moment,' said Bob. 'I can hardly believe that he's truly mine!'

'Oh, but he *is*,' Irene said quickly. Too quickly, she realised, and gave a silly laugh to cover up her mistake.

'I know that,' Bob grinned. 'But it's like magic, isn't it?'

The women laughed at him fondly then, all apart from Megan, who announced that she was going off for a lie down, because she felt sick to her stomach.

'She's been a bit blue, since the birth,' Ma Ada told her son, once Megan had hurried up to the attic. 'It happens to women sometimes after childbirth. I've seen this before. To tell you the truth, I think she's missing you, lad. I think she doesn't want to be on her own with a baby. I think she regrets some of the things she did.'

Bob was frowning. 'I don't think she misses me at all, Mam. I think she'll be glad of seeing the back of me.'

'Nay, lad! Never say that!' Ma Ada was aghast. She looked like she couldn't think of a better, purer soul than her Bob.

Then they crumbled broken biscuits into stewed tea and Bob explained some of the things he'd been doing since he was last home. It was clear that a part of him actually enjoyed being on manoeuvres, being given clear, pragmatic instructions, and fitting into a particular role in a team. Bob tended to like things when they were very clear-cut.

'But you haven't seen any action yet?' Beryl asked in a concerned voice. 'You haven't seen any fighting?'

He shook his head and looked down. The baby was back on his lap and being incredibly, contentedly quiet. Perhaps some of Bob's innate calm had communicated itself to the child, Irene thought.

Then Sam arrived home, in his filthy overalls. 'Bob, man!' he cried, and then was brought up short by the incongruous sight of his brother holding the new bairn.

Bob grinned at his brother.

Eeeh, Ma Ada thought. Look at them there. Never a cross word between the pair of them for all their innocent lives. But now! She shook her head wheezily. Whatever would Bob do if he knew the truth? All that brotherly love between them would be surely killed off in a single instant. Bob and Sam were always the closest and the sweetest of her four boys. To see their love perish would be the death of her, she was sure of it.

That bloody Megan. She'd brought them all close to the edge of disaster.

The best way was to keep all these secrets locked tight away. There was no need for anyone to know.

'I'm glad you're back with the family,' Sam told his brother.

Bob grinned at him. 'Can you believe it, Sammy? Can you even believe this baby? He's *mine*, Sam. I've got me own bairn!'

# Chapter Sixteen

Bob's time at home overlapped briefly with Tom's, and so just for one night, Ma Ada was delighted to have three of her four sons home all at the same time.

'We're going to celebrate that,' she vowed. 'It's a cause for a proper beano!'

The family assembled in the Robin Hood with a few of their neighbours and drank several toasts to their boys. There was a small cake that Cathy Sturrock had managed to whip up out of contraband ingredients, and she even put candles on top of it, though it was no one's birthday. They stood wonkily flaming in the thin icing sugar, looking almost defiantly festive.

Megan had elected to stay at home, babysitting. There was no way she was going to a party in the pub presided over by the woman who'd stolen her man. 'I'll be here with the babies,' she frowned moodily, and Irene had to be cajoled by the others into trusting her with Marlene.

Aunty Madge plonked herself down at the battered, out of tune piano, and got everyone singing along. While Bob looked bemused and full of dread at the thought of leaving home again, Tom – who'd just arrived that morning – was bleary with drink and excited to be back. He kept gathering Irene up in his arms and hugging her. It was like he could hardly keep his hands off her. She laughed like it was all a kind of joke.

'I'll go up into the attic to share with Megan,' Beryl told her, as they stood at the bar, watching Tom waltz his mother around the bare floorboards of the bar. 'You and Tom can have my room while he's home.'

Irene was very grateful to her. 'You're the most thoughtful person in the whole family.'

'I know!' Beryl laughed.

'I mean it,' said Irene. She'd had a couple of brandies, served with great ceremony by the landlady, and she was feeling tipsy and fond. 'Out of everyone here, in this family, you've been about the nicest to me.' Irene beamed at her favourite sister-in-law. Then another thought struck her, 'Do you realise, it's just over a year since I arrived here in the Sixteen Streets for the first time?'

'Is it?' Beryl raised her perfectly plucked and painted eyebrows. 'Well, quite a lot has gone on in a year, I suppose. That tends to make the time fly by.' A year, she thought, privately. Another whole year, and what have I done, except to survive? All I've done is carry on and get through my days . . . Although I've achieved my ambition to become a welder, she reminded herself. I've done that much, at least.

Madge was pounding away at the yellowed ivories, switching from a slow tune to something more cheery and frantic. Her lined face was streaming with sweat, and she'd pause the tune now and then to take a mouthful of stout.

'Do you ever wish that you'd stayed down in Norfolk?' Beryl asked Irene, rubbing her shoulder fondly.

'What?' Irene shook her head firmly. 'Those couple of months I was back there, having Marlene and looking after my ma – that was quite enough, thanks. It was tough getting away from them again. Home gets its hooks into you, you know, but it's good to break out and get away. No, it's better for me up here in the north.'

Beryl was nodding. 'You've changed a lot since you moved up here, hinny. You're much more sure of yourself. You're not scared of sticking up for yourself. You know what you think.'

To be fair, Irene thought, she'd always felt like that on the inside. She had always been pretty good at knowing her own mind. But perhaps she was less nervous about letting other people know how she was feeling now. Perhaps that was how she'd changed.

'I'm glad you're my sister,' Beryl said. 'I always wanted a sister, you know.'

'Ha! I've got dozens of them already,' Irene chuckled, and was about to add something nicer, about feeling close to Beryl too, when there was a loud kerfuffle of someone crashing into the saloon bar. There was a flurry of movement and some shouting going on.

'Eeeh! Is it a fight? What's going on?'

It was Sam. He was late for the do. Everyone had remarked on it, but they knew that he often worked odd hours in the strange, piecemeal work that he did, and so hadn't thought anything of it. Now he was being helped into the pub by the diminutive Mavis, and she looked as white-faced and shocked as he did. He had a trickle of blood down his forehead and his hair was matted and dark.

'Help me with him!' Mavis called out, and was instantly surrounded by folk.

'Sam, Sam, what's happened to you?' Tom demanded, suddenly sober and furious.

Ma Ada clapped her hands to her mouth to cover up the scream of outrage bubbling up inside of her. 'What have they done to you, hinny?'

Sam tried to wave them away. 'It's all right. It was just . . . I don't know who they were. Just blokes. Just fellas. Having a go.'

Tom gritted his teeth. 'Where? On the street? Where did they go?'

Bob was instantly by his side, squaring up and silently getting ready to fight whoever, to defend his brother.

'Don't go chasing after them,' Sam pleaded. One of his eyes was squinched up and swelling horribly, even as they stood there watching him. 'They'll be long gone by now.' He waved everyone away feebly. 'Get back on with the party! Aunty Madge – get playing your piano again. Can I have a drink?'

As the others returned uncertainly to their festivities, Sam tried to sit up straight in the chair by the fire. His mother studied him with a ferocious glare. He felt shifty under her gaze.

'You better not have got yourself into bother by doing anything stupid, Sam Farley,' she growled. She knew him too well, and was watching him quail under the severity of her gaze.

'I haven't!' he protested. 'It was just robbers. Just taking advantage of the blackout, the bastards.' He shivered. 'They gave me a good kicking and left me lying there in the road. Took my wallet, but there was nowt in it. What do I have? Bugger all!' He shook his head miserably. 'Anyhow, I was lucky that Mavis came along when she did. Otherwise I'd be lying in the gutter waiting for you lot to happen by. I'd be waiting for you all to come rolling home from the pub!'

Mavis was standing proudly beside him, glowing with pleasure at being given credit for being his knight in shining armour.

'I shall buy Mavis a drink, then,' Ma Ada said. 'Nothing too strong, of course, because she's a tiny little thing, and we don't want her going daft.' Ma Ada fiddled around with her purse and pulled out some dark coins. 'Here you are,' she told Mavis. 'You go and buy yourself a small drink, as a thank you for saving my foolish son.'

'And I'll have a pint of mild . . .' Sam started, and his mother flashed her eyes at him.

'You'll have nowt! I'm not having you drink after getting a sock in the eye! You'll sit there and be quiet, Sam Farley, and then you're coming home early with me.'

Sam grumbled, and Mavis went hurrying off to the bar, clutching her pennies, feeling incredibly proud of herself.

At the bar Irene said, 'Here, let me buy this for you, Mavis. You did a good thing tonight.'

'Nah, pet, it's all right! Your Ma Ada has given me money!' She waved her reward around. 'But thanks anyway. Eeeh, you should have seen the state of the poor lad.' She tutted and shook her head. 'He was all crumpled up and helpless, lying in the side of the road, in all the wet. I saw him and I realised who it was at once. The fellas were just pelting away from him. I saw them running away.'

'Who were they, Mavis?' Beryl asked her.

'Rough-looking types, I don't know who they were. But, you know . . . your Sam knocks about with some funny fellas in those dockside pubs. You know he does. He's always getting something dodgy, isn't he? Buying knock-off stuff to sell on. Like sugar for Bella. Like chickens at Christmas and nylons. Well, I don't mean nylons for chickens, of course.' She giggled as Cathy presented her with a half of beer and lemonade. 'Eeeh, thanks, pet.' Cathy wouldn't take her money.

'You think he's got himself in bother with his black marketeer chums,' Beryl said. 'That's who they were, wasn't it?'

'I don't know,' Mavis replied, 'but he takes chances, doesn't he? He mixes with a bad sort, down by the docks.'

Irene felt shocked. 'I hadn't even thought about that. What he does is foolish and dangerous. Just for the sake of buying a few pairs of tights and some chocolate.'

'That's our Sam,' said Beryl. 'He's always raced around, poking his nose in, getting into bother. But I don't think he ever realised — some of these blokes really mean business. If they're roughing him up, he must have got in someone's way. It's a wonder they didn't kill him.'

Mavis's eyes widened. 'No! Don't say that!'

Irene clucked her tongue. 'Fancy – British lads hurting each other like that, when we're all at war with a common enemy. It's a disgrace!'

'There'll always be criminals,' Beryl said.

Tom had sidled up to them, and was listening intently to their conversation. 'That daft little bugger. Getting mixed up in nicking stuff. I should have known.' He sighed crossly. 'This is what happens when I go away and take my eyes off you buggers! You all go bloody crackers.'

Irene tried to distract him. 'Come on, you've not danced with me all night, and I'm your wife! Come on, Tom – let's show them all how it's done.'

He whirled her from the bar and into the middle of the floor, just as Aunt Madge finished a romantic tune with a flourish. Then, with her usual impeccable timing, she launched into 'Yes, We Have No Bananas', which wasn't really the kind of song Tom and Irene wanted, but they danced with gusto anyway, laughing at the daftness of it all.

Beryl watched Mavis order a second fizzy beer. 'You like our Sam a lot, don't you?'

Mavis gave her a wobbly grin. 'What? Eeeh, does it show? Can you tell?'

Beryl watched the girl stare across the smoky saloon at Sam sitting by the fire. He looked battered and dishevelled, but as handsome as ever. Beryl had known about Mavis's hopeless crush on him for some time.

'I wish he'd get a job somewhere sensible, like at the biscuit factory,' Beryl said. 'That would suit our Sam more than dock work, and hanging around with all them rough types.'

Mavis nodded. 'That would be lovely, if he worked at Wight's. I'd see him every single day.'

Beryl smiled at her, thinking how straightforward Mavis was. There was no side to her: nothing conniving or sly. She was just a good, sweet person who life hadn't treated very kindly. She wasn't exactly bonny, in fact she looked a bit odd. She walked along in a lop-sided way, like she couldn't wait to get to where she was going, and she talked in that funny, raspy voice. It was like she hadn't quite fully grown up properly. She was innocent somehow, like someone who hadn't been tainted and disappointed by the world.

Beryl wanted to warn her: Sam has his own complications in his life. He isn't as straightforward and sweet as you are. He'll let you down, so don't pin your hopes too hard on him, hinny.

Mavis was thoroughly enjoying her second drink, smacking her lips and watching the dancers whirling around to Aunty Madge's enthusiastic playing. 'Eeeh, I'd love a dance,' she said wistfully.

Beryl plonked down her drink. 'Well, I'll happily dance with you, pet,' she grinned. 'Come on, then.'

There was barely room on the floor by now, as the evening advanced noisily and merrily. The old sawdust boards were shaking and bouncing as the locals forgot their woes and danced them away.

Beryl and Mavis jitterbugged together, laughing their heads off. At one point, Mavis leant forward confidingly: 'I didn't say before, but I *did* recognise those men who roughed Sam up. At least, I think I did.'

'You did? Why didn't you say?' Beryl asked.

'Dunno. Didn't want to worry you all. The thing is . . . I think they were the Mad Johnsons. I think, anyway. They live quite close to us, all their clan. So I kind of know them by sight.'

Beryl stared at her. 'You're kidding? The Mad Johnsons?'

Mavis did a dramatic little shudder. 'They're not nice people. They've ruled over our bit of town for years, and everyone's scared of them. If your Sam's mixed up with them . . . well, then he's got a real problem. He's in awful bother if he's made enemies of the Mad Johnsons.'

# Chapter Seventeen

Afterwards, when they were asked, how did you spend Tom's time at home? They were both lost for an answer.

How *did* we spend the time, Irene wondered? We didn't really have any major plans, or go anywhere unusual or do anything in particular. Nothing out of the ordinary. With the way things were, it would have been hard to do anything special.

They spent time together: that was the most important thing. Tom hadn't seen his daughter for a few months and that little mite drank up a lot of his attention during his few days at home. He sat with her on his lap and stared into her blue eyes, and she gazed back quite calmly at him. There was something very composed about Marlene, and she would stare at people like she was weighing them up. It was unnerving sometimes. The way she looked back at Tom made him feel like she was saying, 'So, you're my father, are you? Yes, I've heard all about you.'

When he told Irene this, she laughed at him, 'You daft thing. She's probably just frowning over a bit of trapped wind.'

Tom went about the house with Marlene in his arms, or over his shoulder, like she was some extra bit of vital equipment or precious kit, that he had been entrusted with. His mother was delighted to see him so taken with the bairn.

'You know what you have to do now, you two. She needs a little brother or a sister. You're best off having shorter gaps between them. Even shorter than I did. Otherwise they get lonely.'

'Mam, man!' Tom laughed. 'I don't think Irene's ready for another yet.' Though he made it plain, the way he was laughing, that the more bairns they had, the better. At least, as far as he was concerned. He made a natural dad. His round, moon-like face just beamed during the whole of his leave home. His mother had never seen him looking so happy.

Those few days, there was time spent with Beryl and Sam, and a shorter time with Bob, who was called away the day after Tom's arrival. They saw him off at the station, and Tom was relieved to be the one watching the train departing, for a change. Poor Bob, though, he still seemed confused by the whole business of going away from home. It was a beautiful, still, clear autumn day in Shields, and he'd have been much happier strolling through the town with the others to the park. Bob looked and felt like he was being punished for some reason.

After seeing off his brother Tom took his small family for a wander through the South Park, pushing the old-fashioned pram through glorious tunnels of changing leaves. Irene felt herself relax completely for once in the cool sunshine and the spangling of goldish green leaves, as they chattered about inconsequential things and nodded hellos to everyone they passed. Then, when they felt like they wanted a sit down, they crossed Ocean Road to visit Franchino's. They were barely through the door before Bella came dashing out to see them, uttering a little scream. '*Tom!*'

'Eeeh, look at you in this place!' he gasped. 'You're doing so well!'

Indeed, the ice cream parlour was almost full today. He was seeing the place at its best. He hardly liked to say it, but it was much more welcoming and less shabby than it had become under the management of her dad, Tonio. Tom wanted to pay tribute to all of Bella's hard graft, but it would be hard to do so without slighting her father's efforts. Instead he just wholeheartedly admired the parlour's decor.

And Bella herself was looking beautiful. Her glossy black hair was up in a fancy chignon, and her black-and-white waitress outfit was just that bit tighter and cinched in than it needed to be. It was a good sign, that Bella was content to look glamorous once more.

With a little flourish she brought Tom a dish of ice cream. 'Don't make a big fuss about it,' she warned him. 'I don't have enough to give everyone.'

He looked at the little smidge of pale cream. 'Is this . . .?'

She nodded solemnly. 'Papa's special recipe, as stolen from Naples, if we're to believe the legend.'

'We should definitely believe the legend!' Tom laughed. 'It's a great story.'

He remembered, years ago, lying on the beach at Marsden Bay, and Bella telling him her papa's tales of old Italy. This was back in their carefree days of spending all night on the beach in the summers when they were kids. He remembered there being a whole gang of them, lighting campfires and drinking cider. He remembered the low throb of Bella's voice, unfolding her family legends with great drama as the night closed in and the shadows of the cliffs lengthened across the sand.

She had told him how her young dad Tonio had once played a game of cards, back in Napoli, with dangerous men, for the highest of stakes. It was – absurdly – for the chance of winning the coveted recipe for the most wonderful ice cream in the world. Tom had laughed, thinking she was making it all up, and how silly it was, but Bella had glared at him crossly.

'No! It's all true, and it's a deadly serious business, this. Now, listen!' And so she had related how it had all gone wrong, and her father's opponents had turned on him. And how the local mafia somehow got themselves involved. Tonio had had to gather up all his belongings and his young family and flee the country of his birth to overseas, putting as much distance between himself and the ice cream gangsters as he could. He had stuck a pin in the atlas at random, and that's why the Franchino clan had pitched up in Tynemouth.

Irene, too, had been treated to the mysterious tales of the Franchino clan in recent months and, like Tom, was never quite sure how much of Bella's stories to believe.

Tom made rhapsodical noises over the ice cream. 'This is just lovely, pet. It's perfect. I can see why they were all shooting each other and chasing after each other over this!'

Irene knew exactly what he meant, though. She'd never had a particularly sweet tooth, but Bella's ice cream was something else. It was just a shame that sugar was so hard to come by right now. Every little portion was a precious amount, and only really doable because of the extra supplies that Sam occasionally managed to bring them.

'Look at Marlene's face!' It had lit up with delight at the taste of the ice cream.

Tom told Bella, 'Do you know what they'll call you, pet? When you go on to become massive and famous? They'll say that you're the Queen of Ice Cream!'

They all laughed at this, but Bella admitted that what she really wanted to do was expand this business that she had inherited. She had been forced to take it over under such tragic circumstances, she really had no choice in the matter. Her whole family had been wiped out in one night, shortly after Christmas.

Sometimes when she closed her eyes she could see them all in the wine cellar under their big house on Simonside. She could picture her old nonna, her brother, her mamma, her papa. She could see them crouching there, terrified, as the planes came up the coast and there was that deadly beat of silence when they knew the bombs were surely going to hit. When they must have known, beyond doubt, that their number was up.

Bella had been away that night. It was the most amazing and horrible stroke of luck. She had been out late, far across town, sitting up with Mavis and Arthur. She'd been drinking brandy with her friends until the early hours. Not something she was given to, but that night it had saved her life. And, although she was plunged into a deep depression as a result of her bereavement, she had slowly come to realise that she had been spared. For some reason she was still alive, out of all of her family. So, perhaps there was a plan for her. Maybe Tommy Farley was quite right, and she really was going to become the Queen of Ice Cream?

Bella smiled, thinking of how delighted her father would be by that idea.

'It's good to see you smiling, pet,' said Irene.

Bella decided to tell them about her plans. Her crazy plans to reopen the kiosk her father had once had on the beach in the 1920s, and where his business had started up, serving ices and coffee to the sunbathers and day trippers. She could picture a time when the hostilities were over and people would be able to holiday and enjoy themselves again. Also, she was thinking of the day when she'd be able to open further branches of Franchino's in other towns across the north-east. She knew she could make everyone hanker after her roasted coffee and her perfect ice cream. 'Just imagine!' she smiled.

'It really will be an empire,' Tom grinned, toasting her with the last of his coffee. And then it was time for them to get on, and carry on with their walk around town before darkness fell.

'Lots of love, Tom,' Bella told him as he left with his young family. 'Come back to us soon.'

They fetched fish and chips from the little shop at the top of the Sixteen Streets, though usually Ma Ada would have refused to eat them. 'They turn my stomach, Betty's fish suppers,' she'd been heard to say. 'I think it's the kind of fat old Betty fries them in. Have you ever seen it? It looks like swamp water, bubbling away. Nah, I wouldn't eat Swetty Betty's chips for nowt.'

'Swetty Betty' was the name painted on the front of the shop. 'Betty's' had been properly stencilled, but some wag had added the misspelt 'Swetty' years ago, and somehow it had stuck. Irene thought it was a terrible advert for the place, but the large, cheerful lady inside didn't seem to mind it one bit. 'Well, I *do* sweat, don't I? I sweat cobs working in here. Anyone would!' Her face was permanently bright red and glowing.

For some reason Tom loved her fish suppers, and they were something he looked forward to fiercely when he came home on leave. His mother gave in grumblingly to his request, on the understanding that he paid for them all and treated them. 'I'm not giving that dirty Betty a penny of my own money,' Ma Ada swore.

Tom loved the portion of hot, glistening scraps that Swetty Betty would include with his supper. He'd relished them since he was a kid: the little nuggets of batter that formed in the fat, sprinkled out over his dinner. To him they were the most delicious part of the whole meal.

Tom and Irene hurried home with Marlene in her pram, and three fish suppers bundled up in their arms. There'd be enough there to divide between the whole household, they reckoned. Sam was going to be out, and Megan was off her food just lately and hated Betty's chips even more than Ma Ada did.

There was a great bustling of energy and excited unwrapping of hot parcels at the kitchen table. Ma Ada brought warmed plates from the oven – she refused to let anyone eat out of paper in her parlour. Beryl helped divide up the portions with scrupulous care, and Lucky sat on one of the wooden chairs, bolt upright and staring with avid, greedy eyes at the perfectly flaky white fish.

They ate very contentedly, and sawed off great hanks of Beryl's homemade loaf, and washed it all down with strong tea.

Then the radio went on, and cheery music stirred the air. They listened to the news with pursed lips, not meeting each other's eyes. Not even wanting to discuss it when the music came back on. It was all talk of manoeuvres and troops and bombing raids. Most evenings entailed some kind of dreadful news. Whenever there was talk of places being razed to the ground Ma Ada would sit there looking stunned at the very idea of so much devastation.

Megan would be punching the air and whooping. 'That'll teach them! They'll learn now! Now they'll know, the buggers!'

But Irene would always be very quiet during reports like this. She hated to think about any of the destruction that was going on, and why it was happening. She'd thought plenty before about the fact that the bombing raids they suffered here on Tyneside were being inflicted on their enemies by their own RAF. And Tom was, of course, a part of that. 'When we cower in our shelters, he's flying abroad and dropping bombs on folk over there . . .' she'd said, and instantly regretted it.

'They're the enemy! They deserve it!' Ma Ada had cried back at her. And, of course, she was right: there was an extent to which, in times like these, everything became black and white. Life simplified itself down to a brutish starkness - us and them. That's how it had to be.

But when Irene heard the news each night . . . she couldn't help thinking about it all over again. She couldn't help thinking about Tom in his plane. He never told her very much. He wasn't allowed to, of course. Loose lips, and all that. But just recently, on this very leave, he had told her that he had a little window.

'A little window?' she asked.

It was right at the front of the plane. He wasn't piloting – he'd told her many times before. He wasn't a pilot, though everyone kept assuming he was, because he was in the RAF. No, he was a bomber.

A cold thrill went through her as he told her this. Irene wasn't sure she really wanted to hear details, after all.

'I'm a bomb-aimer,' Tom told her. Then he explained to her: it was his decision when exactly they would launch their deadly missiles.

Irene wished he hadn't told her anything at all. She had badgered him for details. She had thought, if she could just know a little bit more; if she could understand and share in what he had to do, it would make it more real for her when he was away.

But when he told her – even this tiny detail – about lying in the dark with a circular window that peered down at the smouldering cities far below – it was far too much. She couldn't stand it. She couldn't chase the images out of her head. It was more knowledge than she knew what to do with.

More music played, and they sat peacefully in front of the fire. It was one of the more sedate and pleasant evenings they'd all known in months. Tom was a very steadying presence in the house, Irene realised. There was less bickering and sniping when he was around. Even Megan was contentedly quiet, when she eventually sloped down in her nightie and her curlers for her coffee. She cadged a tab from Tom, and he lit one for himself.

Maybe the presence of the men made the women behave themselves better, Irene wondered?

Then Tom was coughing and spluttering. He sat forward abruptly and couldn't catch his breath for a moment.

'Nasty cough,' his mother said, looking over sharply at him.

He agreed, getting a grip on his breathing again, and taking a long, soothing drag of his Woodbine. 'We breathe in such horrible fumes up there. I spend half my bloody life coughing up my guts. That's why it's so nice to be back home, with the clean sea air.'

'Oh, aye,' his ma laughed. 'That's why folk come to visit the Sixteen Streets! For all the clean, reviving air we've got. Aye, we're like bloody Switzerland here, man!' She chortled to herself, but Irene noticed her watching her son with concern.

Ma Ada was right – that cough of his was horrendous.

# Chapter Eighteen

'Eeeh, well, they're famous where I come from, anyway,' Mavis was telling Irene. 'Infamous! That's the word, isn't it?'

It was the first day back at the biscuit factory following Tom's leave, and Irene couldn't help herself feeling glum. The old routines and rhythms of her work in the packing room were soothing in a way, but it was intensely cold today, and Mavis was chuntering on more than ever. Sometimes her chatter could be endearing, but this wasn't one of those times. Irene loved the girl dearly, but she wanted her to put a sock in it this morning.

The other girls were listening with more interest than Irene was. 'Who are you on about, Mavis?' asked Mary, a plump, confident girl.

'The Mad Johnsons, from over our way,' said Mavis darkly. 'You know them, Mary.'

'Oh, aye. Our Karen went out with the youngest lad. Not for very long.'

Edith and Gladys were taking notice, nodding and soon they were shouting over the noise of the conveyor belt, sharing snippets of their own about the renowned Johnsons.

Irene didn't really want to hear any more just now. If their Sam was getting involved with a bad lot, she didn't want torturing with hearing about just how bad they were. The whole thing made her feel distinctly uncomfortable.

'They've done murders,' Mavis was saying now.

'Oh, shush now!' Irene said. Mavis was going too far.

'It's all true!' Mavis cried. 'At least, that's what I've heard. They garotte their victims and chuck them in the river and they're never heard from again. Oh no, you can't get in the way of the Mad Johnsons, or there's hell to pay.'

All the other biscuit packing girls seemed to agree with her.

Irene tried to stop up her ears and get on with packing her biscuits. She wished the call would come for her to go to the bake house. It was hot and noisy in there, and she wouldn't have to listen to all this bally nonsense.

She missed Beryl being around at the factory. But now Beryl had gone full time at the docks, and was welding all day long. Irene supposed that's what she'd wanted. She'd set her heart on being a welder, but she wasn't half missed round here at the biscuit factory.

Things were changing, Irene thought. Their lives were changing shape every single day, and she wasn't sure she liked it.

Why couldn't there be a bit of stability for a while?

That evening Irene had agreed to go round Mavis's house, to have a little visit and see Arthur for the first time in ages. At first she was keen but it had been a long day and her head was banging with noisy gossip. Now she was beginning to wish she hadn't agreed so readily to visit.

'Oh, I'm that glad you're coming over,' Mavis enthused on the tram ride through the dark after work. 'It's a treat for us, really. Arthur's dead excited about you coming over! He's been going on like it's the Queen of Sheba herself who's promised to pay us a visit.'

The tram was cram-packed with workers going home, squeezed together and clutching their bags and gas mask boxes.

Irene realised that she didn't have anything to give to her hosts when she got there.

'Never you mind about that!' Mavis laughed. 'You've given us plenty. It's our chance to treat you for a change.'

'You should have asked me over when Tom was still at home,' Irene said. 'He'd have liked to see where Bella was living.'

Mavis pulled a face. 'I don't think your fella approves of either me or Arthur. Just like all the Farleys, he thinks we're wasters and peasants.'

'I'm sure he doesn't think that!' Irene gasped, though she knew in her heart that Tom didn't approve of her friendship with the brother and sister at all. He had called the Kendricks guttersnipes, more than once, and Irene had been shocked at his tone. Furthermore, she had been angry that he'd seen fit to tell her who she could and couldn't be friends with.

Perhaps Mavis was right, and it was better that they'd waited until he was back on his airbase before they extended this invite.

The tram battered its way through the biting winds as it drew into the warren of streets closer to the sea. Snow was tumbling down now, flurrying past the lit windows and making both girls shiver involuntarily. 'Soon be home,' Mavis smiled, and jumped to her feet to ring the bell.

As they trudged through the backstreets the snow was falling more heavily, and Mavis was excitedly describing the allotment vegetables Arthur had grown for them and how he'd pickled and bottled all kinds of things in recent weeks. 'I can't imagine Arthur being so domesticated,' Irene smiled, though she had heard before that he enjoyed pottering about on the allotment. The fact that anything edible had resulted from his efforts was news to her.

Her friends' little house at the end of the street looked just as tumbledown and neglected from the outside as it always had. The blackout curtains were up, so that not a speck of light was spilling outside. The streets round here seemed particularly dark and lonely. Irene couldn't suppress a quiver of fear when she thought again about the Mad Johnsons, and how Mavis claimed that they ruled the roost in this part of town.

Stepping into Mavis's house she received a pleasant surprise. 'But it's . . . it's lovely, Mavis!' Irene gasped.

Last time she'd visited, back in the spring, the whole house had been filthy dirty and dusty, and heaped with all kinds of jumble and junk that the parentless siblings had accumulated over the years. It was hard to find anywhere to sit down when you were visiting. There had been dirty plates and dishes left out on every surface, and Hollywood magazines left open, half-read, and dating back to before the war. Stepping into their house was like being inside a bubble in time. A very mucky bubble in time.

Now, though, there was golden light from candles and antique oil lamps. Everything was tidied away and spick and span. The heavy wooden furniture was polished and the cushions had been beaten so that dust didn't come puffing out of them in clouds when you sat down on the settee.

The old wind-up gramophone was playing a crackling 78 and there were delicious savoury smells emerging from the tiny galley kitchen.

'This place is certainly different to what it was!' Irene congratulated Mavis. 'So you got Arthur to live a bit more tidily, then?'

Mavis was shrugging off her massive army coat, and taking Irene's for her. 'It's all down to Bella, really. She's a marvel, Irene. When she managed to stop herself being so sad about her family and losing nearly everything she owned, why that's when she looked around at our house and said, "This place doesn't half need sorting out."'

'It did!' Irene chuckled, remembering the grey and dusty gloom that Mavis and Arthur had once dwelled in.

Mavis went on, 'Bella told us that it was very nice of us to let her stay with us, but if she was going to live here for any length of time, then there had to be some changes.'

And what changes they were, Irene thought! The house was quite beautiful now. It was cosy and warm and filled with interesting-looking knick-knacks and geegaws that drew the eye – rather than seeming oppressively busy and cluttered up.

Bella appeared then, wearing a dress that Irene recognised at once. 'Irene, love,' she murmured, and kissed her on both cheeks. The dress was the only decent one that the Italian girl still owned: the single survivor of her wonderful wardrobe that had been obliterated along with everything else in her family home.

About a year ago Irene had borrowed the gown. Bella had pressed it upon her, and insisted she wore it to a dance they attended at the Alhambra with Arthur, when he was feeling the need of good company and friendly dancing partners. It was darkly glamorous, purple crêpe de Chine. The frock was just about the nicest thing that Irene had ever worn. After the dance she had kept meaning to return it to her friend, and never quite found the correct, tactful moment. It had stayed in her wardrobe until after the bombing, when Bella was left with nothing at all. In the end Irene had filled a bag with things she wanted to give to her friend, clothes she could spare, to see Bella through. She put the sheeny purple dress in with them, folded carefully in tissue paper, feeling slightly awkward about it.

Tonight Bella looked more elegant than Irene had ever seen her before, with her hair piled up and her eyebrows pencilled in like Marlene Dietrich's. She was more buxom and warm-hearted than the German actress, however, and she was delighted to welcome her guest. 'Look! I am wearing the dress, Irene! The dress that you saved from the bomb!'

Irene smiled, and as Bella went to fetch them drinks – it was always sherry they drank round here – a flicker of memory went through her. It was an awkward memory, about that night dancing at the Alhambra. It had been a wonderful night in so many ways, and Irene laughed to remember how Arthur had swung her around that dance floor in front of everyone. She had never danced like that ever before in her life. Somehow his brusque, no-nonsense expertise had made her feel brave and lighter than air.

Anyhow, it was during that evening at the dance that she had spied, across the way and through the potted palms, her sister-in-law Megan misbehaving herself. And Megan had seen Irene observing her, and that had been the root of the trouble between them. Megan had disliked Irene right from the start, but her realising that she was being spied on had compounded that feeling a hundredfold. Megan had shot Irene such a poisonous look it had just about melted her face off, and nothing had been right between them since.

'A year since the dance at the Alhambra!' Bella sighed. She kept her tone light and tried not to think about the changes to her own life that the past year had wrought. 'Well, it's about time that we went out to another dance, isn't it? Surely we're due for one?'

Irene was intrigued by the thought, and basked briefly in the happy memory of dancing foolishly in the cramped saloon bar with Tom the other night. Would he ever go showing off somewhere glorious like the Alhambra? She supposed not. Even down in Lincoln, at the airbase dances with the Land Girls, he had preferred to sit out at the edges with a pint of mild and his ciggies, commenting on the dancers and chatting up the girls.

'I'd love to go out dancing!' Mavis burst out. 'Eeeh, Irene. You must ask your Sam if he'll come out with us. We need all us younger ones to go out together, and I bet he can dance like a dream, can't he?'

Irene said, 'Ay, he can. He was at the Alhambra that night last year. He loves those dances.'

'Well, get him to come out with us.' Suddenly Mavis gave a little scream, like she'd sat on something sharp. But she'd just remembered something. 'There's a dance on at the Albert Hall on Fowler Street. It used to be a picture house for a while, but now they've done it up for dancing again, like it was before, and they reckon it's lovely inside. They've got a night on at the end of the month. We should all go!'

'What's this? What's this?' Just then Arthur made his entrance with his customary aplomb. He was in some kind of costume, as usual. Something he had dug out of his endless supply of cast-off garments that he had salvaged over the years. Tonight he was in the garb of an Edwardian gentleman, with an open-necked shirt and a cricketing jumper. He looked absurdly as if he was about to fling open French windows onto a summer's day and go bounding off across the lawn.

He grinned at them all. 'Are we going out dancing again? Bella, is dinner ready, pet, I'm starved. Did they tell you, Irene, all the vegetables come from my very own allotment? I grew everything we're gonna eat tonight with my own fair hands! It's all vegetarian – well, no one's getting any meat these days, are they? Well, most of us aren't.'

He was gabbling more than usual, and when Irene stood up to hug him hello he paused briefly and took a breath. 'Is your Sam all right? I was that shocked when Mavis told me about finding him . . . lying roughed up in the gutter!'

'He's okay,' Irene said. 'Just battered and bruised still. But it might teach him a lesson, all this . . .'

'A lesson?' Bella frowned, wafting them all over to the dining table, which was folded out and beautifully laid ready for them. She lit more candles and looked questioningly at their guest.

'All this nicking he's been doing. The bad company he's obviously been keeping.'

Bella sighed. 'Oh, I see . . .' And she went off to the kitchen, nodding worriedly.

Behind her back, Mavis said sotto voce: 'Tell you what, without some of the supplies he manages to get hold of, Franchino's would be in a sorrier state, I must admit.'

Irene frowned at her. 'What supplies?' She kept her voice lowered. 'Is this something Bella doesn't know about?'

Mavis sat down at her usual place at the table, nodding firmly. 'Aye, that's right. I'm the go-between, didn't you know that, Irene? I meet Sam in the alley out back, under cover of darkness, when he's got anything for us. I have to dress in dark clothes and everything. He's there with a cart and I fetch the sugar sacks into our house, one at a time, and leave them here under our stairs.'

'Sugar sacks?' Irene asked. 'You mean, all that sugar is nicked?'

Mavis shrugged. 'There's no harm in it. Not while there's a war on, hinny. Everyone has to get by as best they can.'

'But does Bella know she's buying knock-off sugar?'

Mavis shook her head firmly. 'Why, no. But she must suspect, I reckon. The price is so cheap!'

Just then Bella was bustling back into the dining room, with warmed plates and polished cutlery. Mavis asked her, 'Don't we get all our sugar from Sam now, Bella?'

Bella smiled brightly. 'He's like a miracle worker!'

As Bella played hostess, Mavis burbled on about how she and the Italian girl carried the sugar to Franchino's. It was an act that Bella didn't even realise was clandestine. 'Well, me and Bella carry the supplies in, bit by bit all the way to Franchino's on Ocean Road. What did you say it was, Bella? It's a very efficient operation we've got going.'

Mavis sat there looking quite smug and pleased with herself at the thought of her secret missions with Sam. Of course, she didn't tell the others about how clumsy the two of them had been, slipping in the slushy alleys as they hefted the sacks about. Once or twice Sam had lost patience with his young helper and spoken rather sharply, but Mavis brushed those bits of memories away from the picture in her mind. All she could imagine was her and Sam. Bonded in nefarious activity. Smuggling sweetness away down the back alleys all the way from the docks.

Irene wondered if Bella really was ignorant about the dodginess of her dealings with Sam. If she knew the truth, surely she would have massive misgivings about accepting the contraband sugar. It wasn't just out of the kindness of their hearts that Sam and Mavis went to all the effort, and Irene didn't like the thought of Bella being hoodwinked, or being drawn into wrong-doing unawares. From what Irene understood about the Franchino clan, Bella's old papa Tonio might have chuckled about this business, but Bella tended to like everything to be above board.

Mavis's eyes were shining with suppressed excitement. In her mind she was a kind of gangsters' moll. She was mostly just glad of the extra time she got to spend with Sam, literally rubbing shoulders as they manhandled the bags together. And surely it wasn't just her imagination, but she felt that Sam was talking to her more fondly these days? He was coming to see her as a person in her own right.

Irene, however, felt scandalised, hearing the details of their clandestine carrying on. Of course she realised that in practical terms Sam had been keeping Franchino's supplied with sugar for the special recipe ice cream, and even she didn't feel inclined to ask too much about its source. From what she was hearing now, it sounded like a well-run and profitable system that Sam and Mavis had dreamt up between them.

'Is this what's getting him into bother with those thugs, then?' Irene asked Mavis while Bella was out of earshot, and

Arthur earwigged. 'The sugar he brings you?'

Mavis looked delighted at the idea that she was a femme fatale, like in an American movie.

'What he sells us is a tiny amount, really,' Mavis said. 'It's nothing compared to the kind of nicking that goes on down the docks, and the things you see going on round this part of town.'

Irene reflected that both Mavis and Arthur were pretty sanguine about the town's criminal goings-on. Where she came from, Irene had never heard of anything untoward or underhand like that. She felt like something of an innocent, sitting amongst this lot. She looked at the faces of her friends and wondered what other activities went on which she only knew the barest whisper of.

'Look!' Bella swept into the room bearing a steaming tureen. 'It's vegetable stew!'

'I hope it's a big hit with you all,' Arthur said. 'I've poured my life and soul into those carrots, and that marrow.'

'I'm sure it'll be lovely,' Irene smiled.

Irene couldn't help thinking, though, all through their delicious, convivial dinner, about the bags of sugar that Mavis said they had stored under their stairs. Bags of contraband sugar that her brother-in-law had nicked and brought here to sell to Bella, so she could mix up her father's magic-recipe ice cream. And there was Irene herself, serving that delicacy in wafers and glass bowls for unsuspecting customers.

It was criminal sweetness. Forbidden desserts. And Bella's an accessory, and what's more, she realised, with a shock – so am I!

Irene felt herself blushing. She felt the burning dread building up in her chest. She hated having to keep secrets because she tended to blurt things out in moments of stress. Her other friends seemed quite relaxed and happy: they didn't care about stolen sugar, illegal ice cream or criminal gangs of thugs. All of these things seemed everyday and ordinary to them.

I've got to tell Sam to stop it all, she thought. And I've got to warn Bella, haven't I? It might mean the end of Franchino's special ice cream, but that's nothing compared to Sam's safety, surely. And Bella's safety and peace of mind, too. Surely there are more important things than money and ice cream?

Outside, beyond the blackout curtains, snow was sifting down through the November night and settling on the backstreets and the dockyards of South Shields.

It was gentle and soft, but by morning it would be frozen hard.

# Chapter Nineteen

At home, Beryl found that she was doing more than her fair share of work. The scullery at Number Thirteen was a kind of factory where bottles were constantly being sterilised and nappies were stewing and being bleached in buckets, all around the clock.

She'd never been under any illusion that her older, more glamorous sister-in-law was anything but a lazy cow, but Megan was worse than ever these days. These so-called blues she had been suffering since the birth of her bairn were stretching out for months on end, and the only way of treating them seemed to involve lying on her bed reading film magazines and moaning about her life. She barely looked at her own baby. All the endless jobs of feeding and burping and seeing to him had been turned over to Ma Ada and Beryl.

'You two are life-savers,' Megan opined, licking her finger and turning the pages of her magazine. She lived in her night-gown and wafted about the house – whenever she left her attic room – rather like a pale and glamorous ghost.

Ma Ada was looking pale, too. The old lady was being kept awake with night-time bottles and grizzling babes. 'You and Irene need all the help you can get,' she grumbled at three in the morning to Beryl. 'You've got a busy day's work to get through. And Megan's not well enough to do everything she ought to.'

Ma Ada was letting Megan get away with murder, Beryl thought. Why was she being so soft on her?

When they were sharing that attic room, Beryl once asked Megan how far she thought she could push this. Why did she think she could get away with being so lazy and awful?

'Me?' she squawked, with mock outrage.

'You know what I mean,' Beryl said. 'Not pulling your weight. Letting everyone else look after your bairn. What will you do when Ma Ada and the rest of us have had enough of you?'

Megan was all wounded innocence. She sat up in bed in her silky nightgown, her hair all tumbled around her and – damn her, Beryl thought – she looked beautifully unruffled and gorgeous. She had none of the careworn haggardness shared by the other women in the family, and that was because she was getting seven hours' sleep each night. 'But, Beryl . . . It's so hard for me. I feel like that baby of mine isn't even truly mine. I know it is . . . but something in me is rejecting it. It's a horrible, wrenching, punishing feeling. It's a dreadful thing for a woman to go through.'

Beryl wasn't about to indulge her further. 'Get away, lass. You've barely looked at the poor little lad since he was born. Poor Johnny will grow up not even knowing who his mammy is. His real mam can't even be bothered with him!'

Megan shuddered. 'I don't think I'm cut out for this mothering lark, to be honest. I look at him and his red little face makes me feel ill, really. His slobbering and being sick all the time . . . and the shitty nappies – it all makes me want to throw up.'

Beryl flushed at her horrible language, and couldn't believe that a mother would talk like that about her own flesh and blood.

'And when I see his face when he's shrieking and screaming, he makes me think of Bob.' Megan shrugged carelessly. 'Of his big, fat red face when he shouts and bellyaches.'

Beryl burst out: 'Aye, but how can he look like Bob? Cos

he's not Bob's, is he? Bob's not his dad, is he?' The words were out before she could stop herself. She even enjoyed the flash of dismay she saw in Megan's face at her mention of the truth.

'We're not ever gonna say that, Beryl,' Megan snapped. 'That was the agreement, wasn't it? We never say it in this house or anywhere, in order to keep the peace. So just you shut your cake hole, lady.'

Beryl tutted. It seemed to her that plenty of rules got bent and blind eyes were turned on Megan's account. Exhausted to her bones, demoralised, and covered in little burn marks up both arms and shoulders, Beryl was no longer in any mood to indulge her sister-in-law. 'Ahh, you make me sick, Megan. You always get your own bloody way.'

It made her feel strange, sharing the bed with her during the days that Tom had been home. Somehow, because Megan preferred Beryl's company to Irene's, the swap had remained in place even after Tom had gone away again. Now Beryl felt like she was stuck up there for ever, in the attic, and there was nothing she could do. The little baby boy was going to be neglected by Megan, that's how it seemed to Beryl. A part of Beryl felt like she must be there at all times to keep watch over Johnny. Something in her soul reached out to the helpless little bairn. That tiny baby boy. He didn't have a mammy like Marlene had Irene. He wasn't that lucky. Beryl felt anguished and torn about it all, but she felt that he needed her.

The reek of Megan's perfume hung heavily in the darkness, and it made Beryl gag. Gardenia, or something. Megan went to bed in full make-up and perfume, like she was expecting to be rescued by Prince Charming in the middle of the night . . . Just like she fancied that she was in some ridiculous Hollywood movie.

Except she wasn't. None of them were. This was their real life, Beryl thought. And Megan was having a laugh at all of their expense.

'Ma Ada will lose patience with you,' Beryl promised once, after they turned the lights out. 'She won't put up with your sly ways for ever. She'll see through all your pretence.'

'Will she?' Megan said. Beryl could even hear her smiling in the dark. There was something so smug about her voice. Her self-satisfied grin seemed to hang in the air. 'I don't think so. You see, I could take off any day I chose, and I could take that little baby boy with me. And how do you suppose old Ma Ada would feel about losing her only grandson? What do you think she'd say about that, eh? And how would you feel about it, eh, Aunty Beryl? I've seen how attached you are to him. You're devoted to him. You'd hate to see the last of him, wouldn't you? You'd avoid that happening at any cost.'

Beryl lay there, listening hard. Her heart was thumping. She realised that Megan was right. She was holding all the aces. She could do anything she wanted, because she had all the power.

'I mean,' Megan went on, 'it's not like you're gonna have a bairn of your own, is it? You're not gonna give the old woman a grandchild, are you? You've told me that before: it's never gonna happen for you and your lovely Tony. And so you've just got to be content with being a nice aunty. Well, I suggest you carry on being precisely that, our Beryl. And just you stop your complaining about a few simple chores you should be glad to do. And let other people get on with their lives.'

And with that said, Megan turned over and fell asleep almost straight away.

Her words had gouged themselves into Beryl's heart. She lay there quite still, not quite believing the girl could be so cruel. Beryl lay under the heavy bedspread with her heart pounding and her ears ringing like she had some kind of infection from the poison Megan had been pouring into her.

Beside her in the bed, Megan's breathing became deep and even and she didn't wake up, not even when Johnny started whingeing, some twenty minutes later, demanding a feed. Blearily, Beryl stumbled out of bed to see to him.

Megan was right about absolutely everything. She had the measure of them. She had power over them all. That's what she loved. That's why she was living here. The Farley women had to do everything she wanted, for the foreseeable future. She was completely right.

Beryl took the small, still quite sickly bairn downstairs to the parlour to feed him. She sat in Ma Ada's lumpy, worn chair and sobbed to herself as she fed him the bottle.

No one could hear her down here. It was where she did all her crying. And it's where she thought about her past, and wondered how she had ended up being what Megan dismissively called 'just an aunty'.

When he had started courting her, Tony took Beryl dancing in South Marine Park. This already seemed like a hundred years ago: before the war, when the nights were warm and there was a band playing all the time and there were multi-coloured lights everywhere.

He rowed her in a boat across the ornamental lake and made her laugh by dropping one of the oars in the water and getting told off by the man in charge of the boat hut. He told her about his work at the shipyard, where he was a welder, and she was enthralled by his descriptions of the work he did. It seemed amazing and impressive, that he was involved in the creation of important parts of the great big ships that sailed out of the Tyne. It seemed much more important than biscuits.

'We all do the work we have to do,' he told her. 'That's what Ma always says.'

'She's so wise, your ma,' smiled Beryl. They were eating ices, strolling around the wooded perimeter of the park. 'I wish mine was. All mine ever says is, "Have you got the washing in?" or "Have you cooked that fish before it goes off?"'

'Your poor mam sounds like she's had a sad life,' he said. 'Your dad, too. You shouldn't be so harsh on them, pet.'

'I know . . .' she sighed. 'I shouldn't go on about them, complaining. And I never really do, not out loud. But I feel like I can say just what I want to you, Tony.'

He grinned at this, and tried not to feel too pleased with himself. He reached for her hand as they walked under the dappled light that came through the overhanging trees.

Beryl squeezed the large, strong, scarred hand that held hers. The ache was still there in her palm, but her hand wasn't empty any more.

They were married very late that year, in a simple do at St Jude's, the church at the edge of the Sixteen Streets. Then there was a small celebration at the Robin Hood. Beryl cried when she saw her mam and dad there, in their best, outmoded clothes. Looking so old and fragile and out of place.

'You'll be leaving us, then,' her dad said.

'Of course she'll be leaving us,' tutted her mam. 'She'll have had enough of fussing after us two relics.'

'You make your own life, our Beryl,' her dad whispered to her. 'I'm so glad you've managed to get away.'

These were the happiest years Beryl had ever known. She found herself quite content living in the house on Frederick Street with her new family.

She felt like a grown-up in a way she'd never have felt, had she still been living with her parents, and running around after them. Her chores at Number Thirteen were nowhere near as onerous, with four boys living under the same roof, and she found that she loved working at Wight's biscuit factory. She had, for the first time in her life, made proper friends.

One of them was Megan Cook, who was very glamorous and blonde, and who started work on the production line shortly after Beryl did. She came from Hartlepool and had grown up on a farm, and Beryl loved to hear her stories about living off the land. All the girls at the biscuit factory were friendly, but it was Megan who became her special friend. They took to spending time together even after their long hours at the factory.

Beryl invited the newish girl from Hartlepool to come out with her new circle of friends, who she had met through the Farley brothers. Almost nervously at first, Megan came along to their evenings at the local, or down to the beach during the long summer nights. No one ever really had any money, so they would build a fire out of driftwood and sit drinking an old bottle of rum or sherry fetched out of someone's mother's sideboard.

At first Beryl really didn't want to go down to the beach. She hadn't spent any time there for years, even though she had lived within sight of the sands. The beach had bad associations for her. Ones she didn't want reminding of. She just couldn't face it. Even the crash and boom of the surf could bring her out in a sweat.

This was the place that the Farley boys and their gang would come when the nights were mild enough. Sometimes they even slept out on the sands, swaddled in the blankets they brought. They had to be careful that they chose somewhere out of reach of the tide, of course. Somewhere in the rough marram grass, protected and dry on the soft summer nights.

Megan thought this was a lovely idea, and couldn't understand Beryl's initial horror at staying out on the beach. 'But it'll be fun,' she kept urging her new friend. 'There'll be all kinds of mischief. All them lads! That's the whole point, don't you see?'

Beryl smiled at her. She was coming to realise that Megan wasn't as sweetly innocent as she had at first seemed. She wasn't quite as 'man mad' as Ma Ada might have put it, but she certainly had an eye for the boys. Beryl smiled ruefully at the thought of Megan wanting to stay out all night. It was strange, but she herself felt like such an old married lady these days. Those kinds of shenanigans – canoodling on the beach and finding excuses to stay out late – didn't matter a jot to her. She had her Tony, and everyone else seemed so juvenile and silly by comparison.

Megan seemed to read her mind, as they walked along with their hastily packed picnic basket down Ocean Road. 'You're only – what? Nineteen? You're not an old woman yet, Beryl Farley. You're so respectable and boring.'

Beryl merely laughed at this. She glanced at Megan, so cool and composed and mocking in her summer print frock. She was very confident, all of a sudden. Assured enough of her new pal's friendship that she could complain about her attitude, and even mock her like this. Beryl felt a bit stung, actually. Megan didn't really know a thing about her.

It was round about that time that Beryl decided maybe she ought to trust Megan, her new friend. She could explain herself to her. Perhaps, Beryl reasoned, it was time that she divulged the truth of herself. Her long-held secret shame.

And so Megan heard the story from Beryl's own lips. She brought it out like a grand confession, a few months into their friendship, when Beryl felt that she could trust Megan. Beryl had never really had a close friend before. No one had given her this kind of attention or affection and, as a result, she felt she could trust Megan with her very life.

They had been sitting in a coffee bar at the Nook, and Megan had listened with wide-opened eyes. Her reaction to Beryl's worst, most shameful secret had been surprising.

'But it wasn't your fault! And anyway, that was years ago!' Her voice was loud in the chrome and glass coffee bar, and Beryl shushed her.

'Of course it was my fault! And it's the kind of terrible thing that stays with you for ever.'

Megan shook her head, lighting up a cocktail cigarette. It was lilac and gold and the blue smoke that came undulating out of it transfixed Beryl. 'Rubbish,' Megan snapped. 'Look how young you were! How could anyone have coped with that kind of thing at your age?' She sucked elegantly on her cigarette. 'Ooh, these are lovely. They're from that fancy little tobacconist's by the market. Anyway, it's a scandal that your parents let you feel so guilty all these years. How old were you? Eleven years old? They ought to be ashamed of themselves, the pair of them, for the damage this has done to you.'

Beryl simply stared at her new friend. She felt a strange pang of . . . what was it? Relief? Panic? Guilt? All of those. But also a mad rush of something like hero worship for Megan. The things she said were so clear-cut and direct. There was none of the muddle about things that Beryl experienced when she tried to think about her feelings. Megan was telling her to stop feeling guilty and – miraculously – her guilt actually seemed to be lifting away at last, as light as those bluish spirals of fag smoke rising above their booth in the coffee shop.

It was only because of talks like this with Megan, and their growing friendship, that Beryl felt able to join the other young people for their picnic on the beach. She just hoped it wouldn't be too close to Marsden Rock. She couldn't quite cope with that.

They had stottie cakes fresh from the oven and sausages from the famous butcher's in town. They had brown ale and the feasting went on each night as the sun started going down, sending long shadows through the swaying grass and across the gentle sands.

So this was what having a gang of friends was like. It felt wonderful to Beryl, even though she was still rather shy in larger numbers. She was used to keeping away from people her own age, and being set apart, but the Farley boys' gang of friends welcomed her with open arms.

It was funny how Megan slotted right in, easy as anything. She had no embarrassment about jumping right into the middle of things, dancing and flirting and showing off.

'Your friend's a proper live wire,' Tony smiled, nudging his young wife as they sat in the sand and watched the others larking about.

'I didn't know she was as rowdy as this.' Beryl shrugged. 'She was so quiet when she started at Wight's.'

'She's a bonny lass,' Tony nodded approvingly. 'I reckon she's gonna have all the fellas running after her. Our Tom's got a bit of a glint in his eye, look. He can't keep away from her.'

It was true, Tony's younger brother was hovering at Megan's side for much of that evening. He danced with her when there was music. One of the Anderson twins had brought a guitar, and a cousin of theirs had a funny kind of squeezebox thing and could hold a tune. The music became raucous and wilder as the darkness set in, and Megan barely sat down once.

Eventually Beryl said to her husband, 'Can we start off for home now? I don't want to sleep out on the sands all night.'

Tony looked disappointed, but he understood. The others hooted with derision at the old married couple when they announced that they'd have to be getting home. 'Whey, someone has to go home tonight!' Tony laughed. 'If yous are all staying out, our ma's gonna think we've all ran away and left her on her tod!'

All the other Farley boys were staying out. It was one of the shortest nights of the year and it seemed awful to waste that beautiful blue, light night with going home.

Beryl was so glad to return home to Number Thirteen and the room she shared with Tony. It still felt like such a wonderful novelty, sharing a bed with this huge, marvellous man. It still seemed daring and rude to think about it, but she loved the press and the warmth of him against her when they slept. She was thrilled by the almost woolly hairiness of his muscular legs in the bed beside her. This was the best reason for not staying out all night with the gang, and getting home instead. This closeness.

He wrapped himself around her, and she smiled up at him.

'Are we trying for a bairn, then?' he asked her earnestly.

In that instant she went cold. Her heart plummeted. She tried to twist away.

'What is it?' he asked.

She shook her head fiercely. 'I won't have kids. I won't ever have kids, Tony. I can't do it. I can't . . . I can't be trusted with them.'

Suddenly there was a gap and a barrier between the couple. It was like a dark tide had come rushing in between them.

And that's how things had stayed ever since.

Beryl couldn't. She wouldn't have kids.

# Chapter Twenty

As a child Beryl never had a friend she could take to visit her parents. Back when she was at school, the little girls would all drag friends back to their homes, for birthdays and dollies' tea parties, and the like. Beryl had never been invited by them, and she'd never felt like she could bring anyone to hers.

'Not round here! The place is a mess! It's a midden!' Her mother was abashed and hated the idea of anyone seeing inside their house. 'You stay out and play with all your friends round at theirs.'

It had never really bothered Beryl at the time that she didn't have close friends. It was only now, as an adult, that she saw how strange that was, especially when she heard from her sisters-in-law about the way they had been raised. Both Irene and Megan had been brought up in the country, both in villages, in very different parts of the country, but they had always been among a lot of children. They had been allowed to run wild in the woods and the fields near their homes.

Maybe that's why they were so much more robustly sociable and strong-minded than Beryl felt? Oh, she could fake it. She could be chatty and funny and get along with people, but something inside of her cringed at the same time. She was waiting to be rejected, the whole time. She was waiting for people to say that she wasn't good enough, somehow, and that she had failed the test for being an ordinary, decent human being.

It was all down to her parents, she thought. Their oddness and their staying in bed like they had, all those years. But how to explain that to anyone?

Irene had seemed to take it all in her stride, when she eventually went to visit them, in their house overlooking the sea. 'Really?' Beryl had asked, amazed. 'You really want to visit my folks?'

'Why not?' Irene had laughed, sounding quite carefree. 'I'd love to meet them properly. Oh, I know you say they're reclusive, Beryl. But surely they'll love seeing you? And to have two lovely little bairns like this coming to visit them? How could anyone resist?'

Beryl gave a sickly smile, but her spirits rose as she thought more about Irene's idea. Yes, she'd been getting too stuck in a rut lately. These were beautiful bright, wintry days to be explored and enjoyed, and Beryl had stayed home in her free hours wringing out nappies and mashing up baby food.

Perhaps a visit home really was due. And what would her mother think, with her coming round with two babies in tow? Look! Look at these precious bairns! And I'm being trusted with them. Do you see, Mama? I'm being trusted!

So on the next free afternoon they shared, the two sisters-in-law crammed both babies into one pram (how they squirmed and kicked at each other!) and trundled off to the street at the top of South Marine Park.

The sea breeze was stiff and bracing, and the snow was still lying thick and frozen on the pavements. But it was good to be out, and away from Megan and the others, even if it was only to see her parents.

Beryl's mother surprised her, though, by being up and about, and dressed in a smart blouse and skirt when they arrived.

'Mind, you won't see your dad today. He's up in his room and he won't say a word, even to me. It's not one of his better days, I'm afraid. But that's how it is, when you don't ask ahead about coming to visit. You have to put up with how you find us.'

She sat them in the kitchen with a pot of tea and fussed over both children and her eyes went soft and dark with tenderness.

'Long time since there were babbies round here,' she said, picking them up, one at a time, to hold them close. She breathed in the soapy scent of them and looked like she was drawing their vitality into her own bones and sinews. Beryl sipped her tea and felt a great sorrow for her mother, like she hadn't felt in years. She was a woman still suffering, still mourning, and it was plain in every flicker of expression in her face.

They made merry remarks at each other about being busy and having their work cut out for them. They discussed Megan's apparent baby blues, and the complicated arrangements they had, dashing out to work in shifts and fitting all the household tasks around their lives. They even talked about Ma Ada's incredible energy, and how a woman who had seemed so old to them, just a year ago, was up at all hours now, warming bottles, and energetically working the twin tub and the mangle in the backyard. Young life in the house had somehow plumped her full of new energy.

'We could do with some of that energy round here,' Beryl's mother smiled.

Then, just before they left, Beryl nipped out to the privy and Beryl's mum stared intently across the kitchen at Irene.

'Is there something the matter?' Irene asked her, feeling uncomfortable all of a sudden.

'You're being very kind to my daughter,' the older woman said stiffly.

Irene frowned at her. 'Kindness, nothing! She's a great girl. She's been a great support and friend to me since I moved here.'

'I dare say she has,' said Beryl's mum. 'She's a good girl, deep down, I suppose. It's just . . .' Her voice tailed off, and she nibbled at a broken custard cream.

'What?' Irene asked.

The woman locked eyes with Irene and her voice hardened, 'Just never leave her alone with the babies. You hear me? Don't you ever trust her alone with them.'

Irene stared at her and was about to ask what she was talking about when the back door flew open and Beryl came clattering back inside. 'By crikey!' she gasped. 'It's colder than ever out there! Irene, are you ready, pet? We should leave my mama in peace and get on with our day out.'

Irene nodded dumbly, still staring at Beryl's mother, who was looking back at her as if they shared some kind of secret bond.

Irene didn't have a clue what the woman had been trying to tell her. Something nasty, no doubt. She had been trying to undermine her own daughter. Sowing doubt in the mind of her friend. But why do such a thing? Irene's mind was racing as they left the house on the long street above the park, pushing the pram together down the hill.

Unless there was some truth in the mother's warning? Unless there was some actual reason to distrust Beryl, after all?

But, no. Irene refused to believe it. That older woman was cracked, surely. You could see it in the way she went on. There was more wrong with her than was wrong with Beryl. That was as plain as day.

'Are you okay, Irene?' Beryl asked her, after a few quiet minutes of walking back to Ocean Road. 'You're very quiet. I told you we should never have visited that gloomy old house. It would bring down anybody's mood!'

Irene smiled at her brightly. 'Of course not! I'm fine! Come on, let's get out of this chill. Let's have a hot drink and a sit in Franchino's before home.'

'Oh, yes!' Beryl grinned. 'That's a lovely idea. Thanks, Irene. Thanks for this whole afternoon. It's been lovely to get out and about. With the bairns and everything. It was even nice seeing my mother!'

Irene smiled back. But there was a niggle in her thoughts. She couldn't help it. Beryl's mum had planted something there, just as she had meant to.

They had both felt glad to get out of that draughty house just as the twilight was settling over the town. Beryl looked relieved, as if her duty was done for the month, now that she'd checked on her parents. She'd only peered around her dad's bedroom door and exchanged a few words with him in the afternoon gloaming, but it was enough.

'It always makes me feel so sad going round there,' she shrugged. 'They'll never change.'

Irene nodded, not quite knowing what to say. 'Other people's families are a mystery. No one ever really understands, except the people who belong. I can't imagine what you'd make of my lot, if you visited them in Norfolk.' She laughed at the thought, and shook her head.

The two girls were pushing the pram together, and its wheels were jamming and skidding on the hardened ice. Both babies were grumbling and starting to whine.

'Oh, I'd love that!' Beryl said. 'I'd love to see the place you come from. You always make it sound so wild and remote and wonderful. Like something from an old book. All the animals with names and the countryside spread about you for miles. And all your family sound like proper characters. Better than my boring family!'

Irene shrugged. 'Maybe you'd like it. I don't know – the thing about being remote down there is that you're stuck with them. There's one horse and cart out of the village each day, and that's it. You can't just visit for an hour and then hurry off again.'

The sky was a violent kind of purple, sandwiching the lemony yellow of the horizon right down against the humped silhouette of North Shields, far across the harbour. It looked like they could be expecting further snow that night, and it would probably be best to dash home as soon as possible. But first there was time to have a frothy coffee at Franchino's before heading to the Sixteen Streets. Their visit had left them feeling rather flat, and some of Bella's coffee would do them good.

'Proper coffee beans! No chicory!' Mavis grinned at them as they stepped into the steamy warmth of the ice cream parlour. The wonderful smell hit them at once, along with the fierce noise of the coffee grinder.

Beryl looked delighted. 'Real coffee!'

'Where's it come from?' Irene was suspicious. She kept her voice lowered, even though there were only a couple of customers sitting at a booth near the back.

'Sam, of course,' Mavis said, batting her eyelashes at them. 'Your lovely, handsome, brave Sam. He brought a big bagful of beans this morning and dropped it round our house. He came up our back alley like Santa, he did.' She sighed and flomped down on the counter, holding her head in her hands as the coffee brewed. She looked helpless with desire at the thought of him, and the drippy look on her face would have made Irene laugh had she not been so annoyed.

'What's he doing?' she hissed. 'Nicking stuff again! Hasn't he had enough bother?'

Mavis twisted her face. 'He said it was a special delivery for me, because I'd been so good to him. Because I'd found him in the gutter and been his saviour.'

Oh, Mavis was really milking this business of being the one who had found Sam after his roughing-up at the hands of the Mad Johnsons. She was loving his being indebted to her. It was as if he had been forced to take notice of the whey-faced girl for the very first time, and she was relishing every minute of it. 'He'll get himself in proper bother,' Irene worried.

'Here, go and get sat down with the bairns,' Mavis said, 'and I'll bring your coffee over. By, you've got both babies pushed into that pram! They do look snug,' she laughed. 'They look like a hot Saveloy Dip in a bun, crammed in there.'

Beryl and Irene went to sit down, and Beryl saw that Irene was looking annoyed. 'It's all right for Mavis to crow about getting attention and free gifts from Sam,' Irene frowned, 'but she was the one who was telling us how dangerous these Mad Johnsons are. I had no idea about all of that before she said.'

'What's Sam getting up to? Them Johnsons are meant to be proper nasty,' Beryl said. 'I've heard terrible things.'

'And Mavis behaves like there's nothing out of the ordinary about that! Like criminal gangs and all that are just an everyday part of life.'

'Hmmm,' murmured Beryl. 'Perhaps they are, where she comes from?' Beryl didn't mean to sound snooty and judgmental, but she did a bit, Irene thought. Perhaps we both do?

Mavis scooted over with their coffee, bringing an extra one for herself, and some wafer biscuits. She cooed over the babies and parked herself on the banquette beside Beryl.

'Of course,' she said, as if picking up the thread of her own thoughts, 'our Arthur says I'm ridiculous. He says Sam is just being friendly and returning the favour for my looking after him that night. Arthur was quite nasty, actually. We had words, and that's unusual for us. But he said that I'm a fool for thinking that Sam would ever really notice me, you know. Notice me proper. Notice me as . . . a woman.'

Beryl almost choked on her wafer biscuit. 'A woman!'

'Well, aye,' said Mavis, looking hurt. 'I'm a woman, same as you two, you know. You might both think of me as just a little lass, but I'm twenty, you know. I might have had things wrong with me when I was little, and I might have had my growth hampered a bit.'

'You're not that little . . .' Irene said. 'You talk like there's something wrong with you, pet!'

Mavis scowled. 'I know I'm not bonny, like you lot. And I might be almost a midget and skinny, and look young for my age. But I'm still a woman . . . and I've got dreams . . . and needs . . .'

Beryl and Irene exchanged a glance and almost let themselves down by laughing. Irene was glad she didn't. It would have been so hurtful at that moment. Mavis would have been crushed. Yes, she was being earnest and silly, but she was baring her soul to them. They stared at her, and Irene felt her heart go out to the sickly-looking girl as she went on.

'Arthur said that Sam would never look at me in a million years. He said that Sam's got enough on his plate. He says I might as well be a different species to him. Like I was only like a pet or a small animal that Sam might grow fond of. But I really shouldn't get even those hopes up.' By now Mavis was looking tearful. She dragged her lank hair out of her face and tucked it hurriedly up inside her hairnet.

'Those were awful things for Arthur to say,' Irene gasped. 'Fancy! To his own sister, too.'

Mavis shrugged. 'He only pretends to care about my well-being.'

'Oh, surely not,' said Irene. 'You two have been a wonderful team for years. It's been you two against the world, looking after each other. You've always described it like that.'

'I always knew it'd be me by myself, in the end,' Mavis said, blowing on her coffee and then slurping it up. 'He's making plans to go, you know. He's talking about joining up. ENSA. The entertainments. He wants to see the world, he says. It's about bloody time, he says, and that there's basically bugger all for him here in South Shields. Not for someone as special and rare as he is. Anywhere's better than this little town. That's what he's been saying to me lately. Oh, he does sound bitter, our Arthur does.'

Joining up! Irene felt shocked, but another part of herself wasn't so surprised. To her Arthur had always seemed too different and too big, somehow, to fit inside the same town as the rest of them. And yes, he should be using that voice of his, and all his talents, to help people along through the war and to endure their hardships. She had heard him sing a couple of times, and it was incredible. It seemed impossible that a voice so huge and pure could come blasting out of such a skinny, malnourished frame.

'It won't be the same, without Arthur here,' Irene said.

'Another fella gone away,' said Beryl. 'That's what it'll be. There'll be no fellas left, in the end. They'll all go and leave this a town full of women and no one else. A whole country of women.'

'I wish I could go abroad and do something,' Mavis said. 'I wish I could fight. Sometimes I lie in bed and picture myself with a rifle with, like a bayonet on the front. Let me at 'em! I'll sort 'em out!'

When their laughter subsided they drank their coffee peacefully and the babies were quiet and content for a while in the warmth of Franchino's.

'Anyhow,' Mavis suddenly added, remembering. 'Sam's coming to the dance at the Albert Hall with us. He's dead keen. Arthur, too. So, the dance is on! We're having a Christmas night out – the whole lot of us young 'uns!'

# Chapter Twenty-One

Irene and Beryl hurried with the pram round the corner of Frederick Street and were on the alert at once. Something was strangely different. Where was all that noise coming from?

It was a hullabaloo, but not the awful kind. It didn't sound like disaster and horrible stuff for once. It sounded just like . . . music!

'What's going on in there?' someone squawked nearby. 'Sounds like there's a bloomin' party going on!' Aunty Martha was standing at the front doorstep of her own house, raising both eyebrows at the two lasses as they passed by.

'A party where?' Irene frowned.

'At your place! Listen!' The older woman tightened her threadbare dressing gown and looked annoyed. 'There'll be bother from the warden if this carries on much longer. I'm surprised at your ma, pet!'

It sounded like a gramophone playing American jazz numbers as the two girls trundled the pram down the hill. Soon they were close enough to see that the front parlour sash window was up and the curtains were flung open, spilling golden light into the dark and snowy street. Wonderful music was pouring out of Number Thirteen as Beryl and Irene approached, but they were horrified rather than delighted.

'Have they all gone crazy?' Irene gasped. 'What are they playing at?'

'There'll be bother,' said Beryl. 'All that light escaping!'

As they hurried up they saw Lucky the cat, sitting on the windowsill, looking as mystified as they were.

'Ma Ada?' Irene called into the front hall. She advanced warily into the house, half expecting to find burglars in the place, carousing like mad.

'In the front parlour, hinny!' came a welcoming shout.

And there they were, looking dishevelled and warm, despite the chilling breeze that was blowing the lace curtains about.

Ma Ada, Aunty Winnie and Megan were all in the rarely used best front parlour and they were dancing to an up-tempo Cole Porter number. As she hurried into the room in her hat and coat, trying to make herself heard, Irene recognised it as 'Begin the Beguine', a favourite of her Tom's.

The baby pram was out in the hall, and both babies were reacting to the hullabaloo by wailing loudly in dismay.

'What's going on?' Irene yelled at the two older women and Megan.

'They've gone crackers!' Beryl moaned.

Ma Ada was dancing even more energetically than on New Year's Eve down the pub. She had her skirt hoisted up a little way and was practising a dainty jig. Her face was flushed bright red with exertion, and so was Aunty Winnie's, so it was apparent that this little party had been going on for some time.

Megan had a makeshift gypsy dress and turban wrapped around her. They appeared to have been improvised from a tablecloth and antimacassars snatched from the armchairs. She was revelling in the chaotic scene, swaying her hips and whirling about in the middle of the cramped room.

'Eeeh, we've been having a wonderful time!' the old mother-in-law panted at the new arrivals, pausing for a moment. The song was coming to an end and she urged Aunty Winnie, 'Play it again! Put it on again, Winnie!'

'But the light's spilling into the street,' Irene hissed. 'The neighbours are going daft! You'll have the warden knocking on the door and telling you off.'

'Ah, let him!' Aunty Winnie jeered. 'We're always doing just what we're told, aren't we? We're always following bloody orders! We've had enough!'

'We certainly have!' Megan laughed, undulating her hips as the needle hissed into its groove and started the song all over again. 'We've had quite enough of falling into line!'

That's exactly how they looked to Irene: like they had burst out of a straitjacket. After doing as they were told and toeing the line for so long, living in tension and fear, somehow they had liberated themselves and come to irrepressible, noisy life. It was almost frightening to see.

'At least close the window and pull the blackout curtains,' Irene urged worriedly. 'And turn the sound down a little bit.'

'Miss Goody-Goody,' Megan sneered at her, as she tugged at the curtain cord and scooted Lucky out of the way. 'Don't you see? We're sick of being told what to do all the time. Why, it's like the whole place is being run by bloody Hitler already! We might as well give up right now and let the Nazis take over, if we can't even do what we want to in our own homes.'

Megan was being shrill and ridiculous, shouting at Irene as she slammed shut the windows and wrestled with the blackout curtains. Irene didn't even bother trying to argue with her. But she could smell the gin on her breath as she shimmied next to her.

'What's all this?' Beryl cried out, suddenly noticing all the bottles on the coffee table. The women had pulled it to one side, over by the empty fireplace, so they could have the floor for dancing. 'There must be half a dozen bottles open here!'

They were brand new bottles of spirits. They didn't come from the dresser in the other room. These were whisky, gin, brandy, rum bottles. All of them opened and left with their lids off, standing in a forest of smeared glasses. The polished coffee table was puddled with spills. There would be awful stains in the varnish, Irene thought.

'We deserve a little party, we thought,' Ma Ada grinned at them. Her face seemed unfocused and unreal. Neither girl had ever seen her smile so broadly, revealing all of her small, square teeth at once. 'Everything's been so hard and serious for so long. We thought it was time to let our hair down.'

'Come and dance with us, girls!' Aunty Winnie roared. Her hair was a shock of brilliant white. She was like a witch in their front parlour, Irene thought. Perhaps it was she who'd enticed the others into bad ways. Getting them drunk in the early evening and casting all their cares to the wintry winds.

'B-but where did all the booze come from?' Beryl asked, as Megan seized her by the arms and tried to get her to dance.

'Stop asking daft questions! And just enjoy yourself, for once!' Megan hooted.

The party didn't last much longer, thank goodness.

It wasn't very long before a wave of exhaustion passed through the old woman and almost felled her where she stood. She picked up Lucky and ambled through to her back parlour, muttering something about her knees.

Irene pursued Ma Ada down the hall and into the scullery, where she was putting the kettle on the hob and chuckling to herself.

'Eeeh, lass! You and Beryl looked that serious when you came bursting in! You two were like the grown-ups, come to tell off all us young 'uns.' She shook her head and clucked her tongue.

Lucky was mewing impatiently from the cold stone floor. In their haste to enjoy themselves, the women had forgotten his supper.

Soon they were all in the back parlour, catching their breath back and sipping tea. Megan came wading in with armfuls of opened bottles, puffing on a foul-smelling cigarette.

'French tabs! No filters!' she gasped swooningly, and sat down heavily at the table. 'Who's for another drink?'

Ma Ada smilingly shook her head, but Aunty Winnie thrust her dirty glass forward: 'I'll not say no. I prognosticate so much better when I'm three sheets to the wind.'

'Oh, don't let her start prognosticatin'!' Ma Ada laughed. 'That's one thing that's bound to bring the party down!'

'Drink?' Megan asked Beryl challengingly.

Beryl nodded. 'Gin, please. Since it's going. Waste not, want not.'

'Exactly!' Megan snapped, and held out the bottle none-too-steadily.

'But what's it all in aid of?' asked Beryl gently. 'I mean, don't get me wrong. There's nowt wrong with having a little party. But what brought it on?'

'We just thought it was high time we let ourselves have some fun!' Aunty Winnie said. 'I was round here for just a normal cuppa and a catch up with your ma, and then Megan came downstairs and that's when she made her great discovery.'

'My amazing discovery!' Megan slurred. 'It was like magic, wasn't it? It was like a fairy tale, where there's been a visit from the good fairy, and she works wonders with a magical spell.'

'What magical spell?' Irene asked. She didn't trust Megan an inch. She shook her head briskly at the offer of drink, and frowned at her. 'What do you mean?'

'Under the stairs,' said Ma Ada, in a strange tone of voice, as if she half believed that a fairy really had worked its magic and delivered them bottles of hard liquor. 'Megan opened up the little room under the stairs where she used to sleep.'

'I was looking for my old slippers,' Megan shrugged. 'They're thicker for the cold nights. Anyway, I opened the little curtain and – lo and behold! Magic!'

'What magic?' Irene asked.

'Come and see.' Megan lurched into the hall, demanding that Irene and Beryl follow her. 'Tuh-dah!' she cried, and whipped open the braided curtain that was the door to the tiny room under the stairs.

The girls gasped.

There were three crates and each was filled with bottles. There were also boxes of French cigarettes. It looked like dozens of bottles, to Irene's eye, and it looked like hundreds of cigarettes. Foil paper and embossed logos glittered with sophistication in the dim light.

'Santa Claus has come early round this house!' Megan shrieked, tugging on the curtain. She was even drunker than Irene had thought. 'Isn't it magic, eh? Isn't it marvellous?'

By now both babies were screaming fit to burst, agitated by the confusing excitement in the air. 'I'll get them upstairs and settled in the cot,' Irene said, purse-lipped.

'Ah, stop being such a stick in the mud, hinny!' Aunty Winnie clapped her on the back. 'Have a lovely ciggie! Have some lovely gin and vermouth!'

Irene glared at her. She had never quite taken to Aunty Winnie. She thought she was a trouble-making old devil, truth be told. The first time they'd met, Aunty Winnie had started foretelling the future for her, coming out with all this guff about what a sad and terrible life Irene was inevitably going to lead. She wasn't a very nice woman at all, had been Irene's conclusion, though Ma Ada seemed unaccountably fond of her.

'I'm off seeing to the bairns,' Irene said, steadfastly.

'Don't you want a hand?' Beryl asked, dashing to her side, holding her glass a little guiltily.

'I'm all right. Keep an eye on them silly witches.'

'Will do.'

'Where's it all from, Beryl?' Irene was really worried, all of a sudden. 'It isn't theirs. Where have they got all this booze from?'

Fifteen minutes later, with the babies settled in the attic room's ornate cot, Irene traipsed back down the stairs. There was music playing again – a little quieter this time, thank goodness. The radiogram was on, broadcasting dance music from London. Probably some elegant soirée with a big band and ladies and gentlemen wearing divine evening dress, whirling and twirling under brilliant lights.

Somewhere very different to this back parlour, where the dining table was still strewn with dishes from lunch and teatime, and the air was smudgy and blue with French cigarette smoke. Even the bald little cat looked slightly tipsy.

'Ah, we didn't mean any harm,' Ma Ada was murmuring. She had the air of a sulky child, caught doing something bad, flashing out with rebellion. 'Anyway, it's my bloody house, isn't it? I can do what I want – even if there's a bloody war on.' She put down her cup and saucer and barked at Winnie, 'Give us another tot of that gin, pet.'

'That's not a good idea,' Irene said.

The old mother glared at her. 'Who are you to tell me what to do, in me own back parlour?'

Irene quailed. 'I'm not telling you . . . I'm just saying, you might feel the worse for wear, tomorrow.'

Ma Ada snarled. 'Bugger tomorrow. That's what I think!' She curled her thin lips and laughed at her own badness. 'Aye, I do. What's tomorrow ever done for me, eh? The world's just got worse and worse, and darker and darker, and it's taken all me bloody boys off me. So why should I care about tomorrow, Irene? I've spent all me life trying to be good. Fat lot of use that's been!'

Megan smirked through the dregs of her drink. 'She's getting philosophical, ain't she?'

Beryl shushed her.

Aunty Winnie waved her skinny arms in the air, wafting blue smoke about and spilling her drink. 'Ahh, now, pet. Don't go saying anything about tomorrow. You never know what spirits are listening in. You might be tempting fate to do its worst. You might be setting all the unseen forces against you.'

Ma Ada shrugged. 'I don't care. We've been through enough disaster already. Bombs dropping on us. Everyone scared silly all the time. What else is there to be scared of?'

Winnie sank into her chair, looking ghoulishly satisfied as she puffed on her Gitane. 'There's plenty still to be scared of, hinny.'

Irene had heard enough of the old gypsy's maundering on. 'Look,' she snapped, 'those crates and boxes didn't come from nowhere. Someone has deliberately put them under the stairs.'

'Finders keepers!' snapped Megan gleefully. 'I found them. It was my old bedroom, such as it is. They're mine to keep. It's my lovely party!'

'She's right,' Ma Ada nodded happily.

Irene and Beryl stared at each other. They'd both figured out the truth of it at more or less the same moment.

'It's Sam, isn't it?' Irene said. 'Sam hid those boxes there. He thought no one would find them. He thought they'd be safe.'

Megan's eyes blazed and she narrowed them to icy green slits. 'Bloody Sam. Who cares? He's done us a favour.'

'But don't you see?' Beryl grabbed her shoulder. 'This booze and stuff – it must be nicked! It might not be his. He's hiding it there for good reason, probably. And you've just . . . you've just . . .' Beryl stared at the three drunk women and started feeling sick.

'We've been having a lovely time,' said Winnie. 'And we bloody well deserve it, too!'

'But what about Sam?' Irene asked. 'What's gonna happen when he sees what you've done?'

# Chapter Twenty-Two

Irene was first up, early the next morning, dashing around to see to the babies and getting herself ready for work. Beryl wasn't far behind, dressing in the dark and peering out at the snowy street. It looked like there'd been another few inches falling in the night, and she didn't relish the walk down the hill to work.

As she dressed, Beryl took note of those burns on her neck and shoulders once more, from the sparks of her welding. They really looked like they were going to leave a permanent mark on her. It was a horrible thought, and she shivered as she thought about being up on that scaffolding and climbing those rickety ladders. Sometimes she wished she'd never got it into her head to go and work on the ships. She'd been so bullish and determined though, as if biscuit making was too lowly for her. Beryl would only admit it to herself, but since October, when she had dropped her bake house hours and cut her ties with the place, sometimes she longed to go back to working at Wight's biscuit factory.

'Hey, are you ready?' Irene was on the landing, bringing her a mug of tea.

'Are the others not awake yet?' Beryl slurped her tea although it was too hot and, as usual, she was longing for more sugar in it.

'Did you expect them to be up bright and early?' Irene shook her head. 'They'll be in a rotten state when they emerge.'

'But what about the bairns? We can't go if there's no one to see to them.'

'Sam's home,' Irene told her. 'He must have come home in the middle of the night. I never heard him, but he's up and about now, and tidying the back parlour.'

'Oh, crikey – all that mess . . .' Beryl shook her head. 'Eeh, what were they like last night? What were they thinking of?'

Downstairs it was gloomy, and the cigarette smoke from the night before still seemed to lurk in the air. Sam was moving from scullery to parlour, taking bottles and glasses to the sink and emptying ashtrays.

He glanced up briefly at Beryl and Irene when they appeared.

'Were you part of this?' he asked Irene abruptly. She had never heard his voice sound so severe. He didn't sound like himself.

'What?' she asked. 'No, man! We came home and we caught them at it. Drinking themselves daft and carrying on.'

Sam looked furious and terrified at the same time. 'What am I going to do? I'm going to get killed for this. Those silly witches must have emptied half those bottles I'd hidden in there.'

'They can't have had as much as that,' Irene said. 'Come on, sit down and drink your tea.'

He wouldn't be mollified. 'They got through bloody gallons, man. And they opened loads of bottles just to have a taste of each one, by the looks of it.' He sat down heavily and put his hands around his cup. His fingers trembled, Irene noticed. 'You know who all that stuff belongs to, don't you? You know who'll be after me again for this?' He shook his head and fought down his panic. 'They'll have me bloody guts for garters, they will.'

'Who are you on about?' Beryl asked.

'The Mad Johnsons,' he said, lowering his voice, as if they were somehow able to hear him. 'I'm already in enough bother with them as it is.'

Beryl and Irene exchanged a troubled glance. 'What are you doing getting mixed up with them?' Irene asked. 'And why have you even got their stuff in this house? What are you doing, trying to hide it?'

He stood up abruptly. 'Ah, look. You two are never gonna understand. I'm in real bother, right? And what went on here last night has made it ten times worse. A hundred times worse.' He turned and was heading for the scullery again.

'Wait! Where are you going?' asked Irene. 'I thought you were staying here today and looking after the bairns.'

'Of course I am,' he snapped. 'Get yourselves off to work.'

Minutes later the two women were bundled up against the freezing cold of dawn, being careful not to slip on the cobbles.

'Eeh, the state of our Megan, up in that attic,' Irene said. 'She'll have a massive headache when she eventually gets up. She'll be worse-tempered than ever.'

They had discovered Winnie in the front parlour, slumped uncomfortably on the old settee, unconscious with her stays loosened and her corset undone. 'She looked like she'd died in the night!' Beryl was saying. 'I had to check to see she was still breathing.'

'The smell of the booze when I first went down was just horrible,' Irene said. 'The air was still thick with it.'

'What's our Sam gonna do?' Beryl hissed worriedly. 'He seems to have got himself in deep with these Mad Johnsons.'

'Seems to me that he's been doing them favours and he's meant to look after stolen stuff for them. Even after getting roughed up for his efforts.' Irene couldn't understand anyone getting involved in criminal business. Now it felt even closer to home than it had when it was just the sugar that Mavis was smuggling into Franchino's.

It made Irene feel sick to her stomach, just thinking about people coming out of the dark to beat you up, like gangsters in the films that she and Sam enjoyed watching together at the Savoy. Why was he voluntarily getting himself embroiled with real gangsters like that?

'Megan knew,' Irene said, as they came within sight of the biscuit factory gates and it was time for Beryl to peel off. 'When she was drinking and carousing last night, I reckon she knew the whole time, the trouble that Sam was in. She must have known that all that booze couldn't really belong to him. She knew that every swig she took was getting him deeper and deeper into danger.'

'I reckon you're right,' Beryl nodded. 'She was setting out to get him into bother – deliberately.'

'The absolute bitch,' Irene spat, and felt ashamed of herself, for saying it too loud in the street, as others were streaming past.

The two sisters-in-law hugged briefly before splitting up for their separate days at work.

Once more Beryl wished she was heading into the warm, sugary scent of the biscuit factory with Irene.

She thought about the days she had spent simply stamping out ginger snaps and the air filled with the scent of crystallised ginger and sugar. When she went home each night she had felt that her hair and skin were stiff and sticky with all that sweetness.

The work hadn't been too hard, looking back, though the hours were long and repetitive. It was definitely less arduous than the shipyards, and back then she hadn't gone home covered in tiny burns and scars like she did these days.

Oh, I should never have left the biscuit factory, Beryl thought glumly, hurrying down to the docks.

'Ahh, no! That's terrible!' Mavis gasped when she heard the story of last night's impromptu shindig with the black-market booze. 'And Sam looked really scared this morning?'

'I've never seen him looking like that,' Irene told her. The two of them were standing close and whispering, folding and pasting Penny Packets by the conveyor belt, their fingers moving swiftly despite the freezing cold.

'Here, what are you two gossiping about?' It was plump Mary, from over the way. She was always avid to hear about other people's problems. Effie, Edith and Gladys were perking up as well. The morning had been dull so far, and a titbit of scandal was just what they needed.

'It's Irene's brother-in-law,' Mavis said, in her rasping voice. 'He's got himself in bother with the Mad Johnsons.'

Irene shot her a glance. Mavis had no guile at all. She barely had any sense. She'd go spilling out her secrets to anyone who asked to hear them.

'He wants to keep out of the way of that lot,' Mary said. 'I'm telling you, nowt good can come of it. I hear all sorts from their sister, Lily. She's the youngest in that family, and she's all right. Bit of a show-off, if you ask me. But she tells me things that her brothers get up to and honestly, some of the things she says would make your hair stand on end.'

Irene didn't want to hear any further details about the Mad Johnsons' alarming activities. She carried on working steadily and blocked her ears to the women's chatter for the rest of that morning.

At break time Mavis kept chuntering on about the Mad Johnsons, her eyes bright with a strange kind of excitement.

'But it's serious, Mavis,' Irene hissed at her. 'Sam could really be in danger. I thought you liked him?'

The smaller girl's eyes went wide and dark. 'I do! I adore Sam! You know that. I'd do anything for him, if I could.'

'Well, then, stop gossiping with the others about that Johnson lot. It's only stirring it all up.'

But Mavis was thinking things through. She wasn't known for being bright. In fact, some of her friends tended to think of Mavis as being somewhat slow. But she noticed things and remembered everything she saw and heard. So, while her mouth blabbed away about seemingly irrelevant things, from just this morning's chatter in the work room, she had learnt that plump Mary knew Lily Johnson very well indeed. In fact, the two of them were in dispute over a lad they both had their eye on.

'I thought plump Mary had a fella in the army?' Irene asked.

Mavis nodded. 'She does, but he never writes and when he comes home he never bothers with her, so she reckons she's a free agent these days.'

Irene tutted. Poor Mary. Or maybe she preferred being set free from her husband? Irene wasn't sure what any of this had to do with Sam.

Later in the day the two of them finished their shift and clocked out of the factory, finding themselves out in the snowy streets again. 'It might be an idea to get to talk to this Lily person,' Mavis was musing. 'She's the youngest of the Mad Johnsons, and she's the one that all the brothers dote upon, apparently. There's seven of them, and they're all complete brutes. They're all built like brick shithouses, excuse my language. But the one person they all adore is their little sister Lily.'

Irene thought she could see where Mavis was going with this. 'So, if we talk to this Lily, maybe we could convince her to get her brothers to lay off our Sam? To beg them to let him off the hook?'

'It's worth a go, isn't it? We could appeal to her. She might be more sensible than all her brothers.'

Irene linked arms with Mavis and they quickened their pace through the busy streets of town. Here the snow was thinner, but the going was even more perilous with frozen slush. Trams went shunting past, all plastered with snow, and pedestrians were three deep on the pavement, bustling along in hats and coats, all the way down to Ocean Road.

It was dark again, Irene thought. She hadn't seen a single scrap of daylight all day.

'Maybe it's an idea,' Irene said. 'I hate not doing anything when there's a situation on. But how do we get to talk to this . . . Lily, was it? We don't know anything about her.'

'But we do!' Mavis gasped. She was pleased with herself, and the sleuth work she'd been up to all afternoon, under the guise of chattering on with plump Mary and the others. 'She's a singer! That's what Lily Johnson is known for. I've never seen her perform, but she's known for getting up on the stage at clubs and belting out tunes. And guess what?'

Irene smiled weakly. Mavis's batty enthusiasm was infectious. 'What's that?'

'She's due to sing a few numbers with the band at the dance on Saturday night. At the Albert Hall. At our Christmas dance, Irene. We're going to see her on Saturday night. And then we can nobble her!'

'"Nobble" her?' Irene laughed.

'Get to her,' Mavis said determinedly. 'Tell her to call her brothers off. Beg with her, if need be.'

Irene shook her head worriedly. The whole situation seemed much too fraught to her. What if they made things even worse with their meddling? 'I'm not sure . . .'

'I reckon it's a brilliant idea!' Mavis congratulated herself, and Irene couldn't help smiling at her.

Here they were, before the welcoming, golden lights of Franchino's. It was time to dollop froth onto hot coffees and catch up with Bella. Wait till she heard about the drunken, wanton revels at Number Thirteen last night!

'What do you think, Irene? Shall we make it our mission to have a word with this Lily Johnson?'

Irene found herself agreeing. 'All right. I don't know exactly what Sam's got himself into, or what he was planning to do with all that black market stuff, but I want to do everything I can to help him out of bother.'

'Me too,' said Mavis. 'I can't bear to think of him in danger. When I found him lying battered and bleeding in the gutter that night I almost died of fright.' She took a deep and shaky breath. 'I-I think I love him, Irene.'

Irene pressed ahead and hurried into the ice cream parlour. 'I know, pet. But don't go blabbing that out to him. Not yet. He's got enough to contend with.'

'But I do, Irene. I think he's the one for me. I'm obsessed with Sam. I want his babies and everything.'

Good grief, thought Irene. Ah, bless her, though. Little Mavis was worth her weight in gold. Irene hoped that maybe Sam would see her true worth, one day? Otherwise the girl was going to be in for a dreadful disappointment.

Inside Franchino's there was music playing, and there was steam gushing from the coffee machine. Bella was at the counter, welcoming them, and for a few moments at least, Irene could forget all the violence and complications of the world outside.

# Chapter Twenty-Three

'It's not as grand as the Alhambra,' was Irene's first comment, when she arrived at the dance with Mavis, Arthur and Bella. They were late, because there had been a lot of fuss with dressing up for the night, and Mavis not being happy with the way she looked. She could be a proper fusspot, Irene had realised.

'It's true, the Albert Hall isn't quite the same kind of place,' Bella agreed.

'I think it's wonderful,' Mavis said, as they squashed past bodies towards the main dance floor. The small girl looked bonny in her salvaged cream organdie dress, Irene thought. Bella had paid particular attention to making the girl look pretty for tonight, even though Mavis had twisted and complained through the whole process. She wasn't used to having her make-up and hair done so carefully.

All three women were very beautifully dressed – from the dressing up box at Mavis and Arthur's house. They were wearing outfits that had been tailored twenty years ago or more, lovingly restored and fitted by brother and sister working late at night by candlelight. Perhaps they stood out as rather eccentric at the dance, in these outmoded dresses, but they all enjoyed that distinction. Even Irene did, wearing a dress that her mother might have coveted to wear at one of the fancy dances that she talked about going to in Norwich in years gone by. It accentuated Irene's curves, and she loved that, catching glimpses of herself in the mirrored walls as they entered the ballroom. Plus, her dress was emerald green, which really suited her, she realised. She matched the swags of holly and mistletoe that decorated the place, and this even made her feel a bit festive.

There was a small band on the stage at the end of the room, though they could barely see as far as that through the press of bodies.

'Can you see Sam anywhere?' Mavis asked keenly, her eyes darting about.

Irene shook her head. 'Don't go holding out your hopes, pet. These days, he says one thing, and then he goes and does another.'

'But he has to come out tonight!' Mavis gasped. 'I'm all gussied up, especially for him! He has to clap eyes on me, looking my best, and then he'll realise. He'll see that I'm not so dowdy and ordinary after all. He'll fall for me in a flash!'

Her brother nudged her. 'You've seen too many movies.'

'Well, you're the one who sneaks me in for free,' she pointed out.

'But they're not real life,' Arthur said, sounding almost peevish with her. 'He's not gonna suddenly look at you in a new light, Mavis. Don't pin too much belief on that Sam Farley, I'm warning you, pet.'

Irene watched Mavis sag a little bit then, like her brother had stolen the wind out of her organdie sails.

Just at that moment, Bella gave a small cry and clutched Irene's arm. 'Look, there's that girl, coming onto the stage. The one you want to talk to. I've seen her on the street before. Mavis has pointed her out to me. That's her!'

She was a slim girl with dark hair rolled up in a very stylish fashion. Her face was bright with make-up under the lights, and she was wearing a dress in glittery, dark blue material that showed off her pale shoulders. She looked a bit bony to Irene, and her smile seemed rather put on and false as she shimmied up to the standing microphone and bellowed at the audience. 'I'm gonna do one of me favourites now for yer, so I hope you'll all listen!' She cast a glance back at her four-piece band and rolled her painted eyes. 'That's if this lot can get themselves sorted out and in the right flamin' key this time.'

The worried-looking drummer counted them in, and the music started shakily at first. Lily Johnson beamed even more brightly and artificially, jiggling her skinny hips in time to the tune. She began with great gusto: 'Grey skies are gonna clear up! Put on a happy face!'

After a few lines Irene and Bella exchanged a glance. 'She's got a lot of pep,' Bella said.

'Hmm, that's one way of putting it,' Irene said, pursing her lips. She found the girl's voice grating and shrill. Also, there was an occasional whine of feedback from her microphone, which did nothing to improve the number. Neither of these things mattered to the people around them – all those local girls dolled up for Saturday night, and their beaus in army and navy uniforms. They started dancing quite happily in time to the singer's piercing exhortations to be cheerful. Arthur seized hold of his sister without even asking if she'd like to dance, and the two of them vanished into the seething melee of bodies.

'I wish Beryl could be out with us tonight,' Irene said, as she and Bella drifted to the side of the room in search of refreshments. Bella, shielding her ears against the shrieking feedback, took a few moments to realise what she'd said.

'At least, with her staying home, you know that Marlene is being properly looked after,' Bella shrugged. 'After what you said about the old woman and Megan drinking all that booze the other night, I bet you'll never trust them with the bairns ever again.'

Irene nodded ruefully as they queued at a table for paper cups of some kind of fruit punch. But there was more going on in Irene's thoughts about the babysitters than Bella knew. She was fretting about leaving Marlene in Beryl's care. She frowned, remembering Beryl's mother's strange warning at her kitchen table the other day.

*Don't leave her alone with your bairn!*

But Irene had decided to dismiss her imprecations. They were just the ravings of a bitter old woman. There was a reason that Beryl was wary of her mother, and this craziness was surely it.

But . . . wasn't there a niggle still, in Irene's mind? About leaving her baby with Beryl? And hadn't Beryl herself seemed uneasy this evening, when she realised that she was in sole charge of the bairns?

No, Irene shook her head. Beryl was trustworthy. Of course she was. Irene would trust her with anything. She'd trust her with the most precious thing on earth, and that was Marlene.

'Are you all right?' Bella asked, and Irene came back to herself, nodding hastily as they shuffled up the queue for the watery punch. A very plain girl was dishing it out of a vast salver. Irene didn't like the look of the scabs at the corners of her mouth, but she took the drinks anyway.

'Eeeh, Ma Ada is mortified about that night,' she told Bella, switching back to the slightly easier subject of the drunken harpies. 'When she eventually emerged from her room the next day, it was like the mummy coming out of the tomb. She was like Boris bloomin' Karloff, coming down the stairs with a thick head and this guilty look on her face.'

Bella couldn't help laughing. 'She's always so proper, going by what you say. And there she was, dancing around with her skirt up, pie-eyed on gin!'

'And rum and whisky, and all the rest of it. They'd mixed their drinks something rotten.'

Bella sipped her fruit cup and grimaced. 'Mind, they could do with some alcohol in this awful stuff.'

Irene hadn't touched her drink. The girl's cold sores had put her right off. 'Anyhow, Ma Ada blamed Megan for the whole business, and so Megan's in the doghouse again. Apparently she was the envoy of Satan that night, tempting Ada and Winnie into wicked and wanton ways.'

'That sounds true enough,' Bella chuckled.

Irene was glad to hear her friend laugh, and to see her looking so lovely tonight. For a few weeks Bella had been looking rather drawn and exhausted. Irene had started to worry that she was working too hard and the strain was starting to show. Bella had lost almost everyone that was dear to her in one fell swoop, and she had emerged from her dark depression through dint of hard work. However, sometimes it seemed that she was using that work to avoid dealing with her grief: at least, that's how it seemed to Irene, who saw Bella most days at Franchino's and had been keeping a careful eye on her. Tonight, however, the Italian girl seemed – if not happy, exactly – more relaxed than she'd been for months.

'Eeeh, that family of yours.' Bella shook her head. 'The Famous Farleys of Frederick Street.'

Irene was less inclined to see the amusing side of them lately. 'It's a bit tense round Number Thirteen just now, with Sam not talking to Megan, or his mother, and his mother being furious with him and herself and everyone else, and Beryl in this strange kind of mood, like she's in a world of her own.'

'Well, any time you want to move out, away from them, feel free to come over to live with me and Arthur and Mavis,' Bella laughed. 'There's still a spare room in their funny little house. Mind, it's filled with old clothes and jumble, but I'm sure we could make room for you.'

'I might just take you up on that,' Irene smiled, though secretly she couldn't imagine ever leaving Ma Ada's house on

Frederick Street. Her place in the family pecking order there seemed so hard won, and so precious to her, that she simply couldn't conceive of voluntarily giving it up.

Even though it was hardly perfect, she couldn't imagine being anywhere else. She was there, waiting for Tom to come home from war. What would he say if he'd heard she'd waltzed off to some strange, poky house with friends he didn't really approve of, in the least salubrious part of town?

Now the band's tempo had changed and Lily was paying tribute to the coming season by warbling, 'He's the Little Boy that Santa Claus Forgot'. Irene winced at her various vocal flourishes, and the liberties she took with the tune. 'By, I think she's a bloomin' awful singer, don't you?'

'Aye,' Bella agreed. 'But I wouldn't go saying that too loudly round here, pet. Look, there's two of her brothers over there. Watching her adoringly!'

And they were, too. Irene gulped at her first sighting of two of the Mad Johnson brothers in the flesh. They seemed gargantuan to her, both of them dressed up in dark suits like extras from a Jimmy Cagney film. They had squashed, broken noses, fat cauliflower ears and heavy, glowering brows. They were smoking cigars with great concentration, puffing away and conferring in a corner of the dance hall. They would glance occasionally at their songbird sister with what seemed to be incredible pride.

'She'd never be up on that stage if she didn't have tough brothers,' Irene said. 'They look like they're used to everyone doing just what they tell them to.'

Bella nodded. 'That's right. That's exactly the reputation they have.' Her expression darkened and she leant closer to Irene, whispering in her ear: 'I'd never have let your Sam bring us all that knock-off sugar, you know. Not if I'd known he was mixed up with those bastards.'

Irene raised her eyebrows at Bella's vehement tone. She'd rarely heard her speak badly of anyone. 'Oh! So you know about the sugar being knock-off then?' she asked, feeling strangely guilty.

'Mavis confessed earlier today.' Bella pursed her lips. 'I knew there was something dodgy going on. And I'm not sure I like it. I think I'll have to cut off that particular line of supply.'

Irene nodded, and hoped Bella wouldn't ask anything about Irene knowing about the subterfuge. Luckily, Bella was swept away by a sudden memory.

'You know, the Mad Johnsons tried to extort money out of my papa once,' Bella confided. 'They came round the ice cream parlour mob-handed, and said that if he wanted to keep Franchino's open, then he had to pay them monthly. This was years ago – it was probably their dads and uncles who came round. Anyway, my papa was no pushover, of course. He was from Naples! They came round to rough him up, and he suddenly grabbed hold of my nonna's walking stick. Ebony it was, very hard. She was a bit surprised, because she was using it at the time – she was waiting on tables back then.'

Irene stared at Bella. 'You're making this up!'

'I am not! And my papa, he took that stick to those lads. He tanned their backsides, and said "Don't you ever bloody darken Franchino's doorstep again!" Whack, whack, whack! Apparently he scared the life out of them, but that was my papa for you. He never let anyone get the better of him.' As she told the tale over the sound of the sentimental song, Bella's eyes were sparkling with tears which she hurriedly blotted away. 'Anyway, he's the only one in this town, to my knowledge, who ever stood up to any of the Mad Johnsons. Most people just give those brutes exactly what they ask for.'

Brutes, Irene thought. That's exactly what they looked like, those two fellas over there. And there were seven of those brothers, apparently! They were like an army of gorillas, and it seemed hard to know what the average person could do when faced with people like that. Not everyone was as brave as Tonio Franchino, armed with his mother-in-law's ebony walking stick.

'I loved your papa,' Irene said. 'He was so nice to me when I first moved here. All your family was.'

Bella smiled sadly, but she was peering over Irene's shoulder. 'Look, that girl has finished her singing – thank goodness – and it looks like she's heading over to her brothers. Maybe this is a good time to catch her. You could take her a drink and say how you enjoyed her performance – and then you could ask her about Sam?'

Irene took a deep breath. Yes, the skinny girl with the fake flowers in her hair and all that eyeshadow had paused between numbers and was making her way through the crowd. She looked hot and grumpy.

'Okay . . . Here goes,' Irene said, getting ready to approach her. This was going to take some nerve.

# Chapter Twenty-Four

It was strange and rather peculiar for Mavis to be dancing in public with her brother. Arthur didn't seem to mind the hectic crowd around them: he was off in a trance as he whirled his sister around the floor.

Mavis was much less used to making a show of herself. When the two of them practised their dancing, it was in the confines of their cluttered living room and downstairs hall, and that was how Mavis knew all her steps so well, and why they came second nature to her. Arthur had been coaching her in all the old-fashioned dances since she was just a scrap of a thing.

'This is wonderful, Arthur,' she told him. 'Thank you for bringing me out tonight.'

'Well, don't you go showing me up,' he growled at her, narrowing his eyes with mock fierceness.

'Of course not!' As the tempo slowed, and the band played a romantic number without vocal accompaniment, the whole room seemed to take a collective breath of relief. Mavis laid her head gently against her brother's shoulder. 'Eeeh, I'm glad that singing's stopped,' she said. 'She wasn't very good, was she?'

Arthur smirked. 'Lily? She throws herself into it. She has confidence, that's the thing. She couldn't give a nick what you and I or anyone else thinks of her singing. She gets up there and belts out her numbers, and that's that.'

'But she's so shrill . . . and flat!'

'Somehow she carries it off,' he said.

'You should get up there and show them how it's done!'

'Not tonight, pet,' he smiled, just picturing the fury there'd be in Lily Johnson's eyes if he got up on the stage and stole her thunder.

'What will I do, Arthur?' Mavis suddenly asked, looking up at him earnestly.

'Huh? What are you on about now?' But he had a feeling he knew what she was going to say. She was bubbling up with tears. Those pale grey eyes of hers were awash and she was going to start pulling on his heartstrings. His little sister had always had the knack for doing that.

'If you go away and leave me,' she said, her voice rasping against his ear. 'If you do like you said, if you go away and join ENSA. It's not just singing and dancing and dressing up, man! It's the army, Arthur. They could send you anywhere in the world. Africa or Burma or . . . anywhere! And it'll be dangerous, wherever you are. They could blow you up!'

'Let's not go on about it now,' he said tersely. 'We're out having fun, Maeve.'

'But . . . you promised!' Suddenly she sounded very young. Sometimes he forgot how young she really was. 'You promised you'd always be there to look after me. I'm your little sister!'

'I know that, love,' he murmured. Then he frowned. 'Look, you haven't told anyone about my plans, have you?'

She flushed. 'Of course not.' But she had, and he suspected that she had. As usual, Mavis was making his life more complicated.

'I know you're my little sister!' he laughed gently. 'Eeeh, lass. How could I ever forget that?'

She had always been there. She'd been his tender little burden for as long as he could remember. When the two of them had had no one at all in the world, and everyone seemed like they wanted to do them harm, or split them up, or send them to the workhouse, it had been Arthur Kendricks' job to love and protect his sickly little sister.

If he closed his eyes, even for just a second, he could picture how the two of them must have looked back then. Like two filthy bundles of rags. The stuff they had worn when their mother had died and they had fetched up, stunned, alone, hadn't even looked like clothes at all. They spent so long living on the streets they looked like they were dressed in drab sacking and tatters of old cloth. Perfect for going unnoticed in the busy streets, but the two of them had looked semi-human. They were feral children, and eventually they had come to the notice of the authorities.

Mavis's cough! She'd had so much wrong with her back then, but the cough was the worst. She sounded like a great big wolfhound with a sharp splinter of bone stuck in his throat. That cough seemed far too huge and deep to emerge from such a small and puny body. Her eyes were huge and grey and terrified-looking and her body was bent out of shape from rickets and malnutrition. But young Arthur had been terrified, when they took her away to try to make her better, that they were taking her away from his side for good. He had kicked and spat and flailed out at their so-called rescuers, fearing that he was being separated from Mavis for ever.

'Do you remember, Arthur?' Mavis asked him sometimes, and she was asking him again tonight, as they danced at the hall on Fowler Street.

'I remember everything,' he told her. 'And I remember my promise to always look after you. You know that.'

'So you can't go away,' she burst out. 'You can't go singing for troops abroad! What am I going to be like without you?'

'Mavis! Look at all the fellas who've had to leave their families. Look at everyone who's had to cope! All your friends . . . Irene, Mary . . . Effie. All of them have got fellas in the services.'

'I know.' She looked abashed.

'And what about poor Bella? She's lost everything and she's coping, somehow.'

'That's because she's got you,' Mavis protested.

'And you, Maeve. And the two of you will help each other along, if I'm called away.' He smiled at her ruefully. 'Anyway, maybe they won't even have me. There's so much wrong with me, after all.'

'There's nothing wrong with you!' she cried. 'You're my perfect big brother!'

This made him smile. Then he considered and said, 'If you really don't want to live in our house by yourself, you know, you can always get back in touch with old Mrs Kendricks. I'm sure she'd be delighted to hear from either one of us again.'

Mavis was shaking her head firmly and looking frightened. 'No, no way! Are you mad?'

'But she's there, in that big house of hers, all alone.'

Mavis was steadfast. 'There's just no way, Arthur. I wouldn't go back there in a million years. And besides, she's probably left that place and gone somewhere that isn't being bombed.'

'She's still there,' he said. 'And she's still living in that big, old house all alone. She was good to us when we needed help, Maeve. I'm sure she'd welcome you back with open arms.'

'No, Arthur,' his sister said. 'I don't want to.'

He sighed. She might look pale and sickly, but his sister had an iron will. When she'd made up her mind, there was nothing anyone could do about it.

The music was stepping up again, and the dancers around them became livelier. Luckily, the singing didn't start up again.

'Look who it is!' came a familiar voice, booming in their ears. 'Huh?'

'Sam!' Mavis burst out delightedly.

'Oh, you,' Arthur scowled at the sight of the youngest Farley boy, and tried to veer away through the crowd. But Mavis dug her feet in.

'Sam, you look so handsome in your suit!'

'Thank you,' he beamed, blearily.

He's drunk! Arthur thought. He's completely sozzled and soapy-eyed. He can't even focus as he's talking to us, and his breath reeks of some kind of spirits. Probably stolen spirits, too, if Irene's recent tales are anything to go by. 'You're in a right state,' he snapped. 'You want to get yourself home.'

'I'm enjoying meself!' Sam grinned, and put his arms round both Arthur and Mavis, leaning his full weight upon them. 'Can't I enjoy meself with some of me oldest pals in town?'

Arthur went frosty, and tried to disentangle himself. He couldn't stand the thought of Sam touching him. He flinched involuntarily. 'I'm not sure you're any friend of mine, Sam Farley.'

Sam blinked and looked so hurt that Mavis started burbling at him. 'Oh, dance with me, Sam! Come on, you've never danced with me since I was a little lass. Come on – I'm a grown-up woman now, and look at my lovely dress. Don't I look the part? Don't I look lovely?'

The youngest Farley boy was swaying on the spot as he regarded Mavis very solemnly and nodded his appreciation. 'Aye, you do, pet. You look bonny. I'll dance with you. I'll do that, all right.'

Arthur stepped away reluctantly. 'You just look after her.'

Sam grinned at him and swept Mavis up in his arms and launched vigorously into the dance. Perhaps a little more vigorously than the tune demanded, and they found themselves knocking into a few of the other dancing strangers. But Mavis didn't mind. She was breathless with excitement and delight. She was in the strong arms of the man she secretly loved and, even though he was probably not quite in control of all his faculties due to alcohol, she was having the time of her life.

Off they danced, leaving Arthur to retreat to a corner of the dance floor. No sooner had he found a spot and stood there grumbling to himself about the youngest Farley boy and his cavalier attitude, than he felt someone tap him sharply on the shoulder. Whoever it was had powerful hands. He could feel the impression of those peremptory fingers through the shoulder pads of his fitted jacket. Arthur turned to see one of the Mad Johnsons grinning at him. His face was florid, stupid and belligerent-looking and his breath reeked of pickled onions.

'We'd like a word with you, Twinkle Toes,' the Johnson brother growled.

'Hold on, you want me to do what?'

The girl in the gold-green eye make-up had a light sheen of sweat on her forehead and upper lip from being under the hot lights of the stage. She was dabbing her face carefully with a hanky and being careful not to smudge her make-up. It must have taken her hours to put all that lot on, Irene thought, wonderingly. Up close, Lily Johnson looked like something from another world, or from an Egyptian tomb's wall. Her eyes were done up rather like a Pharaoh's, with all that sticky black stuff clagged on.

Irene made herself stop staring down at the small, stroppy young woman and got back to the point: 'I'm asking you as one sister to another. We both love our brothers and brothers-in-law, I'm sure, and we hate to see them getting into any bother. And lads always do, because lads are daft, and that's what they're like . . .'

Lily adjusted the fake orchids in her hair and frowned darkly. 'Get to the point . . . Eileen, did you say your name was?'

'Irene. My name is Irene Farley, and I'm the sister-in-law of Sam Farley.'

'Oh, *him!*' Lily said sniffily. 'Well, he's a right little toerag, that one. A chancer and a thief, from what I've heard from my lot.'

'He is nothing of the sort!' Irene cried out angrily. 'He's a good boy, and he's just got himself a bit mixed up in some dodgy business, and with a funny, rough crowd.'

Violently Lily threw back her head and laughed raucously. She clutched her hair suddenly, and Irene realised that it was a wig, and her hair pins were dropping out. 'That funny, rough crowd happens to be my family,' she snarled. 'Is that what you mean, lady?'

Irene bit her lip. She'd put her foot in it, almost immediately. It was possible that she might be making a bad situation even worse. 'I-I speak as I find,' she said.

'Well, so do I,' the furious chanteuse snapped. 'I speak just as I find, too. And your brother is a conniving, thieving little get, as it happens. He's wormed his way into my brothers' good books, and he even flirted with me, the little devil. And he's nicked God knows how much merchandise from our yard and kept all the profits for himself. We've come to the opinion – my rough lot, that is – that he's a greedy little bugger who needs teaching a proper lesson. Now, what do you think of that, Irene Hoity Toity Farley?'

Lily was just about spitting in Irene's astonished face by the end of her outburst. Irene longed to have something sensible to fling back at her. Maybe she could tell her that her threats meant nothing? Neither she nor any of the Farleys were scared? But that wasn't true. Or maybe she could say that they'd go to the authorities? That Lily and her brothers couldn't get away with trying to intimidate decent folk like that? But she couldn't quite summon up the words to say that, either.

Instead Irene blushed bright red and glared down her nose at the Johnson sister and found herself telling her: 'You know what's wrong with you? It's not just that you're dead common and look like the roughest Christmas fairy I've ever seen. Your biggest problem is that you can't sing for bloomin' toffee and no one's ever had the guts to tell you.'

Lily's painted eyes went wide. '*What?!*'

'You ought to be ashamed of yourself! Squawking like that on the stage, and carrying on like everyone thinks you're wonderful! You've got some brass neck, lady!'

There was a tiny beat of silence before Lily turned on her heel. She hissed through her teeth at Irene: 'You are *dead*.'

# Chapter Twenty-Five

As Irene stood stock still, shocked at herself and her own temerity, the stroppy nightclub singer was marching her way back to the stage. She still had five numbers to sing that night, and she was going to belt them out defiantly. Couldn't sing for toffee, indeed!

'Fantastic diplomacy, Irene,' said a voice in her ear, and Irene looked round to see Bella smiling at her ironically. 'I'm sure you've made the situation a million times better.'

Irene felt a wave of embarrassment and shame go through her. 'Erm . . . Perhaps I shouldn't have lost my temper with her.'

Up on the stage Lily Johnson was seizing control of the microphone again and mangling another Cole Porter song. Despite Irene's feelings about the girl's voice, the dance floor was filling up once more.

'Look at Sam and Mavis,' Bella pointed out.

'They're in a proper clinch!' Irene gasped.

It was true: the two of them were pressed close and dancing in the middle of the room. Mavis would be in her seventh heaven, Irene thought. Dancing cheek to cheek to 'Night and Day' with the boy she thought would never notice her. In fact, Irene had thought Sam would never notice Mavis, too. How wrong she'd been!

'Mavis does look lovely tonight,' Bella smiled. 'Perhaps she's turned Sam's head at last.'

Or maybe, while everyone's attention was turned elsewhere, the two of them had simply grown closer? Mavis had talked about meeting up with Sam to pick up supplies of sugar, for instance. They'd been doing all that clandestine activity together, hadn't they? Perhaps they had developed a rapport and that had led to this moment of what seemed to be genuine romance?

'Oh, Sam . . .' Irene worried. 'I hope he's not leading her up the garden path.'

Of course, it wasn't the first time that Irene had spied Sam in a clinch with someone she knew at a dance like this. Last time, more than a year ago, she had seen him canoodling surreptitiously with his own sister-in-law, Megan, neither of them giving a hoot who saw them getting up to no good. He was careless and profligate in dispensing his romantic favours, Irene reflected, and she really hoped that Mavis wasn't going to be upset in the long run.

'He's kissing her!' Bella gasped. 'And she's kissing him back!'

To be fair, the two of them looked perfect together. Both blond and pale and delicately featured. They were more or less the same height and, just for a charmed instant, they looked very like they matched one another.

Irene thought: well, maybe this is right. Maybe Mavis had the correct idea all along. She knew they were supposed to be together. She's been hankering after him for ages, and now he's taking proper notice. Perhaps this is just how things are meant to go.

Then all at once, Arthur was standing beside Irene and Bella and he saw with shock who they were staring at. He gripped Irene's arm tightly and said sourly, 'Those little idiots!'

Bella smiled fondly, knowing how protective he was over his little sister. 'Ah, leave them be, Arthur.'

'Leave them be!' he cried hotly. 'They're both daft kids. They haven't got a clue what they're doing.'

'There's nothing wrong with it,' Bella said firmly. Arthur could be too protective sometimes, she thought. He needed to loosen those apron strings.

'He's completely pie-eyed, can't you see?' Arthur snarled. 'He doesn't have a clue who he's kissing. Poor Maeve thinks they're having a wonderful moment, but he's away with the fairies. As bloody usual.'

Irene looked harder and thought, yes, he's got a point. Sam was a little shaky on his legs as they swayed to the gentle tune. It looked as if Mavis was propping him up.

'I don't want her being hurt,' Arthur said, in a low, determined growl.

Irene glanced at him and frowned. Was that a bruise coming up on his cheekbone? His face looked red, and there was a graze. His right eye was puffing up and closing to a slit. 'Hey, what's happened to you? Have you been in a fight?'

'A slight disagreement with a burly chap in the street,' he said tersely. 'Fella took me out there to have a menacing word. One of the Mad Johnsons. He got more than he bargained for. But I got a whack in the mush for my pains.'

'What?!' Bella started fussing over him. 'You've been fighting?'

'It was a scuffle. Over in seconds. They wanted to tell me to keep my sister away from Sam, if she knows what's good for her. And they've got a point, too. Sam's bad news.'

Irene felt like she had to defend Sam. 'He's not as bad as that. He's just got into some bad company.'

'He's bad news all right,' Arthur insisted. 'Look at the bother he's caused in your family. He just blunders through things, without thinking of anyone else. I don't want it to end up with him getting my sister up the duff, as well.'

Bella eyed him curiously, but Arthur wasn't in the mood to elaborate further. There was an interlude between songs, and folk were leaving the dance floor as Lily Johnson loudly complained about the quality of the microphone and its incessant screeching. ('She's one to talk!' Irene heard someone quip.) Arthur took the opportunity to go marching right onto the middle of the floor, where he seized hold of his sister's arm.

'Oww! Gerroff, Arthur man! You're hurting me.'

'It's late now. We're going home.'

It was a couple of moments before Sam realised what was going on. He smiled at Arthur before he noticed his one-time friend's stony expression. 'Hey, Arthur! Leave her be!' He tried to prise Arthur's hand off Mavis's arm.

'Oh no, come on, man,' Mavis pleaded. 'You're gonna make a scene!'

'I don't care,' shouted Arthur. That clipped, nasal voice of his really carried, even above the wailing theatrics of Lily at the microphone. 'He's making a fool out of you, Mavis.'

'He was only . . . kissing me . . . a little bit.'

Sam grinned foolishly. 'We were just having a bit of a kiss, man. What's the matter with you? Jealous, are you?' Sam burst out laughing.

Arthur's eyes flashed dangerously. 'Come on, Mavis. We're going. Before I kick this idiot's face in.'

Suddenly Mavis was deciding to stand up for herself. 'No! For once, I'm not going to do what you tell me to do, Arthur. You don't have the right any more to boss me around! Specially not if you're going away to war. What do you care what I get up to?'

Arthur cried out in fury. 'Of course I care what you get up to, you stupid girl!' His face was beetroot red and odd-looking because of the lumps he'd got fighting outside just ten minutes before.

'Leave her be, Arthur,' Sam said, sounding drunker than ever. 'I'll look after her.'

Arthur swung round on him and, from where she was watching across the crowd, Irene feared that he was going to punch him, too. It was hard to make out all the words from this distance, but both Irene and Bella could discern most of what the argument was about. All the dancers were making a kind of island for the fracas, and they waltzed around it, paying great interest.

Irene didn't hear the next words that Arthur said to Sam, but Sam did. They were Arthur's furious parting shot before stalking away, leaving his sister in Sam's arms. 'You hurt her and I'll kill you. I know what you're like. You've forgotten, but I know exactly what you're like. And I will murder you, Sam Farley, if you harm a hair on my sister's stupid head.'

Then he whirled around and left the room.

'What did he say?' Mavis asked Sam. Her voice was quavering with anxiety, with fear, with excitement and . . . yes, even pride. She'd had men fighting about her in the middle of the dance floor, just like other beautiful, alluring women sometimes had, in movies. For once, Mavis had been the star of the show.

'Ah, he was just burbling on,' Sam shrugged. 'I think he was a bit drunk, to be honest. He looked a bit squiffy, didn't he?' Then he held out his arms for Mavis to fall into once more, which she did gladly, and with relief.

As they started dancing again, Mavis felt – very briefly – a stab of disloyalty to her brother. Then she thought: Ah, it serves him right. He wants to leave me here in South Shields all on my own. Our days of being so close are long gone now. He just has to accept me as a grown-up, and as a woman who can make her own choices.

And, look: she was dancing with Sam. She had never felt happier than this ever before.

*

'Arthur Kendricks!'

Bella's voice boomed after him down snowy Fowler Street. It was pitch black, with the few vehicles on the road offering only narrow slits of light from their painted-out headlamps. Nevertheless, Arthur was striding powerfully down the road, skidding slightly and looking drunker with every passing second.

Bella and Irene caught up with him near the marketplace. He took a long, thirsty swig from a hip flask and offered them some. Urgh, it was whisky, Irene realised. It was warming, but she found the taste foul.

'What was all that about?' Bella shouted at him. 'You looked like you were about to start a fight in there!'

He hung his head and sighed out a long plume of frosty breath. 'Have you got any tabs?' he asked, and Bella produced her special cocktail cigarettes. She lit one for him and Arthur smoked greedily.

'Arthur, Sam won't get Mavis pregnant,' Irene assured him, though where her confidence in this matter came from, she had no idea. She suddenly remembered how Megan had told them all – quite disgustingly – how Sam had taken her in the scullery at Frederick Street. She had made him sound rapacious and animalistic, and revealing those sordid details had clearly thrilled her.

Irene reflected that you never really knew what people were like, in their deepest, secret selves. Why, the Sam she knew was just a gentle lad. Misunderstood and clever and frustrated by his life, and tired of always being treated as the youngest and the daftest. To her it seemed fine for him to be left alone with Mavis. But really, what did Irene know?

Arthur was scowling at her, as if he was coming to a similar conclusion. 'What if she does get pregnant by him, Irene? What if Sam has another bastard, eh? And it's my sister's turn. What chance is she going to stand, living in our damp little house with a bairn and me being away, eh? She's not one of the Farleys, you know. She doesn't live with a great big family, who can help her and take over when she's at the factory, or help her with the feeding and all that stuff in the night.'

'You're getting ahead of yourself,' Bella told him. 'Don't get carried away, pet. All they did was share a little kiss.'

His dark expression had the unfortunate effect of making both girls smile. 'That's where it always starts,' he said, and Irene couldn't help laughing out loud at that.

'Eeeh, Arthur. What would you know about kissing and courting and all that, eh?' She meant it fondly, and she meant no harm by it, but her question made Arthur clam up at once. He broke away from them, puffing out plumes of smoke, and heading home.

'Ah, don't sulk with us, man!' Bella called after him, as he went scurrying across the snowy marketplace.

Irene followed after them. It was already arranged that she'd stay at Arthur's place tonight. It had seemed easier than coming home late to Number Thirteen and waking up the household and the babies. Also, she hadn't relished the thought of walking back through the Sixteen Streets so late and alone.

This was to be her proper, happy night out, and that involved staying away overnight as well, enjoying the company of her friends. But Sam's shenanigans and Arthur's horrible mood were pretty much putting the kybosh on the whole thing.

Bella linked arms with her as they walked in Arthur's wake. 'We can have some brandy when we get in,' Bella told her. She'd bought a little bottle from Sam and his secret supply, of course.

'What's Arthur so het up about?' Irene asked. 'This isn't just about looking after Mavis, is it?'

Bella tapped her beautiful nose. 'There's more to it than that, I'm afraid. Much more to it than that. There's business between Arthur and Sam. Old, bad business, from back when they were nothing but lads. But that isn't my story to tell you, Irene. Maybe one day Arthur will explain it all to you.'

Irene hurried along through the snowy blackout. As often was the case, she was in the dark in more ways than one.

She smiled to herself: even with all the fighting and the hullabaloo, it still felt good to be amongst grown-ups, despite all their daft carrying on. She loved being with the babies, of course, but an evening away from them really had done her a power of good.

Everything was quiet at Number Thirteen.

Beryl was in sole charge of the bairns. Marlene and Johnny were good as gold: Johnny with his bottle and Marlene with her mashed up vegetables. There wasn't a peep out of them and Beryl was happy to think that it was because they were content in the presence of their Aunty Beryl. Contented, relaxed and trusting.

Ma Ada and Megan were both having a night off.

'Will you be all right seeing to them by yourself, pet?' Ma Ada asked, looking shattered. Recent days had taken their toll on her.

Megan had her hair up in curlers and a pile of movie magazines and she glanced over at her baby in Beryl's arms like she couldn't have cared less. It was like she hardly even recognised him.

At first Beryl had been daunted. 'Aye, of course. I'll be quite happy.'

Had she imagined it early this evening, or had Irene been watching her very carefully? Just before she went out for her night of dancing, Irene had been staring at her, hadn't she? Beryl had caught a certain look in her eye. Appraising. Watchful. Worried, perhaps?

Beryl was no fool. She knew – she just knew – that her mother must have said something to Irene the other day. Something awful. Something that would wriggle under her skin and niggle at her. It must have been when they visited . . . those brief few moments when Beryl was out in the lav. That's when her mother had pounced. And what had she told Irene?

Beryl hated the thought of Irene not trusting her.

But it was okay. She did trust her, surely. She had left her baby in Beryl's care after all. Whatever Mama had said, Irene had trusted her own instincts and feelings and she trusted Beryl.

Then the evening unfolded beautifully. After waving off the adults for their night out dancing, Beryl turned her attention to bathing both infants in the scullery sink. The two of them gurgled and wriggled and cooed the whole time.

I can do this, Beryl thought. I can do this without panicking. It's easy, isn't it? I'm a natural. I was always good with bairns. I always was, from the very earliest times.

She dressed them for bed in their snuggliest woollens and sang to them. Daft, half-remembered nursery songs. Bye Baby Bunting and wrapping the hunter's bairn in a fresh rabbit skin. That was a rhyme she recalled her father singing to her. And the one about clapping your hands . . . for Dadda coming back up the wagon way, covered in clarts from the pits, with coins in his pockets. When he cuddles you on his return, he'll dirty all your gown . . .

The voices of her parents in her memories seemed so clear suddenly. So young and high. Happy-sounding. They had sung to her and her brother. All those years ago. Back in the far-off days when their family was complete.

Beryl, fastening buttons, was tearing up at the thought of it. Her da and her mama actually singing to her! It seemed hard to fathom, and yet the memory was there. Clear as anything. Beryl sat marvelling in the scullery, hugging both bairns to her, lost in memory. Tears were hot on her cheeks as she sat there quietly.

'You look a proper picture, hinny,' Ma Ada told her, suddenly appearing in the doorway. She eased herself into the room, ready to make her bedtime cocoa. 'Look at you! I wish I had a camera for a picture of you sat there with them two.'

Beryl blushed, feeling self-conscious. 'I was away with the fairies! I was . . . remembering. The songs from when I was a toddler.'

Ma Ada was studying her carefully. 'I imagine your childhood wasn't easy, pet. Nor later on. Both your parents aren't well, are they?'

'Da's never been well since the last war. He came back and he was never right again. He's rarely left his bedroom. He's hardly ever left the house. That was why it was such a big deal . . . when he came to my wedding. Seeing him standing there in the Robin Hood pub, with my mama . . . it was such a huge achievement for him. I could hardly believe it.'

'Aye, I remember it well, pet,' Ma Ada said. 'I saw you with them. I could see that there was a complicated story there, to do with your family.' She put a copper pan of milk on the stove to heat. Just a splash of milk was all that was left. Then she was scraping the cocoa powder from the tin and pursing her lips thoughtfully. 'Your mam's not well either, is she?'

'She had a hard time with the birth of Fred . . . my brother, as was . . .' Beryl said, hugging the babies closer. Marlene squealed a little in protest. 'She had the blues and stayed in bed for ages. It turned her mind, somehow. I was only a youngster and I never really understood it. But she was never the same again.'

Sagely the old woman nodded. 'I've seen that happen before. It's a touch of those blues our Megan's got now, in a way. She's having a hard time adjusting. Motherhood's a big change. We adapt or we don't. Some of us are made for it. Others have to change themselves.'

Beryl watched her mother-in-law study the trembling skin of boiling milk in the pan. The scent of warming cocoa filled the air and she smiled. 'Well, I'd best get these up to the attic and settled for the night.'

'Aye, you go up, pet,' Ma Ada said.

In the back parlour Megan was smoking French Gitanes she'd filched from Sam's secret stash. 'Kiss Johnny goodnight for me,' she said, flipping through the *Picturegoer*. 'He doesn't want my smoke.'

Beryl took the pair up to the top of the house and settled them under their covers without a whisper of protest.

I'm a natural, she thought. All these years, I've been so frightened. I've been a bag of nerves. I thought I was never to be trusted again.

But just look at me. When someone actually has faith in me!

I'm a natural. Ma Ada just about said it down there. I'd make a wonderful mam.

Beryl lay down on the bed in the attic room and listened to the two babies murmuring contentedly as they drifted towards sleep. Her heart was pattering happily. She was letting herself imagine being a mam. She was daring to hope.

Maybe one day. Maybe it's not impossible.

I'd completely ruled it out, she thought. It wasn't something that could happen. I would deny myself that happiness. I must! I had to! Motherhood could never be for me.

But now . . . Well, maybe. Maybe I could? Maybe I should?

The thoughts were making her dizzy as she lay there under the starry attic window. Her thoughts leapt delightfully. The idea of having a baby of her own!

A swelling of joy felt like an ache under her breastbone. Love with nowhere to go. Love for a nameless person that only she could summon into being. It would make her complete at last, wouldn't it? Her and Tony.

Beryl was letting herself dare to hope.

She was almost too excited to fall asleep.

When Tony comes home next. Talk to him. Break the news. Tell him you might have changed your mind. Tell him that things are not impossible after all.

You can tell him that you think, maybe . . .

Maybe it's time . . .

Beryl fell asleep with the bairns in the attic, and her dreams were contented ones. Her dreams that night were wonderful.

# Chapter Twenty-Six

Irene shared a bed with Bella that night, and was soon drifting away into sweet oblivion. She felt vaguely guilty at being away from her baby, but was so delighted to have a peaceful night that the feeling soon melted away.

Bella's room was a tiny one in the corner of the Kendricks siblings' decrepit house, and the Italian girl had done her best to make it liveable and welcoming with her limited resources. Irene could remember the beautiful room Bella had enjoyed in her parents' house on Simonside, with its view of the wild North Sea, and when she thought about that, on top of everything else her friend had lost, it could make her weep.

Bella's losses hadn't turned her bitter or angry, however. Irene couldn't imagine how she herself would cope with the things that the Franchino girl had had to survive. Somehow Bella was calmer and more dignified than ever. Her nature had become sweeter as a result of her cruel losses. As a friend she had become even more loving, as if she had learnt the true value of the ties that bound her to other folk.

Both girls were sleeping soundly following their dramatic night at the Albert Hall on Fowler Street. But some time around one in the morning they were both jolted awake by the clattering of the front door, and noise in the downstairs hall.

Bella sat up swiftly, clutching the bedclothes to her heart. 'Oh God, what is it?'

Irene couldn't make out what she was hearing. 'It's not a raid, is it?'

There were no sirens going off, thank goodness.

But there were footsteps in the hall and muffled voices. Could it be intruders? Could they be under attack?

Bella was listening hard. 'It's OK – I think it's Mavis, back home . . . with Sam.'

'Oh!' said Irene, feeling discombobulated. She looked at the time and wondered about just turning over and getting back to sleep. 'At least he's been a gentleman and brought her back home from the dance,' Irene mumbled.

Bella frowned. She wasn't entirely sure that Sam *was* being such a gentleman.

There came another sudden bang then, as Arthur exploded out of his bedroom and thundered down the stairs, shouting.

'Oh dear,' Bella said. 'We'd better get up, Irene.'

The cold outside the thick blankets on Bella's bed was fierce. There was ice on the inside of the window, Irene noticed, as she pulled on a jumper over her nightdress. 'What's going on?'

Downstairs there was a confrontation in progress. Arthur and Sam were squaring up to each other in the cluttered hallway, and Mavis was sobbing her heart out at the sight of them.

'This is like a house full of crazy people!' Bella yelled at them over their noise, dashing down the stairs. 'What's all the noise about?'

Arthur snarled, 'I caught them! I caught them . . . *at it*!'

Mavis covered her face with both hands and stood there, shaking and frozen in her organdie gown. Sam's coat was over her shoulders, but she still looked frozen to the bone. The wail coming out from behind her hands sounded ghostly.

'Calm down, man,' Sam warned him, looking worried at the wild look in Arthur's eyes.

'What were they doing?' Bella wanted to know.

'It was plain what he was intending to do,' Arthur spat. 'I've lain awake for an hour, listening for her coming in. Fretting like mad about this daft little minx. And then I hear them both coming in here together, and I realise that he's got . . . ideas about what he's gonna do to her. He's got designs upon her . . . *virtue!*'

Irene's mouth fell open at Arthur's highfalutin language. She was poised halfway down the stairs and wanted to laugh. Arthur sounded like he was in some old-fashioned melodrama on the stage. Designs upon her virtue, indeed!

'I had no such thing!' Sam protested feebly, sounding drunker than Irene had ever heard him. He gripped hold of the banister rail and it looked like it was propping him up. His dress shirt was plastered to his skin with wet snow, and Irene thought he'd be getting pneumonia if he didn't warm up soon.

'Can we go and sit in the warm and discuss this?' Irene suggested.

'Good idea. The sitting room will be warmer than out here,' said Bella.

But Arthur wouldn't be assuaged. 'He brought my sister here and his plan was to sneak in and have his way with her. That's what he was gonna do!'

'Nay, Arthur, it wasn't,' sobbed Mavis. 'It really wasn't.'

'You don't know, Maeve,' Arthur dismissed her. 'You know nowt about nowt, you.'

'Arthur, man,' Sam said. 'You've got the wrong idea. Mavis is a canny lass, and I'd never dream of taking advantage of her.'

'Oh, aye,' snapped Arthur.

'I just brought her back home because you lot had left her at the dance by herself. I was trying to be a good friend to her.'

This brought Arthur up short, because he actually did feel guilty for leaving his sister at the dance. Not that she was incapable of getting herself home late at night. They had both grown up on the streets and they weren't at all scared of the blackout. But Arthur could hardly claim to be quite so perfect a brother, having left his sister in the arms of her potential seducer.

'It's true, Arthur,' Mavis said, looking whiter and more worried than ever. 'Nowt bad was gonna go on. Truly it wasn't.'

'I saw him kissing you! On the dance floor, right in front of everyone!'

'Ah, that didn't mean anything,' said Mavis. She slipped the jacket off her shoulders and passed it sadly to the object of her love. 'Sam doesn't really like me in that way. He doesn't fancy me one little bit. I'm not daft. So you've absolutely no worries on that score.'

With that, Mavis slipped past her brother and then up the stairs, mumbling her apologies as she brushed past Bella and Irene in their nightgowns. She vanished like a rabbit into her bolt-hole and slammed the door on them all.

'Ah, bless her,' Bella said. 'And she was having such a lovely night, earlier on.'

Arthur was still gazing at Sam with utter contempt blazing in his eyes. 'I reckon you'd better get home to your own place, Sam Farley. You're not welcome here.'

Sam looked so downcast that Irene felt her heart going out to him. She loved him to bits and hated seeing him like this. He looked confounded and bemused, like he'd been trying to do the right thing, but found that he wasn't trusted by anyone anyway. She felt like crying out to him, or going with him back to Frederick Street, but she stopped herself in time. This was something between Sam and Arthur. She wasn't going to get between two of her best friends.

I don't understand men, she thought, as she watched Sam turn on his heel, pull his damp, clammy jacket on again, and storm out of the Kendricks' house into the darkness.

'I need a nightcap,' Arthur said, once he'd locked the front door, and hurried back to the sitting room.

Irene found him sitting hunched by the almost-dead embers of the fire.

Bella had gone back to her bed. 'I'll leave you to it, if you want to have a word with him,' she said, patting Irene's hand. 'I'm dead on me feet.'

Irene poured herself a little tot of sherry from the fancy decanter Arthur had foraged out of a cupboard, and came to sit with him in front of the warmth.

'I suppose you think I made a proper fool of myself tonight,' he said at last.

'You were defending your sister's honour,' said Irene, smiling at him. 'And sounding just like an old fella with mutton chop whiskers in a Victorian novel. You were sounding like her father!'

Arthur refused to be amused, at his own foolishness, or Irene's gentle ribbing. 'Aw, come on, though. It was clear what Sam was after. And Mavis really means nothing to him. He would use her and chuck her away, and I'd be the one who'd have to deal with all the bother and mess afterwards.'

Irene sipped her warming sherry and sighed. 'I really think you've got it all wrong about our Sam, love. He's a much sweeter, softer lad than that. He'd never use anyone.'

'Oh no?'

'Of course not! I've lived with the Farleys for over a year and—'

'And in that year he's got his own sister-in-law up the duff! Urgh.' Arthur looked exactly like a prim maiden aunt, clutching his pearls.

'Sam says that he felt like Megan forced him into doing it,' Irene said thoughtfully. She was breaking a confidence, she realised, but she was trying to defend her brother-in-law. 'Sam said that he felt like she was bullying him into doing what she wanted. She goaded him. She told him that, if he slept with her, it would make him into a proper man at last.'

Arthur looked at her sharply. 'Is that what he told you?'

'I believe him, too,' Irene said. 'He was upset when he told me all of this. He was still confused about it all. She was telling him that she knew that's what he wanted. The chance to grow up and prove that he was a real man, and not just the little lad they all thought he was.'

'Oh God,' Arthur sighed and shook his head. 'She wrapped him around her little finger. That Megan's a wily, clever one. I'll give her that.'

'But she's also beautiful,' Irene pointed out. 'There's many a fella that would fall over themselves given half a chance to mess around with Megan. Sam must have been flattered and excited by what she was saying to him.' Irene frowned, thinking back to how he'd told her the tale. 'Except, afterwards, when he told me about it all, it didn't seem like something exciting to him. He looked pretty revolted by it.'

'She used him, that's why,' Arthur said abruptly. 'She manipulated him, by the sounds of it.'

'But what kind of man would refuse her?' Irene said. 'What red-blooded fella would turn their nose up at Megan?'

Arthur pulled a face. 'That one gets away with far too much, round at Number Thirteen. I'm amazed your precious Ma Ada has never seen through her. That old woman used to be the sharpest, cleverest old witch for miles around. Everyone said so.'

'I think she still is, too,' Irene said, wondering whether she ought to have another drop of sherry. It would help send her off to sleep, surely. As a rule she disliked alcohol, but right now those heady fumes seemed just the ticket. 'Though I don't think you should call her a witch, Arthur.' She seized the crystal decanter and poured them both a tiny dribble more.

He sighed deeply. 'I do know that Sam is a sweet, soft, loving lad really, you know,' he said at last. 'And I think you've guessed it already, Irene, but there's more to all my anger with him than just protecting Mavis.'

Have I? she thought. Is there? Maybe Arthur was giving her credit for more insight than she actually had. She didn't say anything however, and quietly let him carry on burbling in the firelight.

'You see, I thought for a long while . . .' Arthur smiled and took a deep breath. 'I thought that I was in love with him. Aye, me. I really did. And I thought that he loved me, too.'

Irene choked and spluttered on her sherry. 'It's gone down the wrong hole!' she cried out, coughing hard. Her eyes started watering and she clutched at Arthur's sleeve. 'The sherry! It's gone down the wrong hole!'

For a second she felt like she was drowning. Some picture that would make for the front of the *Shields Gazette* – the young woman who choked to death on fortified wine on her only night out in a year. The shame of it!

Arthur thumped her heftily on the back until she could catch her breath again. She wheezed and her nose and eyes were smarting. She set down her glass thinking, that'll teach me for drinking after midnight.

'Did you hear what I was telling you?' Arthur said peevishly.

'Aye, that you were fond of Sam. Well, that's only right. You lot were all close to each other growing up.'

Arthur shook his head. 'I thought we were made for each other, me and Sam. And once, one particular time, he said just the same. To my face. My heart nearly stopped. I couldn't believe we were thinking the same thing. We were feeling the same way. We were . . . what? About sixteen, I reckon we were. It was like an age ago. We were standing on the beach at Marsden Bay. Standing face to face. So close. Too close to each other. It was only the once, but I've never forgotten it.'

Irene's coughing fit had subsided, but she could still feel her lungs bubbling boozily inside her chest. She was finding it hard to follow what Arthur was confiding in her. It sounded like nonsense to her. 'What are you saying, love?'

'I thought he was mine,' Arthur told her. 'I always thought he was gonna be mine.'

# Chapter Twenty-Seven

Irene awoke to the tantalising aroma of bacon and eggs rising up the stairs from the scullery. She drifted out onto the top landing, all of a sudden feeling absolutely starving. When Bella joined her, bundling herself into a woollen dressing gown, she said, 'I've not smelt bacon in ages!'

The Kendricks' house was absolutely freezing, and Irene's bare feet slapped on the gritty, uncarpeted staircase, but she was so hungry, she didn't care. Her head was banging, too, from taking those last couple of drinks with Arthur.

She groaned, remembering that strange, late night conversation, and the perplexing way it had ended. He had grown embarrassed and annoyed at himself, perhaps for being too candid, and he had seemed almost irked with her, because she hadn't given him the reaction he had wanted. In fact, she had been so stunned by sherry and confusion that she had hardly reacted to his words at all.

Irene still didn't understand what Arthur had been trying to tell her. He had behaved like it was some terrible secret and a dreadful thing . . . but all he was saying really, was that he loved Sam like a brother, wasn't he? In the way that they all, as friends, loved each other, deep down? Yes, it was harder for men to admit to their tender feelings, of course it was. Men were brought up to be tougher than that, and to hide their affections, but maybe Arthur was taking that too hard? Irene could see that it cost him to fall out with Sam, and his upset was painful to her, too. But that was nothing to be ashamed of, surely?

But they had been quite tipsy, of course, and all kinds of feelings get amplified and distorted on nights like that. Perhaps it would just be better to pretend the whole conversation had never taken place?

She did her best to go breezing into the scullery, beaming at the wonderful smells of breakfast, even though her skull was throbbing with lingering pain.

'Oh, how wonderful!' she burst, when she saw Mavis standing sentinel at the battered old cooker in an ancient, frayed wrap of lime green silk. The absurd garment was trimmed with ratty ostrich feathers and had clearly seen better days. Mavis smiled at her as she prodded eggs and rashers of bacon in a skillet two inches deep in bubbling fat.

'I thought we should all have a hearty breakfast as a treat after our big night out!'

There was something tense about Mavis's cheeriness, as if she was at pains to put behind her the more contentious parts of last night's goings-on. She was being bright and determined to rewrite the evening as a lovely time for all.

'Are you doing fried bread, as well?' Bella asked hungrily.

'Ha! I don't know how you keep your figure,' Mavis laughed.

'I don't! Look how I'm expanding. I'm becoming proper buxom!' Bella gave a stately twirl to show off her figure, and Irene had to agree: she was a fine figure of a woman. It was amazing, really, that she didn't have a whole horde of suitors queueing up at her door, begging to take her away. Perhaps there was something in Bella's beauty that intimidated men, thought Irene, and kept them at bay?

'Where did you get all the eggs and the bacon?' Irene asked, dreading the answer. It looked to her like Mavis was merrily frying up a whole week's ration of meat and eggs for an entire family.

'It was Sam,' Mavis admitted, biting her lip. 'He's slipped us a few extra bits and pieces lately.' She looked regretful, as if the scenes of last night were likely to make such treats less likely in future.

Arthur had appeared in the scullery doorway in time to hear these last exchanges. His face looked lurid with bruises and lumps, and one eye was squinting closed. 'A few extra bits and pieces, eh?' he echoed sardonically. 'Well, I won't be touching them. I'll have a tiny piece of dry toast and a black coffee, thanks.' He looked very pale and crumpled. 'I've got an utterly shattering headache.' He sat himself very carefully in a chair at the rickety table and glared at the kitchen, which was completely filled with women, it seemed. 'Tell me, I didn't say or do anything idiotically foolish and irreversible last night, did I?'

They all stared at him, in his pale gold dressing gown with paisley print and his vivid black eye, and all three women decided to simply glide over last night's dramas. They smiled at him, and Bella reassured her friend: 'Everything was fine. And everything is forgotten, dearest.'

'Good,' said Arthur, lighting his first cigarette of the day and hoping it would soothe his fevered head. 'I'm glad of that. I'm glad we could have a lovely evening out together with less drama than usual . . . That really comes as something of a relief.'

Irene smiled and shook her head, and turned her attention back to that delicious-looking breakfast hissing in the pan.

This was Sunday so it was Irene's day off, and she had a feeling that it was frittering away from her, as she sat on the tram heading across town. It was a waste of money, paying a fare when it wasn't that far to walk home, but she was dead on her feet after last night. She sat pressed between women bundled up in their winter coats, gas masks on their laps. She felt rather conspicuous in last night's dress and her dancing shoes.

It was hardly a waste of a day off, she told herself firmly. Eating breakfast with some of her dearest friends, after a night spent dancing under colourful lights. Even if the singing had been awful, and there'd been gangsters about, fighting going on, and all kinds of complications . . . Irene smiled to herself. She realised that she wouldn't have missed any of it for the world.

This was *life*, she thought. This was her real life, and exactly the kind of thing she had imagined for herself when she was a girl down in Norfolk. Now she lived in the city and went to big dances and saw fist fights and heard about love affairs and had friends engaged in grown-up dramas.

Her feet were chilled right through and her shoes were soaked with snow, however, and she was looking forward to getting back to Frederick Street. Not least to see the baby. She counted up and gasped under her breath: it was sixteen hours since she had last clapped eyes on Marlene. And the awful thing was, she hadn't felt the tiniest pinch of guilt more than, at most, three times . . .

Eeeh, she hoped the bairn was all right!

She jumped off the tram at the stop for the Sixteen Streets, beside the pub at the entrance to the dark, forbidding arches, where the railways ran over to the docks. She took in great lungfuls of the familiar smells of soot and coke, and also the wonderfully rich aroma of the biscuit factory as it came wafting up the hill. Then, charged with energy by the frosty sea air, she marched up the steep hill towards her home, her dancing shoes slipping on the frozen cobbles as she went.

Irene was glad to find Number Thirteen relatively peaceful this morning. She was greeted in the parlour by Beryl, who smilingly poured her a cuppa from the vast brown pot. Beryl wanted to know all about the night at the Albert Hall.

'There's loads to tell you,' Irene said ruefully, sitting down with her tea and wrapping her fingers round the cup. 'But first tell me how the bairns were.'

'Angels,' Beryl beamed. 'Honestly, you'd never believe it. I think I've got the perfect touch with them both, for sending them off to sleep. There was never a squeak out of your Marlene. Johnny grizzled a little bit more, but then he always does. He's a little bit sicklier and whingey, on account of his being a bit puny, because of his difficult birth.'

Irene glanced back at the hallway, as if she feared Megan might be creeping up on them. 'Don't let his mam hear you say that! She's not very motherly, but she wouldn't want anyone saying that her baby's puny. She reckons he's perfect!'

'He *is* perfect,' Beryl said. 'He's a lovely bairn, but he's just a bit sickly, isn't he? He's not a bouncing, robust kid like Marlene is.'

Irene nodded at this, gratified to hear her own baby praised.

'Anyhow,' Beryl went on. 'Megan's not here at the moment. She went off at the crack of dawn on the bus to Hartlepool for the rest of the weekend. She's gone to see her parents . . . and I'm glad she's away for a day or two, to be honest. She kind of hangs over the place, doesn't she?'

Irene nodded firmly, and wished there was some sugar for her black tea. 'Her moods take over the whole place, I know what you mean. If she's happy, then everyone has to be happy; if she's in a snit, then everyone knows about it.'

'Hey, you'd better not be talking about me, you lasses!' Ma Ada bellowed as she bundled into the room, swathed in shawls and hugging Lucky to her chest. She looked incredibly tired, and cross at herself for sleeping in.

'We're talking about Megan,' Beryl said, abashed at being caught criticising her sister-in-law.

'Oh, that one,' sighed Ma Ada, settling herself into her customary chair. 'Can you squeeze that pot for a cuppa for me, pet?'

'Of course,' Beryl said, and rushed to fetch a cup. Irene smiled at the old woman, thinking to herself: she's still suffering, a few days later, from her drunken night in with all that purloined alcohol. She still looks a bit embarrassed from being caught dancing around the front parlour with Aunty Winnie.

'And how was your night out?' Ma Ada asked Irene sharply.

'Oh . . .' Irene smiled, and decided not to go into all the particulars and the complications. Ma Ada had a way of ferreting all the details out of you, and Irene didn't feel up to one of her interrogations this morning. 'It was very nice,' she said.

'Nice?' squawked the old mother. 'That's the best you can come up with? It was *very nice!*' She shook her head and her hair was spilling out of its net. 'Good times are wasted on you young set,' she grumbled. 'It's like that son of mine. Sam. He came crawling in . . . what time was it, Beryl? Some ungodly hour. Covered in snow and sneezing and shivering like crazy. I went out on the landing to see if he was all right, and asked him if he'd enjoyed his daft self. And do you know what he said?'

Irene sipped her tea and dreaded to guess what Sam might have told his mum about last night's carrying on. 'What did he say?'

'Same as you did! It was *very nice*, apparently! You boring beggars – is that all you have to say for yourselves?' Ma Ada cackled and slurped her tea, and ruffled up her hairless cat on his shoulders. 'Mind, when I was a lass and we went out, we used to have a fine time at the dances. We really used to let our hair down! You youngsters these days . . . By, you don't know the meaning of the word "fun"! Not compared with us lot, back before the Great War! Eeeh, those were the days!'

Beryl and Irene both smiled at the old woman's relish in her own past. Beryl was longing to ask her more about her salad days, back at the dawn of the century. It was unusual to hear her talk about them in such a positive light. Mostly Ma Ada's tales of the past were about the poverty and the misery, and the diseases and the dirt and the wretchedness of living back then in the Sixteen Streets.

Usually she used the past and all her recollections as a stick with which to beat the younger generation of today: 'Eeeh, you kids don't know you're born! None of you know what real suffering is like!' But today there was a genial smile on her face and her daughters-in-law were left to wonder: was the old dear even starting to mellow at last?

They were interrupted then by a sharp rapping at the front door. 'I'll get it,' Beryl smiled, shutting the middle door on the draught, and intercepting Sam by chance in the hall. The young lad was still in his stripy pyjamas. He looked rumpled and dog tired, mouthing a greeting at her as he opened the front door.

Beryl caught her breath sharply.

There was a telegram boy standing there. No mistaking that dark uniform and cap. The figure was silhouetted against the pale snow on the cobbles of the street. The boy was holding up a square brown envelope and handing it to her.

'Beryl Farley?' he asked.

'Y-yes?' Suddenly Beryl wanted to deny her own name. She wanted to turn and slam the front door on this gawky young lad, who was only doing his job. She was aware of Sam by her side, straightening up, and she imagined she could hear his heartbeat through his open pyjama jacket. It was pounding just as loudly as hers.

'Telegram for Beryl Farley,' the lad said, and pushed it into her hands. It was only as she took it, feeling like she was caught in some horrible dream, that Beryl saw that the envelope had a black trim all the way round the edges.

# Chapter Twenty-Eight

'I'm one of the famous Farleys,' he had said to her, right at the start. 'Us Farley brothers are famous around here.'

And at first Beryl had thought that sounded a bit big-headed, coming from Tony as he stood there in the bar. He looked so cocksure, leaning against the wall, watching the whole place fill up. She had never seen anyone look as at home and relaxed as he did, surrounded by his family and friends and neighbours in the Robin Hood.

It had been her first night out with the girls from the biscuit factory. She'd been a young lass really, she thought, looking back. She was no age. This was, what? Less than five years ago, but so much had happened to change her since then. Back then she had been emerging into the world, making friends for the first time, and learning to stand on her own two feet.

And Tony had been waiting for her, it seemed like. There he was, at the Robin Hood, saying that he was famous in these parts, as one of four fine brothers belonging to the Farley clan.

'Ah, they're good lads,' plump Mary had assured her, when she'd asked about the Farleys the next day. 'It's a decent family, not like some round here. Clean, honest, sober and hard-working. I mean, their father was a drunken old sod, but he's well out of the picture now, and it's their ma who rules the roost round there. And any lass would have to be brave as a lioness to try to snag a Farley brother from underneath Ma Ada's nose.'

It turned out that plump Mary from Horsfield Street had once set her cap at Tom, the second youngest of the boys, and then she had turned her sights on Tony, the eldest, and then she'd been sent away with a flea in her ear before she could start on the others. Plump Mary had been judged as sadly lacking by the stern matriarch.

'There's Sam, the youngest, who's nobbut a lad still and cheeky with it. And Bob, who was knocked on the head by his own dad apparently, and has never been right ever since. And then there's Tom, who's the cleverest, they all say, and going in for exams. And then there's the eldest, Tony, who's the most handsome, I think, and the quietest of the Farley boys. There's just something about him, I think,' said plump Mary, stamping out ginger snaps and going off into a dream. 'You're very lucky. Going out for the first time with the lasses and managing to turn his head. He's quite a catch.'

That had been right at the start of it. Beryl had entered into the world of the Sixteen Streets and the Farleys of Frederick Street, and she never looked back once. There was nothing exotic or exciting about their lives. They lived like most other families in the local area: doing their best and muddling along. They had no more money or ambition or luck than anyone else she knew. They sometimes had a tad more drama than the average household, perhaps, but Beryl found that she relished that, having grown up in a house that had been so quiet and stultified for so long.

The Farley clan suited her. Old Ma Ada had studied her like she was looking at a plump bird in the window of the butcher's just before Christmas. That was how Beryl had felt at the time, and she had been nervous of the old woman. Actually though, Ada had been very kind to her and, in her own way, acted fondly towards her over the years. Beryl was the first of the daughters-in-law, and when she eventually moved in, she was made to feel very welcome.

'You're everything I could have hoped for, for my Tony,' Ma Ada had clucked at the wedding reception – again at the Robin Hood, where all the public rituals of their lives seemed to get played out. 'I'll say, today, that my firstborn is my favourite of all my lads. And other days I'll say different, because in truth I love them all equally, of course. But for a while Tony was all I had to love in this world. In truth, I always hated his father, and so he was all I had, until the others came along, and so he's got a special place in my heart, has Tony. He made a space in my heart before anyone else ever did.' Ma Ada was teary, drawing Beryl closer as she revealed these secrets of her heart and soul. They were things that she would never dream of telling anyone else, but she felt she needed to tell them to Beryl.

'Look after him, lady. Tony might act tough and grown up. That's because he's the eldest of them, and he's had to be the man of the house since he was about nine, and he takes that job very seriously. But underneath all that calm, manly exterior he's still the same loving, kind-hearted lad he always was. He might act like he knows everything and can do anything, but I know how much love and guidance and support he needs.'

Beryl was ready for that challenge. She wanted to be there, giving him any support that she could manage. And so her years at Number Thirteen began, mere months after first meeting her Tony.

The morning that the news arrived Beryl sat in the back parlour and she wouldn't let go of the black-edged telegram. It was as if she was trying to absorb the truth of what it contained through her fingertips, as if words weren't good enough, or clear enough, as if her mind couldn't take them in. She let go of it only briefly, long enough for Ma Ada to read its few brief lines, and then she virtually snatched it back, out of the old woman's crabbed hands. It was as if that flimsy sheet of paper with its strips of grey print were the last physical remnants of her love.

'We'll never get him back,' were the only words that she could frame into a sentence. It felt like hours after the delivery of the news, and hours spent with everyone fussing around her, and shock reverberating through the house. The only words she could coherently chase into order were: 'We will never get his body back. He has gone for ever. Everything that he was.'

When she said them, those words comforted no one. Ma Ada starting moaning and shivering. She sat down heavily in her chair and looked like she was in a dreadful way, as if she was about to expire on the spot.

'She's gone into shock,' Sam said, tucking her shawl around her as she shivered. 'We need to keep her warm. Fetch her cardy from her room, Irene. The big mustard-coloured one that Aunty Madge knitted her.'

'I wish we had more sugar,' Irene said. 'Sugar in her tea. That would help.' But the old woman's teeth were chattering and she couldn't even take a proper sip from her cup without spilling it all down her front.

Tony was dead. Ma Ada tried to take it in. He was dead and gone for ever. Her firstborn son. Her first darling son. She would never see his face again.

It was bad enough when they grew up and became men and their faces changed so that they never looked exactly like their own boyish selves any more. But that was natural, because everyone grew up, and Ma Ada could still see the boys that were inside her grown-up lads. Those boys were still there and would belong to her for ever.

But this was too cruel. He was thirty-five. He'd hardly seen anything of life yet.

'There's a mistake. It's a mistake. Someone must have made a mistake . . .'

Irene and Sam didn't know what to say to that. They knew that it wasn't a mistake. The print in the telegram was so concise and exact. It had the force of truth to it. The HMS *Manchester* had been torpedoed four miles east of Tunisia, in North Africa. One hundred and fifty men were lost.

Before the ship went down, three hundred and seventy-eight were saved and taken captive and sent as prisoners into occupied France. Tony was not among them. Tony had been one of the hundred and fifty who went to the bottom of the sea, east of Tunisia.

The women heard these words and quietly marvelled at them. Africa. Tunisia. A convoy heading for Malta. Italians had fired the torpedoes that had sunk the HMS *Manchester*. It was all exotic-sounding. These places seemed so far-flung and impossible. How could the death of a South Shields lad be tied up with such wonderful-sounding places?

Beryl never thought she'd hate the sound of places so much as this. Africa. Italy. Malta. Tunisia. They could all go to the devil for all she cared. From now on she'd never even be able to hear the word 'Manchester' without being sick to her stomach.

It felt like hours that they sat there, shivering, mostly wordless. Trying to absorb the news. Wondering when the blessed relief of being able to cry might come. But it was like they were frozen in the moment of receiving the news, and the clock on the old dresser would never start ticking again.

Beryl got up abruptly and went to fetch the old, battered atlas from the shelf in the front room. It was one of a set of fine books that took pride of place in that room. Books that were too good to get down very often. A Bible, an atlas, and various improving books. A Dickens that must have been new when Dickens was still alive. *Great Expectations*.

Beryl set the atlas down on the dining room table and flipped through till she got to the northern coast of Africa.

'Oh, don't . . .' Ma Ada moaned. She couldn't bear it, but Beryl wouldn't be dissuaded. Her mouth was set in a grim line as she traced the intricate coastline. She pondered over that pale blue. The atlas smelt both musty and old and somehow still new. It hadn't been opened for years until recently and all the colours were brilliant.

'He's somewhere there, he's somewhere down there for ever,' Beryl said, rocking on the spot and tapping the page with her finger.

She let Irene take her gently by the shoulders and lead her away from the book. She heard Sam carefully put the atlas away. It wasn't doing anyone any good, looking at the exact spot that the *Manchester* had gone to its doom. 'You need a lie down,' Irene told her, and Beryl complied. All her energy and will had been sapped away and she felt like a puppet.

For several hours she lay on her bed and let the house carry on around her. She had no idea what was happening. All thoughts of their usual routines and looking after the babies fled from her mind. Irene would have to get on with it. Beryl found she couldn't even move. And really, she should be helping to comfort Ma Ada. She had lost her son. The two women should be helping each other to deal with the vastness of this loss. And yet Beryl couldn't move from her bed. She lay on top of the candlewick bedspread that she had shared with Tony for so very few years, and she picked out every little thread that she could reach. They came free with satisfying ease: little twists of green wool that she plucked and discarded until the bedspread was ruined.

She kept picturing him. On a ship like the ships she knew so well from the yard. She had worked inside those vast stinking hulls. She knew the metallic smell of them was like blood. She knew the coldness of them.

Had he been alone at the end? She tried to imagine the noise and the screams. Had it been instantaneous? Maybe he wouldn't have known a single thing about it. Surely, surely, that had been the way. It was the way that anyone would choose for a loved one to go, wouldn't they? If they had to go in such an awful fashion. A flash of light and a noise so huge it blotted out everything, for ever. A searing rending of whiteness and a sudden end to everything you've ever known. That was all she could hope for Tony. That was the best that she could imagine for him.

The alternatives were too horrible to imagine. Pain and injury. Terrible injuries. Burns and crushed limbs. Explosions and bodies lying in ruined states. Men blown to smithereens. In darkness and smoke and waiting for their ship to go down. Waiting for the sea to bring them oblivion. Waiting to have their strong, young lives extinguished. And feeling that it would be a relief.

She lay there trying to imagine how that must be: to realise that you are so badly injured there can be no going back. All you can hope for is to die and though it's time to say goodbye to everything, there's no one there to tell. No one to share that precious moment with.

It was the worst thing she could think of.

Beryl lay there, mechanically shredding and destroying the bedspread that had been brand new on their wedding night, and she tried to picture the very worst things that she could.

She pictured him sinking slowly to the bottom of the sea, somewhere north of Africa. She had no idea how deep the sea was. She had no idea what such darkness would be like, or how cold it might be. Maybe it was warm and bright? She really had no idea. And he would be long gone, drowned and heavy and lifeless, but would he still look like himself, as he sank through those depths to the bottom of the ocean?

She tried to picture his face. She tried to see his lovely face, but the only way she could picture it was under the water as his whole body tumbled and vanished and was gone for ever.

Tony was somewhere unfathomable inside the hundreds of pages of an atlas that he had never opened in years.

# Chapter Twenty-Nine

Megan returned from Hartlepool to a house in mourning. For once she came back with a minimum of fuss, and without drawing attention to herself. She merely took up her place and got on with her household chores, helping Irene to keep everything at Number Thirteen moving smoothly along.

The house was quiet, apart from a fairly constant stream of respectful visitors. Tony had known a lot of people and, as was custom, once word was out, they turned up at the front door to pay their respects. Beryl couldn't face more than a handful of visits from these aunties and cousins per day, and it was left to Ma Ada, decked out in ancient widow's weeds in the back parlour, to graciously receive them. Endless cups of stewed tea were poured into the best china cups, and small tributes of cakes and the perennial broken biscuits from Wight's were accepted.

Irene found herself acting like a handmaiden all that week, dashing back and forth to deal with the stream of mourners, then rushing up and down the stairs to see what Beryl might need.

Beryl simply lay on her bed with her eyes closed. She barely ate or drank anything for days. 'This won't do,' Irene warned her, but Beryl just shook her head, without even opening her eyes.

\*

She was thinking about the start of the war. It was just a few years ago. Less than three years, but how young they all seemed in her memory. How keen they had all been.

It had felt like they were all indestructible, back in 1939.

At the time Beryl hadn't been one for keeping up with news or world events. Her parents had never had a newspaper delivered and there was never a radio playing in their house, and so she wasn't used to hearing about what was going on in the world. Certainly her mama and da never discussed such things with her. Dealing with their own problems and getting through the weeks always seemed enough of a carry on for them.

Round Number Thirteen Frederick Street however, the radio was on every evening and current events were hotly debated. Voices were raised in disagreement and Beryl sat there, amazed that affairs in faraway countries might have an effect on people here at home.

Ma Ada had been shocked by her attitude. 'What? Beryl man, if there's war on, then everyone's lives will be affected and turned upside down. Just like what happened last time! Worse, this time, I should think!'

Out of the corner of her eye Beryl noticed Megan's expression. She was pulling faces at everything Ada was saying, just for Beryl's benefit. She sat there with Lucky the cat on her lap, sipping her tea and looking sceptical and satirical as the old woman raged about the possibility of war.

'That Hitler's a madman, and he's going to drag us all into hell with him,' Ma Ada cried.

'Don't upset yourself, Ma,' Tom told her, worried at how agitated she was getting.

'They'll take you all away, don't you see?' his mother shouted at him. 'I've got four grown lads. You know what that means. And I'm scared for us all.'

Beryl frowned, and looked at her beloved Tony, who was nodding grimly at his mam's words. 'Aye, well. If it comes to that, I hope we'll all be ready. The first day they ask, we'll be in the queue at the town hall, putting our names down.'

What? Beryl sat bolt upright. He'd never discussed this with her. He'd given no indication that he thought anything like this would be necessary. She hated the thought of him queueing up anywhere and going off to fight. 'B-but surely that won't happen?' she burst out. 'Surely they'll sort it all out, before it comes to that? You're not a soldier, Tony. You can't go off fighting.'

'I'll do what I need to do,' he said.

His mother glared at him and her expression was a strange, complex mesh of pride and anger. 'That's what they all said the last time. It wasn't so long ago. All of them trooping off down the Sixteen Streets to the town hall. Singing their daft songs, like they were going off on an adventure. And do you know how many came back, lad? Do you even know how many came back in one piece?'

Tony stared back at his mother and nodded. 'Aye, I do know, Ma.'

'And even the ones that did come back, they were changed for ever. They came back like the shadows of the men they'd once been.'

Suddenly Beryl was on her feet and feeling queasy. 'Excuse me,' she muttered, and hurried out of the house via the scullery. She was aware of the fluttering consternation in the room as she made her exit, but she couldn't help dashing out.

All she could think of was her dad. Her ruined, hopeless dad, looking like all the life had been drained out of him. She'd grown up hearing him screaming in his sleep. She'd known all her life that he was a haunted man, and all his ghosts were inside his head, chasing him down through the years.

In the backyard she had lit up a cigarette and forced herself to calm down. Soon she was joined by Megan, who gave her an understanding look. 'They're all still going on about fighting and stuff in there,' she grinned. 'I wouldn't pay them any heed. They just like arguing. It could be about anything.'

Beryl shook her head. 'Doesn't it scare you? What if Bob takes it into his head to sign up with the others, if it comes to that? Wouldn't you be frightened for him?'

Beryl was shocked to see her new sister-in-law shrug. 'Men will do whatever they think they have to do. Whatever they think their duty is. Whatever they think other men will think well of them for doing. That's how they carry on. There's nothing us girls can do to stop them.' She inhaled deeply and stared up at the breezy blue skies above the chimney pots. 'Besides, if Bob marched off to war with the rest, there'd be a little bit more space for me in that rotten tiny box room we have to share.' A dark look flashed across her bonny face.

'I just wish they'd stop talking about war,' said Beryl. 'I feel panicky when they do. As if just talking about it makes it somehow all the more likely.'

All of the boys had signed up in the end and Ma Ada wouldn't speak to any of them for a week. Her youngest, Sam, had something funny going on with both his feet and his heart and he looked downcast because they refused to take him. 'Just you be grateful, you daft little kid!' his mother thundered at him, but Beryl could tell that he was relieved anyway. By now he had left school and was labouring down at the docks, though there was hardly a picking on him. He looked much too skinny to carry any kind of heavy load.

'Same as his old father,' Ma Ada grumped. 'He used to queue up at the docks each morning he was sober, too. Hoping the foreman would pick him to work that day. And our Sam's not moved any farther on than him.' She couldn't keep the bitter disappointment out of her voice.

'But he's not a drunk like Da was,' Tony said, brightly.

'Thank heavens for small mercies,' growled the old mother.

The three older boys, Tony, Tom and Bob signed up for the navy, the air force and the army respectively. There was something odd about Bob's medical and he, too, was initially rejected and sent back home. Beryl supposed it had something to do with his slowness, though everyone was careful not to say anything that would hurt his feelings. Bob was the softest hearted of all the boys. He took the slight from His Majesty's forces quite affably, and returned to his regular work as pot man at the Robin Hood. 'They'll call him up later,' said his mother darkly. 'If this war goes the way I think it's going to, they'll be calling up everyone, no matter what they've got wrong with them. They'll work their way through everyone until there's hardly any beggar left.'

Beryl would never forget the day they all sat listening to old Neville Chamberlain on the radio, announcing that 'this country is at war with Germany'. Beryl really hated that radio of Ada's. It was a wooden hunk of furniture that needed polishing, just like everything else in the parlour. Polishing it was one of Beryl's weekly tasks, and she had to be so careful not to move any of the dials when she buffed it up. The whole thing lit up and crackled and voices came booming out like thunder, like the sound of doom itself.

Whenever that radio came on it was either dreadful news in plummy BBC voices or gloomy old hymns Ma Ada liked singing along with on a Sunday.

Life became a blur of new things to get accustomed to. New things to get used to without Tony at home. They were given gas masks, which were smelly and heavy and hard to remember to carry around in their little cardboard boxes. There were drills and sirens going off, making everyone jump out of their skin, until they became horribly commonplace. There was a huge underground shelter by the town hall at the edge of the

Sixteen Streets, and that was where they were to go, in the event of an air raid. It was still several streets away, and they had to carry blankets and essential supplies, and be ready to sit underground with hundreds of others all through the night.

'I can't do that.' Ma Ada shook her head. 'I'll die of claustrophobia.'

The old woman sat steadfastly under her heaped shawls in her chair by the dresser. Her tiny feet in her old, flat shoes looked as if they were dug in for good. It fell to her daughters-in-law to coax her out of her house, the first time the sirens called them all to the shelter. Luckily, it was only an exercise, because it took quite some time to prise her out of her home.

'It's the safest place for all of us. Think of what Tony would tell you. He'd say you have to go there. You have to keep yourself safe, for him and the others.' Beryl kept saying these encouraging things gently, as they shuffled up their street with the crowd. Everyone else was brisker and more businesslike as they made their way to supposed safety. They waved and encouraged the old woman to join them. 'You'll have to leave Lucky at home, I'm afraid,' Beryl told her. 'They won't have pets in the shelter.' So, that was another drama. Lucky was left on the front room windowsill, staring at them as they made their way up Frederick Street. 'What if we come back and the house is gone? And Lucky's gone?' Ma Ada protested.

There was nothing anyone could say about that, but Megan looked like she had a few sarcastic replies held in reserve. Beryl nudged her. The old woman was frightened, and it was down to her daughters-in-law to assuage her fears. Especially with most of the boys away doing their training.

'We have to be brave, for Tony's sake, don't we?' Beryl kept telling her mother-in-law.

Beryl was coping better with being on her own than she had imagined. It had been hard, waving goodbye to Tony, but so far it had been just for a few weeks. He had a lot to learn if he was going to go off to sea. And his excitement was infectious, she had found. She almost wished that she could join him and the rest of the navy aboard those huge, wonderful ships whose hulls they could see when they stood at the highest point of Frederick Street.

There was something rather fitting and grand about a boy from this part of town becoming a sailor and going off to defend their country at sea in one of the very vessels built here on their doorstep.

Beryl was immensely proud of her husband.

She decided she herself wanted to work on those ships just in order to be closer to him. That was why in the end she had left the biscuit factory and applied to become a welder.

'I know everyone at Wight's is so proud of what they do and all their patriotic biscuits,' she confided in Irene. 'But I want to do more. I want to do something more useful.'

With her Tony away on his ship – wherever he was in the world – her thoughts kept going back to the work he had once engaged in. Surely she could weld and rivet just as well as he'd ever done? It was surely just a matter of learning the right skills and being given a chance to apply herself.

Irene was impressed that Beryl was so determined, even writing to all the shipping firms in South Shields docks and making her case for becoming a welder.

Aunty Winnie the fortune-teller had been round and read the tea leaves for them all, and she'd said: 'Stay at Wight's bikkie factory! That's what the eternal spirits are telling me, Beryl! You'll come a cropper if you learn to weld!'

Irene had never seen the infamous Aunty Winnie go into a full trance before, and she was very impressed. A horrible shiver went through her at the sight. Irene was quite superstitious in many ways. She put it down to being a country girl, and she was easily taken in – as Beryl laughingly put it – by Aunty Winnie's mumbo jumbo.

'Ah, it's all a load of rubbish, man,' Beryl laughed. 'That old witch has been coming round the Farley house for years, predicting death and disaster. She's a disgrace!' Beryl was vastly amused by the serious look on Irene's face. 'And no, that wasn't ectoplasm hanging down her face. She's just got horribly dripping sinuses.'

Despite her own determinedly light-hearted tone, Beryl was haunted by the screeching voice of Ma Ada's old gypsy friend. The death and disaster she predicted that night had filled Beryl's head with queer, nasty thoughts and a feeling of impending doom. For months she had gone about her life expecting a knock at the door at any moment. She lived in dread of the boy coming to give her a telegram to say that her Tony was dead.

'You can't go round thinking the worst all the time,' Ma Ada said, time and time again. 'What you must do is be prepared for the worst, but you must hope for the best, Beryl. That's the best way of living. You listen to me, lass. I know. I've been through the worst of times and you could learn an awful lot from me.'

Up and down to the attic ran Irene, and luckily she had Megan to help her with the changing of nappies and the feeding and bathing of the babies.

Megan still wasn't like a fond and natural mother to her own baby, but when push came to shove, she could still do all the practical tasks in a passable fashion. She was, however, somewhat impatient and brusque. Irene winced when she saw her trying to dress Johnny in a rush, pushing his tiny, stick-thick arms into his little sleeves and making him wail. Sometimes it was easier just to say, 'Here, let me do it,' and take over from Megan.

Downstairs, the priest, Father Michael, took up residence in the parlour, and some of that contraband booze reappeared from its place of shame under the stairs. 'Might as well be hanged for a sheep,' Sam shrugged wearily in the scullery. 'Is that the right phrase? What I mean is, it's open now, and the damage is done. The Mad Johnsons are gonna have my guts for garters, anyway.'

He was talking to Irene, who tried to explain that she'd attempted to talk to the Johnsons' singer sister and she'd tried to get her to call off the thugs.

'That would never work,' Sam sighed. 'She's as crackers as they are. Hard as nails. Doesn't she work at the shipyard with Beryl? But thanks for trying, Irene.'

Irene nodded dolefully. 'What were you doing with their stolen stuff and keeping it in our house anyway, Sam? I don't understand what you were trying to achieve.'

He shrugged. 'I thought I could make a few extra bob, and that they would never notice it gone. They've got so much, Irene. They're loaded, that lot. I thought I could just sneak away a few bottles to sell, and some ciggies, and they'd never notice.'

'You're crazy.'

'I know.'

She looked at his lopsided grin and his soft, pale hair, and felt her heart going out to him, just as it always did. Just as it always had done, since she'd first met Tom's youngest brother.

'The family's going to be different for ever, with Tony gone,' Sam said, his voice roughening. 'Ma Ada will never be the same again.'

'She'll cope,' Irene said hopefully.

'That rotten priest will be getting his hooks into her again. Filling up her mind with stuff about God's plan, and how God is never wrong. She's vulnerable right now. We don't want her going all religious and devout again.'

'Ah, they're just having a drink,' Irene said. 'That priest can really put it away, can't he?'

They were relieved when Father Michael staggered off into the snowy night, singing something festive to himself, and leaving the poor old mother feeling even more desolate than before he'd begun his counselling.

'That old devil,' was all she'd say. 'But still, at least he's been and said his piece.'

'What did he say?' Irene asked.

'Ah, lots of stuff about . . . about our Tony, which was nice. Remembering when he was a lad and sang in the choir with such a pure voice. And what a handsome, fine fellow he'd grown into. And how everyone here in the Sixteen Streets looked up to him. I was glad that old bugger came round and said all that.'

'Did he get all religious on you, Ma?' asked Sam.

'Why aye, of course he did. But I blocked it out, most of it. God's plan and God's this and that. I just nodded like I was listening and taking it all in, but all the time I was thinking: you're just making up any old codswallop, aren't you? I could suddenly see right through all the old rubbish he was coming out with. Because there is no plan and there is no sense to this. There's just nothing. My boy – my firstborn – is dead and gone for ever, and it's for absolutely no reason at all.' Her face crumpled then, and she set aside her drink and put both hands over her face and her shoulders shook.

'Ah, you'll see him again, in heaven, one day,' Irene found herself saying.

'Aye, heaven,' said Ma Ada, wiping her wet face and fixing those keen, glittering eyes on her daughter-in-law. 'And do you believe in heaven, Irene? I know you've said you don't believe half the Bible you were brought up with. I know you said you've left it mostly behind. But do you believe in a place where we'll really be reunited and live together again for ever?'

Irene stared at her. She wanted to give the earnest old woman an honest answer: she deserved one. Perhaps she really needed to hear that Irene still had faith, deep down. Irene took a long breath and said, 'Well, of course I do. What else is there to believe in? We have to hope for that. You'll see him again, Ada. We all will. Your Tony is your brave, strong lad, and he's going on ahead, first of everyone, to make sure that everything is all right, and ready for you.'

Ma Ada looked at her then with such piercing hope in her eyes that Irene almost felt abashed. Her words had certainly hit their mark, but she felt a fraud for saying them. I'm as much of a fraud as that drunk old priest, she fretted. But at least she had brought Ma Ada some kind of consolation.

Aunty Winnie came by, and her hair was dyed a jet black, as if out of respect. She sat down heavily next to her best friend and simply held her hand. Irene was amazed by her restraint and tact. After she'd slurped the last of her cup of tea, she peered down at the leaves, but didn't seem at all tempted to read anything into them. She guessed – probably correctly – that Ma Ada had next to no interest in her prognostications today.

The radio was switched on, as ever, for news of the war, and those voices rumbled on through the evening. They'd switch the dial and get some soothing music. Anything but the softest, lightest strings would grate on the old woman's nerves.

Christmas music played and Irene and Sam exchanged a look. Megan put their thoughts into words: 'Christ, what kind of a Christmas is it gonna be round here this year?'

Megan retreated upstairs when Cathy Sturrock came over from the Robin Hood, her string bag clinking with dark bottles of stout. Always her remedy in times of shock, illness or upset: the stout flowed freely and she sat with her long-time neighbour and they wept together about the eldest Farley boy.

To all intents and purposes, Cathy was another daughter-in-law these days, if not officially so, and Ma Ada found herself being glad of that fact. Cathy might be a little bit old for a daughter, but she was a good woman, through and through. She was worth ten of Megan, though Ma Ada would never actually say this out loud.

Megan stood listening at the top of the stairs as their stout glasses clinked and they chuntered on, and she knew that Cathy was more at home here than she would ever be, and she seethed because of that thought. Aye, but I've had the baby, haven't I? Megan thought. I'm special because I'm the one who's had a bairn. I'll never let any of them forget that.

Downstairs, Cathy was telling Ma Ada, 'At least you'll have Bob with you at Christmas. I just heard from him this morning. He's getting Christmas leave.'

'Oh, that's wonderful!' the old woman cried, and started weeping again. 'Irene, did you hear? Did you hear that, about Bob?'

Irene came out of the scullery, wiping her hands on the tea cloth. 'I did. It's marvellous news.' But she still felt a pang in her heart, because there had been no similar news about her Tom. He was missing his second Christmas at home in a row, and they wouldn't even let him have compassionate leave. He was too busy up in the skies above Europe, aiming his bombs and fighting back.

Irene tried to bury her bitter disappointment as best she could.

It was a couple of days later that Beryl was able to come downstairs, looking pale as old pease pudding. Megan was frying up tripe and onions she had managed to get from the butcher's, and though it wasn't exactly Irene's favourite dish, she was glad the house was filled with the aroma of cooking, and they were all going to sit down at the table together.

Ma Ada said a simple grace and they tucked in.

Then there came a very tentative knock at the door.

'Who the hell's that, now?' Megan groaned. 'Won't those people ever leave us alone?'

Her mother-in-law glared at her. 'I've been very glad of all our visitors these past few days. That's community, that is. That's the old, proper way of doing things. People paying their respects.'

Megan rolled her eyes. 'I just wish we could get our dinner in peace.'

Irene had darted out into the hall to answer the door and at first she simply didn't recognise the thin woman and the old bearded man who were standing there waiting on Ma Ada's immaculate front doorstep.

The woman explained, 'It's Beryl's parents, Irene. Remember? W-we've come to see her.'

Irene gasped and stared at the two of them. They looked so shaky and unsure of themselves. 'Of course!' This was like seeing ghosts standing there and Irene took a second or two to absorb the shock. The old man removed his battered hat, revealing a bald and flaky scalp and somehow the sight of that made her want to cry. They looked so cold and vulnerable standing there.

'Eeeh, you'd better come inside,' Irene gabbled, ushering them in. She was about to call them 'Mr and Mrs' but she found that she couldn't recall Beryl's maiden name. Hopefully they wouldn't notice her lapse in manners as they stepped anxiously into the dark hall and found their way into the back parlour.

Everyone put down their knives and forks at once at the sight of the visitors in the doorway. 'Beryl,' said Irene. 'Your mam and dad have come all the way across town to see you.'

Ma Ada, Megan and Sam all stared at the nervous-looking visitors and then they all stared at Beryl again, to see her reaction. Beryl was mute with shock as she stood up from her plate of tripe and onions.

'Our bairn,' her mother said, holding up her arms.

'Beryl, hinny,' her dad said simply, and there was such aching sadness in his eyes and in his voice. Irene found herself almost breaking down at the sound of it, let alone Beryl.

'Come here, love,' her mother said, and Beryl went to her, and allowed herself to be cuddled by her mum. It was a cuddle like she couldn't remember having for years.

# Chapter Thirty

Her parents' visit seemed to do Beryl some good. They didn't stay for long, and they simply sat with her for a little while, holding her hands. Ma Ada opened up the best front room for them to sit in. The room was chilly and when she drew open the curtains the shadow of falling snow played upon the Nottingham lace at the window.

They sat together in the same room, that little family, in a way they hadn't for years.

'We must get back,' Beryl's mother said at last, standing up and fastening her coat.

Beryl didn't know how to thank them. Her dad had actually left the house for her. He had braved the outside world and come all this way to see her. He looked smart in his outmoded suit. 'Kidda,' he nodded at her, and smiled shakily. 'Y-you know, you can move back home any time you want. You can always come home again.'

Beryl stared at him, and then at her mother, shocked. 'But . . . the thought hadn't even occurred to me . . . Come home?' She looked at them both in perplexity.

'It's the right thing, love,' her da said. 'Come back to us. It's your place.'

Beryl shook her head. She felt dazed by what they were saying. 'But this is my home,' she burst out.

'Not now, though,' said her ma. 'While you were married, yes. But do you really think you still have a place here, with your Tony gone?'

She stared at them. Even with Tony dead and gone and never to return, it would never occur to Beryl that Number Thirteen Frederick Street would ever cease to be her home. She would always feel at home here, much more so than in the place she had started out from. Yes, Number Thirteen was overcrowded, perhaps, and conditions weren't perfect, but this had been her family home for years now, and she couldn't imagine anything different.

The thought of returning to her parents' place filled her with dread, and she felt that she was showing that all too plainly on her face. Her mam and da looked abashed and upset by her appalled reaction.

'They need me here,' she explained. 'To help with the babies and everything. And living here, I'm near the shipyard for work.'

Her mother nodded briskly, knotting her headscarf. 'Of course. It was just a thought, that's all.'

If I went with them, I would just fall into the old pattern of living like we used to, with me looking after them night and day, thought Beryl. There's no way I could slip back into that. I used to thank my lucky stars I'd escaped from them.

And an uncharitable thought came to her: they just want me back to look after them. They're getting older. Even more helpless. They've come to reclaim me. They want me to run after them for the rest of their days.

She let her parents out the front door, into the street, where the daylight was gone, but the snow was almost luminous under the moon.

'Can you find your way all right?' she asked.

Her mother nodded. 'But I wish we could have street lamps again. I feel like everything's just been so very dark, for so very long.'

Her dad gave her a smiling nod. 'See you later, our lass,' he smiled. 'You just think about what we said. Have a think about where you feel you belong. Because we believe, really, it's with us. That's where you should be now.'

Then, off they went, shuffling in the snow like two much older people than they really were.

When she returned to the back parlour, the others were waiting for her. 'Good of them to come,' Ma Ada said. 'I understand it's hard for them, getting out and about.'

Beryl nodded quietly, and went to help Irene in the kitchen. The rest of that evening she spent downstairs with the family. She was easing back into normal life. She found she could even bear to listen to the war news on the wireless, though she flinched and went into a dream when she heard about ships going down in the sea.

She took out her knitting bag and looked at the scarves and gloves she'd been busy with, just a matter of days before.

Beryl was trying to pick up the threads of so many things.

There was a wake at the Robin Hood to get through and really, Beryl would just as soon not have gone. But Bob was coming home, and Cathy Sturrock wanted to make the effort. These public shows of grief were important, she said. Tony was a significant part of their small community, and people wanted to gather and drink whisky and beer at his passing. Beryl grudgingly let them get on with it.

It was lovely to see Bob again, though. To Beryl he seemed slightly different. He'd lost weight, and was standing differently, somehow. Perhaps it was a result of his no longer having to sleep in a cupboard under the staircase? Or maybe it was his being out from under the yoke of marriage to Megan? Strictly speaking, he was still married to her, and he was currently living in sin with Cathy, but no one mentioned that fact.

Megan simply glared at them from her place by the open fire in the corner of the snug, and Ma Ada explained that sometimes, during wartime, things were different. The usual way of things had to be changed. The old woman had to admit that her son Bob was best off living at the Robin Hood with his fancy woman.

'And I don't care what anyone says about it,' Ma Ada said fiercely. 'Let anyone gossip or find scandal in it, and I'll fight them, I will.'

Both Beryl and Irene merely chuckled at the old lady's fierceness, and Irene in particular was glad that the situation seemed to have sorted itself out. Bob and Cathy were obviously happy, though he was home from the front so very rarely, just the same as Tom.

There was the problematic secret of Johnny's parentage, of course, but those in the know were going to keep that a secret for ever. God help us, Beryl thought. Surely that was a time bomb, waiting to go off?

And then there was the problem of Megan herself, who was bitter and cross so much of the time. She moved around the world of the Sixteen Streets like another four-thousand pound bomb that had been dropped and failed to go off. A blonde bombshell that was biding its time.

That evening at the wake, Bob wept openly for his older brother. He folded his tiny mother up in his arms and wailed aloud where everyone could see. The plain sincerity of his grief was good to witness, Beryl thought. Bob was the most honest and straightforward of all of them. His emotions were always open and honest.

This was why lying to him about his supposed son was so terrible, but the women of Number Thirteen knew that the plain truth would hurt him too much, and it was vital that the secret never be told. It was up to the rest of them to protect Bob from his ex-wife's wickedness.

It was a joy to see Bob holding baby Johnny. The bairn twisted and shrieked and went red in the face. He was disturbed by all the noise and the smoky air in the pub. But both babies were in attendance, having their foreheads anointed with a little dab of spirits, as was traditional. Marlene was her usual saintly, almost silent self. She stared with her luminous, beautiful eyes at all the adults carrying on around her, as if she was entertained and amused by everything they did.

Baby Marlene looked as if she was taking careful note of everything that people did. Maybe that was just Irene's fancy though? Maybe she was too much in thrall to that tiny person who had grown inside her, and who still had one strong hand seemingly clutched about her heart?

Irene remembered when she thought of the baby as a mermaid, swimming around inside her, and how, some time around last Christmas, she had stood in this very pub and anticipated a year's time and Marlene being a tiny person in her own right, amongst them all. This was the way time moved on, and the years rolled forward, she thought. These wonderful changes are the best way of marking that: the lives we bring into being, rather than the deaths we have to endure.

Ma Ada was clearly thinking along similar lines. 'It hurts so much. Death and life in the same breath. When my boys were born and we wetted their heads, there were old people dying at the same time. And younger folk. Boys dying in the Great War, getting killed at the yard or down the pits. And I was selfish, thinking: that's just the way of it. Old life makes way for the new. And that's simply the way of the world. I was selfish and glad because my four strong boys were happy and healthy and alive. But I can see now . . . I can see how cruel life can really be.'

*

Arthur sang for them. It was a rare day that he ventured over to the Sixteen Streets, and he dressed soberly for the occasion in one of his immaculate cast-off suits.

He stood by the old piano as Aunty Madge played with her usual plonking gusto and together they performed some patriotic numbers, then some local fishermen's and mining songs and finally showstoppers from recent movies. They got everyone warbling – at first dismally, and then with more enthusiasm. After a few more drinks there was a note of queasy, bibulous joy in their voices as they launched into music hall numbers which everyone seemed to know.

'Isn't it a bit . . . disrespectful, singing like this?' Irene asked Bella, as they watched the others.

Bella shook her head. 'It's always like this here. It's just the way it is. Didn't people sing at wakes down in Norfolk?'

Irene shook her head. The few funerals she had been aware of as a young girl back down home had always been muted, miserable things. There were certainly no performances of 'My Old Man Said Follow the Van'.

Beryl was singing, too, and that surprised Irene. She couldn't imagine herself joining in like that, if she had been in the same position as her, and it was Tom who was dead. There was something febrile about Beryl's mood that night, however, like she was forcing herself to seem as if she was all right. She was being like this to prove something to everyone else.

Later, as the wake became more drunken and noisy, Irene was talking to her sister-in-law and Beryl was saying: 'I want to go back to work. Next week. I'm sick to death of moping around that house. It's driving me insane.'

'Are you ready yet, though?' Irene asked her.

'I have to go back. It's not about my feelings. There's work that needs doing.' There was something much harder and steelier about Beryl, Irene thought. It was as if Tony's demise had annealed her, covered her in something hard and metallic and shut off from everyone else.

'Have you heard this?' Irene asked Ma Ada, who looked rather tipsy as she joined them at the table in the snug. The old woman had unabashed tears running down her face and her hair, which Irene had earlier set with curlers, was hanging down in damp ribbons from the fierce heat of the public bar. 'She wants to go straight back to work next week.'

Ma Ada studied the young widow beside her and nodded firmly. She picked up one of Beryl's hands and pressed it between her own. The work-hardened flesh of her own palms and fingers wouldn't let her feel how scarred Beryl's were already from working at the shipyard, but Irene had noticed. In these days of crying together and holding her, she had seen how Beryl had ruined her hands. She had seen the little pits and scars in the flesh of her shoulders and chest, too, and had been shocked.

'Eeeh, lass,' Ma Ada was saying, still holding Beryl's hand. 'In some ways, y'knaa . . . it's almost a blessing, that it never happened for you. For you'd be left alone now with an orphan bairn to look after. But I do wish you had given him a babby or two. My son . . . he's gone for ever, and he's not left his mark on the world. Well, he has in some ways, maybe. People will remember him. We'll all remember him. Eeeh, but I do wish with all me heart that you'd given him bairns, our Beryl.'

The girl simply stared at her drunk mother-in-law. She was staring at her in appalled, miserable silence. Suddenly Beryl snatched her hands away from Ada's clutches.

'What?' the old woman asked, befuddled.

Beryl was standing, pushing back her wooden chair. She opened her mouth to say something, but nothing would come. She didn't have any idea what to say to her mother-in-law. Where could she even start?

Irene tried to say the right thing, 'Hush now, Ada. It's not the time or place to bring all that up now.'

Hearing this, the old woman made a curious noise. Halfway between a bark and a whine, and it cut through the chatter of the mourners and drinkers closest to them. It was an animalistic cry of pain. She was a mother robbed of her firstborn, and she wouldn't be told to shut up by anyone.

'So, when is the right time, Irene?' she yelled. 'The right time to say I wish he'd left us with his bairns? That would be a comfort now, wouldn't it? Seeing his eyes looking out of his bairns' faces? Thinking that it wasn't all really a horrible, bloody waste? What's the point of it all, eh? What's the point of any of it, otherwise?'

Irene watched as the old woman crumpled forward and started crying at the table. She was caught between deciding which woman to comfort first. But Beryl solved that quandary for her by hurrying out of the Robin Hood at once.

Beryl couldn't stand it a moment longer. Everyone turning to stare at her. She felt like they were all wondering now why she hadn't been able to give Tony any babies.

Such a natural, easy, important thing, and she had failed. Beryl had failed them all.

# Chapter Thirty-One

The days were endlessly cold and dark and Irene found it harder to get up in the mornings and trudge down the hill to the biscuit factory.

'I hear your Beryl's back at work at the shipyard?' Mavis asked her one morning, less than a week after the wake.

'I think she needs to be working and taking her mind off things,' Irene nodded. 'Though she's not herself, really. She's in a kind of a daze, bless her.'

'Aye, that's what that Lily says,' Mavis said, as her fingers worked deftly at the Penny Packet biscuits. 'Lily Johnson, you know. The singer. I saw her in the street and she was saying Beryl's back on the ships with her.'

Irene remembered someone telling her that Lily Johnson was a welder, too. She shuddered at the memory of Lily's burly brothers, and her recollection of the girl's singing voice. 'So, you were chatting with her quite nicely then?' Irene asked, scorn in her voice. 'I thought everyone round your way was scared of the Mad Johnsons?'

Mavis shrugged. 'It's best to be sociable and nice with them. They rule the roost round our way. And they seem to have backed off a bit from Sam, he says. He's no longer top of their list for beating up.'

Irene shook her head. 'And they told you that, did they?'

Mavis cast her eyes down, working busily. 'No, Sam did himself. He told me. Says that the Johnsons have declared a truce, kind of, with him. On account of his loss, and so he'll do a few more little jobs for them.'

Oh, Sam, Irene thought. Why couldn't he just keep himself away from that common lot? 'You've been seeing a lot of Sam, have you then?' she asked Mavis pointedly.

'Oh, yes,' said her friend breezily. 'I think . . . I think things have changed there, too. Since the night we danced, and when we kissed. I think . . . at last . . . he might be starting to take notice of me. As a woman.'

Irene thought: I'll believe that when I see it. Then she felt a bit mean, and so she smiled at Mavis. That poor mite is going to be let down, she thought sadly.

Just then plump Mary broke into their conversation, shouting across the room, quizzing them about their Christmas plans, and Irene was glad to be spared any more of Mavis's coy intrigue.

As the rest of them talked about carol services, men coming home and meat rations, Irene was wondering vaguely if there could be anything in Mavis's words after all. Could Sam really be noticing her at last?

Irene got to observe Sam with Mavis at close hand, as he took her home to tea at Number Thirteen, bringing Arthur as an extra guest.

Megan pulled faces as soon as she saw there was to be extra at the table. 'I'm not sure we've got enough to go round, to be honest.'

'That's all right, I don't eat very much, anyway,' Mavis said.

'And I'm slimming,' joked Arthur, taking off his raincoat and displaying his rail-thin form.

Sam retrieved a bottle of port from under the stairs and checked that his mother didn't mind having extra faces round the table. 'Why, no,' she said, though he had the feeling she wasn't really bothered either way. Like Beryl, she seemed these days to be off in a world of her own.

'Where is Beryl, by the way?' he asked, pouring them all a warming drink.

'Straight up to her bed,' Irene said. 'She's been at work at the shipyard and it's exhausted her. She reckons she's off her food, too.'

Megan slipped out to feed the babies and sneered at Arthur on her way past.

'That girl absolutely hates me,' Arthur muttered.

'She hates most people,' Sam said.

There was thick pearl barley stew made with a lamb bone. It had stood for two whole days, bubbling and thickening on the hob. There was a hank of freshly baked bread, and once it was all out on the table, Mavis fell upon her modest share as if she had never had a hot meal in all her life. Even Arthur looked keen on his food tonight, just about scraping the glaze off the bowl with his spoon.

'Eeeh, this is smashing, Mrs Farley,' Mavis gasped at Ma Ada. 'You're a wonderful cook!'

Don't go gushing at her and lavishing praise on the old woman, Irene thought. She'll only turn up her nose at you.

But Ma Ada simply spooned up her broth and treated Mavis to her kindliest smile. 'That's very nice of you, pet.'

Perhaps the old mother was mellowing with age, Irene thought?

'It's nearly time to put up the decorations, Mam,' Sam reminded her. 'Do you feel like it this year? After Tony and everything?'

She looked at him, scandalised. 'Of course I do! We can't not put out our few bits of tinsel, and the tree. Why, I feel like that would be letting our Tony down, if we didn't. He used to love Christmas, especially when he was small.'

'Maybe we could get all the old things out tonight and put them up after supper?' Sam suggested.

'I'll help!' Mavis burst out, making Irene jump with her eagerness.

'Well, maybe that's a nice idea,' Ma Ada smiled.

Irene piled up the used dishes and took them into the scullery. She felt discomfited and couldn't quite understand why. It was something about the way Mavis seemed intent on ingratiating herself. She was sitting so close to Sam, and gazing at him openly, as if she wanted everyone to know just how much she adored him.

'Well, I love Christmas,' she heard Arthur saying.

'Will you be singing at posh folk's houses again this year?' Sam asked him.

'Nothing planned yet,' Arthur shrugged. 'But that was a good little earner last year. Mind, there seems to be less money about now.'

'You've got a good voice on you,' Ma Ada told Arthur. 'I've seen you a couple of times now, and you're a funny fella, but you put on a good show, I'll say that much for you.'

Arthur nodded at her graciously. 'Thank you kindly, Mrs Farley.'

For some reason Arthur had Lucky the hairless cat sitting on his skinny lap as he sat back and sipped his port. Without anyone even noticing it, the creature had migrated from Ma Ada to the visitor.

'Maybe later we could sing some carols,' Arthur said. 'Old-fashioned ones. Would you like that?'

Ma Ada nodded tearfully. 'Aye, I think I would.'

Irene watched them sitting peacefully in the dim glow of the range, with just a lamp burning on the table and thought: wonders would never cease. She'd never imagine her mother-in-law getting on with Arthur, and yet here they were, sitting like this, after sharing their tea and talking about singing.

'Arthur's gonna sing to the troops in the new year,' his sister suddenly blurted out.

'What's that? Are you leaving us then?' Ma Ada wanted to know.

'Er . . . it's true. I'm off. Well, it's about time,' Arthur said diffidently. 'I'm being posted overseas. It turns out that they'll have me after all, so long as I can sing a few Vera Lynn songs and do a turn every night.'

'ENSA?' Sam asked, sounding surprised. 'You're joining ENSA?'

Ma Ada nodded approvingly. 'I think it's good that you're putting your talents to good use, young man. You'll be doing your bit, in the best way you know how.'

'They'll probably send me to Burma and I'll get jungle fever,' Arthur grinned. 'But heigh-ho. Maybe I'll get a tan.'

'You bloody fool,' Sam muttered.

'I think he's so brave,' Mavis said.

'I think he's mad,' Sam told her.

'Are you sure about this, Arthur?' Irene asked him.

'I've done it now. I have to do my bit, Irene. This is the best thing I can do. And it'll be wonderful, you'll see. I'll come back a great big star, I promise you!'

Something in the conversation galvanised Ma Ada into action, and suddenly she was on her feet. 'Ha'way then, let's get those boxes of decorations out. Megan will help us when she finishes with the bairns. We'll decorate the parlour and make it look all bonny. Maybe it'll make Beryl feel better when she comes downstairs at last.'

Mavis jumped up to help, and Irene suddenly thought, what's she going to do with her brother away? She asked her straight out: 'Won't you be lonely and worried in that house of yours without Arthur?'

'Bella's still there, isn't she?' Mavis smiled. 'She's good company. I won't be lonely.'

'Aye, but she won't be there for ever,' Irene said, as they set out the worn boxes of trinkets and tinsel on the cleared table. 'She'll be looking for somewhere of her own to live, you know she will.'

Mavis shrugged. 'The thing is, you never know what's just around the corner, do you? You never know what big changes are coming.' She was being coy again, and casting glances in Sam's direction. He was busy taking glass ornaments out of the ancient tissue paper. 'I'll be all right, Irene,' Mavis said. Something in her tone made Irene think the pale girl was planning something.

Later, in the dark and freezing outside lav, Irene overheard Arthur and Sam having a smoke together in the backyard.

Evidently neither of them realised she was in there, sitting in the dark, trying not to make a noise. They were leaning right against the privy wall and talking in low, conspiratorial voices. Their cigarette smoke came wafting in, threatening to make her cough. She held her breath and listened hard.

'You're crazy, going away and everything,' Sam told him.

'I feel like I have to,' Arthur said, and there was something so dull and tired-sounding in his voice, Irene barely recognised it.

'Are you going because of me and Mavis?' Sam asked.

'Ha! You think a lot of yourself, don't you?' Arthur laughed.

'You know what I mean.'

There was a pause and, inside the brick-walled lav, Irene was straining her ears and leaning so far forward that she almost fell off the wooden seat. That would have been something, if there'd been a clatter and they'd found her, dropping off the lav!

'Of course it's to do with you and Mavis,' Arthur said quietly.

'But, Arthur, man . . .' Sam began.

'Don't let's go into it all now,' Arthur said. 'You don't want to talk about any of it. You made that clear ages and ages ago.'

'Aww, man,' Sam said.

'Your life is complicated enough,' Arthur told him. 'What with all your nefarious criminal activities and your black market goods, and your knocking about with all those rough types. Not to mention . . . your secret bairn.'

'Shut up, man,' Sam said. 'You're not meant to know about that.'

'Aye,' sighed Arthur, and Irene could hear him blowing out a long plume of cigarette smoke, just like Bette Davis would. She could even picture the sophisticated, quizzical expression he'd be wearing right now. 'There are lots of things I'm not meant to know about, aren't there? Secrets that we share, Sam Farley, eh?'

A tricky, loaded silence followed for a few seconds. 'And they'll stay secrets, too,' Sam said, in a strained, hard voice that Irene had never heard him use before.

'Happen they will,' Arthur replied in a sing-song voice. 'Happen they won't. But you just remember that I know the truth of you, Sam. Never forget that. You can never lie to me. I know who you really are, deep down, don't I?'

'Do you think so, Arthur?' Sam said. 'Nah, man. You might have known me when we were both lads. When we were bairns of sixteen, seventeen. But that's ages ago now. People don't stay the same. Time doesn't stand still.'

'But people do stay the same,' Arthur told him. 'There's a deep down truth to everyone. A secret self. And that never alters, believe me. Everything else is just put on and play-acting.'

'I've changed,' Sam said. 'I'm not the same lad you knew.'

Arthur smoked quietly and thoughtfully. 'Well, I wish you were.'

Sam said, uncomfortably: 'Look, we'd best get back in. You were gonna sing to me mam, weren't you?'

'I like your mam,' Arthur said. 'She's tough on the outside and she's tough all the way through, but sweet as well. Like a pineapple. Do you remember when Bella's dad Tonio had a pineapple that time, at Franchino's? And he cut it into chunks and all us kids tried a bit?'

Sam laughed. 'You do remember funny things, Arthur.'

'I remember everything.' Arthur's voice was hoarse.

'Aye, I do, as well, but the past is gone.' Sam scraped his tab end on the rough paving stone. 'Hey, fancy saying that me mam is like a pineapple! She'll not be flattered by that.'

Arthur chuckled and they were quiet for a moment. Irene started thinking they had gone back inside, and that the coast was clear. She almost started to move when she heard Arthur say, 'You just watch out for my sister. If you hurt her, I'll . . . Well, I don't know what I'll do. But you mustn't hurt her.'

Sam sighed happily. 'I'm going to marry her, Arthur. I'm going to make her mine.'

'I thought so,' Arthur said. 'I could see that coming next.'

'And do you mind?'

'You want my blessing?' Arthur laughed.

'Aye, maybe.'

'Oh, don't even ask me, Sam,' said Arthur. 'Just do what you want to do. You always do, anyway.'

'We'll be, like, family, won't we?' Sam said. 'Me and you, we'll be brothers then?'

Arthur coughed, and even Irene – behind that wall – could tell that he was covering up a sob. 'I thought we already were, lad.'

And then they went back indoors to help with the Christmas decorations.

Irene was left sitting alone in the cold and dark, feeling a shiver go right through her.

Then she remembered something Megan had once told her about the privy in winter: 'Don't sit too long. You'll get rats coming up the pipe to bite you on your bum.'

# Chapter Thirty-Two

'Hey, you. Hinny, you! Yes, I'm talking to you!'

The woman was unrecognisable at first to Beryl. Both of them were wearing their overalls, with sleeves rolled and pinned up, and masks over their faces. They were both on the rickety wooden platform deep within the bowels of the dry-docked ship, supposedly working together, but Beryl was away with the fairies, her mind not properly on the job at all.

Her workmate removed her welding mask and grinned at her. 'I'm talking to you! I'm Lily Johnson – you're Beryl, aren't you?'

Beryl nodded dumbly. She was half aware of Lily as the other female welder at the shipyard, but she'd never really spoken to her before. She had a vague consciousness of her as belonging to the rough family that had some kind of a hold over their Sam, but that was as far as it went. 'What do you want?' Beryl asked brusquely, not even lifting her mask.

'I came over to see that you were okay,' Lily said, her smile dropping a little. She was trying her best to be friendly, but was feeling rebuffed.

Beryl studied the short girl. Her dark hair was up in curlers and bound in a colourful cotton turban. Her face was scrubbed of make-up and her expression was earnest. She was an outgoing, forthright kind of person. 'Oh, I'm fine,' Beryl said shortly. 'I just want to get on with my work.'

Lily nodded. 'You're the one who's lost her man, aren't you?'

Beryl bit her lip. 'Aye, I am.'

'Back at work early. Your mind can't be on your job.'

The taller girl shrugged. 'I can do this in my sleep by now. I just need stuff to do. To stop my mind from going round and round.'

Lily could understand that. She was a practical girl at heart, too. All her life, she'd had to be practical, growing up in an area as rough as she had, amongst all the people and the colourful characters she had known. Hers had been a hand-to-mouth existence, and she had scraped through by sheer force of personality. She was brash as a result, and not to everyone's taste, but Beryl found herself glad that Lily seemed to be looking out for her.

It was a frozen morning in the docks. The very coldest of the winter so far. Beryl found that the bleakness of the pre-dawn light suited her mood perfectly, because she felt drear and hopeless and cold right through to her bones. She found herself asking Lily Johnson: 'Have you got a fella?'

'Aye, just lately, I've started seeing a lad. The butcher's son. From the butcher's on Fowler Street. Alan, he's called.'

Beryl nodded. 'I know him! Big lugs and a nice smile.'

'That's him,' Lily nodded. 'He's soft-hearted. Not the type I pictured myself going with. Not really my kind of man at all.'

'How old is he? He's not even old enough to fight yet, is he?'

'He's not quite seventeen. Soon he'll go.'

'Cradle-snatcher!' Beryl smiled.

'I'm only eighteen, it's not that much older,' Lily said, sounding defensive. 'He's gonna join the Royal Navy.'

'Oh, he is, is he?' Beryl said, and the warmth that had been in her voice drained out of it again. 'Well, just you tell him

. . . tell him . . . to be careful.' But there was nothing else Beryl could advise. What did she even know about the fate her husband had suffered at sea? She had tried to picture it again and again. Her mind had been plagued by the invented pictures for days. All she could think about were torpedoes and explosions, and water rushing in and fiery, horrible deaths. She wanted to tell Lily Johnson to warn her young boyfriend not to bother. Did being a butcher's lad count as a reserved occupation? She wasn't sure. Beryl felt like telling her: Don't let him go to sea. Whatever you do, just don't let him go.

But Beryl minded her own business. 'We'd better get back to work.'

The rest of that morning they worked together on the platform, with the younger girl keeping an eye on Beryl. Beryl tried not to dither and waver with her tools, but her mind kept straying, and that was the worst thing to do with heavy welding equipment. But she loved the fierceness of the torch and the noise it made. 'Here, let me,' Lily told her, firmly, and stepped in to take over.

The hooter sounded for their break and they sat together, chewing on their meagre lunch of bread and dripping. Lily had a hank of corned beef wrapped in greaseproof paper, which she gladly shared with her new friend. 'Look, here's the best thing about knocking around with the butcher's boy!' she laughed.

The corned beef was delicious. Salty and tangy, and Beryl felt it fortifying her straight away, like it was lending immediate strength to her limbs.

Beryl decided to chance her arm. 'You know, your brothers have been making rotten trouble for my family,' she said.

'I know,' Lily nodded. 'Your Irene nobbled me at the dance and tried to talk to me about it, asked me to warn them off. But there's only so much they'll listen to me. They're a law unto themselves, my lads.'

'Don't let them hurt our Sam, though,' said Beryl. 'He's a good lad. He doesn't mean anyone any harm.'

'I'll do me best,' Lily promised, and she smiled at Beryl. Beryl was amazed to find that she was getting along with the tough girl. She remembered what Irene had said about her at the Albert Hall dance, and how Lily had sung with the band, up on the stage. 'What a rotten voice she's got!' Irene had crowed. 'And what a bloomin' nerve she's got, getting up in front of everyone and warbling down the speaker!'

This afternoon, as they returned to work inside the great hollow hull of the ship, Lily sang out as loudly she could. She relished the vast echoes as she stood high above the dry hold. 'The White Cliffs of Dover', 'Sing as We Go' . . . She kept running through her repertoire and her voice was so booming and huge that Beryl could hardly believe it was coming from such a tiny frame.

'Irene said your singing was bloody awful,' Beryl said. 'It sounds pretty good to me.'

The other girl laughed. 'Is that what she said, the cheeky cow?' And it was just like water off a duck's back. She wasn't offended or put off at all. She just carried on singing, clearly loving the way her voice bounced all around the metal walls. Then she started doing her other favourite thing: tale-spinning.

'Let me tell you how my brothers started off on all their wheeling and dealing, and how they got their first fortune,' Lily said, and started relating an elaborate tale about their old grandma, who had brought them all up, and who had hidden a cash fortune inside her wardrobe. 'And she never let on it was there, not while she was alive. It was only after she died that we found all this money stashed away – after she'd brought us all up in dire poverty.'

Beryl was only half-listening, wielding her torch and fixing her gaze on the molten rivulets of metal as she ran the flame down the dark seams in the wall. Lily's strong voice carried even over all the noise, and Beryl found it oddly soothing, to be distracted by the girl's nonsense tales.

'It's not nonsense!' Lily laughed. 'It's family legend this, for us lot. I was only a little girl at the time, but I remember it. I remember going with my brothers to the totter's yard with all my granny's stuff, as they tried to get a bob or two for it. Soon as she was dead they cleared the house of all her old Victorian furniture, but it wasn't worth much. Some of it they couldn't even sell for firewood. Like her old wardrobe, which they had to take to the dump. It was like her coffin that they were going to chuck off the highest heap of rubbish, just for the fun of it: this huge dark wardrobe that had stood in her bedroom for all her life, reeking of mothballs. And all seven of my brothers carried it up to the top of the hill and then they chucked it off the top.'

'And what happened?' Beryl asked.

'Well, when it hit the bottom it smashed into smithereens, but when it did, that's when they realised it had a false back on it, and that's where she'd hidden all her fortune. It was like this great big green cloud of money went up into the sky. We all stood staring at it like it was magic. Then it was like, "Quick! Quick! Grab all of the notes before they fly away!"' Lily laughed and shook her head, remembering the crazy, frantic scene, and all her brothers dashing about the dump, jumping up and grabbing and stuffing their shirts and trousers full of money. Lily had laughed so hard at their antics she had been no help to them at all. 'And so that's how they made their first fortune and set themselves up in business.'

'I don't believe a word of it,' Beryl protested.

'Every word is true!' Lily grinned at her.

*

They worked side by side like this for days on end in the freezing cold of those weeks at the end of the year. Lily distracted her new friend by regaling her with tales of her disreputable brothers and the trouble they all got themselves into. Then she told Beryl more about herself, and her own ambitions to become a proper, professional singer, and how she was really serious about it.

'Oh, I know me voice isn't perfect, and I've never had any proper lessons or anything, but I can carry a tune well enough. And the main thing, you see, is personality, Beryl. It's charisma. That's what audiences respond to. And that's what I've got bags of, isn't it?'

Beryl had to agree with her. The smaller girl had masses of self-confidence, and it was easy to warm to her. Gradually, bit by bit, Beryl found herself making a new friend.

'Our lot at home will go crackers, when they find out I've become pally with one of the Mad Johnsons,' Beryl said.

'Ah, families can be too tribal,' said Lily wisely. 'That's the root of half the bother in this world. People being tribal and sticking with what they know and looking at everyone else like they're the enemy. We're all on the same side, really, aren't we?'

'Aye, hinny, I guess we are,' Beryl grinned back at her. It felt strange, smiling warmly at someone, and really meaning it. It was the first time she'd smiled like that since she'd received the news about Tony. Smiling and relaxing for a moment suddenly felt like a betrayal of him. Oh, but come on, man, she told herself. What are you going to do? Never smile again?

Just then the hooter sounded and Beryl set about mechanically extricating herself from her equipment. Her thoughts were so tangled up in her constantly tumbling mixed feelings that she didn't notice that her boot was caught up in the cabling.

'Hey, Beryl, man!' Lily called out, just as it was too late. Beryl twisted and fell. Luckily she didn't fall far, and it was onto the wooden platform, rather than the unforgiving iron of the hull far below, but she fell hard, with her left arm trapped underneath her. Both girls heard the crack of bone like it was a gunshot, and both felt sick to their stomachs at the sound of it.

Beryl didn't make a squeak of noise. She was too taken up with the pain that came flooding into her whole body on a great tidal wave. She was trapped face down feeling foolish and helpless, with Lily standing over her.

The singer's voice went booming out, calling for help. She was like a foghorn, magnified hugely inside the ship's hull, crying out, 'Help! Help! This silly cow's gone and fallen, and I think she's broken her bloody arm!'

Beryl closed her eyes and bit her lip hard, to stop herself from crying.

'I told you!' Lily yelled at her. 'I told you your mind wasn't properly on the job! I knew you'd have an accident!'

And then others came running to help, and Beryl found herself glad of her gobby, common, pushy new friend.

# Chapter Thirty-Three

'Eeeh, isn't it awful?' Mavis was twittering at their workbench. 'Isn't it awful about your Beryl?'

Irene had to agree. 'Yes, she was only back at work a couple of days, and then she went and had her accident. She's at home now, and she can't even knit. She can't do anything until her arm heals.'

The other girls in the Penny Packets room were listening in, concerned to hear about their former colleague. 'I knew it was a mistake, her working at the shipyard,' Effie piped up. 'Men's work, indeed.'

Plump Mary dismissed her. 'Someone's got to do it, with the men away.'

'It's too much for women.' Effie pursed her lips. 'This proves it. It's too hard.'

'Rubbish,' Irene spoke up. 'Beryl was doing fine up till then. It was just a daft accident. It could have happened to anyone, man or woman.'

Mavis was avid with speculation and gossip. 'Is it true it was that Lily Johnson who pushed her? Lily Johnson tried to kill her, didn't she?'

'Oh, don't be daft, Mavis,' Irene frowned. 'According to Beryl, Lily was very good to her. If it wasn't for her, she'd have been lying there in the cold by herself for ages with a broken arm.'

'Aye, that's what she says,' muttered Mavis darkly. 'But that Lily has probably warned her. She's probably threatened her not to tell anyone the truth.'

Irene rolled her eyes. 'You'll cause bother with your gossiping one of these days, Mavis Kendricks.'

Work was put on pause for a moment then, as there was a rare visit from the factory owner, Mr Wight. The double doors flew open and Mrs Clarke came sailing in, ahead of the diminutive, tweedy little man with the large ears and the bald head. He beamed at them all affably, and Irene remembered what she and Beryl always said about the old man being like the Wizard of Oz, and all the biscuit factory girls being his subjects inside the Emerald Palace.

'I'm bringing round a little Christmas box for all our diligent workers,' he announced. 'To wish you all the very happiest of the season.'

As Mrs Clarke rolled forward a trolley on which were piled small tins, Irene found herself surprised by the idea of it being Christmas. Somehow it had slipped past her, the idea that she should be feeling some kind of festive spirit at this point. Too much had been going on at Number Thirteen and, even though they had the house decorated and their plans made, it all seemed rather sudden to her.

'Thank you, sir,' she said to Mr Wight as he presented her with a small tin of biscuits. The front was printed with their factory logo and a picture of a child that was featured on all the factory's adverts. Possibly Irene had packed this very tin herself, and now it was coming back to her. 'It's very kind of you.'

The old man beamed genially, and Irene remembered how, when she had once paid a visit to his office at the top of the factory, he had seemed to have taken a shine to her. 'It's our young lass from Norfolk, isn't it?' he asked her, tentatively. 'This will be your second Christmas amongst us northern folk, will it?'

Irene nodded. 'Yes, sir.'

'And is your husband getting back for Christmas this year? Ah, no? Well, never mind, my dear. I'm sure he'll be thinking of you.' Mr Wight blushed then, as if he felt he had said something clumsy and foolish. Irene smiled at him as he passed on, handing out biscuits to the other girls. 'Next year, perhaps, the war will be over!' he was telling them all. 'Next Christmas, perhaps all the lads will be back, my sons among them, and our lives will all be returned to normal. What about that, eh? Won't that be lovely? Imagine that!'

Mavis leant in close to Irene and whispered. 'Daft old fool, isn't he?'

Irene nudged her. 'I think he's a lovely old gent.'

'Should have retired years ago, he's past it,' Mavis said. 'He's only keeping on because all his sons are in the army. He's on his last legs, look.'

They watched Mrs Clarke help the old factory owner out of the room, pushing the trolley behind him. 'Return to your work, ladies! No gossiping, and no eating your Christmas biscuits!' the supervisor thundered at them.

Irene said: 'Mavis, I've never heard you say anything as unkind as that before! That poor old fella's just given you your Christmas box!'

Mavis almost looked ashamed. 'I'm sorry. I know it's not like me. I'm just in a funny, awful mood.'

'What is it?' Irene asked, as the two of them started up packing the biscuits again.

'Oh, I can't hold the secret in any longer. I'll burst if I don't tell someone.'

Irene felt alarmed. 'Mavis, what's happened?'

'It's Arthur. He's gone,' Mavis said, tremulously. 'Just like he said he would. Just like he threatened to do. All of a sudden, and there was nothing I could say. He packed one bag and then he was gone, on the train, and that was it. I've no idea where exactly he's reported to, or where they'll take him next, or when – if ever – he'll be back. He barely said a proper goodbye to either me or Bella, and then he was off. My brother has gone!'

'Oh!' Irene gasped. 'Well, that was sudden.'

'We were planning everything we were going to do at Christmas,' Mavis said tearfully. 'He was going to sing at a few big houses in Sunderland and Newcastle and get a bit of money. I've got a rabbit I was going to make into a pie . . . but he's gone! He's upped and gone and left us. Gone to sing for the soldiers!'

Shaking her head and sighing, Irene reflected that Arthur had always been a bit of a law unto himself. 'It's going to be so strange for you and Bella without him.'

'You're telling me!' Mavis gasped. 'He's been warning me for ages that it would come to this one day, and that one day he would have to leave. Whether it was the war or his going off to become a star, it would have to happen one way or another.'

Irene cast a glance at Mavis, remembering what she'd overheard from the outside privy the other night. Had Sam really meant that he intended to propose to Mavis, just like he'd told Arthur he would? Could it be that he'd already asked her to marry him? Had Mavis accepted him and now she was keeping a lid on it for some reason? Surely not! Never in the world! If Mavis had got her heart's desire, and Sam had popped the question, then she'd have been brimming with excitement and delight. There was absolutely no way she'd have been able to keep her trap shut.

No, Sam mustn't have asked her yet. Perhaps he'd gone off the idea. Perhaps he'd only ever said it to put the wind up Arthur.

Irene didn't know. Oh, why couldn't folk be more straight-forward, she wondered? Why didn't they just do the things they said they were going to do, and why didn't they do things right? Why were they forever playing games and making life complicated? Irene prided herself on being a straightforward, honest kind of person. Her Tom was the same. There was no messing on or acting up with either her or Tom. But everyone else seemed to love surrounding themselves in dramas!

'There's nothing you want to tell me, pet, is there?' she asked Mavis, just in case the girl was holding back secrets.

'I don't think so, Irene,' Mavis frowned. 'I tell you every-thing, don't I? Everyone always tells you everything, Irene. You seem to get to know everyone's secrets!' She grinned at Irene's bemused expression. 'Ah, don't look hurt, hinny! It's a compliment. I think it means you're important. People tell you things because they trust you. You're at the centre, at the heart of everyone I know. Anyway, do you want to come to our house on Christmas Day and share our rabbit pie?'

Irene shook her head. 'I can't leave Ma Ada – she'd be cross. I'll have to do most of the work at Number Thirteen. Beryl's going to be hopeless at everything but pulling crackers, what with her arm in that cast. No, I'll tell you what! Why don't you and Bella come to Frederick Street for Christmas Day? I insist. No one will mind.'

'Ooh!' Mavis cried out in delight.

When they left the factory at twilight there seemed to be a kerfuffle of some kind developing right outside the tall iron gates.

'What's going on? I can't see!' Mavis was shorter than everyone, and as the crowd backed up she couldn't even see past the headscarves of the women in front. Everyone was muttering furiously about the hold-up, and great clouds of cigarette smoke were fogging the frozen air.

'It's a fight! There's a fight on!' Plump Mary gasped excitedly, clutching her biscuit tin and her bait box to her chest. 'Eeeh, it's two lasses scrappin' in the streets! What a disgrace! I wish I could see better.'

'A fight!' Mavis cooed, angling for a better view of her own. 'Who is it, Irene? Can you see?'

'Err, no,' Irene frowned. 'And I'm sure I don't care, either. Fancy grown women having a fight in the street. What a disgrace! With all the men fighting for King and Country abroad.'

'Eeeh! It's your Megan!' Mavis broke in, shrill with glee. 'I can see now, can you? Look, that's your Megan. The other one's gone and ripped her headscarf off and you can see all that peroxided hair of hers spilling out of her curlers!'

Irene started pushing her way through the excited, blood-hungry crowd and cried out in dismay when she saw that Mavis was right. 'Megan! Megan – what the devil are you doing?'

But over the noise of the jostling crowd Megan couldn't hear a word Irene was saying. She had her arms locked around the throat of her opponent, a smaller woman whose face Irene couldn't make out. The two of them were tussling on a small patch of the cobbled road, ringed around by raucous spectators.

'Megan's supposed to be at home, minding the babies!' Irene yelled in outrage. 'Who's she fighting?'

Mavis had a keener eye. 'It's that Lily Johnson! She's got her in a headlock, and she's . . . pummelling her!'

Irene groaned. That surely meant there was bound to be more bother between the Farleys and the Johnsons, when Lily's brothers got to hear about what was happening outside Wight's factory gates. 'Megan must have waylaid her as she was leaving the docks,' Irene said. 'What's she doing, though? Why's she attacking her?'

The crowd of women roared its approval then, as Lily suddenly gained the upper hand, wrenching herself out of her opponent's grasp, and raking her face with her nails. She gave Megan an almighty shove, and she landed heavily on the frozen road. Lily gave her a hefty kick in the guts and Megan groaned. Lily then shouted something so rude that it made Irene and several other women gasp.

There was a disappointed groan then, as Mrs Clarke came weighing through the crowd, with her massive chest thrust forward like a battering ram. Her voice roared out with great authority: 'How dare you stand around gawping! How dare employees of Wight's stand there staring at common harlots brawling in the road!'

The crowd of biscuit factory girls parted like the Red Sea before Mrs Clarke, and soon the supervisor was gazing down with great scorn at the two combatants. 'Neither of you are employees of this factory,' she bellowed. 'Though you were, until lately, Megan Farley.'

Megan hung her head, and all her blonde tresses hung down in mucky tendrils around her face. She was clutching her belly where she'd been kicked, and her enemy simply stared back defiantly at Mrs Clarke.

'You can shut your cakehole, you fat old witch!' Lily Johnson snapped. 'You've got no power over me. You think you can parade around, telling everyone what to do, but you're just a nasty old cowbag, do you hear me? You can't tell me what to do! You can't tell me bloody nowt!'

Mrs Clarke looked apoplectic. 'I can call the police, that's what I can do!'

'I've been wrongly accused!' Lily snarled. 'Let's see what the polis will have to say about that! This silly bitch, Megan Farley, she's accused me! She's slandered me in the street! And I won't put up with it. I won't! She's going around saying things about me, and I'll stick up for myself. Especially against the likes of her!'

'Megan?' Mrs Clarke asked the blonde girl. 'Is this true? Have you been telling tales?'

Megan simply glowered sulkily.

'She's been saying I broke her bloody sister-in-law's arm!' cried Lily. 'She's telling everyone I pushed the daft bitch over at the shipyard. But I never did! I was the one who saved her. I helped her. I was the one who went out of my way to look after her!'

Such was the indignation in Lily Johnson's face that Irene found that she believed her at once. And besides, Beryl had told them all the story at home, about how Lily Johnson had been good to her. She had been surprisingly nice to Beryl. So how come Megan seemed to be dead set against her?

'I don't believe a word of it,' Megan sneered. 'You Johnsons are all completely crazy. You're a nasty lot! And you, Lily Johnson, haven't heard the last of this!'

Lily shook her head and started fiddling around in her bag for her cigarettes. 'I think you're the crazy one, love. I pity your bloody family, living under a roof with you.'

The crowd was muttering and starting to dissipate now that it was clear that the actual scrapping was over. Mrs Clarke clapped her hands loudly like a school mistress in the playground. 'Everyone go home at once! There's nothing more to see here!'

Irene surged forward through the crowd, with Mavis tagging along after her. 'Eeeh, we should see how your Megan is. Lily really got the better of her, didn't she?'

Mavis was right, and Irene shuddered at the thought. It was when she was furious and frustrated that Megan was at her most dangerous, as she knew from past experience.

# Chapter Thirty-Four

It was Christmas Eve and the plan was to attend the early evening service at St Jude's. Ma Ada counted it as a triumph that, this year, almost all of the family were planning to come with her. In recent times she had been reduced to going alone. 'Maybe this year we all have more to pray for?' she mused aloud, pulling on her thickest coat and boots and clamping down her hat. She eyed Megan thoughtfully. 'Or more to repent for, hmm?'

Bella and Mavis had traipsed across town for the evening, dressed up in their finest clothes and bringing with them small gifts to put under the tree, and a block of Franchino's ice cream. 'It's still deep frozen,' explained Bella. 'If we stand it in the yard, perhaps it'll stay that way till we get back from church.'

Lucky was given strict instructions to guard the ice cream, but gave no indication of following a word they said to him.

Irene took a look around the cosy parlour, bedecked in festive garb, and said a tiny, silent prayer to herself before they set off. If only Tom were here with them. But she knew she shouldn't complain about his being away, certainly not in front of Beryl, whose own Farley boy was never going to be coming back.

It was enough to know that Tom was relatively safe, and that would simply have to do. Irene's job was to remain cheerful and supportive this Christmas, to be at the heart and soul of the Farley family, and to make sure the festivities – such as they were – all went off okay, for the sake of the rest of the family. Ma Ada was depending on her.

'Are you sure Beryl will be all right looking after the babies?' Sam asked, looking perturbed.

Irene nodded. 'She can do it with one arm tied behind her back, which is lucky, because that's what she's essentially got, with that heavy cast on.'

'She's still not herself,' Sam worried.

'I was hoping Megan would stay with her while we were at church,' Irene said. 'But for some reason she wants to come along with us.'

'Her with her black eye and scratches and her thick lip!' Sam chuckled. 'She's got a lot to pray for.'

'Hmm,' said Irene, who thought the same of Sam, frankly. 'Maybe I should dash upstairs and check on the bairns and Beryl again, and then we can go.'

'Eeeh, there's more cards come through the door!' Mavis announced breathlessly, carrying a sheaf of them into the parlour. She was excited and much less pale than usual. Irene could see that, even with her brother gone, Mavis was looking forward to this Christmas. She had managed to get her feet under the table at the Farleys, and her eyes were sparkling with glee.

'More cards!' Bella smiled. 'You've not got the space for them in here! You've got so many.'

Ma Ada explained, 'I put all the old ones back up again each year, so there's more and more, over time. It's a way of remembering everyone, and keeping them all alive.'

Bella nodded, realising that's why some of the old lacy cards looked a bit yellow and old-fashioned.

'Megan, this one's for you, personally,' Mavis said, waving the envelope around. 'Hey, where's she gone?'

Megan had nipped back up to the attic, where Beryl was sitting with both babies. Her broken arm lay like a dead weight on her lap, and she had Johnny balanced on top of it, while Marlene was bundled up in blankets beside her on the bed.

There was something very peaceful about the image of the three of them, sitting contentedly on the big bed in the attic, and somehow this got under Megan's skin. Something about Beryl's expression of tired, accepting placidness really irked her.

'Well, I hope you'll enjoy your evening looking after the brats,' Megan quipped from the doorway. 'Better you than me!'

Beryl smiled wanly. 'We're all quite happy here. You go off to church. We'll be fine.'

Megan nodded. 'Well, Beryl. I must say, you've come a long way. Time was, you'd have run a mile from being asked to look after bairns. Time was, you'd have done anything but be left like this.'

Beryl sighed and cuddled Johnny closer. 'Aye, well. Things change. Things have to change. We're all learning that. Perhaps I've managed to get over . . . what happened before. It was a long time ago, after all.'

'I hope so,' Megan said, and her voice sounded like it was full of care and tenderness. Then she spoilt it by adding, 'Because that's my precious son I'm trusting you with. I don't want anything happening to him.'

Beryl gasped. 'It won't!'

'That's good, then,' Megan said. 'I think you're to be trusted. I think what happened in your past, it was just a horrible accident. I don't think you should be blamed. Everyone deserves another chance.'

There was something cloying about Megan's voice. She was being smarmy and sickly nice. Beryl stared at her and wondered: is she taunting me? Why would she be doing that?

'I-I told you what happened when I was a bairn,' Beryl said. 'I told you my brother's story. You know what happened, and how I blamed myself, for all those years.'

'Aye, you did, Beryl,' Megan said, absently touching her smarting lips and black eye with her fingertips and wincing. 'And I believed you. When most other people would think you aren't ever to be trusted with the care of bairns again, I believed you. And I trust you now, with the most precious thing that belongs to me.'

Megan came forward and kissed her son on his forehead. Beryl felt swamped by her perfume.

'We'll be fine here,' Beryl said dully, feeling a horrible darkness rising up to swallow her. Megan had knowingly raked up these feelings for her. Why would she do such a thing? 'I do wish you hadn't mentioned Fred tonight, though.'

'Ah well,' said Megan lightly, retreating out of the attic. 'I think perhaps you needed reminding, Beryl. You need reminding who your true family and friends are. The ones who really trust you and love you. The likes of me, for example. Who you told your awful secret to and who still stands by you. Not these other friends of yours, these common guttersnipes like Lily Johnson. She'd never be as good to you as I've been, would she? So just you think on, hinny. Just think on. Now, we'll see you later, after church and the pub.'

'Look, you've had a card through the door!' Mavis called out.

'What are you squawking about?' Megan frowned, hurrying down the stairs and glaring at Mavis. Even with her battered eye and her thick lip, she still managed to look more glamorous than almost everyone present, save Bella.

'This is for you!' Mavis thrust the envelope into Megan's hand. It didn't feel thick enough to contain a card and, sure enough, she found that it held a single flimsy sheet of paper. 'Oh, it's some kind of a note,' she said, and pulled a face. Childish handwriting, spidering across the page. 'It's a death threat!'

'What? At Christmas?' gasped Ma Ada, clutching her bag furiously. 'Who the devil from?'

'It doesn't say,' sighed Megan. 'But it doesn't take a genius to work out who sent it.'

'That Lily Johnson!' Mavis burst out. 'I bet it's her!' She reached out to see the offending article, and Megan let her have it, like it meant nothing to her. Mavis clapped a mittened hand over her mouth in shock and read aloud: 'You have had it, lady! You are doomed! How dare you make a show of me in public! Me and my brothers will get you. And not just you, either. All the Farleys – all you buggers – we're gonna get you all!'

'Christ,' said Megan, putting a cigarette between her sore lips and lighting it.

'Don't you dare say "Christ" like that just before we go to church!' shouted Ma Ada.

Sam groaned. 'I thought they'd backed off a bit. But you've gone and made them worse, Megan.'

'Oh, sod off, Sam,' she snapped at him, and blew smoke in his face.

Mavis was quivering with fear, as if the infamous Johnsons were going to come crashing into the parlour at any moment. 'What are you going to do?'

Irene decided that someone had to be no-nonsense about this. Mavis's hysteria was infectious. 'It's just a lot of rubbish. That girl wants to put the wind up Megan. It doesn't mean anything at all. These people are just full of hot air and bravado. They like to scare people, that's all.'

Everyone looked at her, and Irene was rather surprised to find herself sounding like the most sensible person in the room.

'Do you think so, Irene?' Bella asked. 'I hope you're right.'

'Of course, it's just that Lily being daft. Now, either crumple that note up and chuck it out, or put it away safely for giving to the polis. Either way, forget about it now, and let's get on with our Christmas Eve, as planned.'

Megan stowed the poison pen letter in a drawer, and they all filed out into the hallway. Ma Ada was heard muttering to Sam, telling him off yet again for getting mixed up with 'that rough lot'.

Mavis's thoughts were already elsewhere, looking forward to her ice cream on their return from the service, and Bella was thinking about this being her first visit to any kind of church since the death of her father and the rest of her family.

Tonight Bella would sing in the church and it would be for all the Franchino family, and she knew that they would be proud and pleased that she felt like she could do so again. Something inside her felt like it was stirring and reviving at last, she thought.

The church was draughty and dimly lit and there was something subdued about the music tonight. Of course all the windows were blacked out, and it felt as if the whole place was somehow sightless, or without God's light shining through the old stained glass. That's how Irene felt, but not Ma Ada. For her it could have been pitch dark and have a howling gale rushing through smashed windows and it would still be the church she had known and loved all her life.

Yes, there had been times when she had stayed away, and disapproved of the priest, or wanted to go her own way, but when Christmas came, she had to be here. It was how she marked the passing of the years, and made sense of them all, even when time and events themselves seemed to lack all sense or coherence. Here she could recharge her batteries, it felt like, even when the place wasn't ablaze with light and ringing to the rafters with joy.

She sang and she listened and she prayed, and she remembered Tony. Tony who, dressed like an angel, had once sung in the choir here. Of all her boys, his voice had been the purest and he had stayed here the longest in those old wooden stalls. He didn't simply mouth the words like the others did, like they were just platitudes. He gave his full voice and he knew what it had meant. He explained it all to his mam as they walked home and her heart had glowed fiercely with pride. Her eldest lad – once, she'd even imagined he might become a priest. Imagine that!

But he'd started noticing the lasses, of course, and he'd stopped singing here. Only at Christmas he'd come with his ma and, sitting here – not too far forward, somewhere near the back – the two of them would raise their voices and enjoy the old-fashioned carols. They would come even when the other boys refused; when they were too old to listen to their ma's threats: 'Santa won't come to ours if you don't come to church!'

If she listened, Ma Ada could hear his voice now, singing with her. Tony's deep, confident, wonderful voice. She would hear it always when she listened to these old songs.

But what a dreadful dirge the singing was tonight! The Father looked sozzled. He looked worse than usual, and his voice was barely above a mumble. Her own family weren't much use. Bella had a pleasant voice. Mavis sounded just like Lucky the cat when he was hungry.

Eeeh, everything was going to the bad. That's what Ma Ada thought. Every year was worse than the last, and life was harder and harder and the news was getting worse. It was as much as she could do not to give in.

'Let us pray,' said the priest, and everyone bowed their heads.

Ada found herself thinking of Beryl, back at home, looking after the babies. The old mother was meaning to pray for all the souls who belonged in her care, and all of those who lived under her roof, as well as those away from home, and of course she murmured their names. But the one she was focused on this Christmas Eve was Beryl.

Beryl nursing her broken arm, both babies and her own broken heart back at home.

The poor girl had enough to contend with – more than anyone else – and yet Ma Ada had made it worse for her. The old woman blushed with shame when she remembered her words, right at the end of the wake in the Robin Hood. Oh, I'd been drinking, she thought. What a foolish old sot I was. The drink is like the devil and it loosened my tongue, and before I knew what was what my terrible words were out. The words that I was holding down, deep down for years, and which never should have been said. Out they came in the public bar to taunt that poor girl: 'You should have had his bairn, Beryl. You failed to give my boy a child. That would be some consolation right now. But you failed him. You failed us all.'

Even as she was saying the words Ada could see the damage they were doing. She prayed and tried to recall the exact words she'd said. She had been all drunken befuddlement at the time, and it was hard to remember exactly, but she knew the gist. Oh, she knew the gist all right, and it was hurtful. It was the most hurtful thing she could ever have said to that grieving girl, and she hadn't found the moment yet in which to put it right.

Praying with her old, chapped fingers squeezed together, Ma Ada promised herself that she would put that right this Christmas. She would find a way to tell Beryl how sorry she was.

\*

The Farley clan and their guests walked back up the frosty hill from the church and the sky was dark and cloudy with impending snow.

'When it's light again, it'll be Christmas Day!' Mavis gasped, and her innocently daft and obvious words made the others chuckle. She shrugged, not caring if anyone made fun of her. She was happy. 'That's what Arthur used to say, every Christmas Eve. Just think, Maeve. When the sun comes up again, it'll be Christmas Day!'

Irene hugged her as they walked along, knowing just how much she'd be missing her older brother right now. It was her first Christmas away from him. 'Aye, that's right,' she mumbled. 'We've never been parted, all our lives. Apart from that strange time, with old Mrs Kendricks, the posh lady. When she adopted the two of us, but decided she didn't want us both, just one of us.'

'What's that?' Irene asked, puzzled. She'd never heard this tale before. Mavis glanced at her sideways, as if conscious she had let something slip that she shouldn't have done.

'Oh, I'll tell you some day,' Mavis smiled, as the family turned the corner into Frederick Street. 'Eeeh, I'm frozen, but I'm looking forward to that ice cream you brought, Bella!'

Ma Ada let out a sudden squawk of horror.

'What the bloody hell's going on here?'

She started pegging along on her squat little legs towards Number Thirteen and the others saw at once why she was so upset.

'The door's hanging open! The front door's wide open!'

Megan came to her senses first and set off at a run up the last of the hill.

'But who? Why?' Irene couldn't work out what was going on.

'The bairns!' Megan shrieked. 'What about the bairns?'

Lucky the cat was on the doorstep, staring at them as they came running up the street. He came slinking out of the lit-up hallway and turned a tight circle in the doorway, obviously disturbed by what was going on.

'Beryl! Beryl!' Ma Ada yelled as she hurtled into the hallway. 'Eeeh, where *are* you, lass? And what the devil's going on?'

Irene stood in the downstairs hall and the house felt frozen solid, like the north wind had blown through the whole building, bringing devastation in its wake.

Sam had rushed upstairs and now came thundering back down. He looked completely ashen, gripping the banister as he told them: 'They're gone.'

'Who's gone?' Irene heard Mavis shout.

'All of them. Both bairns. Beryl. The upstairs is empty. I've been right up to the attic.'

'Noooo!' Megan moaned, rushing through to the parlour. 'Are they in the scullery? Is she out the back with them?'

But she wasn't. Beryl was gone and so were both babies.

The front door had been left swinging open like someone had fled in a hurry. Or like someone had broken in.

The occupants of Number Thirteen stared at each other in horror.

'It's the Mad Johnsons,' Mavis said shakily. 'It's them, isn't it? Just like Lily said in her letter. That death threat she sent!'

'Nah, man!' Ma Ada yelled. 'I refuse to believe anyone – even that lot – would . . . would . . . break in and steal someone's bairns!'

Irene felt something crack inside her at these words. It was like something came dislodged inside her chest and all the fear and panic she had been holding at bay suddenly overcame her. 'Where's she gone?' she said. 'Where's my Marlene?'

Bella was keeping the most level head out of all of them. From the hall she reported, 'The pram has gone. Wherever they've gone, they're in the pram.'

'That's good,' said Sam. 'That's good news.'

'Beryl's winter coat and boots are gone, too,' said Ma Ada. 'So . . . I reckon she's gone out somewhere with them. She's taken them out.'

'The Mad Johnsons have taken them all!' Mavis wailed, and Bella nudged and pinched her hard, until she gasped in pain.

'Shut up, Mavis, you're making it worse,' Bella hissed.

'I think I'm going to be sick,' Irene said, and sat down abruptly at the dining table.

'Get her a cup of tea!' Ma Ada shouted. 'We could all do with one.'

'We haven't got time!' Megan cried, with sudden savagery. 'Don't you see? We have to get out there, looking. It's freezing out there! We've got to get out looking for them!'

Everyone stared at each other and knew it was true. But where to even start? Town was pitch black, and it was Christmas Eve. Where could Beryl be?

Ma Ada made a start, rushing back outside and knocking on all the nearby doors, disturbing families as they celebrated Christmas Eve and settled down for the holiest night of the year. Aunty Madge, Aunty Winnie, Mrs Blenkinsop and the Merriweathers. She clattered at their doors and rattled their letterboxes and got them all out on the street. 'Eeeh, I'm sorry to break in on you like this, but something awful has happened. You haven't seen our Beryl and the bairns, have you? We just got back from church tonight – and they've bloody well gone!'

Irene felt helpless, watching the ripples of fear spread along Frederick Street, feeling the thrill of horror and vicarious excitement spread among the denizens of the Sixteen Streets.

'I'm sorry, I can't help you, hinny!'

'We've been in all night . . . we've not seen anything at all.'

'Eeeh, ask in the Robin Hood – maybe someone in there has seen her?'

Irene could barely hear what was being said because of the pounding of her heart, right up inside her throat. This was much, much worse than the last time she had thought her baby was missing. Stupidly she had allowed herself to trust others with her bairn. She tried to fight down the panic, standing in the street and willing herself not to scream. The snowflakes falling on her hot face felt like they were burning her.

Megan stood close by as Ma Ada went whirling up the street, spreading the news and beseeching her long-term neighbours to help.

'If that Beryl has done anything daft,' Megan said, in a low voice. 'I will gladly murder her.'

Irene clutched her sleeve. 'She won't have done anything daft. What could she do?'

Megan shrugged her off. 'She was crazy. You know what she's been like lately. She's off her head, that one.'

# Chapter Thirty-Five

It was murder, pushing the pram with one arm. Her other arm hung heavily in its plaster and weighed her down. Beryl grunted and pushed the pram as hard as she could, battling along Ocean Road, where the heaped snow was frozen into lumps of dirty ice.

At least the bairns were quiet now. They were lying in the pram, in each other's arms, under layers and layers of woolly blankets.

At home they had been awful, inconsolable. They had started playing up, soon after everyone had left for church. Nothing she had tried had been enough to make them settle down. Their screeches and wailing had sawed at her nerves until she found herself standing there, crying back at them.

It was her own mood that had made them like this. Her own gloomy mood, which had taken a turn for the worse after Megan had spoken to her like she had. The babies couldn't help picking up on that darkening mood and screaming out loud at her.

Taking them out had seemed like the only answer. The sudden rush of cold air on their faces and the change of scene and the accustomed, rhythmic bounce of the pram had seemingly done the trick.

Beryl had flown out of the house in a panic. Had she locked the door behind her? She couldn't even remember. At least she'd managed to drag her coat on. She walked and walked through the Sixteen Streets, to the top of the hill, to see all of the docks and the harbour spread out below them in the snowy darkness.

I should go home, I should take them back home . . .

What if the others came home and found her gone, and found the babies gone as well? She had to get back before that could happen . . .

They would think she had gone off her head, of course. They would think she'd turned doolally and then there would be a panic.

She knew that the best thing to do was to get back home before the service was over, and they were finished with their carols and their prayers. The best thing would be for the two bairns to be sleeping like two perfect angels in their cot, and for Beryl to be waiting with a pot of tea brewing, and maybe some broth bubbling away on the hob. Waiting for everyone to come home and reassuring them that everything was all right.

But she didn't feel all right, that was the thing. She felt terrible inside, like something had gone wrong with her, and it would never go back to being normal again. Things she had believed sorted were being dredged up again.

So she kept on walking. She walked into the town centre. It was slippery and hazardous, but she took her time. She walked steadily and carefully, and the business of putting one determined foot in front of the other seemed to soothe her ragged nerves.

And the babies slept on, turning over and mumbling and hugging each other under their swaddling blankets. They weren't at all bothered by being out and about. They were quite content. They were out with their aunty, weren't they? Their poor, widowed, childless aunty.

All she was doing was walking them past the snowy park and down to the beach. Her feet knew the way. This was back where she used to live as a girl, along this way. Every day she had walked down this way. On the days when she was left in charge of her little brother, Fred, she had brought him down here. Mostly it was daytime and mostly it was a lot warmer than this, but the route was the same. She felt a glow of happiness surge through her at the memory. Yes, this was just like it used to be with Fred. Back in the days when folk used to trust her to take a baby out by herself.

You couldn't even get onto the beaches now, could you? They were sealed off and tangled in razor wire, by all accounts. Just in case invaders came sneaking up onto the sands one dark night; in case the Germans brought their U-boats as close as that.

She longed for the feel of the sand under her feet but it would be much too cold and frozen tonight. She'd catch her death, even if she could get down on the beach. She wanted to be down there, though, to feel that soft, crumbly sand between her toes. It felt like heavy, cloddy, unrefined sugar, she realised. Something else it was hard to get hold of these days.

The snow was sifting down now, as she kept on plodding. Her good arm was aching with the effort of pushing the pram, and the pram itself kept veering away and slipping on the frozen snow. Maybe it was time for turning back now? Beryl didn't have a watch on and she didn't know how long she'd been walking about. She'd come much further than she'd meant to.

There was the lighthouse and the pier. Maybe the sands down here weren't as bad as further along? She knew it was impossible to get down to Marsden Bay. All she wanted to do was stay for a while and listen to the sea. The reassuring noise of the sea: it sounded just the same as it always had.

Nothing could change the endless whisper of the sea.

Fred had always longed for the holidays when his big sister Beryl was home from school all day. Her school days seemed endlessly long to the little boy as he sat waiting in the playpen in his mama's room. 'Hush, hush, you must keep hush for your poor old ma. Her nerves aren't well,' Beryl would coach him, urging him to keep quiet all day long. She'd dash back home at lunchtime to feed both him and their parents, and Fred would cry out to be set free, but there was never any time.

He grew to hate Beryl's school days. She had to go to a great big horrible place that ate her up for hours on end. Her school was a grim Victorian mansion that stood not too far away from their house, on that hill high above Tynemouth. He could see it from the window of his mother's room, with its tall windows lit up on the winter afternoons. He could hear the children screaming and playing their games in the yard and he hated the thought of his sister being among them. Why wasn't she home with him all the time?

'I have to be at school in order to learn all my lessons,' is how she explained it to him patiently. Yet to Fred it always seemed like Beryl already knew everything there was to know. He looked at her in wonder. She was brave and fantastically clever. She taught him to talk, to walk, to run and to play.

'Your sister has to go to school,' his mother said from her sick bed. 'Stop grousing and sleep.'

But he hated sleeping in the daytime. He kept quiet though, because Mama would yell at him fiercely from under her covers if he kept up his complaints.

His heart leapt up and started beating like crazy when he heard the front door crash open at four and his Beryl came running up the stairs. Then he was free and they could spend time together.

When Fred was four and Beryl was eleven he was really o~~
enough to appreciate their days out together. Spring and ther
summer rolled around and it was warm enough to spend all
day out, taking an old rug onto the sands, with a bag of paste
sandwiches and a bottle filled with pop.

Later Beryl would wonder about what they had found
to do, to fill up all those hours? They collected shells and
scooped the soft, damp sand into beautiful castles and all the
obvious pastimes. She couldn't remember there ever being
any difficulty in filling up the time. Fred was a good, alert
little boy, interested in everything and he never got bored
or whingey.

Once she remembered him looking cross. It was her suggestion that maybe they should gently encourage Mama to join
them on a day by the sea. Their mother was looking less peaky.
She herself had even voiced the hope that she might get up and
out of the house one day soon. Wistfully she had expressed a
vague desire to accompany her bairns on a trip out to sit by
the sea. The fresh air and the gentle sound of the waves would
be good for her, she thought.

When he heard about this Fred didn't look pleased at all.
He shook his head fiercely and flung his little wooden spade
down on the sand. 'What's wrong with the idea of our mam
coming to the beach with us?' Beryl asked him, though in her
heart she already knew.

The little lad couldn't articulate what he felt. He just looked
peevish. But his sister knew that it was all because this was
their place. This stretch of Marsden Bay, by the great hulking
edifice of Marsden Rock. This was their world and their world
alone. The sickly, pale, tetchy, irritable person who called herself
his mama would not be welcomed here by her son.

Beryl felt vaguely pleased as she watched him amble off
down to the frothing shoreline, picking up and discarding

ack stones and shells. She berated herself for taking pleasure
in her brother's reaction. Poor Mam – rejected like that. But
it was natural, wasn't it, for the lad to want Beryl more than
his mam? After the way he'd been brought up by her?

This little scene stayed with her and ended up haunting
her. With everything that happened not long after, it almost
felt like she was being punished for trying too hard to be a
replacement mother to the boy.

It was one of the last days of her holiday. The sun was
brighter and hotter that day on the beach than ever before. For
some reason the bay was quieter than other days. Maybe the
sands were too burning and blinding? Beryl had the old rug
with her, same as every day. It smelt of their old dog, Sammy.
Long gone, that dog, but his scent lingered not unpleasantly
as she dozed in the sun and her skin toasted scarlet.

Perhaps she was complacent. Maybe even negligent. But
how many days in total had they spent on that beach together
with no one coming to any harm? The boy was little but he
was sensible. He couldn't get lost. There was nowhere for him
to get lost in, anyway, was there?

Only Marsden Rock itself. Only the honeycomb of caves
inside that vast hunk of rock which stood a little way into the
sea. Most of the caves weren't accessible, even at low tide. A
little kid of Fred's age would have to be really determined to
get anywhere near them. He'd have to be a bloody-minded
little bugger, to think about getting into those mysterious inner
caverns deep inside Marsden Rock.

He would have dreamt about them, wondering if they led
somewhere magical, full of treasure. He would have waited till
that point in the afternoon when he knew his big sister would
fall asleep on that old rug on the sand, and then he would
have crept off to clamber carefully on the wet, slippery rock
while the waves crashed all about him. He'd have known he

was going somewhere dangerous. He'd have known he'd be trouble if anyone in charge were to know . . .

He must have known what he was doing. She had warned him often enough. But he had gone anyway.

Beryl woke up with a small, startled cry and he had gone. It took her a few moments before her vision cleared and then she was disoriented only for a second or two. But it was enough for her to realise that her little brother had gone.

All she could hear was the sea pounding against Marsden Rock, and the shrieking of the seabirds roosting on the cliffs. She stood and whirled in a slow circle.

Her heart was pounding really slowly. Dreadfully slowly like it wanted to stop and kill her dead before the news could hit her. Fred wasn't there. And she had lost him.

The worst moment was walking alone away from the beach, back up the steps that were carved into the sheer face of the cliff. Setting off back for home meant that she was accepting the fact that she had lost him.

By rushing back up the cliff, across the grassy Leas and back to their house at the top of the town, Beryl was saying that she had looked as much as she could, and now she was giving up on her little brother.

She ran in a kind of daze, pushing past people as she went by the park gates. It was a beautiful day and the streets were full of people dressed up and enjoying themselves. She was in a cold sweat and all her limbs felt strange and disconnected. There was a lightness to her, and she felt as if she should be carrying something that would weigh her down.

She had left him down on the beach. Somewhere by Marsden Rock. She had abandoned him.

All she could think was that she had to get home and tell her mam and dad. But what was she expecting them to do?

ey were hardly going to rise from their sick beds and rush help her search the shoreline. What did she want them to say to her? There, there, it's all okay. No wonder he's gone missing. It was bound to happen eventually. It's no one's fault. These things happen . . .

She paused to grab the railings and stood bowed over in the street with a hideous stitch in her guts. She retched and she felt as if she was about to vomit or pass out.

'Hey, what's the matter here? Are you all right, hinny?'

People were pressing around her, concerned for the way she looked. She must have seemed wild and out of control, dashing headlong up the hill. She stared at those trying to help her as if she'd never even heard their language before. 'My b-brother,' she gasped. 'My l-little brother . . .'

Her mother never did forgive her. Neither did her dad, though he said much less about the whole affair.

The police and the coastguard were out that afternoon and into that evening, as late as they thought they should keep on trying. They needed to make sure that the little boy hadn't simply wandered off on his own down the beach in the direction of Sunderland. Bobbies were dispatched to scour the seafront going south, searching for the lad. Beryl went back to the beach with them and gave a semi-coherent description of what he'd been wearing.

They all knew, though, that he must have been playing around the base of the rock. The girl had fallen asleep and left him to explore the dangerous caverns by himself. The tide was changing as the day advanced and the grown-ups couldn't get close enough to see. But it was clear from all their faces what they thought. He had been carried off by the waves and had surely drowned. And tomorrow they knew they'd be looking for his body. Sooner or later it would wash up somewhere along the coast.

Beryl saw this look on their faces and she knew exactly wh
it meant. She stood on the sand where she'd left the old dog
rug and she howled. She stood there howling his name until
the frothing water rose and swirled around her feet and they
had to drag her away, back to the cliff steps. She wanted them
to leave her there so she could join her brother. She needed to
go, as well. How could she ever face her mama and da again?
What would she ever say to them?

The polis couldn't help with that, of course. They simply
took her home to the quiet house at the back of the park, and
found that her mother was waiting downstairs in her dressing
gown. She was smoking stale Woodbines that she'd found in
a kitchen drawer.

The polis left Beryl alone with her and Beryl didn't even know
where to start. She watched her mother fall to pieces right in
front of her. And now that she was home, having cried herself
sick on the beach, Beryl just stood there silently, blank-faced
and hollow-eyed, as she watched her mam screaming in the
back parlour.

'I'll never forgive you for this, Beryl,' she swore. 'And I'll
never speak another word to you.'

Then Mama started drinking and got herself good and drunk
on all the bottles from the sideboard. She wasn't used to drinking
at all, and made herself ill, trying to blot all her thoughts out.
Beryl had to clean up after her, following her about the house
as she raged. She listened to her mother noisily lamenting her
angel boy who had been taken too soon from her grasp.

A curious steeliness crept over the girl. Why, you never
wanted him in the first place. You never did owt to look after
him. You lay in your stinking bed every day of his short life.
You left him in that playpen while I was at school. And I was
the one who loved him. I was the one who taught him to talk.
I was everything to our Fred . . .

Her mother ranted and raved and, that night, she invented ne strategy by which she was able to give her daughter instructions while still not, strictly speaking, addressing her directly. She started to use the third person address: 'Is that girl still there? Is she going to help her mother get up to bed? Is she going to bring her some water?'

There was something chilling about being talked to like that. It was like Beryl's mother's mind had gone off to some other place, and she was looking at the world from afar, like a spirit in a table-rapping experiment. Or, thought Beryl, as she dully did as she was bid, it was like her mother couldn't stand the sight of her and hated her so much she couldn't say a single word to her. And this was the way she let her daughter know the depths of her hatred, while still securing her services and making her do everything in their home.

Beryl beetled around in despair, that night, and every night for the rest of that year.

Her father became a ghost. He stood on the landing each bedtime in his night shirt, hovering in the doorway, as if some invisible force let him stray from his bed only so far and no further.

Every night he asked Beryl the same question. 'Have they found the nipper yet, pet? Is he gonna come home to us?'

'Nay, Dad,' she told him each night, and put him back to bed. Each night a little more weary and hopeless than the last. 'They haven't found the bairn.'

And they never did.

# Chapter Thirty-Six

In the Robin Hood Irene grabbed hold of Cathy Sturrock and quickly explained what was going on. The landlady struck the bell and silenced the whole bar in an instant. Closing, already? Shocked faces stared at her. She used the sudden silence to explain the Farleys' plight. Had anyone seen Beryl with the pram? Would anyone help them go and find her?

Cathy was calm and pragmatic in moments like these, though Irene could see that she was as agitated as any of them at the thought of the bairns going missing.

Minnie Hatcher had seen Beryl, she claimed, pushing the pram about an hour ago. She was heading into town, and hadn't responded when Minnie shouted 'Happy Christmas, pet!' at her. 'And I thought then, that wasn't like Beryl, who's normally such a pleasant girl, not like that other one, her sister-in-law . . .' Minnie's words dried up then, as she noticed Megan was actually there, standing behind Irene by the bar and glowering.

'An hour ago?' Irene said.

'Aye, it must have been. I've had two of these brandies and I've been sat here an hour, I reckon?' Minnie looked quizzically at her friend, who nodded.

'I'll come with you,' Cathy told Irene, already reaching for her

., and turning to bark instructions at her barmaid, Sandra, 10 looked annoyed at being left alone.

'You needn't do that,' Irene protested, but Cathy wouldn't hear of it. She marched all the Farleys back into the street, where Sam was remonstrating with his mam.

'Someone needs to be back at the house,' he told her. 'Someone has to be waiting there for when she comes back, or if she comes back while we're all looking. It's no good leaving the house empty.'

Ma Ada reluctantly agreed. 'But it's just because you think I'll hold you young 'uns up, because I can't walk as fast . . .'

'Of course we do!' Megan yelled at her. 'We can go at twice the speed without you, you daft old boot.'

For once Ma Ada let Megan's rudeness go. She simply turned and stumped off towards home again, hobbling painfully on the frozen slush. 'Bring her home again safely,' the old woman cried. 'With those two babbies! Bring them all safely back home again to me!'

'We will,' Bella promised tersely, and was struck by a sudden flash of inspiration. The others were all so upset it was hard for them to think logically, but Bella had had an idea. 'Beryl's mother. Irene, do you remember the address? Where her people live? Isn't it up by South Marine Park?'

Irene nodded. 'Yes, I've been there. I can find it again.'

'What time is it?' Sam tried to see his watch face by the moonlight. 'Nearly nine o'clock? Aren't her mum and da invalids? They're probably up in their beds.'

'That hardly matters,' said Irene. 'If there's anything going on, they'll want to know.'

'Okay,' said Cathy Sturrock. 'You go that way, and I'll go through the middle of town. Mavis, do you want to come with me?'

Mavis looked as if she wanted to stay with Sam, but nodded and did as she was told.

'I'll go through the marketplace and all round the town hall,' Bella said.

'I'll go down the beach front and the White Leas,' said Megan, and hurried off alone, and Irene was relieved to see the back of her for a while.

Sam and Irene parted from the others and made their way to the park and the house at the top of the hill overlooking the sea where Beryl had grown up.

'She must be in a bad way,' Irene said. 'Worse than we thought. Grieving and upset and off her head. To go wandering off like this.'

'It'll all be fine,' Sam promised her. 'Honestly, everything will all be right. Remember that time when Ma was out walking all day with Marlene and you got all worried then over nothing? It'll be just the same as that, I promise you.'

This wasn't all that reassuring to Irene. It just brought back memories of that upsetting afternoon all the more clearly.

Quietly, Sam was also remembering the stories from school about Beryl. The stories that everyone seemed to remember about Beryl growing up. How she'd taken her brother to the beach one day and lost him. Her little brother had never come back, and that fact had hung over Beryl's life and blighted it for all the years since.

But she couldn't have gone down that road again, could she?

It was something she had wanted to do for a very long time.

Impossible to put into words. Hard to even think about. But the hope and the dream of it had played through her mind all her adult life. The fantasy had dragged at her and tormented her.

It was silly, really. Nothing could ever put things right. Nothing could roll back time and change the way things had worked out.

Her brother Fred was long, long gone. Those wounds were scars now, hidden deep within. They itched sometimes and kept her awake.

She played the fantasy through in her mind again and again. When she was feeling low or tired or weak.

It was about walking back home from the beach. Walking all the way up the hill and through the park. She was holding her little brother's hand, and she was taking him home. She hadn't lost him after all.

That was the dream that had plagued her. A happy and, at the same time, very cruel dream.

In her dream it was summertime. It was summer and she was still just a girl. It was a simpler time, before growing up and the start of the war. A time before she even knew who the Farley family were. A time before Tony, and before she gave her heart to someone who could break it by disappearing from her life and never coming back.

Tonight it was freezing and dark and the snow was whirling down quickly now. It was Christmas Eve, and in a way, Beryl was lucky, because she didn't have strong feelings about Christmas one way or another. Growing up, it had never seemed all that special. She didn't have warm and happy associations with any part of Christmas time. It was just a few days of palaver, as far as she was concerned.

But there was a spark of something inside her tonight. A strange glimmering. I could make that dream of mine come a little bit true, she thought, as she pushed the pram along. That daft dream. That dream that stood no chance of being real. They weren't even her own babies. She'd stolen them, in effect. Stolen them? Was that true? She'd been trusted. She'd been trusted enough to look after the bairns. She was worthy of trust, and that made her heart glow warmly as well, just that simple thought.

I'm a woman who can be trusted with other people's bairns, she thought. At last! At last, I'm that woman.

And her dream was of taking them home to her mama, in the house on the hill at the top of the park. Taking them home safely, in the way she had failed to bring her brother home, all those years ago.

Such a simple dream. A straightforward fantasy.

Beryl's heart quickened as she pushed the pram towards her former home. The bairns were stirring hungrily in their blankets. They were waking each other up with their twisting. It was time they were fed. Perhaps the cold was even getting to them. It was time they were indoors . . .

Would her parents even be awake, this time of night? They were a law unto themselves in their habits, and the hours that they kept.

But when Beryl went up the front path and put her old key in the latch, she had a feeling that her mama was up and about, at least. Of course, no light struck out through the blackout curtains. Still, Beryl had a feeling that there was a welcome waiting for her indoors.

'Beryl!' Her mother was shocked to see her in the hall, covered in snow, bringing the pram into the warmth of the kitchen. 'What are you doing? Why are you here, pet?'

Beryl could barely express herself. She couldn't easily explain. She took off her coat and got her mum to help her extricate the wriggling bairns from the pram. 'They need feeding and changing . . .' Beryl said, in a whisper. Suddenly she felt like she was on her last legs. All the strength was ebbing out of her.

Her mother clasped Marlene to her and looked wary. 'What were you doing out in the snow with them? It's a hideous night out there!'

'It's a beautiful night, Mama,' Beryl smiled. 'I've just been out a bit too long, that's all. But I've brought them back to you, haven't I? I've brought the babies to see you.'

Now, as her mother bustled around hastily, Beryl's dad came down the stairs in his dressing gown. He looked pale and worried. 'What's going on? What's happening, is there trouble?'

'No trouble, Da,' Beryl smiled, going to kiss him for Christmas. 'I was a bit confused and a bit unhappy there for a while. And no wonder, too! But I think I'm all right now. No harm done. Happy Christmas, Da. It's good to see you up and about.'

His wife looked harassed. 'She's brought the babies here!' she told him.

'Oh!' said the old man. 'What can you give them? Are they eating proper food? Will they have some Christmas pudding, do you think? Or some sherry, maybe?'

Beryl couldn't help laughing at him. Her old, befuddled dad. It really was good to see him standing up in the kitchen, downstairs, on Christmas Eve. He looked delighted that there were babies there. So did her mum. They sat with them and cuddled them, and made both the bairns laugh, and gave them milk and basked in the tender warmth of them.

This was the right place to come tonight, Beryl thought, relaxing in the glow from the old kitchen stove. She had done something good, in the end. It wasn't a disaster at all.

There was peace for a little while, and then the front door was all clatter and bang.

It was Irene at the door, with Sam. All in a panic, of course.

Irene hugged Marlene to her, so hard she started the baby grizzling with temper. 'Oh, thank God. Thank God they're all right . . .'

Beryl's mum and da stared at the newcomers and felt relieved and dismayed all at the same time. 'Well, it's good to see you, Irene,' the mother said.

Beryl was sitting with a hopeful smile on her face, with little Johnny cradled in her lap.

'What were you thinking of, Beryl?' Sam asked her gently. 'You slammed out of the house and left the door wide open! No note, nothing. You never said where you were going.'

Beryl frowned. 'Didn't I? I . . . I don't remember . . .'

Sam and Irene exchanged a quick glance. 'Well, there's no harm done,' Irene said, though her heart was still pounding twenty to the dozen. She didn't like the glazed, vague look on her sister-in-law's face. She had never seen her smiling like that before and it disturbed her.

'Ah, Beryl's fine,' her mama said. 'She's a good girl. She'd never do anyone any harm. Least of all children. You can see she dotes on these babies.'

'I do,' Beryl said brightly. 'I love them both.'

'Well, Megan will be going bananas, as you can imagine,' Sam said. 'So, we'd better think about getting them both back to Number Thirteen.'

'Eeeh, I'm sorry,' Beryl said, looking teary. 'I'm sorry for being the cause of all this fuss tonight.'

They tried to reassure her that everything was fine. There was no harm done.

'I am sorry, though,' Beryl said. 'I never wanted to cause any bother.'

Sam was hugely relieved not to be the source of all the anxiety this time. He was used to being the cause of all the trouble and tonight it was a pleasant change to be seen as one of the sensible ones.

The others all agreed that they'd best drink up their tea and hurry home to Frederick Street. As they dallied, however, there came another great rumpus at the front door, and it was Megan. Her face was frozen and puce with fury as she came storming up the hall into the cosy kitchen at the back.

'What the hell do you think you were playing at?' she thundered at Beryl. She wrenched her child out of Beryl's mum's arms and set him off wailing again. 'You kidnapped him! You kidnapped both our bairns! You're not fit to be left alone with them! You've had some kind of brainstorm or a breakdown, or something.'

'Now, now, Megan,' Sam broke in diplomatically.

She sneered at him. 'Just you shut your mouth,' she said, through gritted teeth. The baby was wedged between them and suddenly Irene was struck by the startling thought, that Johnny was Sam's own baby. That's why he stuck with me tonight. We were both searching for our own babies together. It's a secret and no one must ever know, but he still feels so attached to baby Johnny. Right now Sam looked like he wanted to take the bairn right out of Megan's arms. She was too angry, too reckless, to be trusted with a baby.

'We should all calm down,' Beryl's dad said.

'Megan – everything's okay,' Irene tried to tell her. 'Honestly, the babies are safe.'

But Megan took a long time to calm down. She gulped hot, sweet tea and clutched Johnny and glared at all the others. 'I thought she'd taken you,' she whispered to her baby. 'I thought that you were gone.'

'Everything is fine,' Beryl said.

# Chapter Thirty-Seven

It was late by the time the Farleys reconvened at Number Thirteen.

By then Ma Ada was almost beside herself with worry. But back they all came, shaking snow off their shoulders and stamping their feet. All the young 'uns and their friends, and most importantly of all – the two Farley babies. Her grandchildren.

Having them safely back indoors was the greatest Christmas present the old woman could have asked for. All the searchers were back and everyone had fussed over the bairns and got themselves warmed through again. Cathy had returned to the Robin Hood, with their thanks ringing in her ears. Once Beryl was sound asleep in her old room and Megan was fuming and sulking in the attic, the others gathered peacefully downstairs.

Ma Ada sat with both drowsy babies held protectively on her tiny lap in her throne-like chair in the parlour till after midnight, Christmas morning. She was fierce and wouldn't let anyone take them out of her arms.

'Happy Christmas, Ma Ada,' Irene told her, and the old woman smiled. She looked exhausted and triumphant.

'I've got me little family together,' she said. 'As much as

I can have, for now. As much as this bloody war will allow. But everyone who can be at home is here, tonight, at Number Thirteen, and that will just have to do.'

Irene agreed with her with a heartfelt sigh, bending to kiss the old woman on the forehead. 'Shall I go and put the kettle on?' she smiled.

Out in the yard, Sam and Mavis were having a heart to heart.

The snow had slowed for a moment and the moonlight was poking through the dark blue clouds. The frozen yard glimmered silver and it looked almost pretty out there, by the privy and the coal hole.

'But do you think this is the right time?' Mavis was asking. Her voice sounded huskier than ever as she smoked the end of his last cigarette for him.

'I do,' he smiled.

'Ah, Sam, man,' Mavis smiled up at him. She beamed at his handsome face staring at her. She could hardly believe the way he was looking at her and no one else. 'I can't think of anything I'd rather do in the whole wide world.'

'So?' he grinned.

'But is this really the right moment? After all the hullaballoo and the upset there's been tonight?'

Sam shrugged. 'Mavis, there's always something going on round here. When you belong to the Farley clan, you come to understand that. There's not a day or a night goes by without there being some kind of bloomin' drama.'

Mavis gave her queer little rasping laugh. 'I'm starting to understand that! I do know what you mean.'

She shivered, just as a breeze whirled through the backyards, up from the depths of the docks. It brought with it a new flurry of snowflakes that danced around the two of them as they stared at each other.

The moment was frozen for ages and ages. As far as Mavis was concerned, that moment could last for ever.

Sam said, 'It's Christmas. I want to kiss you. All the panic has died down. You're happy, I can tell. And it's my favourite night of the year, you know.'

'Is it?' Mavis blinked and felt snowflakes melting on her lashes. 'Do you really want to kiss me? For real, this time? Not just showing off, like at the dance?'

He kissed her. It was real.

'Oh!' she said. She had never really been kissed before. That's what had been so odd about the kissing on the dance floor. He had been so drunk. He didn't mean it. He'd hardly even known it was her he was kissing. It hadn't counted.

But this kiss did.

Sam loved her.

Mavis held her breath and counted the snowflakes whirling by like they were wishes.

'Hey, hey, what are you bubbling for?' he asked her.

'Do you mean it? Do you really want to marry me?'

He held her fast. 'Ah, Maeve. Of course I do. I love you loads, pet. I feel like a daft lad for not saying it before. Now, you just say yes, and let's go indoors and tell everyone before they all go off to bed. Come on now.'

'If you don't tell your mother first she'll go crackers,' Mavis chuckled, blinking her tears away.

'She will! And she's up having a last cup of tea and a cuddle of those babies. So come on, come back inside with me and let's tell them all the news.'

'Eeeh, Sam,' Mavis sighed. 'Maybe you're right. Maybe it's a perfect night for this. All the upset is over and everyone is all right for now, and safely home. Thank goodness for that. Maybe it's the perfect time to tell them all . . . our happy news.'

He kissed her cold nose. 'Ha'way, then, pet.'

'All right,' she said.

Then they turned as the scullery door opened, to see Irene letting out Lucky the cat. 'Hey, what are you two plotting and planning out here?' Irene laughed.

'Just you wait!' Mavis laughed happily. 'You'll never believe it, Irene!'

'What is it?' Irene asked warily, as the two of them came hurrying in from the cold. 'You both look so happy!'

'I am!' Mavis cried. 'I've never felt so happy in all my bloomin' life!'

# Acknowledgements

Thank you to my agent, Piers, and my editors, Victoria and Lucy, and to Olivia, Amber and the team at Orion.

Thanks to Rita, Peter, Stuart, Jon, Nick, Georgie, Patricia, Steve, Jamie, Johnny, Rylan, Stephen, Matt, David, Mark, Mike, Darren, Mags, Caroline, Nick, Jim, Sue, Katy, Anthony, George. Thanks to all the Fambles gang.

And thanks to my Mam, my Big Nanna, and all the women of my family for being inspirational.

Thank you to Jeremy and to Bernard Socks.

# Credits

Orion Fiction would like to thank everyone at Orion who worked on the publication of *The Biscuit Factory Girls At War* in the UK.

**Editorial**
Lucy Frederick
Victoria Oundjian
Olivia Barber

**Copy editor**
Kate Shearman

**Proof reader**
Linda Joyce

**Audio**
Paul Stark
Amber Bates

**Contracts**
Anne Goddard
Paul Bulos
Jake Alderson

**Design**
Debbie Holmes
Joanna Ridley
Nick May

**Editorial Management**
Charlie Panayiotou
Jane Hughes
Alice Davis

**Finance**
Jasdip Nandra
Afeera Ahmed
Elizabeth Beaumont
Sue Baker

**Production**
Ruth Sharvell

**Publicity**
Ellen Turner

**Operations**
Jo Jacobs
Sharon Willis
Lisa Pryde
Lucy Brem

**Sales**
Jennifer Wilson
Esther Waters
Victoria Laws
Rachael Hum
Ellie Kyrke-Smith
Frances Doyle
Georgina Cutler

*Don't miss the first heart-warming*
*Biscuit Factory Girls saga about war,*
*family and the importance of friendship . . .*

**Can Irene find a new home by the docks?**

Newly married to dashing RAF officer, Tom, Irene Farley leaves behind her safe countryside life to move in with his family by the docks in South Shields. Little prepares her for the devastation the Jerry bombers have wreaked on the Sixteen Streets or that they would be living under her mother-in-law's roof, alongside Tom's three brothers and two wives!

Irene's only escape is her job at the local Wight's biscuit factory packing up a little taste of home for the brave boys fighting for king and country across the channel. As the threat of war creeps ever closer to the Sixteen Streets, the biscuit factory girls bond together, because no one can get through this war alone . . .

**Available in paperback, eBook and audio now!**